echoes of guilt

L.T. Ryan

Laura Chase

LIQUID MIND MEDIA

chapter
one

VIOLET CARVER SMILED as she spotted the bouquet of violets on her doorstep. Their velvety petals and sweet fragrance brought a grin to her face. Her favorite flower, and her namesake. She bent down to pick them up, burying her nose in their softness and breathing deeply.

Her heart fluttered with excitement. She didn't need a note to know who they were from. The guy she'd been talking to online had been so sweet, so thoughtful. These little gestures were exactly what she'd always wanted in a relationship.

Carrying the bouquet inside, Violet set it down on the counter. She reached for her phone and sent a quick picture of the flowers to her sister, Sarah, along with a text:

"Look what my secret admirer sent me! Aren't they beautiful? 😊*"*

Her phone buzzed almost immediately with Sarah's response:

"Violet, you really don't know this guy. Be careful, okay? I'm serious."

Violet rolled her eyes, smiling to herself. Sarah had always been the cautious one. Sure, they'd only been talking online, but this guy seemed genuine. Sweet. Romantic.

"Relax, Sarah," she muttered, placing her phone down next to the bottle of perfume he'd sent her earlier that week. She gave it a wistful glance. Her favorite scent. He really paid attention to all the little details.

She filled a vase with water and arranged the violets carefully, stepping back to admire them. They were perfect, just like the connection she felt with him. The thought of meeting him in person made her stomach flutter.

A sharp knock at the door interrupted her thoughts. She glanced at the clock—9:37 p.m. A bit late for visitors, but maybe... was it him?

Her heart raced with anticipation as she made her way to the door. She peeked through the peephole but saw no one.

Frowning, she opened the door and stepped out, looking up and down the hallway.

"Hello?" she called softly, her voice filled with curiosity.

There was no answer, just the faint hum of the building settling around her. She laughed at herself, shaking her head. Maybe it was a neighbor or someone messing around.

Closing the door, Violet turned back toward the kitchen. But before she could take a step, a gloved hand clamped over her mouth.

Her scream was muffled as she thrashed against the grip, panic surging through her. A rag was pressed firmly to her nose and mouth, the pungent smell of chemicals filling her senses.

She tried to fight back, her arms flailing, her nails clawing at the attacker's arms, but they didn't budge. The strength behind the grip was overwhelming, and no amount of struggling seemed to make a difference.

Her vision blurred, her limbs growing heavy. Her knees buckled, and the attacker guided her to the floor as she fought to stay conscious.

The world around her darkened, her thoughts growing foggy. The last thing she saw before everything went black was the bouquet of violets on the counter, their bright petals a cruel reminder of how wrong she had been.

chapter
two

CLAIRE STEVENS FROZE mid-sentence as her office lights abruptly blinked out, plunging the room into complete darkness. The tapping of her fingers on the keyboard ceased, and the glow of her monitor dimmed to black. She blinked, disoriented, gripping the edges of her desk as her heart thudded against her ribcage.

Moments ago, she'd been buried in an appellate brief, the words blurring after hours of revision. Now, her office—a sanctuary of routine —was unrecognizable. The faint hum of the building's air conditioning continued, but it only amplified the silence that followed. The window behind her reflected nothing but her pale silhouette against the void.

The inky blackness stretched further than she expected, swallowing the faint light from the hallway. She stood slowly, her chair groaning against the wooden floor as she pushed it back. Her knees wobbled, but she steadied herself with a deep breath. *Focus.* She reached for her desk lamp, fumbling over loose pens and stacks of paper, but its switch clicked uselessly under her fingers.

Her mind spiraled into irrational possibilities. *Power outage? Or... something else?*

Her breaths quickened. She'd always hated the dark, hated the way it made every sound sharper, every shadow more alive. When she was a child, her mother's voice used to scold her for leaving the hallway light on at night. *There's nothing there, Claire. Just your imagination.*

"Is someone there?" a voice called out from the hallway, startling her.

The tension in her chest surged, and she took a shaky step toward the door. She squinted, trying to make out the source of the voice.

"Yes!" she replied, her own voice trembling. She placed a hand over her heart as relief crept in. "Please turn the lights back on!"

A few seconds later, the fluorescent bulbs flickered, then buzzed back to life with a faint, mechanical hum. The sudden brightness forced her to shield her eyes, which had adjusted to the gloom. Her office looked utterly normal again—her cluttered desk, the unfiled legal briefs in neat stacks near the window, the framed certificates on the walls. Yet, her pulse hadn't slowed.

The sound of shoes on carpet brought her attention to the hallway. A man appeared at the door. His blue coveralls were familiar, and his expression was one of mild embarrassment.

"So sorry about that, ma'am," the janitor said, scratching the back of his head. "I assumed everyone had already left for the evening."

Claire managed a thin smile, exhaling through her nose as she sat back down. "It's fine. No harm done," she replied, though the ache in her chest said otherwise.

As the janitor made his way out of the room, Claire used the opportunity of broken focus to get up from her desk and stretch. She tended to get completely consumed by her work, and in the few short years she'd been an attorney, it had started to take a toll on her health. Her shoulders ached constantly from hunching over briefs, her wrists were often stiff from hours of typing, and her once-dependable sleep schedule was now a patchwork of restless nights and groggy mornings. The dark circles under her eyes had become permanent fixtures, and the nagging tightness in her chest reminded her that she hadn't exercised in months. Even the simple act of stretching sent a sharp pull through her lower back, a reminder of how little she moved during her twelve-hour workdays.

She looked at herself in the mirror hanging from the back of her office door. Her grey wool skirt fit her a little more snuggly around the hips than she'd have preferred. The plain white blouse was tight around her shoulders. Her unruly brown hair was tucked into as neat of a bun as she could manage and thick reading glasses were perched on her nose. Claire sighed, knowing she looked far older than her actual age of 28, but given her work schedule, her personal appearance had been the first thing she'd lost her grip on.

She had thought that she would end up practicing corporate law in New York City. Ironically, it was easier to stay healthier there than it was in Savannah, Georgia. New York City almost required you to walk everywhere, while people in Savannah still drove a fair bit. Claire had tried to buck that trend when she'd moved back. While she owned a car, it sat mostly unused in her apartment's parking lot.

Her gaze caught on the stack of papers on her desk, all courtesy of Bob Hayes, the managing partner of Savannah Legal, P.C. She should have been grateful to the man for the job in the first place. Given how things hadn't worked out for her in New York, she was fortunate to land on her feet. That still didn't mean she enjoyed working until—she looked at her watch—8:30 p.m. on a Friday, especially when everyone else at the firm had left at 5.

After law school, she'd taken a job in New York City, which had only lasted a year until she had to leave. With no other prospects, she had to fall back on her family ties to get her a job—a bitter pill to swallow for someone who hated relying on anyone else and prided herself on handling things on her own.

Her father, Roy Stevens, had been an extremely successful trial attorney. The Stevens didn't have a long pedigree like many of the families in Savannah did. What they did have was money, and under certain circumstances, that could serve someone just as well.

Some people would have been happy to take a job with their father's old business partner, but that hadn't been the life Claire wanted. She'd wanted to go somewhere she could build a name and reputation for herself. She especially did not want to remain in her hometown if she could help it.

Hometowns were a lot like cemeteries. Everything may have been buried, but that didn't mean the ghosts of the past didn't linger. But perhaps the worst thing about moving back home for Claire was the weekly family dinner.

The walls of her office were decorated with her various accomplishments reduced to sheets of paper. A Bachelor of Arts from Augusta University, a Juris Doctor from the University of Georgia, both *suma cum laude*. She rolled her eyes at the papers. Neither of them could seem to get her away from Savannah.

Her cell phone vibrated on the table, startling her. She picked it up and answered without looking at the caller ID. "Hello?"

"Claire, it's Jamie."

Her stomach sank as soon as she heard his voice. "Hi," she replied.

Jameson Pierce was her boyfriend of three months, though she still hesitated to use the term. They had met at a charity gala her firm sponsored, where his effortless charm and polished demeanor had initially won her over. He was the son of a prominent state legislator, and his life seemed to glide along a path paved by privilege. She was supposed to call him when she left the office—a habit he insisted on under the guise of concern for her safety, though she sometimes suspected it was more about control.

"Let me guess," he said, "you're still at the office?"

"Twenty points?" Claire said in a teasing voice, hoping to lighten the mood.

Jamie sighed. "You really don't know the meaning of 'work-life balance,' do you, Claire?"

Claire twisted her lips at his words. It was easy for him to say. He had never needed to worry about maintaining or succeeding at a job; his ticket had been written the day he was born. Unlike Jamie, whose life aligned with Savannah's old Southern ideals—complete with traditional gender roles she often chafed against—Claire had spent her career fighting for every inch of ground she gained.

Claire's family, on the other hand, had built up their influence among the Savannah social elite, but it was nothing like the Pierces'. Despite her father getting her this job, it didn't come with a lifetime guarantee. Which meant long nights at the office and missed dates.

"Sorry," Claire replied. "I'll make it up to you. Dinner tomorrow instead?"

"Yeah, that should—"

"Wait. I've got another dinner planned and I can't get out of it."

Jamie sighed on the other end of the phone. She clenched her eyelids shut and wondered how long he would put up with her difficult schedule.

Jamie's voice carried a hint of frustration when he said, "Alright, well, shoot me a text tomorrow and we can try and plan something for next week."

"Okay. Sorry again," Claire said, but Jamie had already hung up.

She put the phone down and took that call as a sign to start packing up. The pile of legal briefs that needed editing would sadly still be there for her tomorrow. She grabbed her leather tote bag and began gathering her things. The bell on the front door to the office chimed.

She figured it was the nighttime janitor returning. Stepping out from her office, she called out to him. "Don't worry about locking up. I'll take care of it when I head out."

But rather than the janitor's friendly response, her calls were met with the sound of soft, slow footsteps against the carpet. A chill ran up her spine as the steps approached her office. It wasn't until their owner rounded the corner that Claire felt like she could breathe.

An older woman with perfectly coiffed grey hair and piercing blue eyes stood in front of her. Whereas Claire's clothes had been purchased off the rack, it was clear this woman had spent a considerable sum having her ivory pantsuit custom fit to her size and shape. The luxurious blazer and matching trousers draped effortlessly over her long, slim silhouette and exuded sophistication.

Claire recognized the woman instantly. Dolores Bates was something akin to a matriarch in Savannah. The Bates family was not only wealthy, but extremely interconnected, with a longstanding pedigree. The Bates were about as close as one could get to southern royalty.

That was until their son Anthony had been convicted of a string of heinous murders. Savannah Legal represented him in his initial trial. Specifically Claire's associate, Daniel Harding. It'd been a grueling affair that captured national attention and lasted for over a week. After the jury had taken another week to deliberate, the trial had ended up in a conviction. Since then, Savannah wasn't quite sure what to make of the Bates.

Claire lifted her chin slightly. "Sorry, the office is closed."

"Perhaps you'd make an exception for an old woman." Dolores cocked her head to the side, her blue eyes twinkling. It was clear she knew she was going to get her way.

Claire took a deep breath and nodded, gesturing for Dolores to follow her into her office. "How can I help you, Mrs. Bates?"

Dolores pulled out the chair opposite Claire's desk. She sat gracefully, her back straight and hands folded in her lap. "I'd like to speak with you about a legal matter."

"Okay." Claire could feel a knot forming in her stomach. Whatever Dolores Bates asked for, she got. And she never asked for anything simple.

"As you know, my dear son Anthony has been convicted of a number of crimes he did not commit. We intend to appeal the verdict." The woman's southern twang was gentle and unassuming, her words honeyed with a practiced grace that could easily disarm most people. Claire, however, saw through the charm to the steel underneath—Dolores Bates didn't ask for things, she commanded them. "I would like you to represent him on appeal."

The knot in Claire's stomach became a deadweight in her core. "Mrs. Bates, don't you think Mr. Harding would be better suited to handle the appeal? He is, after all, much more familiar with the facts of the case."

"No," Dolores replied. "You're the lawyer we intend to hire. I'm sure you understand we have a longstanding relationship with this firm. I don't see it being a problem."

Claire pressed her lips together and held back a sigh. Mrs. Bates was politely telling her that she didn't really have a choice in this matter.

If it weren't for the truly horrific nature of Anthony's crimes, Claire would have said yes. Taking on such a high-profile case would give her the prestige, not to mention the hours, she needed to meet the firm's milestone for partner. Once she made it to partner, her life would be a little bit of her own again. At least, that's what had been promised to her by those above her.

However, up until Anthony's conviction, he'd been the beloved playboy of Savannah. Tall and blond, his blue eyes were just as piercing as his mother's, and he'd used them to his advantage. Having grown up rubbing elbows with some of the most prominent figures in Georgia politics, he knew how to command an entire room.

His arrest had taken the entire city by surprise. When he pled not guilty, it had split the city in two. His victims—seven in total—were all beautiful young women he'd stalked and subsequently murdered.

Or didn't, if his mother was to be believed.

Representing him on appeal was a risk. Taking the appeal could make her a lot of enemies, and losing could do significant harm to her already tenuous reputation.

Winning, however, would be a total gamechanger.

"I appreciate your confidence in me, Mrs. Bates," Claire said, "but I will need some time to think it over."

A smug smile formed on Dolores' lips. "I'll expect your response by five p.m. tomorrow."

Without another word, the woman stood, ran her hands over her blazer, and left the office, leaving Claire alone in stunned silence.

chapter
three

CLAIRE BREATHED a sigh of relief as she clicked the door to her apartment shut. She switched on a light and tugged her sneakers off her tired feet. If there was one thing she hated most about the legal profession, it was that everyone felt the need to wear full-blown business suits daily. She wore sneakers on her walks to and from work, but the rest of the day required her to suffer through three-inch heels. Add to that the somewhat antiquated expectations of the South—always polished, always presentable, and never showing a hint of fatigue—and daily discomfort was the result.

Claire rubbed a sore spot on one of her ankles before padding through the hallway, the plush carpeting a welcome relief against her bare feet. Her loft apartment was a short walk from the office, just a few blocks from Franklin square. She liked being in the middle of everything. It certainly wasn't New York, but the city had a certain charm to it nonetheless.

The loft was one of the few things Claire enjoyed about being back in Savannah. The apartment was open and airy, with tall ceilings and exposed beams. The walls were mostly exposed brick, and the wide windows let in plenty of natural light and a view of the quaint cityscape.

She set her leather bag down on the green velvet sofa and made her way into the kitchen. Her sister Fiona had helped her decorate the loft when she'd moved in last year, having brought over the sofa, a patterned accent chair, and a large rug to tie it together. Fiona's tastes were a little more eclectic than Claire's, but she appreciated the inspired pops of color.

Claire grabbed a bottle of wine from the cooler, grasped the corkscrew, twisting it into the cork, and pulled it free with a satisfying pop. The rich aroma of dark berries and oak filled her nose. She poured the deep red liquid into her favorite wine glass.

She plopped onto the sofa and took a luxurious sip. Closing her eyes, she savored the warmth in the back of her throat. Her muscles had almost started to relax, until she remembered Mrs. Bates' visit.. Claire's eyes shot back open and she sighed, her mind heavy with memories of the Bates murders.

The trial had been ongoing when Claire had joined the firm. While she hadn't been involved, she'd still been privy to a lot of the facts and details of the case. The particulars

of the crimes he'd been accused of committing would never leave her mind.

She caught a look at herself curled up on the sofa from one of the accent mirrors across the loft. She let out a sad chuckle and rubbed beneath her eyes. Dark circles had become her new norm and no amount of caffeine patches or eye cream could help them. She was hunched in on herself, intent on protecting whatever dignity she had.

Claire had never been one to turn down work when it was offered to her. Not that she had much choice as an associate. But this sort of assignment was different. And appeals were almost never successful. Who could she talk to about this? Who did she trust enough not to start rumors and also appreciate just how difficult a decision this was?

She leaned over the coffee table and picked up her phone, intent on calling Fiona, but hesitated as she was about to press the call button. Fiona was currently seeing Daniel Harding, the associate who'd handled Bates' trial and lost. Claire was almost certain word would get back to Daniel if she asked for Fiona's opinion. Besides, it wouldn't be entirely fair to put Fiona on the spot like that.

Claire started scrolling through her contacts, her thumb hesitating over names that felt more like distant acquaintances than true friends. As she did, she idly wished she had a stronger group of people in whom she could confide—friends who truly understood her. But sadly, all work and no play left very little time for friendship, especially after the mess she'd left behind in New York. Starting over in Savannah hadn't exactly been her choice, and the circumstances of her abrupt departure were still a raw wound she avoided revisiting. Whatever the reason, it had made it harder to trust people, leaving her feeling more isolated than she cared to admit.

She scrolled until she found Meredith Porter's name. Meredith and Claire had become fast friends after sitting at a communal table at a local coffee shop. Claire and Meredith had discovered they'd attended the same undergraduate institution. They'd only overlapped by one year and had never run into each other as far as they knew. Meredith had gotten her degree in psychology and recently finished her doctoral work to become a licensed clinical physiologist. If anyone could understand the weight of this sort of decision, it would be Meredith.

Decision made, she pressed "call."

She drummed her fingers on the edge of the coffee table, her gaze flicking to the nearly empty wine bottle on the counter as the dial tone hummed in her ear. The silence of the apartment, broken only by the faint ticking of the clock, pressed down on her.

Meredith's warm voice greeted her after a few rings. "Hey, Claire!"

"Hi Meredith." Claire tried hard to keep the anxiety out of her voice. "I hope I'm not bothering you. I sort of need someone to talk to about a pretty big decision."

"Of course! I'm glad you called me. Did you want to talk now or is it something you wanted to discuss in person?"

Claire adjusted the throw pillow behind her back, shifting restlessly on the sofa. Her fingers traced absent patterns over the soft fabric as she considered her words.

Claire took another sip of her wine, hoping it would give her some renewed confidence. "I wish I had time to talk in person, but I'm sort of on a tight deadline."

"No problem. What's up?"

Claire took a deep breath and leaned back against the sofa, putting down her half-empty wine glass. "It's about a case. You remember Anthony Bates?"

"Yeah, of course. Everyone remembers him."

"His mother wants me to represent him on appeal."

"Whoa." Claire could imagine the way Meredith's eyes would widen with this information. "Why you?"

"That's a great question. I'm not sure, but she was insistent."

"Didn't your colleague handle his trial?"

"Yeah, and Anthony was obviously convicted."

"Right. Maybe that's why she doesn't want him handling the appeal? Since he lost the case in the first place?"

"I guess so." Claire got to her feet and grabbed her glass, deciding she need another round.

The bottle clinked faintly against the countertop as she poured. The swirl of red liquid filled the glass, its rich aroma briefly grounding her.

"How do you feel about it?" Meredith asked, hitting home on Claire's inner turmoil.

Claire exhaled slowly as she poured herself another glass. She tried to organize her thoughts into something moderately articulate.

"I guess I'm worried about the potential consequences. If I'm not successful in defending him—and there's a pretty big chance I won't be —that could have serious implications for my professional reputation. Not to mention the emotional strain of trying to defend Anthony Bates."

Meredith was silent for a moment. "Do you think he's guilty?"

Claire took a long sip of wine before answering. "I'm not really sure. I'm never sure that anyone is. I mean, he did confess originally. Why would someone confess to crimes they didn't commit?"

"Sounds pretty damning to me."

"But if I won the appeal, this could literally make my career."

"But then you'd have to live with the fact that you got him off the hook when you're not really sure about his innocence at all."

"So, you see my predicament." Claire sank back into the sofa, her elbow brushing against a stack of unopened mail she hadn't touched all week. She turned away from her reflection across the room. "All of this is complicated by the fact that I'm not even sure I have a choice if I want to keep my job."

"What do you mean?"

"Dolores Bates made it pretty clear that her family has a long-standing relationship with the firm. I wouldn't be surprised if she's already let Bob know."

"Bob?"

"The managing partner."

"Right. Well, who cares about what Bob or Dolores want? What do *you* want? At the end of the day, you have to be comfortable with the decision you make. You shouldn't let other people sway you one way or another."

Claire took a sip. "The thing is, I'm terrified I'll lose my job if I don't take this case."

"So what if you lose your job?" Meredith said. "You'll find another one."

Claire gave a lifeless chuckle. "It's not that easy in the legal field. If a lawyer is out to find a new position, firms always assume it's due to a problem with them." Plus, she doubted she'd find anyone willing to take a chance on her, having stayed in New York less than a year before returning to Savannah.

"I understand," Meredith said, her tone gentle. "But I still don't think that should sway your decision."

Claire fidgeted and sighed. Her fingers brushed over the glass rim absentmindedly, leaving faint smudges in the condensation. She stared down at the swirling liquid, her thoughts a tangle. "I don't know. I still feel so torn."

"Alright, let's approach this in a more clinical way. I'm going to throw some fancy terms at you, but just bear with me."

"I think I can handle it."

"Good. Now, there's something in the psychology world that's called a 'heuristic,' which is just a shortcut for people to make decisions or judgments quickly."

"Okay, I'm following."

"Now, one way to approach decision making is to determine how likely something is. This is called the 'availability heuristic.' For example, if you were deciding whether you should speed in order to make an appointment on time, and your fear is that you will get a ticket, you might approach that decision by thinking about how many times you've seen other people get a ticket for speeding."

"Okay, but I'm not sure I understand how that helps me with my situation."

"What I'm wondering is, in your situation, what is the one biggest thing holding you back from taking this case?"

Claire closed her eyes and took a deep breath. "I guess it would be actually working with Anthony. Then becoming one of his victims."

"Okay, good," Meredith said. "Now, can you think of any other examples of when a defendant of this nature attacked their lawyer?"

Claire scrunched her face as she tried to think. Like most women her age, she was a bit of an avid true crime junkie, but she'd never come across this fact pattern.

"I can't think of any."

"Right. And what about Daniel? He worked with Anthony. Has anything bad happened to him?"

"No, but Daniel doesn't fit the target demographic. And Anthony is in prison right now."

"True. Now if you take all that into account, do you think it'd help you make your decision?"

The outcome was inevitable. Claire took a gulp of wine to fill a forming void. Her free hand clenched the throw pillow beside her, its plush texture grounding her for a fleeting moment. "I should take the case."

"I think if you didn't want to, you wouldn't have called me to talk it over."

"Maybe you're right," Claire said, a small smile forming. "This is why I say you've saved me a fortune on therapy. Having you as a friend might be the best decision I've ever made."

"I didn't go to school for the last decade for nothing."

Claire chuckled. "I guess that's true. Thanks, Meredith. I really appreciate it."

"Sure thing! Hey, before you go, there's an event over in Augusta next week. I was wondering if you wanted to go with me. It's a conference for us psych majors, but it might be nice for you to get out of town for a bit."

Claire finished the rest of her second glass of wine and placed it on the table. "I'm not sure what my schedule will be with taking this case on, but I'll fit it in if I can."

"Just let me know."

"Thanks again," Claire said. "I'll let you get back to your Friday evening."

"Of watching Gilmore Girls reruns?" Meredith laughed. "You're too kind."

As the women hung up, Claire straightened with a renewed sense of excitement. Her gaze drifted over to the unopened laptop on the table. If she really was successful in pulling off this appeal, this could be the lucky break she needed to make a name for herself.

chapter
four

"I SEE someone was busy this weekend." Bob Hayes stood at the threshold to Claire's office holding a steaming mug of the office's notoriously bitter coffee; He sipped it casually, completely unbothered by the acrid aroma that made Claire's stomach churn. He looked the way he always did—a short man with bushy white hair and a matching mustache, wearing a crisp navy suit, a white shirt and red tie. The uniform of a Southern Republican.

Claire plastered on the fakest smile she could muster. "Glad I could get it all done for you, Bob."

"Good work, putting in the hours," he said, stepping a little further inside. "This job is more about commitment than it is about talent."

Claire stifled a groan and instead nodded her head, trying to seem enthusiastic. "Did you see my email over the weekend?"

His face contorted in exaggerated confusion. "Afraid not."

Claire held back a sigh. Of course he hadn't. Yet if she was even a minute late to reading one of his emails, he wouldn't let her hear the end of it for a month. She really wanted to say, "so much for commitment over talent," but stopped herself. Bob was much more of a, "do as I say, not as I do," sort of mentor.

"Well, Dolores Bates stopped by Friday evening," Claire began, sitting straighter as Bob paced back and forth in front of her desk.

He lifted an eyebrow, not breaking stride. "What did she want?"

"She's requested that I take Anthony's appeal."

"You don't say." Bob finally paused, his tone as unfazed as if she'd mentioned a traffic ticket. "And what did you tell her?"

"That I'd think about it," Claire replied, careful to keep her tone neutral. "But she only gave me a twenty-four-hour window to consider." She hesitated, glancing at Bob to gauge his reaction, but he simply gestured for her to continue. "When I didn't receive your response to my email, I felt compelled to go ahead and accept the case."

Before Claire could get another word in, Bob cut her off with a dismissive wave. "That's great news, then," he said, finally stopping his pacing and flashing her a smile. "I would have done the same. Good to keep the business under the same roof."

Claire bit back a sigh. Bob had a habit of cutting her off mid-sentence, something he liked to chalk up to his years in New York. But Claire had worked in New York, too, and the excuse didn't hold water. In truth, it seemed more like he just enjoyed the sound of his own voice.

Still, his approval eased some of the tension in her shoulders. She'd been anxious when he hadn't responded to her email, her mind spinning with worst-case scenarios about the fallout of making the decision alone. With Bob's blessing, at least she wouldn't be in hot water for stepping on any toes.

"Wait just a minute." Daniel Harding's voice interrupted from the hallway, his sharp tone heralding his arrival as he strode into her office at precisely the worst moment.

Claire had a feeling that losing out on the appeal would not be a convenient thing for Daniel. Since she and Daniel were the only two associates at the small firm, they were in constant competition for work and prestige. Daniel was Claire's senior as far as time at the firm went, but they otherwise had the same number of years practicing on their resumes.

Daniel's face was flushed and his movements were sharp with frustration. "Why should Claire get this assignment? I represented Anthony at trial. I know the case like the back of my hand."

"That is true," Bob said, ever one to stir the pot. He looked at Claire expectantly, as if it were her responsibility to argue Daniel's point.

Claire glared back at her mentor. "I said exactly that to Mrs. Bates."

"Wait." Daniel stared at her in disbelief and sputtered. "You already met with the client?"

Claire held up her hand. "The client's mother. She came to the office late on Friday night and asked me to take the case. I suggested she contact you for the appeal instead, given your history with it. But for some reason she said she wanted me."

"Seems entirely too convenient to me." Daniel scoffed and ran a hand through his thick brown hair. He adjusted his glasses and gave Claire a piercing glare. "It sounds like she came in looking for help on her son's appeal and you snaked this case from me."

Claire took a deep breath and resisted the urge to put her head in her hands. If only this man knew the absolute anxiety she experienced over whether to even accept Mrs. Bates' request, he wouldn't be saying these things. Unfortunately Daniel, like most lawyers, was entirely self-absorbed. It didn't bode too well for her sister's budding relationship, but Fiona was going to have to figure that out for herself.

"Daniel, I give you my word that I did no such thing."

"Your word means nothing to me, Claire."

She ground her teeth together and fisted her hands under the table. It was this sort of behavior that made Claire really hate working with lawyers, let alone be one.

"Alright now." Bob placed a hand on Daniel's shoulder. "I know you're disappointed, but we need to keep the client happy. Especially a client like Dolores Bates."

Daniel shoved Bob's hand away. "This is ridiculous! Dolores Bates didn't ask for Claire. She's not even a defense attorney. She handles the firm's corporate work!"

Bob shrugged his shoulders. "You're welcome to call Dolores and confirm her request."

"I plan to do just that," Daniel said, all but pushing past Bob to get in front of Claire. He stepped up to her desk and leaned over. "Get her on the line."

Claire bent forward, suddenly feeling protective over her small piece of the office. "Excuse me?"

"We're going to call Dolores Bates together. Right now. And confirm what really happened."

"You've got to be kidding me."

"Do I look like I'm joking?" Daniel asked. Claire looked him up and down. He actually looked to be in a murderous rage.

Claire couldn't stop herself from rolling her eyes. She wasn't quite sure why her sister liked this guy so much. He had average looks and a bad temper. Not to mention a questionable work ethic. He never stayed at the office much past five and was never here on the weekends. She questioned whether he ever really put enough time into his cases and secretly wondered if that's why he'd lost the Bates trial.

"Fine," Claire said, knowing just how this was going to end. She turned away from Daniel and dialed the number Dolores had given her, placing the call on speaker for the room to hear. The woman picked up on the second ring.

"Yes?"

"Mrs. Bates, it's Claire with Savannah Legal."

"Claire, good to hear from you."

" I'm here with my colleague, Daniel Harding—"

"Claire, I thought I made myself clear on Friday. You are the one I want on this case, not Daniel."

Claire didn't need to turn around to know just how red Daniel's face had gotten. She could almost feel the smoke blowing from his ears.

"Daniel has a lot of experience with the facts of the original case, Mrs. Bates. Are you saying you don't want him working on this at all?"

Dolores took on a clipped tone. "What I'm saying, Claire, is that I am hiring you, and you alone, to represent my son in the appeal. I have great respect for Savannah Legal and the other attorneys who work there, but I don't want them working on this."

"Okay," Claire replied, feeling more apprehensive than she'd anticipated. She hadn't understood that this woman had wanted her in a complete vacuum. Nor did she understand Dolores' reasoning for that.

Daniel cut in before Claire could say anything else, his tone akin to a used car salesman. "With all due respect, Mrs. Bates, I think you're making a mistake. No one is more familiar with your son's situation than I am. Besides, not to discredit Ms. Stevens here, but she's never done defense work before. She handles our corporate affairs."

"I appreciate you trying to talk yourself back on the case Mr. Harding, but, it's useless. I'm well aware of Ms. Stevens' background. I would never have asked her to take the case if I didn't think she was capable. And if you were so familiar with our son's case, then perhaps we wouldn't have lost the trial to begin with."

Claire's office became deadly silent. Her lips pressed into a thin line and she didn't dare look at the man behind her. It was clear that Daniel didn't have a defense for Dolores' unexpected attack.

Dolores continued, her tone terse. "Do you have any other questions for me, Claire?"

"No," Claire replied quickly, looking forward to ending the conversation. "Thank you."

"Excellent. I expect weekly updates on your progress. Speak soon."

Claire turned to Bob, who was still sipping his coffee as if the two associates who worked under him weren't completely at war.

"I guess that settles it then," he said, completely oblivious to Daniel's impending meltdown. "Danny, go and grab Claire the Bates files from your office when you get a moment."

Daniel managed to sputter an "Okay," before storming out of the office.

Bob watched the man leave in a fiery rage and shrugged his shoulders. "Don't worry about him. He'll come around."

"Sure," Claire said, sarcasm dripping from the word.

Bob made his way to the door and tapped the other side of the frame. "Looks like you've got a lot to do, then. Holler if you need anything."

"Thanks," Claire mumbled as he left her to her fate.

Her phone buzzed within seconds and she picked it up to see a text from her sister.

No need for lunch today.

Claire furrowed her brows. She and Fiona had a standing weekly lunch date, a tradition they'd started when Claire returned to Savannah from New York. It had been Fiona's way of reconnecting, insisting they carve out time despite their hectic schedules. Fiona had recently graduated with a degree in journalism and landed a job at the local newspaper—not exactly the Pulitzer-caliber reporting she'd dreamed of, but it gave her plenty of juicy gossip to share over coffee.

She picked up her phone and dialed her sister's number.

"What do you want, Claire?" Fiona asked, her tone dripping with derision.

"I'm just a little confused."

"What's there to be confused about? I'm canceling our lunch."

"Why?"

"Seriously?" Fiona said, the scowl clear in her voice. "You can't figure it out?"

Claire pinched the bridge of her nose. "Are you seriously canceling lunch on me because of the Bates case?"

"You completely stole it out from under him, Claire!"

"No, I didn't! I don't know what he's told you, but we just got off the phone with Dolores herself. She wanted to hire me and only me! If it had been up to me, I wouldn't be involved at all."

"Yeah, that sounds really convenient."

"Are you seriously going to side with your boyfriend, who you barely know, over your sister?"

"I'm not siding with anyone," Fiona said. "I'm making up my own mind."

Claire scoffed. "And then siding with your boyfriend."

"Think whatever you want, Claire. But for now, I need some space."

"Real nice," Claire said. "Just at the time when I need the most support, my own family pulls away."

"Feel free to get your support from Dad. He always liked you better, anyway."

Fiona hung up without another word.

"I wonder who that could be?" Daniel said, a smug smile on his face as Claire looked up to see him with one of the Bates boxes.

She locked eyes with the man. "I'm not sure what good poisoning my own sister against me does for you."

Daniel feigned innocence, saying, "Not sure what you mean."

Claire got up to grab the box he was holding. As she took it, she looked down at the contents. Attorneys generally had legal assistants organize case files into binders. But this box looked like it had gone through a tornado.

Daniel all but sneered. "The boxes must have dropped at some point, so none of the files are organized. Too bad Dolores wants you to work on the case completely by yourself. I'd have been able to help you put it all back together, but—" he shrugged, his lips tugged into a smug smile. "Good luck."

Claire decided that causing a scene or getting huffy with Daniel was only going to waste her energy. Instead, she put on a smile and said, "Thank you."

chapter
five

THE HEAT of the summer was oppressive as Claire rounded the corner onto Whitaker Street. Her parents had recently moved from their larger home in Ardsley Park to a smaller one in the Southern Historic District. The house had been built in 1895 and while it had been tastefully updated, the structure was a little garish with its two-story latticed balconies and large bay windows.

As she walked up the porch steps, she glanced at the wicker seating arrangement, complete with perfectly stitched cushions in a loud floral fabric. If the house was garish, her mother's sense of decor was downright ostentatious—an aesthetic that had sparked more than one argument between them. Claire could still hear her mother's voice ringing in her ears from last Christmas: *"Honestly, Claire, beige is not a color. It's a lack of personality."*

As the oldest daughter, Claire seemed to bear the brunt of her mother's attention and criticism, a fate her sister had seemed to escape. Fiona may have claimed that their father liked Claire better, but Fiona shared a much closer relationship with their mother, one filled with mutual admiration rather than constant judgment.

According to her mother, Claire wasn't supposed to become a lawyer. She was meant to become a doctor. She had come from a long line of doctors and consistently said it was a shame that no one followed in their noble footsteps. How Claire was supposed to become a doctor when she fainted at the sight of a papercut was a riddle her mother refused to answer.

Claire steeled herself as she grasped the large brass door handle and entered the home. The moment she walked in, the scents of Sunday dinner were all around her. Weekend dinners were always an affair for the Stevens', complete with hired chefs who started cooking in the wee hours of the morning.

"Hello?" Claire called out as she slid out of her sneakers in the foyer.

"I want the Cornish game hen to be golden brown this time, not burnt like it was the last time you cooked it." The melodic voice of Gretchen Stevens scolding the kitchen staff drifted on the air, making the house feel like the home Claire remembered. "Claire!" Gretchen exclaimed as she floated into the foyer. "So glad you came!"

Claire resisted the urge to roll her eyes. Her mother said that as if she had some choice in the matter. If Claire didn't show to Sunday dinner, there would be hell to pay. She knew, because she'd paid it before.

Gretchen was a 65-year-old woman straight out of a Country Living magazine. Her blonde hair had a shine straight from the salon—a shine that also did a good deal to cover up her grays. Her A-line dress was a loud floral pattern that rivaled the outside sofa cushions and a simple pearl necklace hugged her neck. Gretchen compensated her shortening height with classic leather pumps, despite that wearing them around the house required annual refinishing of the wooden floors.

"Happy to be here, Mother."

"Dinner's almost ready. Come say hi to your father while we wait."

Gretchen all but pulled Claire into the sunroom where Roy Stevens was smoking a cigar. The smoky haze floated in the air against the sunbeams glowing from the windows on every wall.

Claire sighed. "Dad, those are so bad for your health."

For the first time since Claire had returned home, she could see her father's age finally catching up with him. Roy was nearing 73. Whereas Gretchen did what she could to cover up her grays, Roy embraced them wholeheartedly, complete with a full head of white hair, matching beard and mustache. As he stood, Claire noticed that he was a few pounds thinner. But he was never one to skip out on a meal, so it definitely wasn't from dieting.

"Don't deny an old man his pleasures," he said, putting the cigar out and waving away the smoke. A big grin spread across his face and he held his arms out. "Are you too old to give your dad a hug?"

Claire smiled back and eased into her father's embrace, a little less tight than it used to be. The cigar smoke lingered against his clothing.

"Come on and sit," he said as they parted. Claire sat across from him on one of the sofas. "How's the new job going?"

"Dinner's ready!" Gretchen sang from down the hallway, not allowing them a chance to reconnect in peace.

Roy gave his daughter a small roll of his eyes and then a wink. "We better get going. If we don't sit down right away, we'll never hear the end of it."

Claire nodded and the pair moved into the dining room. As to be expected, the table was set meticulously. A burgundy satin cloth covered what Claire knew to be one of her mother's most prized heirlooms, the dining table to an eleven-piece set by Theodore Alexander. Not that anyone ever got to see it, because it was always covered by a tablecloth.

Two gold candlesticks graced the center, flanked by matching gold and crystal dinnerware. The napkins were folded into intricate fan designs and a gold platter filled with hors d'oeuvres was placed at one end. A selection of wines and spirits were on the matching buffet on the opposite wall.

Roy made his way over to the buffet to pour himself a brandy. "Don't mind if I do."

"Cigars *and* brandy? Aren't you the least bit worried about your health?"

Roy chuckled to himself. "If the internet is to be believed, at any time I can go vegan and I'll suddenly look forty and all my ailments will be cured overnight."

Gretchen scolded as he took a big swig from his drink. "Honestly, Roy."

Roy winked at his daughter and the three sat down to what Claire knew would be an uncomfortable dinner.

"So," Gretchen began as she placed her napkin in her lap with practiced poise. "You were about to tell your father about how your new job is going. How long have you been there now, dear?"

Claire wished she was having this conversation with just her father alone. He showed a genuine interest in her life and well-being. If her mother ever showed interest, it was to gather ammunition.

"It's going well," she replied. "Thank you for asking, Mother."

"Is Bob still a right bastard?" Claire's father asked with a laugh.

"Roy!" Gretchen exclaimed. "Please watch your language at the dinner table!"

The two waiters who were always present for these dinners brought out the first course. A salad with an array of colors and textures. Golden yellow sautéed squash and deep red roasted beets fanned the edges, interspersed with delicate curls of parsley and sprigs of fresh rosemary. While her family's Sunday dinners were absolutely not her favorite pastime, the food was far better than the microwave dinners she routinely ate at the office.

"Sorry, dear," Roy said, a bit of sarcasm coating his voice. "I meant to say, how is working for Bob?"

"It's alright, I guess."

"Alright? You guess?" Gretchen moved the lettuce around with her fork and barely putting any of it into her mouth. "Why, what's wrong?"

"Nothing's wrong, Mother," Claire said through gritted teeth. "Being a lawyer isn't an easy job."

"Well, it's the job you wanted."

Claire took a deep breath. She knew what was coming.

"You would have made such a good doctor. You got an 'A' in Advanced Chemistry. It's really a shame you didn't follow through on that path."

"Yes, thank you." Claire shoved a fork full of lettuce into her mouth.

"The medical community isn't what it once was these days," Roy said, frowning at the beet on his fork. "Too many lawyers sniffing around hospitals looking for a payday."

It was ironic of Roy to say that, given he'd made the family's fortune being one such lawyer. Claire could never understand why her mother was so preoccupied with her becoming a doctor when her father had done such a good job elevating the family's name and status by being a lawyer.

It hadn't always been easy and for a time Roy had struggled to get cases, living paycheck to paycheck when Claire and Fiona were younger. But after the Savannah River Site litigation finally took off, Roy was exceptional at winning cases. Watching her father's drive and dedication was what made Claire change her mind about becoming a doctor and pursue a legal career.

Claire absently chewed on her fingernail as the conversation spiraled. She wasn't even aware of it until her mother's voice cut through.

"Claire," Gretchen said sharply, her eyes narrowing in disapproval. "I wish you'd get rid of that wretched habit. It's unbecoming of someone in your position."

Claire dropped her hand to her lap, her face heating. "Yes, Mother," she muttered, biting back the urge to say something sharper. She focused on the vibrant salad in front of her instead, pushing the roasted beets around her plate.

Gretchen shoved a sprig of lettuce into her mouth and shook her head. "Such a shame."

"Anyways," Claire said with a sigh. "I actually picked up a pretty large case on Friday."

"Oh?" Roy said, deciding to put the beet back down on the plate and take a sip of brandy instead.

"I'll be representing Anthony Bates on his appeal."

"Oh, Claire!" Gretchen all but wailed, throwing her fork onto the plate with a clatter. "You can't!"

The waiters brought out the second course and the three fell into a tense silence as everything was placed in front of them. Claire always thought it a curious thing, that her family refused to speak in front of the kitchen staff. It's not like they were unable to hear the entire conversation from the kitchen.

A butternut squash soup garnished with pepitas and rosemary was placed in front of her. The smell was mouthwatering and Claire wished she could just enjoy the soup in peace and quiet, but she knew that was a pipe dream.

"Why can't I?" Claire finally asked when the staff left.

Gretchen looked between Claire and her husband. "Roy, please! Talk some sense into your daughter. She is talking about representing a murderer."

"He's appealing his conviction. I'll be representing him on his appeal."

"He confessed to the police. Everyone heard the story. Plus, he was convicted. An innocent man doesn't just confess to murdering seven women. Claire! It's dangerous! You could become a target." Gretchen turned to her husband. "Roy? A little help here."

Roy shrugged. "She's a lawyer, dear. She deals with people who break the law."

Claire smiled at her father who was hiding his own smile with a sip of brandy. .

She tasted her soup and glanced at her mother. "I'm honestly a bit surprised that you're not more excited by this."

Gretchen sat back in her seat, clearly giving up on the prospect of eating entirely. "Why on earth would I be excited about you representing a psychopath?"

"The Bates hold a lot of sway in this city."

Gretchen shook her head. "No, dear. They *used* to hold a lot of sway in this city. Until their son was convicted of murdering seven young women. Everyone talks behind their backs."

"Including you, I suppose."

Gretchen glared at her daughter. "I don't understand why you couldn't do a different type of law."

"If you recall," Claire muttered, "I was trying to practice corporate law in New York."

"And you let everything that happened your senior year of high school reenter your life and ruin that for you," Gretchen bit out. "After all this time, almost a decade, and you still can't seem to get over it. Honestly, Claire, how long are you going to let it control your life?"

Claire gritted her teeth and stood. Her chair screeched against the floor, giving voice to the anger inside of her. "I've lost my appetite. I think I'll head home."

chapter
six

GRETCHEN OPENED her mouth to protest, but Roy intervened. "Gretchen, enough!" Then turned to his daughter, his tone softer. "Claire, please sit down."

Claire knew better than to disagree with her father. She took her seat and crossed her arms, facing away from her mother.

"Everyone in this family is so dramatic. Would it be possible to go one whole dinner without someone threatening to leave?"

The blood in Claire's veins began to boil. "I'm tired of Mother constantly bringing it up."

"I understand, but the matter is dead and buried, which means you need to move on from it."

"Could have used a different turn of phrase, Dad."

"*Moving on,*" Roy said, "I've got something I'd actually like to discuss."

The kitchen staff brought out the main course. Individual Cornish game hens with a variety of sides placed in the center of the table.

Roy took a long drink from his glass as he waited for the family to be alone again, his eyes moving between his wife and daughter.

Claire and Gretchen looked back at him expectantly as soon as the wait staff were back in the kitchen.

"Yes?" Gretchen finally asked her husband impatiently.

"I've been reading this book on World War II." Roy all but grinned. "And I wanted to tell you both about it."

Claire laughed into her fork at her father's antics.

"Some other time, dear," Gretchen replied gently, thinking he was serious.

Roy chuckled to himself and grabbed the leg from his hen. "Speak to your sister lately?"

Claire sighed. "Yes, and no."

"Why do you say that?" Her mother asked, not even considering touching the food on her plate. "What's wrong?"

"Maybe you should ask her," Claire remarked. "Which by the way, why doesn't she have to be at Sunday dinners?"

"She's very busy with her journalism job, sweetheart."

"And I'm not busy working as an attorney in private practice with a billable hours expectation north of 2200 a year?"

"No one said you weren't busy."

"I'm just tired of the double standards when it comes to this family. She's the younger sister and seems to get away with everything. She even got to pick her own career."

"So did you, dear."

Claire closed her eyes. "Glad we managed to come full circle in our dinner conversation." In that moment, she decided it might just be better for her to stay silent the rest of the dinner.

"Speaking of," Roy said, "how do you intend to represent the Bates kid on this appeal? If he confessed, that's gonna be tough to argue against, no?"

"Confessions and guilty verdicts are two different things," Claire replied. "Appeals are all about procedure. Did the Court follow the correct procedure throughout the entire trial? If they didn't, did their mess-up prejudice the defendant?"

"Sounds complicated." Roy downed the rest of the liquid in his glass. "This is why I never handled the appellate stuff. I liked to get my hands dirty with the actual trial work."

"It is fun to go through the record and figure things out. It's a bit like being handed a huge bag of puzzle pieces. You don't know what the thing's supposed to look like at the end, or even if the pieces are all from the same puzzle."

"Yep." Roy smiled proudly at his daughter. "Sounds horrible. But I know you're up to the task."

Claire returned his smile.

The two locked eyes and Roy winked at his daughter. "So, do you get to read about all the murders?"

"Yes," Claire responded. Her father glanced at her mother from the corner of his eye. He was clearly trying to rile her up. One of his favorite pastimes.

"How many were there again?"

"Seven."

"Seven murders," Roy said slowly before whistling.

Gretchen fidgeted in her seat, pushing bits of food around her plate and putting none in her mouth.

"I remember the news saying something about him being systematic in the way he killed people."

Gretchen's eyes widened but she kept her gaze trained on her plate.

"Yes," Claire said, nodding dramatically. "Serial killers often are."

"What exactly did he do? Tell me *all* the gritty trial details you've uncovered so far."

The facts of Anthony's trial were pretty well-known. While not as widely followed as the Depp-Heard trial, it had the same sort of notoriety around Savannah. Something about a young attractive man killing young attractive women in Savannah's elite seemed to capture the interest of society. But Roy was asking not because he hadn't been paying attention, but because he wanted to fluster his wife.

And Claire was all in. "He clearly stalked his subjects for some time."

"How do you figure?"

"He knew a lot about them. Their interests, whereabouts, hobbies. He used that information to send them items. Five in total. Each one unique to the victim in some way before they received the last gift, which was accompanied by the actual murder."

Gretchen remained silent, a rarity at Sunday night dinners. Claire relished in this.

Roy took a swig of his brandy. "Walk me through one of them."

"One of the murders?" Claire clarified and Roy nodded his head.

"The first of his victims was Olivia Parker. She was finishing her senior year of undergraduate studies at Florida State University, but her family lives here. No one actually knows how she met Anthony. Depositions of her friends suggested it may have started online and then become an in-person thing when she moved back."

"What were these gifts he gave her?"

Claire placed her fork down on the table. "The first always started off with a personal letter. I can't remember the exact details of hers, but it was something akin to a fan or love letter."

"A fan letter?"

Claire shrugged. "Apparently one or two of the victims had big social media followings."

Roy nodded, and Claire continued. "The second gift was always something the victim had a present interest in. For Olivia, this was a gold bracelet."

Roy let out a whistle and took a bite of his hen. "An expensive one?"

Claire laughed. "I don't know what the appraised value of it was, Dad."

"Man knows how to court. Okay, keep going."

"I found the third gift to be the creepiest. It was something that indicated Anthony was watching the victim. In Olivia's case, it was a ticket stub from a concert she'd recently attended."

Roy wrinkled his nose. "Agreed."

Claire looked at her mother, who was still looking down at her plate. Her fork was barely moving by this time.

"And the fourth gift was always something about their past. Olivia's was a pompom. I guess she was a cheerleader back in high school."

Roy shrugged. "And the last gift?"

"Always a bouquet of flowers. Their favorite kind. And they were always found dead with it." A chill ran up Claire's spine. She wanted to brush off people's concerns about representing a man like Anthony, but she was still nervous about it.

"How'd she die?" Roy asked.

"Most of the time it was some form of drug introduced to their system," Claire said, finally taking a bite of her dinner.

"How'd the police know they didn't administer it themselves?"

"None of the victims had any history of drug use," Claire replied. "Plus, with all the calling cards Anthony left with each one, coupled with his confession, made for a pretty easy conviction."

"Do you know if there are pictures of the victims?"

"Roy!" Gretchen finally blurted out, unable to take it any longer. "Sweetheart," she said, turning to Claire. "Please, reconsider. You can't really be thinking of representing a man like this. He's hurt our community. I don't care what the Bates family is offering to pay you. You don't need to worry about your reputation by refusing this case. They don't hold that sort of sway anymore."

Claire shook her head. Of course her mother thought that her only motivation for taking this case was because it might impact her social standing. "It's not about popularity. No one should make a decision like this based on what it will do for them socially."

" I think you should at least consider it." Gretchen huffed. "While you may not be concerned about what it does to your social standing, did you ever think about what it could do to our family name? If you agree to represent this lunatic, we all will suffer because of it."

Claire held up her finger. "First of all, he's not a lunatic. He's a serial killer. There's a big difference."

Roy smirked behind his empty glass.

Gretchen turned to her husband. "Please help me here."

"The girl's mind is made up, dear," he said, shrugging. "She's all grown up now. There's nothing either of us can really do. I think it best to just support her."

Gretchen stood up from her seat. "Sometimes I honestly think your goal in life is to drag this family's name through the mud, Claire."

Claire didn't respond. When her mother got upset, she got nasty, and there was no reasoning with the woman. Claire had learned that the hard way.

"All this talk of *murder* has ruined this dinner and made me lose my appetite. I'm retiring." Her heels clicked against the shining wood as she made her way up the stairs.

Claire and her father waited until they heard the upstairs door click shut. Roy looked at his watch and tapped the face of it. "We made it a full two minutes longer this time."

"Two minutes longer till what?"

"Until someone huffed away from the dinner table."

"You track that?" Claire asked in a mix of amusement and disbelief.

"What else am I supposed to do to entertain myself at these dinners?"

Claire pushed her full plate to the side. "So, you don't like them either, huh?"

"It's not that I don't like them." Roy leaned back in his chair. "It's just that they've become a little contentious over the past year."

"A little," Claire chuckled.

Roy leaned forward and caught his daughter's gaze. "Your mother does have a point, Claire. This man Anthony Bates is clearly very dangerous. I am worried about you getting close to him. What if you get him off the hook and he turns on you?"

"I did consider that," Claire replied, nodding. "But then I decided that that would be a pretty nasty way to repay your lawyer for saving your neck."

"But as you said, the man's a serial killer. That's what he does."

"I know, Dad." Claire shivered, feeling the weight of her decision more than ever. "But if no one agreed to represent people society deemed dangerous, then the system would break down. Everyone deserves representation, and everyone deserves a fair trial."

"I know, Claire Bear," Roy said, his voice lowering to a whisper. "But just be careful."

chapter
seven

Claire wove her way through the crowded hallway of Mingledorff Hall, taking the gleaming birch stairs two at a time. She, like many of Savannah's social elite, attended the Savannah Country Day School. The hall had been recently updated. Large white columns were illuminated by modern LED lights overhead. She rather liked Mingledorff Hall. Even though she wasn't focusing on science or math, she didn't mind walking over to find her friend.

This was her senior year and as much as she enjoyed her time here, she was looking forward to moving away for college. Her relationship with her mother was starting to degrade. Gretchen very much wanted Claire to go to medical school, but Claire had already told her that just wasn't going to happen. And, when Gretchen didn't get her way, she made her displeasure known.

Claire had told her mother that even if she had to pay her own way, she would make her career choice work. Her father had told her in confidence he would make sure she got the support she needed. He said to be patient with her mother, that eventually she would come around.

Claire was still waiting.

As she got to the second floor and made her way down the hallway, her eyes scanned for a familiar face. She spotted Matthew at his locker, his sandy blonde hair styled perfectly and his crisp button-down shirt tucked into designer jeans. He looked up when she got closer and flashed a charming smile.

"Hey there, Claire Bear," he said, teasingly. He'd heard her father say it to her one time and that was it. She would never escape the nickname as far as Matty was concerned. "What brings you to my neck of the woods?"

"Just wanted to see your pretty face, Matty." She rolled her eyes. "What's on the agenda for next period?"

"Biology," Matty said, his eyes gleaming with excitement.

"Ugh." Claire scrunched up her nose. "Sounds like a nightmare. I don't think I'll ever understand why plants need to go through photosynthesis."

"You literature snobs. I wish I could be interested in old books like you."

"Speaking of which"—Claire leaned against the locker next to him, folding her arms—"have you made any progress with your dad yet?"

Matty's expression darkened. "Not really. He's still pushing me towards Emory and a business degree. It's like he doesn't even care about what I want."

"That sucks. I'm sorry. I guess he's still intent on you taking over the family business?"

The Hodges family had a long history in Savannah. They were one of the first families to open up a paper mill and still ran a successful business manufacturing paper goods.

"Yep. He's convinced I'll be the next great marketing genius or some shit." He sighed. "I just want to study science. Find a cure for cancer or something."

"Don't you have an older sister? Why couldn't she take over?"

Matty made a face and lowered his voice. "She's my half-sister. Out of wedlock, before Dad's arranged marriage with my mother was finalized."

Claire twisted her face. "It's pretty antiquated of your father to hold his mistakes against her."

Matty nodded his head. "I agree. She wasn't even allowed to take his last name."

"That's gross."

"But she's super awesome. I'm actually sort of glad for her." He shrugged. "She'll get to do what she wants with her life. Right now she's a junior in college studying psychology."

"That's a pretty cool perspective. In some ways I feel the same about Fiona. Like, on the one hand, I'm jealous that she hasn't had to experience the same pressures from our mother that I have, but I'm also glad for that."

"Your mother's disapproval isn't something I would wish on my worst enemy."

The two shared a laugh. When they'd first met, Claire and Matty had bonded over their apparent failure to live up to their parents' expectations. For Claire, it was her mother's expectations and for Matty, his father's. It gave them something to commiserate over.

"Why don't you just tell your dad how you feel, though? I finally had that talk with my mom the other day. She's not happy about it, but she can't actually *make* me do anything I don't want to do. And, I told her as much. Life's too short to spend it doing something you hate."

"It's not that simple, Claire." Matty's tone took on a tinge of bitterness. "You know how it is. Our families have these expectations, these legacies we're supposed to uphold. Can't exactly disappoint the old man, can I?"

"I mean you could," she said, "but I know it's not in your nature. Still, you shouldn't have to sacrifice your dreams for someone else's idea of success."

He scoffed. "Easy for you to say. At least you know what you want to do with your life."

Claire shrugged. "Maybe? If I'm being honest, sometimes I wonder if I'm just planning to go to law school because of my dad. Or, because I just don't want to go to medical school." She brought her fingers up to her mouth to chew her nails.

"Ah, the age-old question of whether we're living our own lives or someone else's," Matty mused. "Deep stuff, Claire."

"Shut up," Claire grumbled, but couldn't help but smile, lowering her hand. "Anyway, I'm having a party this weekend while my parents and sister are out of town. You're coming, right?"

Matty closed his locker and gave Claire an exasperated look.

"Don't be like that. This party is really important to me!"

"I can't understand why. I've heard people talking about it. All you did was go around and invite the most popular kids in the school."

Claire looked down, suddenly interested in her own shoes. " So?"

"So, I don't understand why you think you need to impress anyone. Why not just be yourself? Like you said to me just a moment ago."

Claire huffed. "We graduate next week, Matty. I need to make a name for myself before I leave for college."

"Make a name for yourself?" Matty made a face like he was dry heaving. "You sound like one of *them*."

"I just want to fit in."

"You fit in just fine with me."

Claire shrugged, feeling her face warm. "We're not always going to be in high school. My mother keeps reminding me of that. Sure, we'll go to college, but at some point we'll all come back here and I don't want to be outside of the social circles."

"Being outside of the social circles sounds amazing," Matty said wistfully. "And if you're trying not to become like your mother, you're doing a pretty poor job of it."

Claire stomped her foot. "Just say you'll come to my party!"

"I honestly don't know if I'll be able to handle the people you invited. You know how I feel about 'high society,'" he said, making air quotes.

"You're part of that crowd, too, you know."

Matty stuck his tongue out at her and she laughed.

"Plus, you didn't invite just the popular crowd. You had to go and invite the jocks, too."

"What's wrong with that?" Claire asked. "They know how to keep things lively."

"Gross," Matty muttered, making a face.

"Just come over early. We can pregame so you'll be buzzed when everyone you hate shows up."

"You mean everyone you invited?"

Claire rolled her eyes. "Okay, when *everyone* shows up then."

Matty was silent for a moment, studying his friend. "I'll consider it."

"Just give in. You know I always get my way."

"You're going to make a really great lawyer someday," Matty said, trying to hide a smile.

The bell rang, giving them both a five-minute warning to head to their next class.

"Hey! Claire!"

Claire turned to see Kendra waving at her from down the hall, motioning for her to hurry up so they could walk together to their next class.

Claire nudged Matty in the shoulder. "So, you're coming?"

Matty groaned. "Fine. But don't expect me to talk to anyone."

Claire shrugged. "That's fine. Everyone thinks you're weird and antisocial anyway."

"Don't ruin my reputation. It's all I've got."

"Later, Matty!" Claire slung her bag over her shoulder and headed toward her next class.

"Later, Claire Bear."

chapter
eight

PRESENT

Claire reached for the box that was about to topple over, teetering on the edge of her desk. She'd spent the better part of the afternoon in her office organizing the document binders Daniel had given her. It was obvious he'd dumped them out and thrown them into the box haphazardly.

As just an associate in the firm, Claire didn't have a dedicated assistant or paralegal, so most of the administrative work fell on her. Which was all non-billable. She didn't quite understand how Daniel made his hours requirement with how little he worked.

Daniel kept walking up and down the hallway outside her office throughout the afternoon. Claire had gotten tired of seeing his smug face as she worked on the binders and decided she needed a change of scenery. Even if that meant carting her newly organized boxes two blocks to the Chatham County Law Library.

She'd taken one of the firm's document carts, stacked her organized boxes onto it, and made the walk to the library. She had certainly attracted several confused stares from passersby. Getting to work on the case in peace and solitude without Daniel at every turn was worth it.

The scent of musty books and the faint hum of the florescent lights greeted her as she pushed her cart inside the building. The law library had become one of her favorite places since joining the firm, often providing her an escape. The office environment could feel stifling.

Except, this time, the familiar surrounding did little to ease the butterflies in her gut. The more she sorted through the piles of documents at the office, the more she started to feel overwhelmed about the appeal. And having to handle the entire matter on her own.

"Claire!" a loud whisper from behind one of the bookstacks caught her attention.

Joy, the librarian, emerged with a smile. Joy was in her mid-thirties, with blonde hair pulled back into a loose ponytail. Her bright blue eyes were always filled with a mix of curiosity and intelligence, making her an asset when it came to legal research. Claire had often relied on her to bounce ideas or research case precedent.

"Hi, Joy," Claire replied through a yawn.

Joy smirked. " Something tells me you worked all weekend."

Claire shrugged. "You know the life."

"Only by watching you and others. Thankfully, I avoided all that by choosing the research route." She gestured to the cart full of boxes. "What's all this?"

"I'm taking a new case. Just needed to get out of the office."

"Do you need some help?"

Joy had been instrumental in helping Claire on a few of her cases in the past. She more than took the place of a paralegal and assistant combined.

Claire hesitated. "This case is a bit different from others."

"Different how?"

Claire looked around to make sure no one would overhear her, but she still kept her voice low. "I'm taking the appeal for the Anthony Bates trial."

Joy's eyes widened. She ushered Claire into one of the side study rooms, helping her maneuver the cart of boxes through the narrow doorway.

Joy shut the door behind them and kept her voice lowered. "How did that happen? I thought Daniel was lead on that case?"

"He was," Claire said, "for the trial. But Dolores Bates specifically asked me to represent Anthony on appeal."

"That's a little odd, don't you think?" Joy tilted her head. "I mean not to say you aren't a great lawyer and don't deserve the case, but you haven't handled any major trials on your own, not here anyway. Why would she ask for you?"

Claire swallowed the lump in her throat. She knew all of that, but hearing Joy say it out loud only served to spike her anxiety.

"Your guess is as good as mine," she finally said.

"Aren't you nervous to represent him? I mean, there could even be more victims we don't know about!"

Claire's gaze drifted to the boxes filled with all the morbid details of Anthony's conquests. "I am a little nervous. But I don't really have a choice in the matter."

Joy nodded, her expression softening. "My offer to help still stands."

"Are you sure?" Claire said. "I have a feeling this appeal is going to be just as contentious for the city as the trial was. The politics involved might get super messy."

Joy shook her head. "That stuff doesn't bother me. I certainly didn't go into this profession to become popular."

Relief flooded Claire's system. "That means a lot, Joy. Thank you."

The two women began unloading the cart. They took out all the trial binders and spread them across the large wooden table that took up almost all of the small study room.

When they finally had everything pulled out and organized into piles, Claire's heart rate increased as she looked at all the documents.

"I have to start at the beginning and go through everything," she said. " While I know the basics as much as anyone else does, I'll really need to get in the weeds on the procedural aspect."

Joy skimmed through the binder closest to her. "When is the brief due?"

"Two weeks."

"Two weeks!" Joy exclaimed, her face paling a bit. "That's not much time at all."

Claire nodded. "I know. But Mrs. Bates let some time lapse after the conviction. No one thought they'd appeal." She paused. "The whole thing is... odd."

"Who else at the firm is helping you on this?"

"Just me."

Joy blinked a few times. "What do you mean, 'just me?'"

Claire shrugged. "I'm on my own. Mrs. Bates specifically said she didn't want any other attorneys working on this."

Joy shook her head in disbelief. "This is really bizarre."

Claire nodded, pushing down the waves of nausea threatening to crash into her throat.

JOY MOVED a sheet of paper across the table. "Take a look at this."

Claire looked up from the deposition testimony she was reading. "What is it?"

"The original mental health report ordered following Anthony's arrest."

Claire looked it over and started to flip through the pages. Moving past the boilerplate, she looked for the diagnosis.

"That's odd." She reread the words on the page confused as to what she was seeing.

The subject displays no signs of any disorders commonly affecting serial killers, to include Antisocial Personality Disorder (ASPD), Narcissistic Personality Disorder (NPD), Borderline Personality Disorder (BPD), Sadistic Personality Disorder, Psychopathy, or Schizophrenia.

Joy's eyes were filled with obvious intrigue. "What do you think?"

"This makes no sense."

Joy nodded. "Keep reading."

Claire shook her head and continued on.

The subject does display classic symptoms of untreated Post Traumatic Stress Disorder (PTSD). Further evaluation is recommended.

Claire paused to process what she just read. "He gruesomely murdered seven people and doesn't have any personality disorder? Just PTSD?"

"I haven't even shown you the best part yet," Joy said, giddiness in her voice.

Claire winced. "What's the *best* part?"

Joy slid another report over to her. Claire looked over the document and furrowed her brow. "Another psychological evaluation?"

"Keep reading."

"Dated one week after the initial report." Claire flipped back to the older report. "By a different doctor."

Joy was almost squirming in her seat.

Claire turned the pages to find the diagnosis.

The subject displays classic signs of Antisocial Personality Disorder (ASPD), Narcissistic Personality Disorder (NPD), Borderline Personality Disorder (BPD), Sadistic Personality Disorder, and Psychopathy. All of which are mental disorders commonly associated with serial killers.

Claire blinked in confusion several times, flipping the report back to the first page. "This doesn't say it's an updated report."

"Exactly."

"So, two doctors came to completely different conclusions just one week apart, and only the latter report was admitted at trial? Was there even a mention of the earlier report in any of the trial documents?"

"Not that I've seen so far," Joy said. "So, what do you think? Have you ever seen anything like this?"

"Honestly, no," Claire responded. She leaned back in her chair. "I don't understand why Daniel didn't object to the entry of the second report. I think it's highly prejudicial to Anthony's case to stick him with all these diagnoses. At the very least, the first report should have been submitted for the jury to consider."

"I think we're going to find a lot of holes in his defense, unfortunately."

Claire shook her head. "I just don't understand why. It's not like he's a bad lawyer. Lazy, yes, but he knows how to win cases. Why mess up so bad on such an important case? You'd think he'd be worried about his reputation."

"More than that, what about the doctors?" Joy asked. "What's the deposition say about the discrepancy?"

Claire got up and moved over to one box at the end of the table. She started flipping through the files only to reach the end, unsuccessful. "That doesn't make sense." She flipped back to the beginning, searching through the files again.

"What is it?"

"There's no deposition of either doctor."

"Are you kidding? Who was the second doctor? The one who issued the second report?"

Claire walked back around the table to look at the report. "Doctor Elizabeth Brown. Says she's over at Augusta Medical, where he's being held right now."

"Can you call over there?" Joy asked. "See if you can talk to her?"

"Yeah, good idea." Claire pulled the number up on her phone and pushed the call icon.

"Augusta Hospital," the woman on the other end of the line answered.

"I'm calling for Dr. Elizabeth Brown," Claire said.

"One moment please."

Claire looked at Joy, both of them a bit on edge.

"I'm sorry," the receptionist said, "but Dr. Elizabeth Brown is no longer practicing with us."

Claire clenched her eyelids shut. She should have figured. These sorts of positions did have high turnover rates. "Did she leave any contact information?"

Claire heard a few more keys click on the other end. "It doesn't appear so," the woman said.

Perhaps the author of the first report could shed some light on the situation. "Is Dr. Susan Fields employed with you?" Claire asked.

"Not currently, but I can give you her contact information."

"Please." She jotted down the phone number the receptionist provided. "Thank you for your help."

Claire ended the call and met Joy's expectant eyes. "Well?"

"Neither doctor is currently employed there, and Dr. Brown didn't leave any follow up details."

Joy made a face. "That's inconvenient."

"But the receptionist did give me Dr. Fields' information." She stared down at the phone number she'd jotted down. "I suppose it's worth a call. Even if her report wasn't used, maybe she can tell us why."

Joy shrugged. "If she's honest."

Claire nodded and dialed the number. It rang a few times before a woman picked up. "Dr. Susan Fields?"

"Yes?"

"My name is Claire Stevens and I am an attorney working on the Anthony Bates case. I know this is out of the blue, but do you have a minute or two to discuss his case?"

The doctor did nothing to hide her sigh on the other end of the line. "I do, but just a few. I'm about to see a patient."

"Of course, I understand," Claire said in a sweet voice while making an exasperated face at Joy. "I was just hoping you could clear up some procedural items for us. It looks like you were the original psychologist to issue Anthony's report, but it was never used during trial and you were never deposed."

"That's correct."

"Do you know why? That's a little irregular, if I'm being honest."

"As far as I understood it, the prosecutor requested a second evaluation of the defendant following a recommendation from another psychologist. It wasn't my place to question why."

"A recommendation from another psychologist?" Claire repeated. "Was that by chance"—she flipped to the second report—"Dr. Elizabeth Brown?"

"I honestly couldn't tell you," Dr. Fields replied. "I was seeing so many patients during that time. When I was told I wasn't on the Bates case anymore, I didn't have the time or interest to find out who it was reassigned to."

"Okay. Thank you for your time," Claire said and hung up.

"What did she say?" Joy asked.

"The prosecutor had requested a second evaluation. I guess it was a recommendation he received from another psychologist."

"Is that normal?" Joy asked.

Claire pinched the bridge of her nose. "I'm a little out of my wheelhouse when it comes to criminal procedure, but I've never heard of anything like this before."

"And I guess you don't want to ask Daniel about it?"

Claire scoffed. "What good would it do? He wouldn't lift a finger to help me."

"Yeah, you're probably right."

Claire sat down heavily in her chair. "I'm just not sure I'm up for the task of unraveling all of this."

"Of course you are," Joy said in an encouraging tone. "You're just in the 'overwhelmed stage' right now. Things will start to make more sense the further in we dive."

"Either that," Claire said, "or we get stuck and can't get back out."

"Stop that," Joy chided gently. "You're just tired. We should probably take a break. It's nearly dinnertime, anyway."

Claire leapt up out of her chair and looked at her watch. "Oh no."

"What's wrong?"

"I'm supposed to meet a guy for dinner." She hastened around the room, shoving papers back into binders. "I'm already fifteen minutes late."

"Don't worry about the files," Joy said. "Just go! I'll make sure everything is locked up."

"You're a life saver." Claire hugged the woman and rushed out the door. "Coffee's on me tomorrow!"

chapter
nine

CLAIRE BURST INTO THE RESTAURANT, the scent of roasted garlic and freshly baked bread hitting her immediately. The soft murmur of conversation and the occasional clink of glasses surrounded her, but she barely noticed the strange looks from the few patrons already seated and enjoying their wine. She knew she looked disheveled—her blouse wrinkled and hair slightly out of place—but she hadn't stopped to fix herself before hustling over.

She scanned the room quickly, spotting Jamie seated near the window. His eyes stayed fixed on the menu in front of him, his posture calm and unbothered. The hostess, poised behind her stand, opened her mouth to greet her, but Claire gave her a brief smile and headed straight for her seat across from him.

He didn't look up from the menu, his expression devoid of any emotion.

"Jamie, I am so sorry."

Annoyance was written all over him. He simply nodded, eyes still scanning up and down the menu. He flipped to the next page.

"I just got caught up in the new case," she tried to explain. "I lost track of time."

He finally looked up and shrugged. "It's fine," he said curtly. "I'm just glad you made it at all."

She wished he had just not acknowledged her existence at all in that moment.

"Right," Claire responded slowly, settling into her seat. "I'm really sorry."

"Can we just order something?" he asked. "I've been waiting a while and I'm starving."

"Okay," Claire said, grabbing her own menu and trying to keep her hands from shaking. "What do you think looks good?"

Jamie signaled the waiter. "I'll get another glass of the house red and the prime rib.".

"And you?" the waiter asked, looking at Claire.

"Um." She tried to read the menu quickly, landing on the easiest option she could find. "The grilled chicken looks good."

"And to drink?"

"Just a white of your choosing," she replied.

"Of course," the waiter said, taking their menus and making his way toward the kitchen.

The two sat in silence for a moment, and a waiter brought by a basket of bread. At the sight, Claire's stomach responded with a soft grumble. She hadn't realized how hungry she was, having spent all day at the library. She reached for the bread and broke it open to swipe it with butter. Jamie stayed still.

"I started diving into the Bates case today." Claire said, after a bite. Her growing hunger was immediately eased.

Jamie's eyes widened. "Bates, as in Anthony Bates?"

Claire nodded. "His mother came to the firm and specifically gave the case to me."

"And you're taking it?"

Claire nodded again.

Jamie stared at her for a long moment. "Are you sure about this, Claire? He's as dangerous as they come."

"He still deserves a fair trial," Claire said. "And given the evidence, I'm not sure that he got one."

Jamie raised his eyebrows. "Is that right?"

The waiter returned with their glasses of wine, breaking up their conversation. Jamie took a gulp of his instantly. Claire took a smaller sip of hers. "I'll admit, I really wasn't sure what I was going to find when I started digging into this case. In some ways I thought that I would really struggle to find an issue that was appealable, but now I don't think so."

Jamie scoffed. "And what went so wrong at trial that a murderer deserves to walk?"

Claire leveled him a steely look. "For starters, we've got two different medical reports dated within a week of one another, that contradict one another. And neither doctor was even deposed."

He shrugged. "So what?"

"Only the second report, diagnosing him with personality disorders associated with psychopaths, was admitted into evidence. The first report didn't have the same findings. Don't you think the jury should have known that? Don't you think the doctors should have been questioned about it?"

"The man confessed to killing those women. At that point, I don't think any of the nitty gritty legal stuff really matters."

Claire furrowed her brow. "But it *does* matter. That's the whole point of our judiciary." She shook her head, spinning the stem of her glass between her fingertips. "I'm hoping it will make more sense when I drive out to see him."

Jamie's voice was firm and a bit startling when he said, "I don't want you doing that."

Claire looked up from buttering another piece of bread. "I'm not sure you really have a say in what I do."

"That's pretty rich."

"You're going to need to give me a better reason for why I shouldn't go see my client, Jamie," Claire said. "I'm sorry, but even if the doctor situation didn't exist, I have an ethical duty to speak to him about his case."

Jamie dropped his voice low. "What if he tries to hurt you when you visit?"

"Doubtful."

Jamie's eyes took on a wild rage. "How can you say that? He was convicted of violently murdering seven people. All women, around your age."

"But I don't really fit the profile, other than age and gender. Most of those women had some sort of social media presence or following or if they didn't, they were—" Claire paused. She was going to say "attractive," but she thought better of it. "Popular," she said instead. "I'm just a boring attorney."

Jamie shook his head, took another gulp of his wine. The glass was now half-empty. "I think you're being foolish."

Claire broke off a piece of bread and shoved it into her mouth. Claire swallowed her bread and tried to suppress the sigh that crept up her chest. "I understand your concerns, Jamie. But please understand that I really have no choice in this."

"That's entirely untrue. You don't have to represent anyone. You could back out of this tomorrow."

"And lose my job. Then what?"

"You and that stupid job," Jamie muttered.

Claire blinked her eyes several times. "Excuse me?"

"I'm just saying, all it does is get in the way. You're late to every single one of our dates, if you even make it at all. It's all you care about."

"Well, it is my career, after all."

"You really don't need a career."

Claire cocked her head, her expression contorting into disgust. "I seriously cannot believe I'm hearing this. How do you figure that *I* 'don't really need a career' I've worked tirelessly for years to get? What if I actually enjoy my work, huh?"

"You have connections, Claire! You have me now. I know the whole New York thing didn't work out but I know *why* you had to come home. Don't you think it'd be easier if you had more time to worry about yourself instead of a job?"

She scoffed. "Is that really how you feel?"

"I guess it is."

The two sat in a heated silence, glaring at one another. The din of conversation filled the room. Occasional laughter. Sweet nothings shared between significant others. The juxtaposition would have made her laugh.

Claire was the first to break the silence. "So, what then?"

"I guess I just thought that if we were going to take things further, your job wouldn't be an issue anymore. You know who my family is. It's not like you'd need to work."

"Well, if this isn't just the sweetest hint at a marriage proposal I've ever received," Claire said sarcastically. "I'm really shocked at how anti-quated you're being. I thought you would be proud of me, a self-made attorney who values doing something with her life."

"I am! And you'll always be an attorney, and that's something to be proud of." He shook his head. "But that doesn't mean you need to practice."

The waiter returning with their food had them falling silent again, each looking down at the table now.

"Let's just eat and try and enjoy the dinner," Jamie said.

"Fine," Claire said, too hungry to pass up the chance to eat her first proper meal for the day.

The rest of the time passed in silence. Claire thought she might bring up more about the case, but every time she opened her mouth to say something, she thought better of it. He wasn't able to hear anything she said right now. Jamie had already been hurt by her tardiness, and then he'd insulted her entire career. She realized she wouldn't be able to tell him anything, ever.

WALKING out into the muggy night air of Savannah, Claire sighed as she turned to Jamie. "Look, I don't know what to tell you. It's obvious that my commitment to my career bothers you. But I'm not going to quit. And I have no intention of being a kept woman, either. There's nothing wrong with that life. It's just not for me."

"I understand," Jamie replied.

Claire wrapped her bag around her shoulder tighter. "So, where does that leave things?"

"I honestly don't know," Jamie said, running a hand over his hair. "Can we just take some time to think about it?"

"Okay," Claire said. "Just to be clear, I'm still going out to Augusta."

Jamie let out a long sigh. "Yes, I know."

He leaned forward to give Claire a quick kiss on the cheek before opening his car door for her.

"Thanks," she said. "But my apartment isn't far. I think I'll just walk."

"You sure?" he asked, his expression softer now than it had been all night. "It's late."

Claire nodded. "I know my way."

Jamie looked like he wanted to argue and then thought better of it. He nodded and climbed into his car, driving off into the night without even looking back at her.

Claire began walking, suddenly weighed down by the three-inch lawyer heals clacking against the concrete. She found a nearby park bench and grabbed the sneakers out of her bag, swapping out her heels for them. She briefly considered returning to the library to work on the case more, but Joy had likely locked up and left for the night.

As Claire walked back to her place, it wasn't the conversation with Jamie that floated through her mind. Instead, it was the facts of the case. She realized that she actually didn't know a lot about the victims. She wasn't sure that anyone really did, other than what the newspaper had reported on them.

She shuffled up to her apartment building and let herself inside, then made her way to her front door, unlocking it and letting herself in. A quiet reprieve from the rest of the day. She kicked off her sneakers without placing them on the shoe rack, instead padding into her kitchen. She poured herself another hefty glass of wine before she made her way to the laptop on her small desk in the living room. The screen provided the only light besides the streetlamps reflecting outside the windows.

She opened her browser and typed, "Anthony Bates Murders," into the search bar.

Several articles pulled up and she clicked the first one, which listed the victims' names in order.

Olivia Parker, Emma Johnson, Mia Martinez, Violet Carver, Ava Cooper, Isabella Thompson, and Charlotte Davis.

She clicked on Emma's name and an article about her appeared in the window.

Tragic Loss: Promising College Student and Yoga Sensation Emma Johnson Murdered in Savannah

Savannah, Georgia — The vibrant coastal city of Savannah is in shock today as it mourns the senseless loss of 22-year-old Emma Johnson, a college student and rising Instagram sensation known for her inspiring yoga videos.

Emma's life was tragically cut short in a shocking act of violence that has left the community reeling. As a college student, she had dreams of making a difference in the world through her education, and her Instagram following, which reached thousands, attested to her captivating yoga talent and positive influence on social media.

Her friends and family remember Emma as a beacon of positivity and a young woman with a bright future ahead. The investigation into her untimely death is ongoing, with authorities urging anyone with information to come forward.

As Savannah grapples with this heartbreaking loss, the memory of Emma Johnson lives on through the lives she touched and the inspiration she brought to countless individuals on her journey.

Emma leaves behind a mother, father, and older brother. The family asks for privacy during this difficult time.

Pressing the back button, Claire moved next to Mia Martinez, to read a surprisingly similar article.

Savannah Grieves: Tragic Murder During Spring Break Marks Second Unsolved Homicide

Savannah, Georgia — The idyllic charm of Savannah's historic streets has been shattered once again as the city grapples with the devastating murder of 21-year-old Mia Martinez, the second unsolved homicide to rock the community in recent months.

Mia, a college student from Florida, was visiting her family during spring break and had dreams of entrepreneurship, studying business with aspirations to open her own candle shop. Her promising future was cruelly stolen in a heinous act that has left both locals and authorities stunned.

As the investigation into Mia's tragic death intensifies, it casts a dark shadow over the city, still haunted by the memory of the previous unsolved case, Emma Johnson. Savannah's residents are left searching for answers and demanding justice as they mourn the loss of another young life.

The community's heart goes out to Mia's grieving family as she leaves behind her mother, father, older brother, and younger sister. Law enforcement officials are urging anyone with information to come forward. Savannah remains a city united in its resolve to find closure for Emma Johnson and the other unsolved case that have shaken its sense of security.

Unease settled in her stomach and warred with the bitter wine and undigested contents of her dinner. Talking to Meredith had put her nerves to rest about the prospect of Anthony coming after her. But as she read about each of the young women who had their lives cut short, she started to wonder if maybe Jamie had a point.

That, coupled with the conflicting medical reports, and other unexplained abnormalities in the case, had her head reeling.

She looked at her glass of wine. Maybe she'd had one too many and needed to just go to bed. She'd be able to think about things with a clear head in the morning.

chapter
ten

CLAIRE TUCKED her thermos of coffee under her arm and pushed the law library's glass door. She stepped inside and scanned the room, taking a moment to adjust her eyes to the florescent lights. The law library was never particularly busy. Most of the large tables that made up the center aisle of the first floor were empty. Occasionally, you might find a desperate attorney or an inquisitive citizen searching through the racks of books that towered up to the ceilings, but that was often a rare sight.

Spotting Joy at the receptionist desk, Claire made her way over.

"Morning!" she said. "Ready to dive back in today?"

Joy looked up from the computer screen, her face apologetic. "I'm so sorry, Claire, but I can't today. My boss is unexpectedly in town and I'm swamped."

Claire bit her lip, trying to mask her disappointment. "I understand."

"I've left everything in the room set up for you, though," Joy said. "And you can continue to leave your materials there each day so you don't have to haul them back to the firm. I've blocked you off for a few weeks. Hopefully I'll be able to help you some tomorrow."

"Thanks, Joy," Claire said, forcing a smile. Joy's inability to help hadn't been her fault. This was her actual job, after all. She would help when she could. Claire let go of any hard feelings and made her way back to the study room.

As she entered the room, her eyes fell on the many boxes and binders spread out on the table. It didn't seem so intimidating when Joy was there working with her, but now, facing it all alone was overwhelming. The whole world was against her on this case. Anthony was a divisive figure for the city, but she hadn't thought everyone she spoke to would be against his fundamental right to appeal his verdict. Joy had been her only real support in this.

The more she thought about this case, the more she wondered if it was just a boulder hiding something unsightly beneath it. Claire wondered whether she really had the skill to uncover it all herself. She still didn't understand Dolores' request that she be the only attorney to work on this. For most clients, it would be to save money. But that was an unlikely case for the Bates family.

Perhaps Dolores was strategic with her request. After all, Daniel had lost at trial and Bob had overseen that loss. But generally when something like that happened, wealthy families would hire an attorney to come down from someplace like Washington, D.C. to handle the appeal. Choosing Claire, and only Claire, was an odd request.

Claire shook off the nagging self-doubt. Dolores had confidence in her for some reason, otherwise she wouldn't have given Claire the case. After all, the Bates family name had more to do with Dolores than her husband. Claire tried to take some assurances from that.

She took a long drink of coffee from her thermos, the bitter warmth spreading through her chest and momentarily chasing away her fatigue. The faint aroma of stale office paper lingered in the air, mixing oddly with the rich scent of her coffee. She set the thermos down and grabbed the first box to sift through its contents.

She laid it all out in front of her and paused, pondering where to even begin working through this on her own.

"I need to get a better understanding of the chronology," she muttered to herself. "What led to his arrest in the first place?"

Starting from the very beginning with Anthony's arrest seemed the most logical. She began to pull out documents and lay them in front of her. A police report dated the night of his arrest was buried all the way in the bottom.

"Says here an anonymous tip was phoned in, giving the description and whereabouts of the defendant." Claire furrowed her brow and rifled through the box, looking for any other police reports of tips.

"The one and only tip the police get and it's an exact match for time, place, and description?"

A red flag waved in her head and her heart started to pound. It didn't make sense. In cases like this, especially high-profile ones, tips usually flooded in—some from well-meaning citizens grasping at straws, others completely off the mark, or worse, deliberate hoaxes. Investigators typically sifted through dozens, if not hundreds, of dead ends before stumbling upon anything useful. But here, the only tip was perfectly tailored, as if someone had handed the police exactly what they needed on a silver platter.

Every detail she read about this case made things feel more and more . . . purposeful.

She put the tip paperwork aside and moved to the next set of events. "They get the tip, then they make the arrest. He's taken into custody and interrogated..." Her voice trailed off as she read the interrogation report.

She looked over the single sheet of paper multiple times, making sure she was seeing it correctly. "This has to be a mistake," she said to herself, getting up to look through the other boxes for missing pages. She picked through each box, one by one, laying out all the papers and files in front of her, scanning each and every one. She found no other pages to go with that report. Sinking back into her seat, she blinked her eyes in confusion.

"There should be a recording," she said, shaking her head in disbelief. "A transcript, something more than just, 'The defendant was taken into custody, interrogated, and confessed to all seven crimes.'"

Her fingers trembled as she held the paper and the hairs on the back of her neck started to rise. There was just too much about this case that seemed vague, convenient.

"Daniel should have caught this. The holes in the police records, the conflicting psych reports. Why didn't he investigate all this further? Bring it out at trial?"

She added another point to her growing list about the interrogation, realizing it might be very long by the time she made it through all these documents.

"Alright, so then he's arraigned, and"—she looked over the paperwork for the arraignment—"he pleads 'not guilty?'" She tapped her pen to her lips several times. "Within the span of twenty-four hours, he confesses to all the crimes and then pleads 'not guilty.'" She shook her head, making another note.

She moved to his psychological evaluation ahead of the trial, pulling the two reports close to her again. She leafed through the documents, but their conflicting stories hadn't changed since yesterday.

"I've got to find out who this Dr. Brown is," she said to herself. "Try and make sense of what is going on here."

At the very least, she could ask one of the paralegals at the firm to do a little digging into Dr. Elizabeth Brown. At the moment, there were only two paralegals working. Claire pulled up the number for Janet. She'd been working there the longest, having even worked for Claire's dad back in the day.

"This is Janet."

"Janet, hi. It's Claire."

"What can I do for you?" The woman's no-nonsense attitude was just what Claire needed.

"I need some help on the Bates matter. I've got two psychological reports, dated within a week of one another, but only the second was used at trial. Issue is, the doctor who issued the report can't be found."

"Can't be found?"

"Yes," Claire replied. "I called the hospital where she supposedly worked. The author of the first report indicated the prosecutor had requested the second report, but the hospital didn't have any follow-up information for her. She'd never worked there formally."

"If you give me her name, I can try and look into it. But I'll be honest, medical records are a tricky thing. They're normally under a tight seal."

Claire nodded. "Yeah. I don't think the first report was ever sealed because it was never admitted, but the file says the second report was admitted under seal. I only have access to it because we have a copy of all the files."

"You're lucky," Janet said. "My guess is that if you had to file a motion to access it, Judge Miller would drag his feet. I don't think he really wants this verdict overturned."

"Seems like no one wants to give this man due process of law."

Janet chuckled. "He is a contentious figure. I'll see what I can dig up. What's the name?"

"Dr. Elizabeth Brown."

"Got it. Give me a few days."

"Thanks."

Claire ran her fingers through one of the reports as she put her phone down. She still needed someone to walk her through the intricacies of this report. It's possible there was something objectionable in it that shouldn't have been allowed into evidence, but without more experience in criminal work, Claire wouldn't be able to spot it.

Under normal circumstances, an associate would go to an older partner for this sort of guidance when working on a case. She briefly considered asking her father for help but reconsidered. Her father dealt with civil mesothelioma cases. He'd have never run into anything like this during his years of practice. Her friend Meredith was an obvious choice, but she'd already asked for her help. Claire scrolled through her contacts to find her friend, hesitating on the call button. She never wanted to come across as too much, too needy. But desperate times and all that. She hoped her friend wouldn't be exasperated by another request.

The phone rang a few times before finally Meredith answered. "Hey Claire!"

"Hey Meredith!" Claire replied, trying to match her friend's energy. "Mind if I pick your brain a little more?"

"Of course not," Meredith replied, her tone warm. "I'd be happy to help. What do you need?"

"Well, I took that case we talked about."

"The Bates case?"

"That's the one. In the course of reviewing everything, I've found that it involves a psychological report, and I'm a little out of my wheelhouse."

"Of course! I'd be happy to help," Meredith replied warmly.

"It's sort of a lot to go over. It might be better to meet in person, if you have the time?"

"I'm actually free tonight. Want to meet for dinner?"

chapter
eleven

CLAIRE LOOKED DOWN at the open live map on her phone to make sure she was headed in the right direction. The evening air was warm, carrying the scent of fried seafood and sweet pralines as she strolled past Savannah's charming shops and restaurants. The storefronts were a mix of brightly painted facades and historic brick buildings, their windows showcasing everything from handmade soaps to quirky antiques and local art. The glow of string lights hanging between the buildings cast a cozy ambiance over the bustling street, where couples and small groups wandered leisurely.

She passed a bustling café with outdoor seating, the clink of glasses and laughter spilling onto the sidewalk, and then a boutique with vintage dresses in its window. Finally, she came to a simple white door, almost hidden in the rough texture of a brick wall. Looking up, she spotted a modest sign above the door that read, "Alley Cat Lounge."

Pushing the door open, an eclectic vibe surrounded her. Different colors lit up the brick wall behind the bar, red booths dotted the restaurant floor, and people were milling about, engaged in lively conversation. The atmosphere felt jovial, even for a Tuesday evening.

Claire hesitated for a moment, taking it all in. She wasn't entirely comfortable in places like this—loud, bustling, and full of strangers who seemed at ease in the lively chaos. She preferred quieter settings where she could blend into the background, but tonight wasn't about comfort. She squared her shoulders, reminding herself she had a purpose here, and stepped further inside, searching for Meredith.

Taking a moment to soak it all in, Claire couldn't help but feel a little out of place. It'd been a long time since she'd been to a place like this. Her work life in New York never really gave her the time to go out and nowadays, she mostly kept a low profile in town.

Her eyes scanned the room, searching for Meredith.

"Claire!"

Claire turned toward the sound to see a bright-eyed redhead waving at her. Meredith had always been attractive with her naturally thick red hair and infectious smile. Even though Meredith was a few years older, Claire had always felt like her own life experiences had aged her more.

As Meredith made her way toward Claire, she could see heads subtly turning, people taking second glances at the striking redhead. Meredith had always had that effect—effortlessly drawing attention with her confidence and natural beauty. Claire forced a smile, but the feelings of jealousy were hard to suppress, no matter how much she hated herself for it.

It wasn't just Meredith's looks; it was the way she carried herself, with an ease and assurance that Claire had never quite mastered. She couldn't help but compare it to the years of her mother's sharp critiques, picking apart everything from Claire's posture to the way her hair never quite laid flat. "*You'd look so much prettier if you just put in a little effort,*" her mother would say, a phrase that still echoed in her head more often than she cared to admit.

Claire knew she shouldn't feel envious toward her friend—it wasn't Meredith's fault, after all. But as those familiar insecurities surfaced, she couldn't stop herself from wondering what it would feel like to be the one who turned heads instead of fading into the background. Taking a deep breath, she pushed the feelings aside, reminding herself that Meredith wasn't her competition; she was her friend. "It's so good to see you," Meredith exclaimed, wrapping her arms around Claire. She stiffened inside the hug before awkwardly trying to return it, her arms almost limp around her friend.

"You too. It's been too long."

"Come on," Meredith said, gesturing to the back. "I've got a booth tucked away."

With a nod, Claire followed her through the lively crowd, the hum of conversation and bursts of laughter blending with the clinking of glasses and loud music.

She sat down to find a drink already waiting for her.

"I ordered you something sweet," Meredith told her, gesturing to the drink in front of Claire.

Claire eyed the glass, taking in its vibrant pink color and the sweet, citrusy aroma that wafted up from it. She hesitated a second before taking a sip. The scent alone had promised something refreshing, and it didn't disappoint. To her surprise, it was delicious—a blend of fruit, club soda, and just a kick of alcohol.

Claire set the glass down, licking her lips. "It's really good."

"Glad you like it! I'm sort of a regular here. The bartenders let me experiment." Meredith took a sip of her own. "Anyway, I'm so glad you reached out! This new job's been kicking my butt. I'm actually grateful to have a reason to get out."

"I can completely commiserate," Claire agreed. "I just started working on this case, and I don't think I'll be getting any sleep anytime soon."

Meredith leaned back in her chair, swirling her drink casually. "When do you have to, you know, turn in all the lawyer stuff?"

Claire chuckled at the vague phrasing, finding it a welcome break from the usual legal jargon. "The appeal brief? Two weeks."

Meredith's eyes widened. "Yikes. That doesn't sound like much time."

"Tell me about it," Claire replied. "Normally judges will issue a bit more time for the briefs, but no one seems to want this appeal to succeed."

Meredith frowned. "That doesn't seem completely fair."

Claire shrugged. "It's fair so long as it's within the rule of law. Judges don't have to grant extensions. They just normally do it out of courtesy."

Meredith rolled her eyes. "Sometimes lawyers lose sight of what's actually important. I've learned that with this new job."

Claire raised an eyebrow, curious. "Wait, what's the new job? You haven't told me about it yet."

Meredith grinned. "Oh! I'm working for the federal system now as a clinical psychologist. I do evaluations and write reports for defendants. It's a lot of digging into people's minds—fascinating and sometimes a little unsettling."

Claire blinked. "That sounds intense. And kind of perfect for you."

Meredith laughed. "It is. I mean, some of these cases are wild. You'd be amazed at what people admit during an evaluation."

"Well, if you've got all these juicy cases to work on, maybe you can share one or two with me," Claire said, smiling as she tried to relax.

"Juicy cases? Oh no, that's your job," Meredith teased. She leaned in with a playful glint in her eye. "So, tell me what *you've* found on this case you're working on!"

"The more I dig into the file, the more inconsistencies I find. The biggest I'm trying to wrap my head around right now are his psych reports. I've got one from a Dr. Fields that says he doesn't have any diagnoses other than PTSD. Then I've got another report dated only a week later saying he's got a host of conditions."

That can happen," Meredith said. "Sometimes clinicians disagree."

"I get that, but why issue the second report in the first place?"

"If the prosecutor didn't like the first report, he might have asked the court for permission to get a second one. Probably fishing for something more favorable."

"That would make sense," Claire mused. "The second report definitely paints the picture of a more deranged and unstable man. But, why not have both admitted into evidence?"

Meredith shrugged. "I'm not a lawyer, but from what I've seen, they're generally both admitted, unless one of them has some glaring error that would prejudice the defendant. Did Daniel not get the first one admitted?"

Claire shook her head. "No. I've seen no motion to admit it. It's as if he tried his best to lose this case."

Meredith chuckled. "He was successful in that."

"Yeah. He didn't even depose either psychologist."

"Now that is strange," Meredith said, raising an eyebrow. "I've not been deposed yet since I just started, but I had to go through a lot of training in orientation for it. It's sort of par for the course with this sort of work."

"Exactly," Claire said. "And he does a lot more criminal work, so he should have known better."

"Have you talked to him about it? Asked him why he decided not to?"

Claire shook her head. "Not yet. I want to make a list of everything I need to discuss with him. Honestly, I'm not sure what the point is though. I doubt he'll be helpful."

"Why's that?"

"He's not allowed to work on the case."

Meredith furrowed her brow. "Not allowed?"

Claire leaned forward and lowered her voice. "Dolores Bates specifically forbade him from working on the matter. I think it bruised his ego."

"I'll say," Meredith clucked. "Didn't you say your sister was dating him?"

"Yeah."

"Can't she get any info for you?"

"She completely sided with him on the whole thing. She won't even speak to me."

Meredith gave Claire a look full of sympathy. "I'm sorry. This all sounds really hard."

"It's not been the easiest," Claire admitted, before forcing a smile. "But I'm sure it'll all work out."

"That's the spirit!"

"I'd love to be able to speak to the doctor who issued the second report," Claire said, returning to the facts of the case. "But I called over to Augusta and they don't have any contact information for her."

"What was the name?" Meredith asked.

"A Doctor Elizabeth Brown?"

"Do you want me to ask around and see if anyone knows her? It's sort of a small world, us clinical psychologists."

"That would be great. I have one of the paralegals at the office trying to find out more, but I'm not too hopeful."

"If you want, I can take a look at the report."

"Could that get you into trouble?" Claire asked.

Meredith shook her head. "I don't see why it would, as long as neither of us tell anybody about it."

Claire hesitated for a moment, weighing the potential risks of accepting Meredith's help. A lot of the trial records were now public, but psychological reports generally remained sealed. But if Meredith was already working in the court system, then she would already have access to the reports if she wanted them. And since Meredith wasn't assigned to the case, Claire couldn't see why it would be an ethical violation on her own end.

"If you wouldn't mind, that would be great."

"Happy to! So, what are your next steps?"

"I should probably go see Bates."

"Are you sure that's a good idea?" Meredith asked.

Claire flinched at the question. Every time she brought up going to see her client to anyone, they seemed against it. It made Claire feel as if no one thought she could fully handle this.

Meredith reached her hand across the table.

"I don't mean to say you can't handle it or shouldn't," she said, seemingly a mind-reader. "I just mean, are you really prepared for that sort of thing?"

"I'm not sure I really have a choice," Claire replied. She sighed and the words started to flow before she could stop herself. "I'm not going to lie to you, I am nervous about it. Everyone keeps telling me how dangerous he is. It's not like I don't already know. I've read the reports and even seen the photos from the evidence file. Even the guy I'm seeing doesn't want me going out there." She shook her head, looking into the distance. "But I feel like I have to."

Meredith nodded in understanding. "I get it. When I first started this job and was assigned to defendant interviews, I was really nervous.

And for a while, it weighed on my mind, especially at night. What would happen if someone tried to cross the line, or made me a target? Was I really going to be able to handle meeting with these sorts of people? But I think if you prepare yourself for what you might see and hear, then you should be okay."

Claire shivered a little. "I'm not sure how to prepare myself, honestly. At first I was pretty comfortable with handling the case. Excited even. But now I feel isolated and strangely anxious. The whole thing is just making me feel really on edge."

Meredith's eyes softened and she reached out to give Claire's hand a squeeze. "I get it. It was tough in the beginning for me, like I said. But over time, I found that there was a lot of value in the job I was doing. Maybe you'll feel that way too when all of this is over."

"Thank you. It means a lot to have someone who understands what this feels like."

"That's what friends are for, right?"

chapter
twelve

CLAIRE STEPPED inside the firm's lobby. It'd been a few days since she'd been here, and as much as she wanted to return to the solitude of the law library, she needed to save face.

She made her way over to Janet's desk, hoping against hope that the paralegal had found something useful.

"Hi Claire," Janet said, not really looking up from her computer.

"Hey, Janet. Were you able to find anything useful on the psychologist?"

"Honestly, I haven't," Janet replied, typing furiously on her keyboard. "I'm in the middle of a closing right now. When I finish up here, I'll email you what I did find, but it's not much."

Claire nodded. She'd figured as much. Had she found anything useful, Janet would have let her know immediately.

" Thanks, Janet," Claire said, trying to hide her disappointment.

She then turned to head toward her office.

"Fancy seeing you here." Daniel's sarcastic tone made his way to her as she passed the communal kitchen.

She turned on her heel to look at him. He was pouring himself a cup of coffee, his expression smug and begging to be punched as always.

"I do work here," she replied.

"Could have fooled me. Some reason you can't make it to the office these days?"

"I've been working on the Bates case over at the library," Claire remarked, not sure why she felt the need to defend herself.

"That's right. The precious Bates case." Daniel sneered as he looked her in the eye and sipped his steaming coffee. "How's that going, by the way?"

"Fine, thanks." She started to walk back to her office. It was obvious that she should just give up on trying to ask Daniel for information about the trial details. He was clearly not going to help.

"Find anything amiss?" Daniel called after her.

His question had her stopping in her tracks. She turned back to look at him.

"Amiss?"

"It's an appeal, yes? You'll need to find *something* that went wrong at trial."

"Right," Claire said, trying to hide her suspicion. "Still working through everything."

She retreated to her office, hearing Daniel's final say from down the hall. "Can't wait to see what you find."

She shut the door and moved to her desk. Daniel's words still rang in her ears.

Maybe he was just asking if she'd found an appealable issue, but she couldn't help but think he knew more. Daniel had made a fair number of errors at trial. Unfortunately for her, a trial attorney's incompetence didn't necessarily give rise to an appealable issue. If the defendant's lawyer didn't properly preserve the issue for appeal, there was nothing that could be done. As far as Daniel was concerned, Claire was still trying to figure out if he'd just been sloppy.

Her office phone ringing brought her back to the present.

She picked up the phone and answered, "Claire Stevens."

"Claire." Dolores Bates' voice filled the other end. "How are you progressing with my son's appeal?"

"Good," Claire said, her heart rate increasing. "As I'm sure you can appreciate, it's a large file and I haven't involved any other attorneys, at your request."

"Yes. Your discretion is appreciated." She paused a moment. "Have you visited Anthony yet?"

"No, ma'am," Claire replied. " I was planning to soon."

"Great. I'll be sure to let him know to expect you. That's all for now."

The line went dead. Claire put the phone back with a soft click and stared at it for a time. She hadn't quite anticipated making a visit out to see Anthony so soon. But it was obvious that his mother wanted things to move faster.

She pulled out her calendar. She still had a little less than two weeks before the appeal had to be filed. But she probably shouldn't wait until the last minute to get his side of the story.

Doing a quick search online, she pulled up the phone number for the Augusta State Medical Prison, where Anthony was confined. Taking a deep breath, she picked up the phone to make an appointment.

"YOU'RE GOING TO SEE HIM?" Joy asked with wide eyes.

"I have to," Claire replied, putting a few files in one of the boxes.

"Are you sure it's safe?"

Joy wasn't saying anything Claire wasn't already feeling but hearing it out loud also wasn't helping her nerves about the situation.

"Does it matter?" Claire asked. "I have to. Besides, he's in prison. What's he going to do?"

"I guess that's true," Joy said. "It's just that the whole thing feels creepy. His mother doesn't want you working with anyone. Then calls you and pushes you to go see him?"

Claire shrugged. "It'd be a pretty weird move for a mother to want her son's defense lawyer to get killed before she wins his appeal."

"Unless," Joy said, jabbing her finger into the air. "She doesn't want him out."

Claire gave her an exasperated look. "Are you seriously suggesting that Dolores Bates set her son up to be arrested? The entire trial dragged her family's name through the mud. "

"Okay, but what if she decided she liked the peace and quiet of him being in prison? I mean, Anthony was known for causing scenes at times. And since the family name was already ruined..."

"She hired me to throw the appeal?" Claire gave her an exasperated look, feeling a pang of hurt at the insinuation.

Joy blushed. "I'm sorry. I was just having fun and getting carried away."

Claire sighed. "I know. But maybe we can keep things out of the realm of the fantastical?"

Joy nodded. "Deal." She hesitated before asking, "But let's assume Dolores is trying to protect her family's reputation, why file an appeal at all?"

Claire met her gaze, her voice steady. "Not filing would've been worse for the family's reputation. Can you imagine what the tabloids would've done with that? Headlines speculating about why the Bates family wasn't fighting for their son's freedom? Dolores is trying to salvage whatever shred of dignity they have left."

Joy tilted her head thoughtfully, nodding. "I guess that makes sense. I hadn't really thought about it like that."

"Exactly," Claire said, her voice softening slightly. "It wasn't about getting Anthony out of prison as much as it was about protecting the family name." She leaned back in her chair and absently ran her fingers along the edge of the worn conference table. "Anyway, I was intending to go see him at some point. Might as well do it sooner rather than later. Maybe talking to him will give me some answers."

"Or maybe he'll find you so interesting that he decides to stalk you and you'll be his next victim if you manage to get him out," Joy muttered.

"Joy!"

Joy's eyes softened. "I should probably just keep my mouth shut from now on."

Claire shook her head. "It's okay. It's what everyone else is thinking."

"Are you worried about it?"

Claire could feel a knot form in her stomach. "Not really," she lied.

"That's good then," Joy said. "Just, be careful."

"I will." Claire lifted a box of documents and headed for the door.

———

AS SHE WALKED BACK to her apartment, the small box of documents under her arm, she thought about what Joy said. As nonsensical as her accusations against Dolores were, she still needed to consider every angle. She'd been in the legal world long enough to understand that when someone's behavior didn't seem to make sense, it was usually because you didn't have all the pieces of the puzzle. Often, what appeared to be irrational actions were rooted in perfectly rational responses to emotions or circumstances you weren't aware of.

Maybe this was the real reason she was so apprehensive about this case. Everywhere she turned, there was another person she wasn't sure she could trust. Not to mention Joy's point about winning the appeal.

If she did win the appeal, Anthony could be released. The prosecutor might decide to retry, but in high-profile cases like this, they might cut their losses and move on rather than risk a not-guilty verdict. That, and a second case would likely get caught up in jury selection for months. Pretty much everyone had an opinion about Anthony Bates.

Could Claire really become a target? She told herself she didn't fit the profile of his victims. For starters, she was older than the oldest of his targets, most of them were college-age. But as the thought settled, she grimaced, realizing that was just about the only factor in her favor.

If she were being honest, she actually fit the profile in more ways than she wanted to admit. She was young, female, and had grown up in Savannah. On top of that, all the victims came from well-off families—another box she reluctantly checked. The more she thought about it, the less comfort her initial reasoning gave her.

Claire shook her head and tried to reason with herself. Why would anyone want to off the lawyer who got them out of prison? He'd have no reason to kill her, and killing without a reason was irrational behavior.

Do serial killers need a reason to kill? A little voice inside her head asked.

Claire tried to shush the intrusive thought away, the weight of it pressing heavily in the back of her mind. As she walked up to her front door, the faint scent of magnolia lingered in the humid night air, and the soft buzz of cicadas filled the quiet neighborhood. She paused for a moment, taking a deep breath, the familiar warmth of Savannah's evening wrapping around her like a damp blanket. Spinning her wheels about it on her own wasn't going to help.

The metal of the doorknob felt cool against the muggy air as she stepped inside. She kicked off her shoes by the entryway and flipped on the kitchen light, the faint hum of the bulb breaking the silence. By the time she dumped the box onto her marble countertop, the faint scent of old paper rising from its contents, she already had her phone in her hand and was calling Meredith. "Hello?"

"Are you busy? Do you mind if I vent?" Claire asked, plopping herself down on the sofa. She usually would decompress with her sister, but that obviously wasn't going to happen right now.

"Always. What's up?"

"Dolores Bates called," she said. "She wants me to go visit Anthony."

"Are you going to?"

"I have to at some point. No sense in delaying the inevitable."

Meredith made a noncommittal noise. "I can tell you're anxious about it."

"I am," Claire said, turning to look out the window. "A friend put it in words for me earlier. She asked what happens if I get him out of prison and he comes for me. How do you deal with this sort of worry?"

"First thing's first, and I don't need to tell you this because you already know. Just because you win his appeal doesn't mean he's out of prison. There could be a new trial."

"Maybe." That was the most likely scenario, but not the only one.

"As for how I deal with this, I just try and remind myself that I am helping these people. People make mistakes and do the time for their crimes. If we judge them on their past indiscretions, then we doom them not to move forward."

"Yeah," Claire said, "but he's a serial killer, Meredith. That's different than someone who sold drugs."

"True. But I've worked with all different types of people. I've never experienced a problem."

"Not to make you worry, but you really haven't been doing it for that long."

"Not here in Savannah," Meredith replied. " I was in school for a long time for this career. I had to go through internships and rotations, some within the prison system. Nothing's ever come back to haunt me."

"That's good to know," Claire said. "Thank you."

"So, where is he?"

"He's over in Augusta," Claire said. "At the medical prison."

"Wait," Meredith said. "Augusta?"

"Yeah, why?"

"When are you going?"

"I have an appointment for tomorrow, but I can be flexible if I need to."

"I'm heading out there tomorrow," Meredith said, excitement in her voice. "There's a conference back at our *alma mater*. I think I told you about it. Would you feel better having some company?"

"Absolutely," Claire replied, breathing a sigh of relief. "That would be so nice to have someone to go with. Did you want me to drive? I'm pretty sure my car still turns on." Claire laughed, realizing she hadn't even started her car's engine in about two weeks.

"No need. If you don't mind one that's a little beat up, we can take mine. It's not as fancy as your ride, but I'll have to drop you off and then head to the conference so I'd feel more comfortable in my own car."

"I totally understand. I can't tell you how much I appreciate this, Meredith."

"It's no trouble. I'll pick you up tomorrow morning around nine. Text me your address, okay?"

"I will, and see you tomorrow," Claire said.

"See you!"

chapter
thirteen

THE AUGUSTA STATE MEDICAL PRISON waiting room was a sad, sterile place, with faded linoleum floors and walls painted an unremarkable shade of beige. It was eerily quiet yet the room hummed with an undercurrent of activity, as if there should have been more noise. The somber atmosphere weighed heavily against Claire.

On the drive out here, Claire had been honest with Meredith that she was a little nervous about this interview. She'd never done anything like this before and almost didn't know where to start. Meredith told her not to think of Anthony any differently than her other clients. Just to be careful about when to press for more information or when to back off.

"Better to try again another day," Meredith had said, "than to ruin the relationship and not get any information out of him. At least, that's been my experience."

Claire flipped through her notes as she waited in the lobby. She had a few key questions for Anthony during this interview. For starters, she wanted him to walk her through his arrest. Then she wanted to sus out why he confessed to the crimes before later turning around and pleading "not guilty." Claire had a feeling the second ask was going to take a little bit more time, if he would even give her a truthful answer at all.

This was also assuming that Anthony would be in the state of mind to even speak to her. Inmates weren't sent to a medical prison by choice, but because they needed physical or mental health treatment. There was no indication that Anthony had any physical ailments, so the two psychological evaluations he'd undergone likely had something to do with it.

She'd brought this up to Meredith on the drive and her friend had agreed. Even if Claire were able to uncover something damning based on Anthony's testimony, it could easily be attacked depending on what he was currently being treated for. It seemed that everywhere she turned, she hit another roadblock. Claire closed her eyes and tried to let the hum of the florescent lights calm her racing heart.

"We're ready for you," a guard said, interrupting her reverie.

She opened her eyes to see a large white man with a thick brown mustache standing at the other end of the waiting room. Claire stood and made her way over to him. He handed her a badge that said, "GUEST," with a lanyard attached to it. She put it over her head as he buzzed them through the first set of doors, then through a series of bleak corridors lined with cinderblock walls and nondescript doors until they reached a small, equally dismal room. Claire glanced through the small window in the door. Sitting inside, wearing a prison uniform but devoid of handcuffs or restraints, was Anthony Bates.

Claire eyed him up and down. He was in his early forties, but he appeared younger here, his features still blessed with a boyish charm. His blond hair was thick despite the mandated prison buzz cut. His blue eyes seemed to hold a hint of mischief, his demeanor exuding an air of nonchalance, as if he were completely at ease in this confined setting.

"Is it safe?" Claire asked hesitantly, glancing up at the guard.

"Y'all are free to talk," the guard replied, "but I won't be leaving the room."

Claire nodded, glad for his presence and the two entered the room.

Anthony's posture was relaxed, straightening slightly as they entered. He leaned back in his chair with an easy confidence that seemed completely out of place, which only emphasized his effortless charm. His mouth stretched into a beam she wouldn't have expected a prisoner to muster.

"Good morning, Mr. Bates," Claire said, trying to sound confident as she sat down across from him. She opted not to extend her hand for a handshake, unsure of what the protocol here was. "I'm Claire Stevens, the attorney for your appeal."

"Very nice to meet you, Claire," Anthony said, his eyes cheerful. "I'm grateful you came to see me."

There was something magnetic about him, a charisma that radiated from him. Even as he waited patiently at the table, she found herself drawn to him, despite her better judgment reminding her of the gravity of the situation. Claire could see how he was able to woo women into trusting him. It was a disarming quality, she realized, that could easily sway the opinions of those around him. Yet she couldn't shake the feeling that, beneath that charm and those piercing blue eyes, he had a secret he wouldn't be willing to share.

Claire nodded. "I know discussing these events might be difficult, so if at any point you don't feel like continuing, please let me know and we can stop for the day."

That charming grin of his didn't waver. "Thank you. I appreciate your consideration."

"If you don't mind, let's dive right in."

"Of course."

"Let's start with the night of your arrest," Claire said, keeping her tone neutral.

Anthony tilted his head, curiosity sparkling in his eyes. "But wouldn't you rather hear about the nights of the murders?"

Unease ran through Claire's spine at his question and the look of excitement on his face.

She cleared her throat and tried to keep her voice even. "An appeal is different from a trial. We need to focus on the legal aspects of your case, not the crimes themselves."

"Ah, I see. As you wish." He leaned back in his chair again. "The police arrived. No doubt because I was dancing in the street."

"Dancing?" The report had only indicated a disturbance, and of course that someone had phoned in a tip. There'd been no details of Anthony's activities at the time. "Why were you dancing?"

"The real crime, Claire, is that none of us dance anymore."

Unsure of what to make of his response, Claire jotted it down and pressed on. "So, you were arrested while you were dancing?"

"Not quite," Anthony said, holding up a finger. "I was taken to a hospital for evaluation first."

"Under police escort?"

"Yes."

"Were you told that you were being arrested at this point?"

"No. But I've been taken to the hospital before."

Claire made another note. "Did the police stay with you at the hospital?"

Anthony nodded his head. "This time, yes."

"Can you remember who came to talk to you while you were there?"

Anthony cocked his head to the side, as if in thought. "The names are a bit fuzzy. I can't say I was completely of sound mind during the time. I do recall a detective. Her last name had something to do with the law."

"When you say you weren't completely of sound mind, what do you mean by that?"

Anthony's gaze drifted momentarily, his brows furrowing in concentration. "It's like... there were moments of clarity, you know? But they were fleeting, overshadowed by a fog. Like trying to see through a murky window. I remember flashes of the night, but they're disjointed. Fragments."

Claire leaned forward, her curiosity piqued. "And in these moments of clarity, what do you recall?"

He paused, his expression clouding over with a mixture of frustration and confusion. "I remember feeling agitated. Restless, like something was gnawing at me from the inside. It's hard to explain. And then there were these flashes of anger, intense and consuming. But they weren't directed at anyone in particular, just an overwhelming sense of rage."

"Do you recall being on any substances?"

Anthony threw his head back and laughed. "Of course I was."

"What substances would those have been?"

"Magic mushrooms."

Claire paused and looked up at him. "Magic mushrooms?"

"Psilocybin if you want to be scientific about it."

Claire leafed through her notes and files. She found the arrest records and ran her finger down until she found the toxicology report. "But you didn't test positive for any substances?"

"Of course I didn't. Hospitals test for things like alcohol or opiates. They don't test for psilocybin."

Claire nodded and made a note. "Why'd you take them?"

"The experience is unlike anything you could ever imagine." Anthony closed his eyes, as if savoring a bite of the juiciest steak. "Sure, it can start out scary, horrific even, but once you push through and get to the other side, it's like the equivalent of swimming through all the love in the universe."

Claire's eyes widened as she jotted down more notes. She needed to follow up on whether Anthony's contention was true that psilocybin wouldn't show up on a toxicology report.

"Interesting," Claire said. "So back to the detective then. Was her name"—she flipped her notes over—"Lawson?"

"Yes, that's her. I was just coming down from my trip when we arrived at the hospital. The woman had so many questions for me. She seemed trustworthy, so I told her what she wanted to hear."

Claire paused from making notes to look up at Anthony. "Can you tell me what you mean by that?"

"Detective Lawson seemed genuinely interested in me," he explained, his voice steady and confident. "She asked a lot of questions. It was nice to have someone so invested."

"She was investigating murders and thought you were a suspect, Mr. Bates. She was interrogating you."

"It didn't feel that way. That's why I felt that I could open up to her." His blue eyes met Claire's, his stare unsettling.

"During your time with Detective Lawson, did she ever tell you that you were under arrest?"

"No, not that I can recall."

Claire raised an eyebrow. "Did anyone read you your Miranda warnings? You know, the things the police always say on television—'you have the right to remain silent,' and so on?"

He chuckled softly. "No, no one said that to me."

"Okay," Claire said, her mind racing. "Did you ask to leave?"

"What would have been the point? The police were standing at the door. They wouldn't have let me."

Claire scribbled furiously on her pad. "What did you tell Detective Lawson?"

"What she wanted to hear."

Claire looked up and into his mischievous gaze again. "And what did she want to hear?"

"About the crimes, of course."

"You confessed to them."

"Yes, she was looking for who had committed them."

"And you claimed that you had committed them?"

"At the time, yes. It was so obvious she was desperate to hear someone confess. I wanted to make her happy."

Claire shook her head, confused. "So, are you saying you didn't commit those murders?"

"Yes," he said, throwing back his head in exasperation, as if this were the most obvious thing in the world. "You're my defense lawyer. Did you really think I killed all those people?"

Claire rubbed one of her temples. "It doesn't really work that way. Just because a lawyer defends their client doesn't mean their client is innocent."

"Oh." Anthony shrugged and smiled again. "Well, I am."

"To be clear, you confessed to murders you didn't commit," she said, "to make the investigating detective... happy?"

"Like I said, I was coming down from a beautiful trip."

Claire took a deep breath. She didn't want to press him too far, but his story wasn't adding up. Anthony had provided specific details about the crimes during his interrogation—details that hadn't been released to the public. How could he have known that information if he hadn't been the perpetrator?

She decided to approach it from a different angle. "Okay, so you confessed to murders you didn't commit to make a woman you'd just met happy, and that's why you eventually plead 'not guilty?'"

"I didn't think I should go to prison for what happened," he said, his tone suddenly serious, the grin wiped clean off his face. "It wasn't my fault."

"Not your fault?" Claire asked, baffled. "People were murdered, Anthony. You gave the detective the details of those murders and admitted to them."

"Yes, but that doesn't mean I killed those people."

"How did you know about the murders, then?"

"A friend," he replied, his eyes never leaving hers.

Claire shook her head. "A friend? Who?"

Anthony smiled. "My friend only talks to me, Claire Stevens," he said. "If you need a friend, you should find your own."

Claire could sense that he was getting to his limit. His mood and demeanor had shifted, as had his body language and answers were becoming more and more unhinged. In any event, she had what she needed as far as an appealable issue.

"This has been really helpful, Anthony." She rose from the table. "Thank you for your cooperation."

"You know," he said, eyeing her up and down. "You remind me a lot of my mother."

Claire stopped to look at him, but his eyes gave nothing away.

He sniffed the air slightly. "I think you both even wear the same perfume."

"I'll take that as a compliment."

Anthony cocked his head to the side. "Hmmm, wasn't thinking of it that way."

"Well, thank you for your time today."

She tried to turn around but his voice caught her attention again, his tone hopeful. "Will you be coming to see me again, Claire?"

Claire found herself unable to meet his gaze for a second time, merely looking over her shoulder in acknowledgment. "It's possible."

"I'd like that very much," he said. "It seems like you need a friend. I think I'd enjoy getting to know you better."

Claire nodded at the guard and hurried out of the room. As she walked back through halls of the facility, she tried to maintain her composure.

Upon entering the waiting room, she reached a shaking hand into her purse and pulled out her phone to text Meredith, the screen wobbling as she typed her message.

Done with the interview. Can you come pick me up?

Meredith's reply was fairly quick.

Sorry. Conference still going on. I can be to you in an hour. Is that okay?

Claire looked around the room, the small, sterile waiting room starting to suffocate her. She wanted to leave. Now.

I'll grab an Uber. Meet you back at the hotel.

Meredith gave her a thumb's up, but Claire was already requesting a car, not wanting to spend another minute in the place.

chapter
fourteen

CLAIRE STARED at the scribbled text on her notepad as she sat on the hotel bed. Her wet hair dripped down her back and soaked into her shirt, but the sensation didn't even register against her skin.

She'd reread her notes so many times now she basically had them memorized, but nothing added up. At this point, she wasn't even worried about the appeal. While she had to follow up on a few administrative things, she was confident his Miranda rights had been violated. Daniel should have brought this up before trial even began, and she intended to confront him about why he hadn't, but it wasn't something he had to preserve for appeal. Not to mention the fact that he'd been tripping on some new-age version of LSD. Anything he'd said during the police interrogation should have been thrown out. Especially his confession. She sighed and replayed their conversation in her head, the way he had casually mentioned the murders, as if they were inconsequential. He'd claimed he hadn't committed them, despite his confession, and only knew the details from a "friend," who only spoke to him.

Anthony was starting to sound a lot like Son of Sam, and Claire idly wondered if his "friend" was a talking dog, encouraging him to commit heinous murders.

Claire's stomach knotted. What had he meant, she reminded him of his mother? She made a note to look into his family background.

Having met the woman, she didn't see any sort of resemblance in mannerisms, demeanor, or otherwise.

She was starting to realize that the Anthony Bates rabbit hole might have been a lot deeper than she'd thought.

Her phone buzzed on the hotel bed, jolting her from her thoughts about Anthony. It was a text from Meredith.

On my way back. Dinner?

Claire stared at her screen, hesitating before typing a response.

Not feeling up to it.

The phone rang with a call almost instantly. Claire heaved another sigh and picked it up, throwing her notepad onto the bed.

"Hey, I get it," Meredith said. "Today was rough but take it from me. You shouldn't shut yourself in. You need a break or you'll get lost in work—or depression."

Claire's chest tightened. She knew the darkness of depression all too well. Her friend had a fair point. "Fine."

"Great! Be down in ten." The call ended without another word.

Claire glanced in the mirror, taking in her reflection. Her short brown hair was still wet, her eyes bloodshot and surrounded by dark circles. She looked like she hadn't slept in days. She got up from the bed and rifled through her weekend bag for something to wear, but her phone dinged again. Casting a glance at it, she read the message that Meredith was outside. Now in a rush, she decided to throw on what she'd worn earlier. Inhaling deeply, Claire ran a brush through her hair and made her way to the lobby.

Meredith waited in the pull-through. As Claire slid into the car, her friend greeted her with a warm smile.

"How was the conference?" Claire asked, buckling her seatbelt.

"Good!"

Claire nodded, allowing time for her friend to give her details. But Meredith didn't take it. So she changed the subject. "Where are we going for dinner?"

"Farmhaus," Meredith answered. "Meeting someone from the conference who didn't know anyone. Thought you wouldn't mind if she joined us."

"Of course not," Claire said, attempting a smile. Inside, though, she wished they could talk privately about everything that had happened today.

It was a short drive to the restaurant and the minutes passed in silence as Claire stared out the window.

"Ready?" Meredith asked her. Claire blinked and turned her head from side to side as she realized they had already parked.

"Sorry, yeah."

As the pair walked into the restaurant, the retro vibes stirred memories for Claire. The glossy red counter was the main attraction, accented by chrome stools with worn vinyl cushions. Black-and-white checkered tiles lined the walls, giving the place an unmistakable old-school diner feel. The air was thick with the mouthwatering aroma of sizzling burgers and fresh-cut fries, underscored by the faint sweetness of milkshakes being blended behind the counter.

The interior offered only a few seats, most of them taken by groups chatting over baskets of food. Meredith glanced around, then turned toward the door. "Let's wait for my friend before we order," she suggested, nodding toward the inviting outdoor seating.

Claire followed her back outside, where red picnic tables were scattered under strings of twinkling café lights. The evening air was crisp, and colorful planters dotted the patio, adding a welcoming touch. Meredith scanned the area for their third companion as they picked a spot to wait.

Claire nodded, her thoughts drifting back to Anthony and the unsettling things he'd said. She attempted small talk with Meredith, trying to distract herself. "So, the conference, what was it about?"

"There were a host of panels on all different topics. It was mostly a PR thing for the university." Meredith looked up from the menu she'd been scanning. "Trying to get donors and fresh blood."

"Makes sense," Claire said.

"Hey," Meredith called out, waving at someone who just walked in. "Over here!"

Claire followed her gaze and locked eyes with a familiar face. The woman stopped in her tracks. "Oh my God! Is that Claire Stevens?"

Claire's stomach dropped. She hadn't seen Kendra Miller since her senior year of high school. Her shoulder length auburn hair was the same as it was back then, along with her round face and cheeks full of freckles.

"Hey Kendra," she said, standing to greet her old friend.

Meredith looked between the two women. "You two know each other?"

"Do we?" Kendra exclaimed, reaching out to give Claire a hug. "We were basically best friends in high school. It's been ages."

Claire tried to smile again, but her lips wouldn't cooperate.

"Okay, this is crazy," Meredith said. "Let's order, and then we can all connect."

"Sounds good to me!" Kendra said with a beaming smile.

Claire trailed slightly behind the two women as they made their way back into the restaurant, pretending to study the menu posted near the door. The scent of sizzling burgers and fresh fries hit her again, mingling with the chatter of customers and the faint hum of a milkshake blender behind the red counter. She glanced over at Kendra a few times, her mind wandering.

The longer she was in Georgia, the more of her past seemed to resurface, unbidden and unwelcome. Memories stirred with each familiar accent, each nostalgic sight and smell, and she couldn't quite shake the feeling that her past was catching up with her.

Kendra's presence reopened the Pandora's box of memories she'd worked so hard to bury deep down.

The food was prepared quickly and the three made their way outside to sit.

"Have you two seen each other since high school?" Meredith asked. Claire wished she hadn't.

"No!" Kendra said, slapping her hand down on the table, the thud causing a few fries to tumble off the edge of her plate. She quickly popped one into her mouth, brushing crumbs off her fingers. "Can you believe we've run into each other after all this time?"

Claire forced a tight-lipped smile, her hands idly fidgeting with the wrapper of her burger. "What are the chances, right?" She took a small bite, chewing slowly, trying to mask her discomfort.

"I heard you moved to New York," Kendra said. "I didn't know you moved back! Did you miss home?"

"In a way," Claire answered tersely, desperate to move away from the past. She reached for her drink, the condensation leaving damp rings on the table as she picked it up. "What have you been up to?"

"I went to Southern Coastal University for college and now I'm a social worker, mainly working with kids."

"That's great!" Meredith chimed in, pausing to take a bite of her burger. She gestured enthusiastically with a fry in hand. "Sounds like rewarding work!"

"Yeah! I really love it." Kendra leaned forward, resting her elbows on the table as she turned to Claire. "What about you?" she asked, dabbing her mouth with a napkin. "Do you love being a lawyer?"

Claire tried not to grimace. "I have mixed feelings about the profession."

"It's pretty awesome that you were able to get into law school and all that. Honestly, after everything that happened, a lot of us were really surprised when we'd heard the news."

The blood in Claire's face drained out and her lips pressed together. Her legs seemed to move of their own accord and she stood. "Excuse me, I'm not feeling well."

Before her friends could protest, she bolted for the bathroom, seeing the sign for it instantly. She pushed the door open and it slammed shut behind her as she fought to catch her breath. She slid the lock to the right, ensuring no one would enter behind her.

She tried to slow down her breathing, tried to keep the panic attack at bay, but the deep breaths were useless. Thoughts and images began to swirl in her mind.

A shed. A gun. Blue and red lights. Police sirens.

She released her grip as her hands started to shake and backed up to the wall, sliding down. She crouched on the cool tile floor, not caring about the germs. Clamping her eyes shut, she wrapped her arms around herself, wanting to escape into her own private cave.

A gentle knock sounded on the door. Claire tried to respond, but her voice failed her.

"Claire?" Meredith's concerned tone seeped through the door. "Are you okay?"

"Fine," she managed to croak out. "Something I ate."

"Want me to take you home?"

"No," Claire said. "I'll be out soon."

Meredith's footsteps retreated, and she stayed in the bathroom for another fifteen minutes trying to fight off the panic and get control of her mind.

By the time she emerged, Kendra was saying goodbye to Meredith. Oblivious to the turmoil she had caused, she gave Claire a big hug. "Sorry you're not feeling well. Hope you keep in touch!"

"Sure," Claire said and Meredith waved goodbye. She turned to Claire and her eyes softened. " We can talk in the car if you want."

Claire nodded, the knot in her stomach tightening as they walked toward the car in silence. The cool night air carried the faint scent of pine and damp asphalt, mingling with the distant hum of traffic. The chatter and laughter from the restaurant faded behind them, leaving an uneasy quiet that seemed to amplify Claire's swirling thoughts.

Once inside the car, Claire remained quiet, gripping her seatbelt as if it might steady her. She had no idea where to even start. Her mind churned with half-formed sentences, none of them feeling right. Instead, she let herself gaze out the window, the blurred glow of streetlights and neon signs reflecting off the car's glass. She let herself gaze out the window, watching the Augusta nighttime pass by.

Finally Meredith ventured. "Do you want to talk about anything?"

"Unsure," was Claire's reply.

"Do you think your interview with Anthony caused your sickness?"

Claire nodded her head, grateful Meredith hadn't made the connection between her response to Kendra's reminiscing.

"Talk to me, Claire. Don't bottle it up."

"I can't, really," she replied. "It would be a breach of attorney-client confidentiality."

"I understand," Meredith assured her, "but you know I'm not going to tell anyone."

Claire took a deep breath. Maybe talking about the interview would help keep her mind off her past. Both things were upsetting, but one was slightly less so.

"Anthony was . . . odd," she said. "Charming. Unbothered by being locked up. He wanted to talk about the murders like he was interested in them, like I would be too. Almost as if he wanted to relive them. And was disappointed when I told him I wasn't there to talk about them."

Meredith parked the car in the hotel parking lot, but neither woman got out.

"He talked about dancing in the street," Claire continued. "Said he was on magic mushrooms at the time of the arrest and that I reminded him of his mother." She shook her head, trying to clear her thoughts. "I'm sorry, I'm not making any sense. The whole thing just made me feel so anxious."

"I understand," Meredith said.

"He also said he wanted me to come visit again. That he wanted to get to know me better." Claire twisted her hands in her lap. " Do you think I'm paranoid for worrying about becoming a victim? I've dismissed it, but now, I just don't know."

Meredith put her hand on Claire's shoulder. " I don't think you're paranoid. What you're feeling is normal and valid."

"I found an appealable issue. And it's pretty bad. Like, bad enough to get him a whole new trial. But if I get him out, will he come after me?"

"I can't answer that question," Meredith said. "No one can. You have to trust your gut on this."

"My gut says that I have a duty to defend him. And if I don't bring this appeal correctly, I could risk losing my law license. Not to mention help perpetuate denying someone their rights under the Constitution. Can I really live with myself if I do that?"

"Is there really no one else you can talk to about this? Maybe someone at your firm? Or a family member?"

Claire shook her head, then paused to consider her boss. "There's really no one. Bob was more effective in his heyday when he was working with my Dad. Besides, Dolores doesn't want me sharing this with other attorneys at the firm. Even if I could, Daniel makes me almost as anxious as Anthony."

"What do you mean?"

"I went into the office yesterday and he was fishing for information. His questions made me think he already knew what he was looking for." Claire sighed. "Maybe he was confronted with the same decision I am and decided to keep someone truly dangerous in prison."

"It's possible," Meredith replied. "And that might be why Anthony's mother doesn't want you talking to anyone at your firm."

"Could be. Fiona and I used to talk, but with her and Daniel an item, things are still on the rocks between us."

"I understand," Meredith said.

"You're really the only one that I've been able to share things with," Claire confessed. "I'm really grateful to you for it."

Meredith waved her hands. "Don't even mention it. I'm always here to listen. I'm sure I'll be coming to you with something sooner than later, too."

"Thank you," Claire whispered, wiping tears from her eyes.

"I think you're totally exhausted," Meredith said, shutting the car off. "And so am I. Let's get some sleep. You'll feel better in the morning."

"Okay," Claire agreed, and the two women stepped out of the car.

chapter
fifteen

FLASHBACK

Claire opened the door to find Matty in a white button down and Bermuda shorts, looking as surly as ever with his unmoving scowl. He was clutching a bouquet of peonies in his right hand, his left dangling by his side in a fist.

"I made it. Happy?" He shoved the flowers at Claire. "These are for you. Thanks for playing host to impending stupidity."

"Thank you," she laughed, taking the bouquet and ushering him inside. "How did you know peonies were my favorite flower?"

He gave her a flat stare. "I know everything about you, Claire. You told me your favorite flower a long time ago."

Claire hid her blush as she sniffed the flowers, and the two made their way through the house. Matty whistled as they walked into the kitchen. Claire filled a vase with water and put the flowers inside as Matty looked around.

"I forgot how crazy nice your place was," he said.

Claire's father had purchased the historic Tudor Revival house in Ardsley Park from some developer who'd gotten in over his head with trying to renovate it. He'd managed to get it for a steal, boasting endlessly about how it was the kind of deal you couldn't pass up—an investment that practically paid for itself. Roy always had a thing for real estate. Most lawyers did.

Claire remembered walking through the house for the first time, her father beaming as he pointed out the original woodwork and stained-glass windows, while her mother only saw the endless potential for upgrades. It wasn't long before the property became a canvas for her mother's ambitious vision.

With her family's newfound wealth, her mother had spared no expense in the renovations of the home, yet all of its historic elements remained intact.

"I just don't get why your parents decided to live so far from downtown."

Claire shrugged, walking over to the fridge to grab them each a beer. "I dunno that it's that far. Besides, I sort of like that it's secluded and out of the way. It's nice to get away from it all at the end of the day."

"You sound old when you say stuff like that," Matty laughed, cracking his can open.

Claire stuck her tongue out at him.

"You should convince your parents to move," Matty said, looking around at the architecture and high ceilings. "This place is way too pretentious."

"Yeah, they really went all out. But if my mother gets her way, they eventually will move. I know she feels a little disconnected from the world out here."

"Like mother like daughter."

Claire frowned as she cracked open her beer. "What's that supposed to mean?"

"Your mother has been desperate to be accepted into the tighter social circles of the city." Matty shrugged. "Everyone knows it."

The two made their way to the solarium. Claire kicked off her shoes and sat on the side of the pool, letting her feet dangle in the cool water. There were beach balls and pool floats already strewn across the lit-up water, just waiting for the party to begin.

"That's easy for you to say. You come from old money. My family's had to work twice as hard just to be noticed."

"Notice me, senpai," Matty joked in an ultra-feminine voice.

Claire kicked her feet, splashing him. "Watch it or I'll throw you in the deep end."

Matty laughed and sat down next to her.

"God, why are we friends again?" she asked, shaking her head.

"Because I'm the only one who can tolerate your terrible taste in music."

They both chuckled. Matty let his legs hang into the water next to Claire's as he took a sip of his beer. It was quiet except for the steady hum of the pool pump.

Claire was the first to break it. "Do you remember when we first met?"

"Of course I do," Matty replied, turning his head to look at her. "You transferred to Country Day. You got assigned to be my lab partner. The entire day you tried to boss me around during our lab. It made me think you were just some stuck-up rich girl. I was one-hundred percent correct."

"Thanks a lot for that trip through memory lane," Claire said dryly. "That was a tough time for me. My dad had just made it big with all the asbestos cases he was litigating and my family was getting torn apart by the media attention." She swung her feet through the water. "I thought I needed to be the perfect daughter and the perfect student, because I thought everyone was watching me. I didn't know who to trust."

"Except for me." Matty nudged her lightly with his elbow. "I was your ride or die from day one. I saw through your perfectionist facade. And look at you now! Throwing parties when your parents are out of town."

A lump formed in Claire's throat, her voice softening. "I don't know what I would've done without you."

"Hey, stop that. What's brought all this on?"

"It's just going to suck with us going to different colleges. You're going to Emory and I'm going to Augusta. I mean, who's going to keep me from doing something stupid or turning back into a mean girl?"

Matty laughed. "Don't get dramatic. We'll still talk and text all the time."

"I don't know," Claire said. "I'm just nervous to have to go to a new place and try and fit in all over again. You know that I don't make friends easily. It feels like I'll be starting from scratch again."

Matty sighed, placing his beer can on the concrete floor next to him. "I get it. But college is supposed to be about finding yourself, figuring out what you want to do with your life. You can't do that if you're constantly worried about fitting in."

"You've never had to worry about fitting in, Matty. Your family owns practically half of Savannah." She took a sip of her beer, the crisp bitterness hitting her tongue before the cool liquid slid down her throat. "People just make room for you."

"Maybe," Matty conceded. "But that doesn't mean I don't understand how you feel. Besides, I make it a point to *not* fit in."

Claire rolled her eyes. "Yeah, I've noticed."

Matty laughed. "You should try it sometime. It's liberating. Not worrying about what other people think of you. Just living your life for yourself."

"Even though everyone wants to stay on your family's good side, they think you're weird and antisocial," Claire said. "They're just too afraid to tell you."

"Perfect. Exactly how I want it." He tried nudging Claire a bit, but she still wasn't feeling chipper. "Look, we may not be going to the same school, but that doesn't mean we can't still be there for each other. We'll figure it out, okay?"

Claire eyed him for a moment, but finally relented with a nod. "Yeah. Okay."

"And who knows, maybe I'll come visit you in Augusta. My half-sister goes there, so it'll give me a reason to visit."

"Ugh, please don't. I don't need my roommate thinking I'm some kind of loser who can't make real friends."

"Trust me, you won't have trouble making friends. You're smart, funny, and drop-dead gorgeous. What more could anyone want?"

Claire blinked in surprise as she looked at Matty. "You...you really think so?"

He downed the rest of his beer and tossed the can behind him. "Duh."

Something came over Claire upon hearing Matty say those words. A sense of confidence she'd never felt before. She leaned toward him, intent on showing him how she'd felt about him for so long. Maybe his words were encouraging her, or maybe just the fact that she wouldn't be able to do this once they left for college. Plus, seeing him end up with someone at Emory would tear her apart.

She'd never wanted him to just be a friend.

As she leaned closer, Matty pulled away.

"Claire, I..."

"Matty," she said, not able to look into his eyes. "I've had an enormous crush on you basically since the day we first met."

Matty's eyes widened for a moment. "Claire." He breathed heavily for a moment, his gaze staring into hers when she finally looked up. "I'm sorry, but I can't."

Claire's face flushed with embarrassment. She pulled away, her stomach dropping with rejection.

"It's not you," he said quickly, putting his hands up.

Claire shook her head, eyes watering. "What do you mean?"

"Claire." Matty sighed and slid a palm down his face. "I'm gay."

Claire blinked as she tried to take in his words. She couldn't believe it. All this time, she had been harboring feelings for someone who didn't even like girls.

"Wh-why didn't you tell me?" Claire stammered, feeling tears prick at the corners of her eyes.

"I haven't told anyone," Matty said, looking away. "Savannah isn't exactly the most welcoming of this sort of thing."

Claire looked at him in disbelief. "What? You think I'd share something like that? Is that what you're saying?"

Matty put up his hands again. "No, no. I-I don't know." He fumbled over his words. "I guess I just wasn't ready to tell you. I didn't want it to change things between us."

"That would never change things between us, Matty. But keeping a secret from me? Not trusting me? That would change things."

Matty's eyes flashed with a mixture of hurt and anger. "That's a little hypocritical, Claire. You just admitted that you've been crushing on me since the day we first met. How is that supposed to make *me* feel? How is that not a betrayal of our friendship and trust?"

A wave of anger and sadness washed over Claire. She had thought about admitting her feelings to him so many times. She just never thought that he would throw it back in her face. She had always prided herself on being accepting of everyone, but now she couldn't help but feel betrayed by her best friend.

The doorbell rang and she stood.

"Whatever," she muttered, wiping away her tears.

"Claire, don't be like that!" Matty stood up and followed her. "It came out wrong! I didn't mean it like that!"

"I hope you enjoy not talking to anyone at my stupid party," she said. He grabbed at her arm, but she shrugged him off. "I'm glad we had this talk so I could find out how you really feel."

Matty didn't follow behind her as she walked off.

Claire felt like she was about to explode. She didn't know what to do or say, and worst of all, she didn't know how to handle the fact that her closest friend had kept this secret from her.

All she knew was that her life would never be the same again.

chapter
sixteen

The highway stretched ahead in an endless ribbon of asphalt. Claire wrung her hands, her knuckles turning white as she glanced over at Meredith, busy with one hand on the steering wheel and one fiddling with the radio.

"Hey Meredith," she said hesitantly, "do you mind if we stop at the medical center before heading back? It's just the next exit."

"Okay." Meredith's fingers paused on the radio dial. She raised an eyebrow and glanced at Claire, curiosity evident in her green eyes. "But why?"

Claire hesitated, a familiar knot of anxiety forming in her stomach. "Um, there's something I need to do there. I just remembered."

"Are you sure?" Meredith asked, clearly not convinced by Claire's explanation.

"Something I forgot to ask the staff." Claire insisted, forcing a smile as she stared straight ahead. "I need Anthony's up-to-date charts."

"Okay." Meredith turned on her blinker, guiding the car toward the exit.

Claire's mind raced as the prison came back into view. She needed those records, hoping they contained some clue about what had happened to Anthony while he was in custody. The police records were so sparse. She wondered whether extraneous reports had really gone missing, or whether Daniel hadn't served proper discovery on the prosecution.

Her heart pounded in her chest, betraying her calm exterior.

Meredith pulled up to the front door, the car idling as she looked over at Claire, eyes filled with concern. "I'll wait here," she said softly.

Claire nodded, forcing another tight-lipped smile before stepping out of the car.

"I'll be right back," Claire said, her voice wavering slightly as she got out of the car. The door closed with a soft thud behind her.

She stepped into the hospital once more, the sterile scent and harsh fluorescent lights igniting that familiar ball of anxiety within her chest. Her heart raced, her breaths shallow and quick.

"Ms. Stevens?" The receptionist peered up from her computer, her face lighting up in recognition. It was the same woman who had been there yesterday. She was in her early forties, a bit heavy set with graying brown hair. She looked like she truly didn't want to be here. "Are you here to see Mr. Bates again?"

Claire shook her head, her fingers digging into the strap of her bag. "No, I was actually hoping to get a copy of his medical files. I should have asked yesterday, but it slipped my mind."

"Ah, I see." The receptionist's eyes narrowed, her fingers tapping rhythmically on the desk. "We can't release the files without authorization from the patient or, in this case, the patient's guardian."

Claire gritted her teeth, frustration bubbling inside her. "Is there anything I can do to expedite the process?" she asked, her voice tight.

The receptionist frowned. "You'd need to speak to the guardian directly. If they grant permission, then we can release the files to you."

Desperation creeped into Claire's voice when she asked, "Who is the patient's guardian?"

"I'm sorry, but I can't give you that information."

Claire's hands clenched into fists, her knuckles turning white. It was the curse of this case. At every turn, a new person was standing in her way. She could try and push a motion through the court for access to the files, but with less than two weeks until the appeal was due, it was unlikely she'd get them back in time.

"Please," she said, her voice barely above a whisper. "This is important."

"I wish there were some way I could help you," the woman replied, her expression softening. "But I cannot break protocol, especially with medical records."

Claire exhaled sharply. She fished her phone out of her purse, realizing she already knew the answer to her question. She pulled up Dolores Bates' number.

The phone rang once, twice, then Dolores picked up. "Claire. How can I help you?"

"Good morning, Dolores." Claire's voice was steady, masking her frustration. "I'm actually here in Augusta. I met with Anthony yesterday."

"Is that right?" Dolores replied, her tone cool and detached.

Claire continued, her eyes flicking back to the receptionist who stood behind the desk, watching her expectantly. "I need a copy of Anthony's medical records. I believe they might contain crucial information for our case."

"Is there an issue obtaining them?"

"Unfortunately, they won't release them without authorization from Anthony's guardian."

"Very well." Dolores replied, her words clipped and efficient. "Do what you must."

"Would you mind speaking to the receptionist? They need to hear it from you directly."

The sigh on the other end betrayed a hint of impatience. "Fine. Put her on."

Claire handed the phone to the receptionist, watching as the woman nodded and exchanged polite pleasantries with Dolores. After a brief conversation, the receptionist handed the phone back to Claire.

"Thank you, Dolores. I appreciate your help."

"Of course. Do keep me informed of any progress."

Dolores ended the call without a goodbye.

"Please give me a few minutes," the receptionist said, standing up from her desk and disappearing into the depths of the facility.

Claire found a seat and stared at the sterile walls. She hated being alone with her own thoughts. Her brain seemed to be hardwired to use the opportunity to run through worst case scenarios. What if there wasn't anything in the medical records that was helpful? Or worse, what if the records actually hurt their case or contradicted Anthony's recollection of the events?

The receptionist reappeared in front of Claire, extending an envelope filled with the coveted documents. "Here you go."

"Thanks," Claire muttered, her grip tightening on the envelope. She rose from her seat, legs shaking but resolved.

Sunlight streamed through the glass doors as Claire exited the building, clutching the envelope. Meredith's car still idled at the front parking lot.

"Got it?" Meredith asked as Claire slid into the passenger seat.

"Got it."

"Alright then," Meredith replied, shifting gears.

Claire stared out the window, watching the blurred landscape whip by. Her breathing was shallow, her chest rising and falling with each quick intake of air. The envelope of documents felt heavy on her lap.

Meredith glanced over at her, concern etched across her face. "Are you okay?"

"Fine," Claire snapped, immediately regretting her sharp tone. "I'm just...thinking."

"About Anthony?"

Claire pressed her forehead against the cool windowpane. "About everything."

"Would you feel better if you looked through that file now?"

Claire looked down at the envelope. It wasn't too thick and they had a few hours' drive before they'd get back to Savannah. But as soon as she moved to open the file, her anxiety spiked again.

"You don't have to," Meredith said, keeping her eyes fixed on the road. "But if you have questions as you go through it, I can give you my input. We can talk about the other reports I went through as well."

As much as Claire just wanted to put her head back and go to sleep, Meredith's offer was too good to pass up. She cracked open the envelope with her index finger and pulled the contents out onto her lap.

"I'm not even sure what I'm looking for. Something to corroborate his story? Or something else entirely."

"Let's start by looking at his medical history. Sometimes patterns emerge and can shed light on certain behaviors or conditions."

Claire nodded, flipping through the pages until she found the section labeled, "Medical History."

Claire ran her finger down the page. "I don't have the report in front of me, but it doesn't look like he's got nearly as many diagnoses as the psychological report from the trial."

She turned to the next page and nodded. This list was definitely shorter.

"That's something I wanted to talk to you about," Meredith said. "The first report seemed fine, the one issued by"—Meredith snapped her fingers—"what was the first doctor's name?"

"Fields?"

"Right. The Fields report was more in line with what I'm used to seeing. I'll be honest, the sheer number of diagnoses on the second report was a little mind boggling."

"Mind boggling how?"

"I'm not saying it's not plausible to suffer from all of those issues, but it is rare to manifest them all simultaneously. And for a clinician to be able to actually diagnose them all after one interview." Meredith frowned and shook her head. "It just seemed odd to me."

"So, it's something Daniel should have objected to?"

"That's a bit out of my wheelhouse."

Claire nodded. "Dr. Fields said the prosecutor had requested the second report. Said it was issued by a psychologist with a history of seeing Anthony, Dr. Brown." She flipped through the chart and sighed. "But I'm not seeing anything here about Dr. Brown."

"What about the two reports? Can't you use that in the appeal?"

"Not really," Claire said, leafing through the rest of the documents in her lap. "Daniel should have objected to both reports during trial.

Since he didn't, he waived Anthony's right to use the issue during an appeal."

"That hardly seems fair."

"And is the very reason to choose a competent trial lawyer."

"Does Daniel not have a good reputation?"

"As far as I know he does. Losing the Bates case didn't hurt him all that much because no one really wanted Bates to win."

Meredith rolled her eyes. "More unfair."

"There's a lot of that going around," Claire remarked, getting to the last page of the documents. She sighed as she shuffled them back inside the envelope. "Nothing useful."

"I still think it was worth the effort." Meredith cast her a glance and smiled. "This way you know for sure that there aren't any ghosts lurking, ready to jump out at you."

"I'm more convinced than ever that there are more." Claire shook her head as she looked out the window. "Ghosts have a way of never leaving me."

chapter
seventeen

DETECTIVE ERIN LAWSON was seated at her desk in the bustling precinct, the faint smell of burnt coffee lingering in the air as papers and open case files cluttered her workspace. The overhead fluorescent lights cast a dull glow, accentuating the exhaustion etched into her sharp, angular features. Her dark brown hair was pulled into a tight ponytail without a hair out of place, and her gray button-up was still wrinkle free despite the long shift that had stretched well past reasonable hours. She had the lean, wiry build of someone who spent more time on the streets than behind a desk, and her sharp green eyes, shadowed by fatigue, still held a relentless intensity. She was midway through reviewing a suspect's statement when her desk phone buzzed, cutting through the low hum of conversation around her. With a sigh, she picked it up.

"Erin, there's someone here to see you," Officer Grayson said on the other end.

She glanced at her calendar, her brows furrowing. "I have no meetings scheduled today."

"I know. It's an impromptu visit," Grayson replied, his tone even.

"Tell them I'm busy," Erin said, a note of impatience in her voice. She turned to place the receiver back in its cradle, already turning her attention back to the document spread across her desk, her pen tapping against the paper as she refocused. But Grayson's voice stopped her.

"I tried," was the response. "Her words were, 'She's welcome to talk with me now, but if she chooses not to, I'm happy to send her a subpoena or notice of a deposition.'"

Lawson groaned. "Who is she?"

"Claire Stevens. Says she's working on the Bates case."

Lawson paused. "That case has been closed."

"I didn't stick around to ask more questions."

"Fine," Lawson said, standing up. "I'll go take care of this."

Lawson hung up the phone with too much force and made her way out to the front of the station. A woman in her late twenties was sitting in the waiting area. Her brown hair was cut short and not really styled. The woman attempted to exude confidence and professionalism through demeanor and posture. As she looked up at Lawson's approach, her eyes betrayed a hint of apprehension. She was nervous, that much was clear to the detective.

"I'm Detective Lawson," Lawson said curtly, crossing her arms over her chest. The woman met her gaze but didn't smile. She stood and introduced herself.

"Claire Stevens. I'm working on the Anthony Bates case, and I would like to ask you a few questions."

"Let's talk in here," Lawson said, gesturing to the conference room to the right.

She didn't wait for Claire to follow her through the oak door to the worn conference room, and didn't bother to hold it open for her. Lawson took a seat in one of the leather chairs strewn around a large circular table. Her visitor sat a few seats down.

"So, are you a journalist?" Lawson asked, feigning ignorance. She was the sort of detective who liked people to tell her things, rather than the other way around.

"No." Claire passed a business card down. "I'm Anthony Bates' attorney."

Lawson looked at it briefly and resisted the urge to roll her eyes as she silently read, "Claire Stevens, Counselor at Law, Savannah Legal."

She tossed the card back onto the conference table. "Hate to tell you that this case has already been tried."

"Yes, I'm aware." Claire made no attempt to hide her exasperation. " I'm handling his appeal." Lawson watched as she took a few papers out of her folder along with a notepad. " I'd like to talk to you about the night he was arrested."

"Ask your questions," Lawson said, doing nothing to hide her own irritation.

"Please recount the night of Anthony's arrest for me."

"Not sure if this is your first time doing criminal work, but every-thing about the night of the arrest is in the police reports. Did you get a chance to read them?"

Claire gave Lawson a measured look. "As I'm sure you're aware, the police reports are pretty limited. Seems as if there's a fair amount missing from them, actually."

Lawson sighed. "As far as I remember, I received a call about someone having a psychotic episode that fit the description of the suspect for the murders. We picked him up and took him to the hospital where I asked him a few questions. He seemed more than happy to talk to me."

"Were you aware that he wasn't read his Miranda rights when you started speaking with him?"

"I wasn't aware someone needed to be read their Miranda rights to be admitted to a hospital."

"That is true, but when you're held in a hospital by the police, unable to leave, and questioned by a detective, that starts to look a lot more like an arrest. Especially when those questions lead to a confession."

" I've been doing this for quite some time," Lawson said, "and that was not my evaluation of the situation."

"I'll be sure to include that in my brief," Claire said under her breath. "Do you recall what questions you asked him?"

"All of that should be in the report." Lawson stood from her seat. "As I'm sure you can appreciate, I actually have other work to do and don't have time to relive the past."

"Funny thing," Claire said, also standing up. "As I mentioned, the report is unusually bare. There's also no recording of your interrogation."

"Likely because he wasn't under arrest at the time. So, it wasn't an interrogation."

"As you said."

"Well, if there's nothing else—"

"There may be," Claire said, gathering her things. "But I'm happy to notice a deposition if there is."

"Great," Lawson said, her voice dripping with sarcasm before walking out of the conference room, leaving the lawyer inside.

She walked back to her desk and sat down heavily, leaning back in her chair and closing her eyes.

"Something the matter?"

Lawson cracked an eye open to see her supervisor, Paul Richardson, standing in her doorway.

Richardson stood about six feet tall, with bright white hair and a mustache to match. His eyes were kind, but his expression often let others know not to bother him.

She rubbed her temples. "Just a lawyer fishing for issues."

"What case?"

"Anthony Bates."

Richardson cursed and ran a hand over his head.

"Yeah," Lawson replied.

The Bates case hadn't been easy for the station to handle. There were a lot of politics in policework and arresting the son of a prominent Savannah family and charging him with seven heinous murders was not great for business. Not when said family was such a big donor to law enforcement and held a lot of political sway.

"Think anything will come of it?" Richardson asked.

"Honestly, it's hard to know. I'm not a lawyer, but her questions made me a little uncomfortable."

"Just what we need," Richardson grumbled, taking a sip of his coffee.

"We'll deal," Lawson said. Internally, she wished she could leave

Savannah. She'd dreamed of working in larger jurisdictions—Atlanta, maybe even D.C.—where high-profile cases and resources were plentiful. But those opportunities required the kind of experience she was still building. For the time being, she was stuck here. She needed more experience before she'd be able to apply for a bigger jurisdiction.

"Just keep on it," Richardson said. "And don't take any more impromptu meetings from her."

"Why not?" she asked. "I'd rather her fish for information off the record."

Richardson shook his head. " Don't make this easy for her. There are costs and paperwork involved with depositions."

Lawson scoffed. "Not like the Bates family can't afford it. And I've never known a lawyer to shy away from billing for useless paperwork."

"Just do your best to keep her at a distance, but make sure you know what she's up to."

"Great," Lawson said, rolling her eyes. "Thanks for another impossible task, as usual."

Richardson nodded and walked away to leave her alone with her thoughts.

Lawson's stomach twisted, knowing she hadn't been completely honest with Claire about the night Anthony was arrested. The call had come in from an unknown informant, letting her know Anthony Bates had been out in public and acting strangely. The informant had suspected he may have been involved in the murders. Lawson found him and took him to the hospital with the intention of interrogating him.

When they'd arrived, he was coming down from a mushroom trip, his behavior alternating between being cooperative and borderline violent. The hospital staff ended up strapping him to the bed. He'd clearly been agitated and was sweating profusely. That's when Lawson began to ask him questions. At first he wouldn't say much, insisting that he, "loved everyone," and, "why would he ever murder someone?"

Lawson had a feeling that he was lying, so she'd pressed him harder. Eventually, he broke down and started talking. Confessed to everything.

Lawson had kept the reports from that night light. If she had included how everything had happened, a competent lawyer would get the case thrown out. She'd been a nervous wreck the entire trial, expecting the defense team to depose her and question the police reports from that night, but they never did. For a while, she'd struggled with the guilt, drinking herself to sleep each night. But when the verdict was announced, she'd thought the whole ordeal was finally over.

Lawson had justified her tactics to herself after Bates' conviction. The police had been receiving daily calls from concerned citizens, essentially turning against the force while the murders remained unsolved. No one could understand just why there hadn't been an arrest yet.

Following the conviction, Dolores Bates had withdrawn the substantial Bates' family donations to the police force. Lawson and Richardson had agreed there wasn't much else that could be done. Better to have one family angry with the force than the entire city.

But now, with this new lawyer digging around, that familiar unease from the entire trial was starting to return. If the truth came out, it could ruin her career and reputation. She needed to find a way to keep Claire at bay, even if it meant bending the rules.

chapter
eighteen

IT HAD TAKEN her all night, but Claire finally had all the evidence she needed for Anthony's appeal. Joy had let her stay overnight at the library, locking her inside to let her continue working. Claire had scoured through case after case until her eyes stung from staring at her bright computer screen and her back ached from hunching over all night.

The Georgia Code, like most states, required a confession of guilt to be voluntary to be admitted into evidence. While that was a good starting place, Claire wanted to find a case that matched Anthony's fact pattern.

It was less than an hour before dawn when she'd finally found the one ruling she needed. A ruling from the Georgia Supreme Court that overturned a defendant's guilty verdict in the case of a tainted confession. The Court had held that a "Miranda-tainted statement was not admissible as evidence of the defendant's guilt or innocence and the trial court's failure to *sua sponte* disregard such statement was grounds for a new trial."

This wouldn't be the easiest appeal brief to write, but if she argued it correctly, the Court of Appeals would be helpless not to overturn the verdict. What she wanted to know now was how everything she had uncovered over the last few days had been ignored during the trial.

Thankfully, an error like this didn't require an objection at trial. The courts considered something like this so fundamental to the concept of justice that whether the trial court raised it was irrelevant. However, Daniel should have spotted it. Had he moved to exclude the first confession ahead of the trial, the outcome could have been very different for Anthony.

As soon as Joy was in to unlock all the library doors, Claire barreled out intent on getting answers from Daniel. She almost ran Joy over in her haste to get out the door.

"Whoa!" her friend exclaimed, catching her thermos of coffee. "I guess that means you found what you needed?"

"Yeah," Claire said, looking at her watch.

"I can't believe you actually stayed here all night," Joy said. "Can I get you some coffee before you head out?"

Claire shook her head. "Thanks, but no. I really need to talk to someone as soon as possible."

Joy gave her a knowing smile. "When you get passionate about something, there's no stopping you!"

Claire chuckled. "Something like that. I'll catch up with you later."

Joy waved her goodbye and Claire all but ran towards the law office. She ignored the odd stares from people as she weaved her way on and off the sidewalk to avoid the slower pace of others.

She didn't even bother to change out of her sneakers or groom her appearance as she made her way into the firm, her hair likely a frizzy mess and her eyes lined with deep dark circles.

"Morning, Claire!" Bob tried to say as she whirled past him.

"Not now," Claire said in response. Her attitude surprised even herself. Normally she would never be so rude to a colleague, let alone to her boss. Maybe it was her lack of sleep or maybe she was just legitimately tired of being lied to by everyone around her.

If her suspicions about Daniel were correct, then there was no way Bob wasn't in on it. Bob was always deeply involved in every major case the firm handled—his fingerprints were on everything, from strategy sessions to client meetings. He prided himself on knowing every detail, no matter how small. If something shady was happening, there was no chance it had slipped past him. Either way, she wanted answers, and Daniel was about to give them to her.

She shoved open his door to find him reclining in his leather chair, his feet crossed on top of the desk, the morning paper stretched out in front of him. She'd never realized just how much the man bothered her. Maybe it was the velvet loafers, or the way he combed his hair over, or his stupid red tie. It made her sick to think of him living such a privileged existence when he'd so thoroughly screwed his client, who was now sitting in prison.

"Daniel!" She all but barked.

He lowered the paper and gave her a confused look. "Can I help you with something?"

She stomped inside the room. " You can help me understand why you blatantly ignored the fact that Anthony's confession was tainted and should have been excluded from evidence."

Daniel's face turned from confused to concerned. He threw his paper to the side and stood, quickly rounding his desk to close the door. Claire expected him to return to his seat, but he didn't. He stayed uncomfortably close to her, forcing her to take a step back.

"Lower your voice," he said in a forced whisper.

"Why should I?" she replied, her loud tone remaining.

His expression was morphing into one of anger now. "Because there are bigger things at play here, and I don't need you screaming about a tainted confession for everyone in the office to hear."

"Bigger things?" Claire asked, shaking her head. "What could possibly be bigger than something like this? Anthony gave me the entire story. He was taken to the hospital by the police, kept there against his will, then interrogated. That not only was his confession tainted, but I'm pretty sure he was high at the time he gave it."

Daniel opened his mouth to speak, but Claire put her hand up to stop him. "I'm not done. I spoke to the detective who interviewed Anthony too. You never even deposed her. Had you, the truth would have come out. She's been with the force long enough to know she didn't follow protocol. Seems like everyone knew Anthony's confession should have been excluded except for his own lawyer. Now, how could that be?"

Claire cocked her head to the side, waiting for Daniel to give her an answer.

Daniel sighed and pinched the bridge of his nose. "Look, what do you want me to say?"

Claire blinked in disbelief. "What do I want you to say? I want you to say the truth! That piece of information was staring you right in the face. Also who doesn't depose the arresting officer? Why didn't you move to exclude the confession?"

Daniel let out a deep sigh. "Let's just say it was better for everyone that Bates went to prison."

"Everyone except Bates." She took a step back from him, putting some distance between them as unease crept over her.

"He's a murderer, Claire. Just let it be. Do what you can to make it look like you tried with the appeal and then wash your hands of it."

Claire scoffed. "You think I'm going to throw the appeal?"

"Yes," Daniel said slowly. "You're going to throw the appeal, Claire."

"I don't know where you get off Daniel, but I am certainly not going to do something so unethical, and for no reason."

"I told you there was a reason."

"Which is?"

Daniel leveled her a sinister look. "That it's better for all of us if he stays in prison."

"Why, Daniel? Why risk your law license and your reputation?" Claire shook her head and just about screamed when he didn't answer her right away. "Tell me why!"

"Better risk that than my life," he replied quietly.

Her heartbeat sped up and she furrowed her brows. "What are you saying? Did someone threaten you?"

"Just leave it, Claire. And be thankful that you haven't received the same treatment."

"Daniel, if someone threatened you, you should have reported it."

"No," he snapped. "I've seen enough of these thing go wrong. Better to just handle it. Do what they say. Bates belongs in prison, anyway."

Claire shook her head. "How can you say that? We took an oath when we became lawyers. This flies in the face of what we're charged to do."

Daniel scoffed. "God, you're so annoying, Claire. Even in high school, getting up onto your high horse. Acting like you're better and more righteous than everyone else. It's laughable, given what happened, too."

Claire's eyes darkened. This was why she had tried to get out of Savannah. Anyone who had the opportunity threw her past back in her face.

"How did you know it wasn't just someone playing a harmless joke?" Claire asked, brushing off his comment.

"When is threatening someone's family ever a harmless joke, Claire? It was made clear to me that whoever this person was, they were serious."

The hair on the back of Claire's neck rose. "Made clear to you how?"

Daniel's expression soured further. "They knew things. They were watching me."

"Who was it, Daniel?" Claire asked, her voice shaking with concern. "Who threatened you?"

Daniel hesitated before answering. "I can't say for sure, but I have my suspicions."

"Dammit, who?"

He glanced around the enclosed room, as if someone might be listening in. "Someone working for the other side."

"Someone from the prosecution?"

Daniel nodded. "I can't prove it, and I don't want to take any chances."

"You really think they would do that?"

"Absolutely. They have connections with the police force, who were highly motivated to get someone booked and behind bars for these crimes. With those connections, they could provide the surveillance needed to make the threat credible. Their motives line up perfectly, and to me, it just wasn't worth the fight."

Claire's mind raced. If someone from the prosecution was willing to threaten a defense attorney, what else were they willing to do? And was it possible they had done something to tamper with the evidence in Anthony's case? Is that why the police records from that night were so sparse?

"I need to know everything you know, Daniel," Claire pressed, her tone firm. "You might not want to help, but you have an ethical duty to do so. You worked this case; you were involved. If there's anything we're missing that could help Anthony's case, it's on you to make sure it's brought to light." Her eyes locked on his, unyielding. "This isn't about what you want—it's about what's right."

Daniel shook his head. "I'm not getting involved, Claire. If you want to get yourself or your family killed, that's on you, but I'm not making myself a target just so you can throw a little party in the name of justice. Just drop it."

"I already told you I'm not going to do that."

"Don't be an idiot, Claire." Daniel's eyes turned dangerous. "If you take this any further, I could be dragged into it."

Claire folded her arms against her chest. "Is that why you were angry you didn't get the appeal?"

He seethed. "I just knew you were going to be a goodie-two-shoes about the whole thing. The only time you've ever bent the rules was to get admitted to the bar. Daddy pull some strings for you after things didn't work out in New York?"

Claire's eyes darkened. "That's quite enough."

She turned to leave, realizing she wasn't going to get any further with Daniel. A tug on her arm had her looking back at him.

"I'll give you one piece of advice, Stevens." His gaze burned with intensity, a mix of warning and sincerity that left her unsure which to trust. "Be careful. There are people who will stop at nothing to make sure this case stays closed."

"And are you one of them?" she asked, looking down at his bruising grip on her arm.

He let go of her rather quickly, leaving the question unanswered.

chapter
nineteen

CLAIRE'S APARTMENT door creaked open and Meredith stepped inside, meeting Claire in the kitchen. She handed her friend a full glass of wine without a word and poured herself a large one, the dark liquid sloshing against the sides.

Meredith raised an eyebrow. "Are we celebrating or trying to drink away our sorrows?"

"Finished Anthony's appeal brief," Claire said, her voice strained. "Submitted it this afternoon."

"Wow, that was fast! Did you find what you needed?"

Claire nodded, her short brown hair swaying with the motion. "Anthony's confession was tainted. It changes everything."

She shuffled into the living room, Meredith close behind, and plopped down on the sofa, her wine spilling over the edges a little as she moved. Meredith sat in the patterned chair across from her. They each took a sip. Claire took another.

Meredith frowned, her confusion evident. "I don't know much about tainted confessions. What does it mean?"

"Basically, Anthony was found and admitted to a hospital by the police where they questioned him. Just because the police don't say, 'you're under arrest,' doesn't mean you aren't." She went on to explain that they hadn't read him his Miranda rights either. "The appeal court could overturn the conviction, because his confession should never have been allowed into evidence."

"Couldn't Daniel have brought this up already?" Meredith asked, taking a slow sip from her glass.

Claire tensed, a death grip on her wine glass. " I confronted him about that."

"Okay, and...?"

Claire stayed silent. How could she tell Meredith that Daniel blew the case because someone had threatened him? And worse, he thinks it was someone at the district attorney's office. She wasn't even sure whether *her* knowing that information put her in danger.

"Look, I don't want to push you," Meredith said. "You don't have to tell me if you don't want to."

"No, it's not that. It just makes me nervous." She took a deep breath, deciding to just be honest with her friend. "Daniel claimed he didn't object to the tainted confession because he was threatened."

Meredith's response was barely a whisper. "Wait, threatened?"

"Yes. But you can't tell anyone, okay?" Claire locked eyes with her friend, seeking reassurance.

"Of course, who would I tell?" Meredith responded earnestly. "What did he say? About the threat, I mean."

"He wouldn't give many details. Just that his family would be in danger if he didn't keep Anthony locked up."

"Does Daniel know you submitted the brief? And that you might win the appeal?"

Claire's grip on her wineglass tightened further, betraying her anxiety. She nearly drained her glass with a large gulp, the liquid warming her insides as she tried to escape from her thoughts. "Yeah," she said, nodding. "Hence the large glass of wine."

Her words hung heavy in the air.

Meredith's brow furrowed in concern. "Are you worried he might come after you?"

Claire shook her head, yet a sliver of uncertainty still lingered. "Daniel? No, I don't really think he'd do something like that."

"I'm not so sure, Claire." Meredith's eyes darkened. "I've seen people you'd never expect do really heinous things."

"Great, thanks. That makes me feel loads better."

"Sorry," Meredith said sheepishly, and they sat in silence for a bit.

Claire absently swirled the remaining wine in her glass, the rich red liquid catching the dim light as her thoughts shifted to Anthony. Would he be released? The possibility felt distant, almost surreal, after all the twists and turns the case had taken. She had worked hard to build a solid case for his appeal, pouring countless hours into combing through evidence and piecing together arguments. Yet, even with all that effort, doubt lingered—a quiet voice reminding her how unpredictable the system could be. Now, she had to live with whatever the outcome was, whether it brought closure or opened a whole new set of questions.

"Do you think Anthony will get let out?" Meredith asked, as if reading her mind.

"It's hard to know," Claire admitted, biting her lip. "The Court of Appeals could ask for oral arguments, or they might just issue their ruling based on the briefs."

"If they rule in his favor, do you think there will be a new trial?"

Claire pondered the question, taking another sip of her wine. "It depends."

"What do you mean?"

"It sort of depends on *how* the Court of Appeals rules," Claire explained. "Their reasoning in the decision will play a big part. If they find significant errors in the trial, the prosecution might feel the case isn't strong enough to retry. But if the issues are more procedural, they may decide to pursue it again."

"Wouldn't that be double jeopardy or something?" Meredith questioned, her voice laced with surprise. "Being put on trial for the same crime twice?"

Claire hesitated, her thoughts racing as she considered the implications. She had focused so much on the appeal itself that she hadn't afforded much thought to the aftermath, at least the legal side of things. She'd certainly let her anxiety run rampant about getting a supposed serial killer out of jail.

Claire grimaced as she considered the possibility of double jeopardy. "It's such a rare thing to have happen because usually, cases don't get to this point. But you're right, if they tried to bring him up on the same charges, we could move to dismiss for double jeopardy."

"Then what happens?"

Claire sighed, running her fingers through her hair. "Then he goes free."

"Are you feeling any better about that?"

She hesitated, her mind whirling with conflicting emotions. "I'm honestly trying not to think about it. Right now, I'm more focused on the fact that Daniel thinks I'm a traitor, and also that I probably won't have a job soon."

Meredith furrowed her brows again. "You think you'd get fired?"

"There's no way Daniel acted unilaterally on this. Whether or not he told Bob about the threat, he definitely got Bob to sign off on not objecting to the confession. I figure if Bob had a hand in the decision, then I've just become a thorn in his side. He won't want information like that coming out. So close to retirement, it could completely ruin his reputation."

Meredith frowned, swirling her drink thoughtfully. "But then why would Bob even let you take on the appeal? Wouldn't it be easier for him to keep you away from it altogether?"

Claire sighed, leaning back in her chair. "He probably didn't have much of a choice," she conjectured. "Think about it—Dolores Bates has a lot of influence, and she specifically asked for me. If Bob outright refused, it would look suspicious. He has to keep up appearances, especially with someone like Dolores. It's better for him to let me take it on and try to control the fallout quietly than to risk raising any red flags."

"Can't you talk to your dad about it?"

Claire pursed her lips. " I could, I guess. But I'm not sure that would really change anything. My father retired and sold his interest in the firm to Bob. Then Bob hired me more as a favor to my father rather than out of any actual use to the firm. So, yeah, I'd say my time there is probably limited."

"Hey, you don't know that yet." Meredith reached out to squeeze Claire's hand. "You shouldn't worry."

Claire nodded. "Thanks. It's just..." She took another sip of wine. "I had hoped that things with this firm would have gone better than my time in New York."

Meredith eyed her for a moment and asked, "What happened in New York?"

The wine had loosened Claire's tongue. "I was trying to escape my past, but it followed me there just the same."

Meredith leaned forward, her interest apparent. "What do you mean?"

Claire waved her hand dismissively, having no desire to relive the painful memories. "There was an issue with my bar application," she said carefully, deciding to circle around the issue. "After studying for months, interviewing, and getting a job at a really prestigious firm, I ended up having to resign. My dad helped me start over here."

"That sucks," Meredith replied, her tone soft and genuine. "I can sort of relate."

"You can?" Claire asked. She didn't know a lot about Meredith's past. It was one of those things she never asked about because she didn't want people asking about hers.

Meredith nodded. "Yeah. I was originally planning on going to medical school. I took the MCAT and everything. Even got admitted to a few different places."

"So, what happened?"

Meredith shook her head. "Sort of the same thing as you. Something caught up with me and I needed to change paths." Meredith looked far off for a moment before her eyes returned to her wine. "But I'm actually glad for it. I think things turned out better this way. Maybe in time, you'll feel that way too."

Claire sighed and looked at her friend, grateful for the support that Meredith had always provided. "Maybe."

Meredith smiled and walked over to the kitchen. She grabbed her purse and came back, fishing her hand around inside of it. "Listen, you know this isn't like me, but I hate seeing you so distraught." She walked back over and sat down next to Claire. Meredith held her palm out, displaying a bottle of pills.

Claire gave her friend a confused look and Meredith waved her hands in front of her face. "It's nothing crazy, I promise. Besides, I am technically a clinical psychologist. I'm licensed to write prescriptions. But to save you the trouble, I think these might help."

"What are they?" Claire asked, taking the unmarked orange bottle.

"They're super mild antidepressants," Meredith said. "I've had lows just like what you're going through, and they just helped even me out a little bit so I could get through the day. Nothing crazy."

Claire nodded her head. "Okay, thanks." She popped open the lid and Meredith put a hand on the bottle.

"But don't take these when you've been drinking. That would not be a good interaction."

"Oh." Claire put the lid back on the bottle and tightened it. "Okay." She placed the bottle on the coffee table and tucked her legs underneath her.

"You know what? Let's celebrate getting the appeal in by finishing this bottle of wine and worrying about everything else later."

Claire grinned. "I'll drink to that!"

chapter
twenty

CLAIRE'S HEART beat heavily in her chest as she stared at the email at the top of her inbox entitled, "New Filing in Bates v. State." The soft hum of her computer filled the quiet office, blending with the faint buzz of the overhead fluorescent lights. A mug of cold coffee sat forgotten at the edge of her desk, next to a stack of legal briefs she had yet to review.

Claire held her breath as she clicked the link to pull up the document. The seconds it took to load felt like an eternity, her stomach twisting with anticipation. Outside her window, the muted sounds of Savannah traffic drifted in, but they barely registered over the pounding of her heartbeat in her ears. It could be the Court ordering oral argument, a signal that there was still time to shape the case, to plead Anthony's cause in person. But it could also be the ruling—the decision that could either validate all the hours she'd poured into this appeal or bring it to a crushing halt.

She bit her lip, her mind racing through every possible outcome as the document finally opened on her screen.

In the matter of Bates v. State, *The Court of Appeals of Georgia hereby finds that, looking at the totality of the circumstances, a reasonable person in the defendant's position would have experienced a restraint on his freedom of movement normally associated with an arrest. Thus, the trial court erred in admitting the defendant's confession. The trial court's judgment is reversed.*

Claire blinked her eyes in shock. She leaned back in her chair, her eyes scanning the document over and over again, but the words didn't change.

She'd won the appeal for Anthony.

The question now became whether or not the prosecution would attempt to retry him.

Even if they did, Claire was confident that she could get him declared mentally unfit to stand trial. In that way, the prosecution's second report stunt coupled with his current medical history would work against them. The fact that he hadn't been declared mentally incompetent the first time was obviously Daniel's doing.

Her phone ringing brought her back to reality.

"Claire Stevens," she answered, her voice cracking slightly.

"Claire, we've seen the ruling." It was Dolores Bates, emotionless as always. "Job well done. We can't thank you enough

"Thank you, Ma'am," Claire replied. "I'm glad we were able to set things straight."

"Once Anthony comes home and readjusts, we'll be throwing a celebration. Something small and private, but we'd appreciate your attendance."

"Yes, of course," Claire said, her stomach churning at the thought of seeing Anthony again. Claire didn't have the heart to tell the woman that this wasn't over. She still needed to talk to the prosecutor and see what their intent was for a new trial. But for now, she'd let Mrs. Bates enjoy the win.

"Great. I'll be in touch with the details. Until then."

The line went dead before Claire could say anything more. She replaced the phone on the receiver only to hear a knock on her door.

She looked up to see Bob, drinking his never-ending cup of coffee, looking extremely pleased with himself.

"What can I do for you?" Claire asked him. She'd been dreading this conversation ever since she'd filed the appeal brief. Daniel accused her of being a goodie-two-shoes, but he'd follow any boss straight off a cliff. Bob wasn't one to hover over his associates' caseload, but like she'd told Meredith, the chances of Bob not knowing that Daniel threw the trial were slim.

Besides, Bob wasn't the sort of man to keep a trial lawyer around that would ruin the firm's reputation. A loss was still a loss, even if it was for Anthony Bates. Whether Bob knew Daniel's justification for throwing the trial was another matter.

She more than expected to be fired if she'd won the appeal, and she wasn't sure her career could take another hit like that.

"Nothing, nothing," Bob mused. "Seems like you've done more than enough."

Claire tried to read him, but Bob was one of those people who always had a smirk on his face.

She sighed and leaned back in her seat. "I'm not sure how to take that."

"You won the appeal, Claire." He chuckled and took a sip of his coffee. "How's it feel?"

"I guess it hasn't really set in yet," she said, shrugging.

Bob nodded. "I remember the first time that I won my first big case. Changed everything."

Claire stayed quiet, not sure what the outcome of this conversation was going to be.

"In any event, no doubt you'll be fielding a lot of calls from the media once they've all figured out what the ruling means."

"I guess," Claire said.

She hadn't really given much thought to that, but she realized it was something she'd have to address.

"We're all real proud of you, Claire," Bob said.

Claire looked at her boss in shock. "You are?"

Bob looked back at her, furrowing his busy white eyebrows. "Of course. Why would you think otherwise?"

"No reason."

Could she have been wrong? Had Daniel actually acted alone when he'd thrown the trial? Everything she knew about Bob said that couldn't be true, but his response to her winning the appeal was not what she'd expected.

Claire's phone rang and Bob nodded toward it. "Looks like the calls are already starting. We'll get you an assistant by Monday to help manage your caseload."

Claire looked at the flashing light on her phone, swallowing a lump in her throat. "Thank you."

Bob didn't say anything else before he tapped the doorframe and continued his daily stroll.

The phone continued to ring, and Claire moved to pick it up. Just as she put it to her ear, Daniel barged into her office.

"One moment," she said, stabbing the hold button. She looked at Daniel expectantly.

"I hope you're happy," he all but spat. "And I hope you know that this doesn't just put me in danger, it puts your sister in danger, too."

Claire's stomach churned. She hadn't spoken to Fiona since she'd agreed to take the appeal. Not for lack of trying, but her sister was still convinced she'd thrown Daniel under the bus to get the case. She wondered what Fiona would think of Daniel throwing the case intentionally. Would she have supported that decision, given the anonymous threat? Claire wanted to tell her sister, but she was afraid that would just make things worse.

"I'm sure it won't come to that," Claire replied softly.

Daniel shook his head. "Only time will tell. Congratulations on getting a crazed man out of jail, Claire. Murderer or not, he's still a danger and clearly so are the people he's connected to. Stay safe."

He vanished from the room without another word, leaving Claire in stunned silence. Was he threatening her? No, he wouldn't. She was obviously just on edge from the whole thing. That had to be it. Her finger moved to the hold button when she realized she was still holding the phone.

"Hello?" the person on the other end of the line said. "Is anyone there?"

"Yes, sorry," Claire replied, finally turning her attention back to the call.

"DO you think they'll attempt to retry him?" Meredith asked, taking a sip of her wine.

Claire had called her to meet up as soon as she was able to break away from the unending calls from the media plaguing her at her office. The two had agreed to meet for dinner to celebrate Claire's win. But Claire wasn't sure she felt much like celebrating.

The two were seated at a small corner table in one of Savannah's quieter restaurants, the dim lighting casting a soft glow over the rustic wooden tables and exposed brick walls. The faint murmur of other diners' conversations mingled with the occasional clatter of dishes from the open kitchen nearby. A basket of warm bread sat between them, the inviting aroma of garlic and herbs wafting into the air.

"Not sure yet," Claire said, shoving a piece of bread into her mouth. She chewed as she tried to think it over. "The first trial wasn't a slam dunk. Without that confession, they might risk an acquittal. Not to mention how divisive it was in the community. If I were at the prosecutor's office, I'd have to really think about whether it was the right thing to do."

Meredith nodded in understanding.

Claire left out the part where Daniel thought it was someone at the prosecutor's office threatening him, potentially even the district attorney herself. Claire didn't want to believe it, but she agreed with Daniel on one question: who else had the proper motivation?

Her mind drifted to Detective Lawson. The detective would have had the same motivation as the district attorney for getting Anthony convicted. Given what Claire learned recently about the woman's interrogation tactics, she may have had even more reason to want such an outcome.

Claire tucked that thought into the back of her mind.

"Have you heard anything around town?" Claire asked Meredith, already wincing in anticipation of her answer.

Meredith moved her head from side to side, as if considering her answer. "A bit. Seems like there are people on both sides. Some are happy, and some are really upset."

Before Meredith could elaborate, their server arrived, setting down plates of steaming food with a polite smile. The rich aroma of Meredith's pasta and Claire's juicy steak wafted up, briefly pulling Claire's attention away from the conversation. She picked up her fork, twirling it absently.

"Yeah, figures," Claire said, her tone laced with resignation. She hesitated for a moment before adding, "Anything about me?"

She hoped the question didn't come off as conceited. What she actually wanted to know was whether people were speaking negatively about her, because that's what she was expecting.

"You know how people are," Meredith said, clearly trying to soften the blow.

"Yeah, that's what I'm worried about." Claire pushed the food around on her plate. "I was so focused on just getting through the appeal, I never really planned for what would happen if I won. At least not in terms of public opinion. It sort of seemed like a pipe dream at the time. I'm not sure I really want all of this attention."

"I get that."

"And if I'm being honest," Claire said, lowering her voice, "I'm terrified that Anthony is going to be released."

"I know how you feel. But like I said, I've worked with a lot of criminal defendants. I've never had anything happen."

"You've worked with people who did their time, were released, and were generally mentally stable," Claire said. "Not to mention, non-serial killers."

"I guess that's true now. Even still, I don't think you're in any real danger."

"I hope you're right. I still can't shake what Daniel said to me."

"I wouldn't worry too much. He's acted like a child through this entire appeal."

"That much is true," Claire said, forcing herself to eat a bite of her far too expensive steak. "But what he said, and just the way he said it, felt very much like a threat."

Meredith waved her fork in front of her face. "Maybe someone was playing a joke on him. Or maybe someone was just trying to see if they could influence the trial but wouldn't actually follow up on the threat. There's a host of possibilities for what motivated that phone call."

"I guess. You know though, he came to my office once he heard the news."

"I'm sure that was pleasant."

"I'm not going to say he outright threatened me, but he told me to 'stay safe.'" Claire shuddered as she thought back to it.

"Look." Meredith set her fork down. "I work with dangerous people on a daily basis. Daniel doesn't strike me as someone who would act on one of his impulses."

Claire shrugged. "People said the same thing about Anthony, too."

"Oh, Claire," Meredith said, reaching forward. "It's going to be okay. Just try and enjoy your dinner and the win."

"Yeah," Claire said, pushing her plate away, unable to eat anymore. "Okay."

chapter
twenty-one

CLAIRE WALKED INTO HER APARTMENT, the quiet stillness of the space broken only by the faint hum of her refrigerator. She kicked her sneakers off, one landing near the door and the other spinning to a stop halfway across the kitchen floor. Tossing the stack of mail she'd grabbed on her way up the stairs onto the counter, she reached for her phone, the screen lighting up as she thumbed through her recent emails.

The news had officially broken about Anthony's appeal. He was set to be released tomorrow and the media couldn't get enough of it. The firm had actually had to take Claire's email address off their website, because the number of emails she was getting was flooding their servers.

As she scrolled through the various messages, it was obvious the city was still divided on the Bates matter, even now. Overall, more people were against his release than for it. Most of the subject headings in her inbox said things like, "How could you?" or, "Thanks for putting a murderer back on the streets."

She sighed, clicking the phone screen off and pushing the device away from her. People had warned her this would happen—that taking on a case like this would make her a target. She thought she'd prepared herself for it but experiencing it firsthand was a different story. The flood of criticism and scrutiny felt overwhelming, more personal than she ever expected.

This was supposed to be a big moment for her career, and instead, it just seemed like everyone hated her. But that had always been her plight. Even when she tried to do the right thing, people got angry with her. Told her she was being foolish.

She tried to push the self-doubt out of her head, deciding she needed a distraction. She'd already had enough to drink at dinner, so television it was. Grabbing her mail, she flipped on the TV and sank onto the couch.

She'd been so busy working on this appeal that her mailbox had really piled up, to the point where the courier left a sticky note on the front of her mailbox asking if she'd moved.

As she flipped through the past-due bills, breaking news coverage interrupted what she thought might be a quiet evening to inform the citizens of Savannah that, "Anthony Bates, the man who had pled guilty to murdering seven women, has been released thanks to the efforts of Claire Stevens."

Claire pressed the button to flip the television off, the angry voices of pundits and commentators cutting out mid-sentence. The room fell silent, but the knot of frustration in her chest only tightened. She resisted the urge to grab the remote and hurl it at the screen, her pulse racing from the barrage of negativity she'd just endured. The media frenzy surrounding Anthony's case wasn't just professional anymore—it felt personal, their biting critiques and smug assumptions chipping away at her composure.

Her phone rang, the sudden vibration breaking the tense stillness. A knot of anxiety formed in her chest as she glanced at the screen, half expecting yet another reporter or angry email notification. When she saw the caller ID, her shoulders relaxed, and she let out a long breath of relief.

"Hey, Dad," she said, putting the device to her ear, her voice softer now.

"Heard you won the case!" he boomed through the phone. Claire pulled it back just a little and smiled at his theatrics.

"Yeah. I'm guessing that's not all you heard."

"There are always gonna be people who have something critical to say about everything. Even when I was representing people who were dying from a horrible disease, there were still people on the other side saying the company shouldn't have to pay for it."

"I don't think they're just saying something about anything, Dad." Claire sighed, looking at the refrigerator, its contents holding another bottle of wine. "I think they're saying very specific things, and they're saying them about me."

"Do you feel like you did the right thing?"

Claire's willpower broke, and she padded over to the fridge to grab the bottle. She set the phone between her ear and shoulder, uncorking the bottle and pouring herself a glass as she tried to think through her answer.

"Yes? Maybe?" She shook her head. "I dunno, Dad. I was so focused on my goal that I never thought about what would happen if I achieved it."

"What do you mean?"

"I mean Anthony. Everyone kept warning me about him, but what was I supposed to do? Throw the appeal? That's not the sort of person I am."

"I know it's not, Claire Bear."

"And I kept dismissing my anxiety about him getting out of prison while I was working on this, but if I'm being honest, I'm not entirely comfortable knowing that he's going to be free. I met him, Dad. He seems—" she hesitated. "A bit unhinged."

"He's not free, free, right?" her father asked.

Claire took a large drink from her glass. "I don't follow."

"I mean, you won his appeal, but don't you think with all this buzz that the prosecutors will try and go for another round?"

"Honestly, I'm not sure they have it in them. Sure, public opinion is totally against Anthony, but that doesn't mean there's enough evidence to convict him at this point, not without that tainted confession."

"You don't think they'll try again anyway?"

Claire took another sip of wine. "I think public opinion is so strong right now that they may not risk trying again, because if they do and they lose, that could be really bad for them politically."

"Look, kid." Roy shuffled around on the other end of the line, likely switching his sitting position. "I still think you did good. It was a hard-fought case and at the end of the day, you did the right thing. You weren't the one making the decision. Those people in robes were. So you shouldn't blame yourself."

"What if someone else gets hurt, Dad?" Claire asked. "What if *I* get hurt?"

"That's not going to happen," Roy said, his voice full of conviction. "I never let them come for you in the past, and I won't let them now."

A dusting of a smile made its way across Claire's lips. "Thanks, Dad."

"Now, go make sure your door's locked and get some sleep."

Claire chuckled. " Thanks. See you on Sunday."

The two said their goodbyes and Claire decided to turn off her phone. Her father's words gave her a bit of comfort, but she still went over to her front door and made sure it was locked.

Sitting back down on the couch, she flipped through the rest of her mail quickly, intent on heading to bed soon. A few more bills, some junk mail, and an envelope that didn't seem to fit with the rest of the bunch.

Claire placed everything else on the coffee table and studied the mysterious envelope. She turned on the side table's light to see better. It was plain white, slightly heavier than the others, with no return address and her name written in an unfamiliar script. She ripped it opened and unfolded the sleek paper. The writing was tidy and concise, matching the front.

Dearest Claire,

I must congratulate you on today's win. I've been following you since Mrs. Bates approached you to take this case and have been silently rooting for you. Despite the difficulties in your background, I knew you would do the right thing and not cave to the pressure from those around you.

I read your appeal brief and found it to be flawless. There was never any question in my mind that the Court of Appeals would rule in your favor. I'm sure Anthony is also extremely grateful and I hope the Bates family has expressed their gratitude to you for doing what no one else agreed to do.

I, for one, am happy to know that there are still lawyers with morals in this world. Whatever the press may say, know that you did the right thing.

Your admirer.

Claire's heart nearly stopped when she got to the bottom of the letter. She turned it over in her hands, looking for who sent it.

Nothing.

Then she grabbed the ripped envelope to look at the front. No return address. Not even a stamp or a postmark.

How could this person have sent this letter so quickly? The news just broke today. How did they get it into her mailbox without sending it through the mail? How were they able to read the appeal?

Claire's stomach dropped and her throat went dry, despite the wine she had just been drinking. Racing over to her phone, she quickly pulled up an old news article about Anthony's victims.

Police discovered that all of the victims had been stalked in a similar fashion. Bates first lured the victims into a false sense of security by sending them letters and gifts, before finally going in for the kill.

"No, no, no," Claire muttered as she tried to find a news article that explained the details further. She had deliberately tried not to look at his crimes during the appeal, knowing that could influence her judgment. At the time, she also found such information to be entirely irrelevant to her work.

She tried to remember where she'd read about his crimes in detail. Her eyes scanned the room and spotted something in the corner.

Claire all but ran over to the file box sitting in the corner of her kitchen. She dropped to her knees and popped the top open, searching through the papers, praying the document she needed would be there. Grabbing the pre-sentence report, she flipped through it roughly, before finally landing on the page she needed.

"The subject's propensity for sending letters of admiration to his potential victims could be a symptom of his borderline personality disorder."

chapter
twenty-two

LAWSON LOOKED up from the report at the sound of her office phone ringing, the sharp tone cutting through the stillness of the nearly empty precinct. The faint hum of fluorescent lights above her and the distant clatter of a janitor's mop bucket in the hallway were the only other noises accompanying her late-night solitude.

She stared at the blinking green light for a few seconds, wondering who could possibly be calling her at this hour. Lawson enjoyed staying at the office late to work on her cases after everyone else had left for the day. The quiet was calming, the usual buzz of phones and chatter replaced by the soft rustle of papers on her desk and the steady tick of the wall clock. It was the only time she felt like she could truly sort things out.

She didn't recognize the number, and if she didn't pick up on this last ring, it would go to voicemail. However, curiosity got the better of her. She put the phone to her ear and answered. "Detective Lawson."

"I'd like to report a crime."

"If this is an emergency, please hang up and dial 911," Lawson replied in a flat tone, her pen tapping absently on the edge of her desk.

"No, please!" the voice on the other end of the line begged. "Don't hang up."

Lawson cocked her head. She recognized this voice. But from where? "Who is this?"

" Claire Stevens."

" What on Earth? Why are you calling me?"

"I didn't know who else to call."

The girl sounded desperate on the other end of the line, but she really didn't have much sympathy for her. Especially not after the way her entire appeal brief threw Lawson's reputation under the bus.

"As I said, you can call 911," Lawson repeated, ready to hang up the phone.

"Please, just hear me out. It's about Bates. I made a mistake. He's going to kill again."

Lawson shook her head in disbelief, pinching the bridge of her nose. Claire Stevens had to be kidding. "What makes you say that?" she asked, more out of curiosity than any sense of duty.

"I got one of his letters," Claire replied, sounding almost out of breath.

"One of his letters?"

"He always sent them a letter of admiration before the other gifts."

"You know it's from him?" Lawson asked, her skepticism rising.

"Well, not exactly."

"Is there any identifying information on the letter?"

"It's a letter of admiration, Erin! Who else would send me something like this?"

"I don't know, how about someone who sided with Bates during the trial, but didn't want their unpopular opinion to be made public?"

"I don't think so." Claire's paranoia was tangible, even through the phone. "I think this is more than just a simple letter from a fan. Lawyers don't tend to have fans."

Lawson chuckled at that. "Yeah, you guys aren't very well liked."

"Please help me with this."

Lawson sighed. "Bring the letter to the station tomorrow. I'll take a look at it. But if you want my advice? Get some rest."

"You're there now. Can't I just bring it by now?"

"No" Lawson said without explanation.

Claire huffed. "Why not?"

"Because it's past hours and honestly, I just don't want to deal with this tonight."

"How can you say that?" Claire sounded frantic. "I might be his next victim."

"I seriously doubt that."

There was silence on the other end of the line for a beat. "You don't know anything about this letter, do you detective?" Claire's words were slow and measured.

Lawson was taken aback. "Please tell me you're not asking what I think you're asking, Ms. Stevens."

More silence.

"No. You're right. I'm just tired and confused, that's all." Claire was silent for a moment. "What time should I come in tomorrow?"

Lawson was about to answer, but Claire cut her off. "It doesn't matter. I'll head to you on my way into the office."

"Great," Lawson said with a roll of her eyes before hanging up the phone. She closed her eyes and rubbed her temples, trying to fend off the impending headache. The last thing she wanted to deal with was a paranoid defense attorney.

CLAIRE SHOWED up to the precinct the next morning far too early. Lawson could tell by the state of her appearance that she had not, in fact, taken her advice and rested. In fact, the girl looked like she had been up all night, anxiously pacing a room.

Lawson was exhausted herself, having only gotten a few hours of sleep between their phone call and the next morning. She clutched her cup of coffee like a lifeline, taking a big sip of it before walking up to Claire.

"Ms. Stevens," she said, trying to keep the annoyance out of her tone.

"Can we talk in your office?" Claire asked, looking over her shoulder.

"Let's talk in here again. " Lawson gestured to the conference room next to them.

She opened the door and Claire rushed through, sitting in the seat nearest to the door. Lawson turned around and watched as the woman smoothed the crumpled paper against the table.

Sitting down across from her, Lawson took another big sip of her coffee, but Claire started up before she could even ask a question.

"This is the letter that Anthony must have slipped into my mailbox yesterday," Claire said, pushing it forward so that Lawson could see it.

Lawson slid the letter closer to her, running her eyes over it briefly.

"And you know that Anthony, who as of yesterday was still sitting in jail waiting to be processed out, was the author behind this letter, how?" Lawson knew she wasn't doing a good job keeping the exasperation out of her voice, but this is not how she wanted to start her morning.

Claire reached into her purse and pulled out a rather thick document. She thumbed it to a certain page and then pushed it forward, pointing at a paragraph.

"Because right here," Claire said, "this is the first thing he would do to a victim. Send them a letter of admiration. It says it right here."

Lawson looked over what she realized was Anthony's pre-sentencing report. She pushed both documents back at Claire and sighed.

"Ms. Stevens, I can understand your concern, but your theory doesn't make sense. Anthony Bates isn't being released until today, that's if he's lucky and receives his medical clearance. There's no way that he could have slipped this into your mailbox."

"Then someone else," Claire said, wringing her hands. "Someone who is copying him. Or someone who's upset with the fact that I got him out."

"That is a bit more likely," Lawson mused. "But still not as likely as someone just telling you they thought you did a good job. Not everyone thought Anthony was guilty, which was the unpopular opinion. Maybe someone just wanted to express their gratitude."

"But how would they know my address?" Claire asked.

Lawson shrugged. "That stuff's pretty easy to find these days."

"I just don't think you're taking this seriously," Claire said, her eyes following Lawson as the detective stood.

"You're right, Ms. Stevens," Lawson replied. "Because I don't think this is a serious matter."

"I think you're wrong."

"Lawson held the door open. "I've been doing this for a while, and I've got a pretty good gut instinct about things. I hope for your sake that I'm not wrong. But if anything else happens, it's obvious that you know where to find us."

"That's it?" Claire asked in disbelief. "You're not even going to file a report?"

"I'll have your visit recorded."

"This is retaliation," Claire said, standing up. "You're not taking this seriously because you're angry I got the conviction overturned."

Lawson scoffed, although if she were being completely honest, Claire Stevens wasn't her favorite person. She didn't say anything else. It was obvious Claire was looking for a fight. In her eyes, all lawyers loved to argue and she didn't have the time or energy for it.

Claire tried to stare her down, but Lawson just stood there calmly, sipping on her coffee.

"Fine." Claire gathered her papers in a heap and put them in her bag. "If you won't help me then I'll have to figure this out myself."

"Good luck," Lawson said, feigning a smile.

Claire blew past her and Lawson let the door close behind her rather than follow the woman into the lobby. It was meetings like these that made Lawson really miss drinking.

She walked over to the phone tucked away on a desk at the side of the room. Picking it up, she quickly dialed an extension.

"Hey, it's Lawson. Can you get me an update on Anthony Bates' whereabouts? Thanks."

She placed the phone in the receiver and looked out the conference room window. Even though she didn't think that Anthony was to blame for Claire's fan mail, that didn't mean his return to the city wouldn't present a danger to its citizens. The appeals court could do what they wanted, but Lawson had been around the block a few times. While she'd been nervous for her professional career regarding the way she'd handled Anthony's interrogation and conviction, she'd never felt guilt over her methods.

People liked to believe that everything in the criminal justice system worked according to the rules, but that just wasn't the reality on the ground. Lawson always believed that keeping people safe was more important than following some inane amount of red tape designed to let people like Anthony Bates off the hook. But that was exactly what happened anyway.

And now, she had to worry about a serial killer back on her streets.

All thanks to Claire Stevens.

chapter
twenty-three

IT WAS SUNDAY. Usually Claire bemoaned her weekly family dinner obligation, but today she was grateful for the company. Anthony's release was scheduled for today and as much as Claire felt better about the secret admirer after she'd gotten some sleep, she still wasn't entirely convinced she was safe.

Walking up the steps and through the front door, she kicked off her sneakers with a careless flick, earning the familiar sound of her mother's disapproval. Her mother, arms crossed and lips pursed, was waiting just beyond the foyer, her eyes narrowing at the offending footwear.

"Claire, honey," Gretchen said, her tone both saccharine and sharp. "You're a well-known figure in the town now. Are you really letting yourself be seen in those old things?"

"Good to see you too, Mom." Claire opted to give her mother a kiss on the cheek, choosing not to engage in her criticism. Gretchen's posture softened slightly, and she seemed all the more grateful for the gesture, even if she wouldn't admit it outright.

"Hello, Claire."

Another voice caught Claire's attention and she looked up to see her sister standing in the living room.

"I didn't know you were coming today," Claire said, making her way to give her sister a hug. But instead, Fiona stepped back.

Claire furrowed her brow at Fiona's coldness. Was she really still mad at her? Claire could only imagine what Daniel told her after their last confrontation.

"I'm a member of this family too," Fiona said, pointing her nose a little higher.

Claire nodded her head. "I never said you weren't."

"Where's Claire?" Roy's booming voice asked.

Claire turned around to see her father with a big smile on his face. She walked over to greet him, sharing an enthusiastic hug. She could smell the cigar smoke hanging off him and she shook her head but decided not to say anything.

"Let's all stop moping in the foyer," Roy said. "Come on and sit down while we wait for your mother to finish stressing over the food."

"I heard that, Roy," Gretchen called out from the kitchen.

"You do a great job, honey!" Roy yelled into the other room before giving his daughters a wink. Claire laughed at her father's antics, but Fiona rolled her eyes.

"Actually, I think I'm going to go help mom," Fiona said, making her way to the kitchen.

"Suit yourself," Roy responded. "Your funeral." But Fiona was already out of earshot.

Roy chuckled and took a seat in his favorite recliner. "So, how are you feeling after your big win?"

Claire sat on the sofa opposite him. She worried her lower lip, wondering how much she should tell her father. She didn't want to worry him, but she was pretty spooked from receiving that letter.

"Honestly, Dad? I'm a little anxious still."

"I don't blame you. A lot of people are pretty upset about the outcome."

Claire leaned back into the embrace of the sofa, blowing a bit of hair out of her face. "I guess that's supposed to make me feel better?"

"Not make you feel better," Roy corrected, a finger in the air. "Just make you aware."

"I was already aware. I knew that when I took the case. I guess I just didn't fully appreciate how I would feel about it." Claire ran her hand over the couch cushion beside her. "Bates gets released today."

"Is that so?" Roy said, lighting up a cigar. "Like I told you, I'm not going to let anyone hurt you."

Claire smiled. "I appreciate the sentiment, but what do you really think you'll be able to do?"

"Just let a dad be a dad, would you?"

Claire nodded her head. "Okay, Dad. Thanks."

She chewed her lower lip and stared off into the backyard beyond the window. The lawn was immaculate, as always. Her mother's prized gazebo sat amid a perfect gardenscape. As impractical as it was to move it, the family had that gazebo to every new place they'd lived.

As a kid, it had been her favorite escape. Tucked away in the quiet corner of the backyard, surrounded by towering oaks and the soft rustle of leaves, it had felt like her own private sanctuary. She'd take her favorite books, sprawling out on the soft grass or curling up under the shade of the trees, losing herself in stories that took her far from the expectations and pressures of her life. It was the one place where no one could find her, where she could dream, imagine, and be herself without judgment. Sometimes, she'd close her eyes and pretend she was in a completely different world—one where she made the rules. It had been her safe haven, her retreat from the chaos of family dinners, her mother's critical eye, and the weight of trying to be perfect.

Those days seemed so far away now. After the trajectory Claire's life had taken, she yearned for a time where she had no worries and wasn't always looking over her shoulder.

"You still seem worried about something," Roy said, waving a bit of smoke out of his face.

Claire took a deep breath. She desperately wanted to tell her father about the letter, but her conversation with Detective Lawson was fresh in her mind. If she really was just being alarmist, would it be fair to her father to make him worry for nothing?

Plus, if she did tell him, he would probably demand she move back home, and as much as she enjoyed her father's company, her relationship with her mother was much more strained. There's no way living under the same roof as Gretchen Stevens would work for either of them.

But Claire hated keeping secrets from her father. Even when the world had turned against her years ago, he had never judged her for what'd happened. Instead, he helped her and got her set back on the right path.

Keeping this from Roy in many ways felt like a betrayal. But it was also the right thing to do.

"Just tired, that's all. This last week's just been a lot."

Roy nodded, accepting her explanation. "Just make sure you take a little time for you."

"Dinner's ready!" Gretchen called out from the dining room.

"I'll still never understand why we eat dinner at 2 p.m. on Sundays," Roy chuckled as he put out his cigar.

"It's Sunday one-meal, Dad," Claire replied with a small smile. Her mother always made such a big ordeal of the meal that it became the only one served on Sundays. If you said you were hungry in the morning, Gretchen would wave you off, insisting, 'We'll be eating in just a few hours.' If you dared to mention being hungry in the evening, she'd counter with, 'We just had a big meal!'

"I think the word you're looking for is 'Brlinner.'"

Claire suppressed a laugh as they made their way into the dining room.

The pair quieted down as they entered. Claire sat opposite Fiona, as was always the seating arrangement, but this time it was far less comfortable to be staring at her sister. The rift that had formed between them had also taken a toll on her, she realized, but she couldn't concede to carrying the blame for it.

The first course was brought out, and Gretchen began the conversation. " Fiona, what articles have you been writing recently?"

Fiona's lips twisted into a knowing smirk, and she glanced at Claire, whose fingers unconsciously tightened around her wine glass. Her voice was laced with provocation. "I've been delving into the legal system. Its flaws, to be exact."

A rush of blood flooded Claire's cheeks. She shifted in her chair, trying to maintain her composure. Fiona's words were far from an innocent update.

"What an interesting topic," Gretchen said with an oblivious smile, nodding her head. "And what have you found?"

Claire and her father shared an exasperated look.

"Quite a bit," Fiona responded. She leveled her gaze at Claire, her eyes searching. "For instance, the Bates case. There's a prime example of our justice system's shortcomings."

Claire blew out a frustrated sigh and put her wine glass down after taking a gulp. She had never been one to shy away from confrontation. "I was under an ethical obligation to expose the truth, Fiona. The man didn't get a fair trial," she said firmly. "Not to mention the inconsistencies in the evidence itself," she added, her thoughts drifting to the psychological reports. They had raised more questions than answers, glaring holes that the prosecution conveniently ignored. "It wasn't just about him—it was about the integrity of the system."

Fiona scoffed. "Ethical obligation? Everyone knows he murdered those women. What about your ethical obligations to the victims, their families, and society?"

Claire's chest heaved as she fought to maintain her composure, her nails digging into her palms beneath the table.

"Justice isn't about what 'everyone knows'," she snapped, unable to keep her voice level. "It's about what can be proven. It's about ensuring that everyone gets a fair trial, even Anthony Bates."

"Fair?" Fiona rolled her eyes. "Tell that to the dead. Tell that to their families."

"You wouldn't understand," Claire said finally, her voice low.

"I understand just fine," Fiona said with a laugh. " I know more than you think."

Claire's pulse quickened and her insides churned. Did Daniel tell Fiona that he was threatened?

Claire pushed herself back from the table, the scrape of the chair legs on the hardwood suddenly the only sound in the room.

"Excuse me." Claire got up and exited the dining room.

"Claire!" Gretchen called after her daughter. "Come back and sit down!"

Ignoring her mother, Claire bent down to slip on her sneakers and tie the laces. She looked up at the sound of footsteps approaching her. Roy had his hands in his pockets and an expression full of sympathy.

"Claire Bear," he said, his voice soft and understanding. "Try not to let it get to you, okay? Whatever help you need, just let me know."

Claire wiped the tears from her eyes and stood to look at her father. "Thanks, Dad. I'll be okay."

"I know you will."

Roy started to laugh, and Claire gave him a confused look. "What is it?"

"We didn't make it nearly as long this time before someone huffed away from the table."

Claire couldn't stop the smile that cracked her lips. She reached out and gave him a quick hug, the faint smell of his cigar lingering in the air. "I'll call you later, Dad."

She made her way through the front door and stepped out onto the porch. The soft creak of the wooden boards beneath her feet echoed in the sultry afternoon air. For a moment, she lingered, letting the warm breeze brush against her face. The distant hum of cicadas and the faint aroma of honeysuckle from her mother's garden filled her senses. The house behind her glowed faintly, the sounds from inside fading as she descended the steps. She had always felt a mixture of comfort and constraint in this place—safe in its familiarity but burdened by its expectations.

The walk back to her apartment was short, but Claire dragged it out. The exercise helped settle her swirling thoughts. In some ways, being outside on the street felt safer than being alone in her apartment. At least out here, she could see people, hear the murmur of distant voices, the occasional bark of a dog, and the hum of cars passing by. Being outside around people felt like a shield against the encroaching unease that crept in when she was alone.

She wondered how much Daniel had shared with Fiona. If he had revealed that he had been threatened, why not come to Claire about it? What else was he keeping from her?

She wandered aimlessly, her shoes scuffing softly against the pavement. The sky, a blanket of muted gray, began to glow faintly with the streetlights flickering on overhead. Claire blinked in surprise, realizing she had been walking around, lost in thought, for hours. Begrudgingly, she made her way back to her apartment.

She hesitated as she passed by her mailbox. It stared at her like a silent judge, daring her to uncover whatever awaited inside. She decided not to check it this time, quickening her pace toward the door, eager to leave the shadows of the street behind her. If there was another letter, she'd rather not read it before she went to bed. She entered the front door and immediately switched on all of the lights, as was becoming her new habit.

Her heart hammered in her chest as she walked through each of her rooms, checking that she was well and truly alone. When she confirmed it was just her in the small space, she let out her breath and sat on the sofa.

She switched on the television, then got up to get herself a glass of wine, vowing that this time she wouldn't drink herself into another bout of paranoia.

The local news started to play as she uncorked a bottle of red. Claire froze as she listened to the newscaster announce, "A local woman has been found dead in her home."

chapter
twenty-four

THE WINEGLASS TREMBLED in Claire's hand, liquid threatening to spill over the edges as she rushed towards the television. The screen changed to a press conference, Detective Lawson walking to the podium outside of the police station.

Reporters jostled for position as the newscaster turned to the conference.

"Detective Lawson," one reporter shouted above the din, "what can you tell us about the victim?"

"Out of respect for the victim and their family, we won't be releasing any details."

Lawson scanned the crowd before pointing to another reporter.

"Do you know anything about the perpetrator?"

"At this time, all we know is that it appears to be someone who was following the victim for quite some time. They sent letters and gifts before committing this crime. All of that evidence is in police custody."

Claire's stomach dropped at the revelation, her thoughts returning to the letter sitting on her kitchen counter. She gripped her wine glass tighter, her hands beginning to sweat from nerves.

Another reporter pushed his way up to the front, waving a notepad. "Do you think Anthony Bates is responsible? He was released today, wasn't he?"

Claire's eyes widened at the question, her breathing heavy. Detective Lawson pursed her lips, obviously uncomfortable with the question. "We cannot comment on who we believe the perpetrator might be at this time. However, if anyone sees anything suspicious or has any information, they should report it to my office directly."

Claire felt a lump form in her throat. Could it really be Anthony? Was there even time for him to commit a crime between his release and now? And how would he have sent letters and gifts to the victim? He couldn't have been stalking her while in prison.

She swallowed hard, trying to dispel the panic in her body. Lawson put up her hands, indicating no further questions, and the screen switched back to the newscaster, indicating that they would keep the public informed as they learned more about this breaking news.

Claire switched the television off and stared at the black screen for a few moments. What if the killer was Anthony? What if he wasn't?

Was she next?

She had tried to tell Lawson about her own letter and had been summarily dismissed. It was obvious the detective didn't think there was any merit to Claire's concerns, but this changed everything.

The idea of being alone in the apartment started to make Claire's insides squirm. She put down her wine glass and grabbed at her phone. Desperation drove her to dial Jamie's number. Maybe she could invite him over, at least until she felt more settled.

"Hey," Jamie said, his voice sounding a little surprised on the other end. "What's up?"

"Do you want to come over?" Claire all but blurted out.

She could almost feel Jamie's hesitation on the other end of the line. "Claire, is everything alright?"

"Yes? No? I'm not sure. I'm just really anxious right now."

"Why?"

"I just got something in the mail that...it just made me anxious, okay?" she replied defensively.

"What did you get in the mail, Claire?"

"A letter," she said, matching his annoyed tone.

"Why is that something to make you anxious? You're a lawyer. You must get letters all the time."

"This one was different. And now, with what's happening in the news, and the other woman who got murdered receiving a letter, I'm just getting a bad feeling from the whole thing and don't really want to be alone."

"Let me get this straight, you get a letter in the mail and you're worried someone might murder you now." Jamie's tone was beyond harsh now. "So, you want me to come over to what? Fight off your murderer? Get murdered with you?"

"Well, when you put it like that—"

"Look, I'm sorry you're dealing with this, but it is just too much. I told you from the start that you shouldn't take the Bates case, and this is exactly why."

"What are you trying to say?" Claire asked, already knowing the answer.

"Don't make me spell it out."

"Fine. Don't say it. Have a nice life."

She clicked the phone call off, feeling more vulnerable than ever. She wrapped her arms around herself as the walls of her apartment pressed down and she tried to catch her breath. Not only was she worried about being the next victim, but she also had gotten dumped. Life was just great sometimes.

She looked at the full wine glass in front of her. Reaching forward, she grabbed her laptop off the coffee table instead. "Fine," she muttered to herself. "I'll figure this out on my own."

She opened the device and logged in, her fingers moved rapidly over the keyboard as she tried to find out more information about the recent crime and victim.

She scrolled through the pages of articles and reports, but all of them said mostly the same thing. Then Claire noticed an Instagram post by someone claiming to be a friend of the victim.

Her eyes darted back and forth across the post, absorbing every detail.

"Started with a letter of admiration...gifts personal to the victim..."

she read aloud, her voice trailing off. The parallels between the victim's case and her own experience made her shiver.

But my friend was a social media influencer. So no one thought it was weird at the time. In hindsight, the items sent weren't things my friend shared online, so the signs were there.

Claire worried her lower lip as she continued reading.

Anthony Bates was released today and the way my friend was murdered was just like his crimes. I don't know if it was him, given the timing, but maybe it was someone inspired by his twisted actions due to the publicity surrounding his release.

The words gnawed at Claire. Had she not agreed to take the appeal, would this person not have been murdered?

A soft ping drew Claire's attention from the post, and she glanced at the right corner of her screen. An email notification hovered in the corner, the subject line reading "Anthony's Welcome Home Party - RSVP Now!" The sight of the email twisted Claire's stomach into knots, and she hesitated for a moment before clicking it open.

"Join us this Wednesday to celebrate Anthony Bates' return home!" the message proclaimed in bold letters, followed by details about the venue and dress code. Claire's hands trembled as she read. She tried not to look at the photo of Anthony that accompanied the invitation, with his disarming smile and piercing blue eyes.

The thought of attending the party alone filled her with dread, but she really had no one to go with.

Claire wracked her brain, trying to think through who she might ask to be her guest. Just then, a text buzzed her phone and Claire jumped. She looked down to see it was from Meredith.

Checking in. How are you holding up?

Claire picked up the phone to respond.

Got a second to chat?

Her phone rang almost instantly.

"Hey," Claire said, trying to keep her voice even.

"Hey, what's going on?" Meredith asked her, her concern in her voice evident.

"Other than being dumped by Jamie this evening, finding out about this new murder, and getting an invite to the Bates' welcome home party for Anthony, nothing much."

"God, Claire, I'm so sorry!" Meredith sympathized. "That's a lot to unpack. Let's break it down. What happened with Jamie?"

"Things were pretty shaky for us anyway," Claire admitted. "But when I tried to tell him how anxious I was about this new murder, he said he couldn't take it anymore and ended it."

Claire could hear Meredith sigh through the phone. "That's a pretty unfortunate response. He was supposed to be your boyfriend. I don't see why supporting you through a difficult time is all that much to ask."

"Thanks," Claire breathed out. "I know all I've been doing is fixating on this Bates case over the last few weeks, and he didn't want me to take it in the first place, but I really felt like I had no choice."

"I know," Meredith said. "You can talk to me about this. I don't mind."

Claire smiled. "I'm not sure what else there really is to say. I'm just totally spooked by this new attack, and I'm sure people in town are going to blame me."

"Let's try not to jump to conclusions," Meredith said. "I haven't seen much about it. What happened?"

"Some Instagram influencer was murdered and the perpetrator's actions match the Bates murders. And I tried to tell Detective Lawson about the creepy letter of admiration in my mailbox, but she didn't want to hear it." Claire sighed. "Now look what happened to someone else."

"Wait, you received a letter? And went to the police?" Meredith asked, concern lacing her voice. "Why didn't you tell me?"

"I don't know. I feel bad for bothering you so much with this stuff."

Meredith's voice took on a slight tone of authority. "Look, Claire. You're not bothering me. You're my friend. If something is happening to you and you're stressing over it, I want you to tell me about it. Deal?"

Claire nodded. "Okay, deal."

"Good. Now, what about this Bates party?"

Claire turned back to her computer to look at the invite. "It's on

Wednesday. Dolores asked me to go, but I really don't want to. The guy really gives me the creeps."

"I'll go with you," Meredith volunteered.

"No," Claire said, shaking her head vigorously. "That's a really generous offer, but what if Bates really is behind the new murder? I don't want to put you in danger."

"I appreciate the concern, but honestly, I don't think it's him."

Claire blinked for a moment. "Why do you say that?"

"The timing just seems way too close. Someone gets murdered the day he gets released? I've worked with a lot of detainees. I just don't see it."

Claire worried her lower lip. "I'm not sure if that makes me feel better or not."

"I get it. Either way, I'm going with you to the party, okay?"

Claire sighed. "I really can't argue with you, can I?"

"You could, but it would be a waste of time."

chapter
twenty-five

CLAIRE HURRIED out of her apartment, having overslept by a few minutes. She was just thankful that she had been able to get any sleep, given how anxious she'd been the entire night. As she grabbed her keys off the kitchen counter, she stared at the letter, its presence like a weight pressing against her chest, silent but oppressive. Gritting her teeth, she grabbed it and stuffed it into her bag, deciding she would get to the bottom of who sent it today.

She rushed down the stairs, her shoes scuffing lightly against the worn steps, then slowed as she caught sight of the mailboxes. The faint smell of cleaning solution lingered in the narrow hallway, and her heart pounded hard in her chest. She needed to check it today. If she didn't, the nagging worry would follow her all day.

Claire walked over to her mailbox and slipped the small key inside its slot, the faint scrape of metal against metal echoing in the quiet space. Holding her breath, she turned the key, and the small door creaked open. A few letters lay inside, and she grabbed them with slightly trembling hands.

A water bill, an electricity bill, and a grocery ad. That was all. She shoved the mail back inside the box, the tension in her shoulders easing slightly. She let herself breathe again, the exhale steadying her nerves. Closing the box with a soft click, she glanced at her watch and sighed. No time to grab coffee on the way to work. She'd have to settle for the gross office drip coffee again.

Claire quickened her pace, the morning air cool against her skin as she walked faster than normal. By the time she made it inside the office lobby, she was slightly out of breath as she pushed through the glass doors. Keeping her head down, she made her way to her office and barely had time to put her bags down before Bob appeared at her door, his usual brisk energy already radiating off him. His voice boomed when he greeted her. "Claire!"

"Hi, Bob," she said, looking up. Of course he had never had a problem drinking the office drip.

"Glad to see you here today," he said with a grin. "Got some good news for you."

Claire eyed him. "Okay."

"Congratulations on your promotion to 'Of Counsel.'"

It was a title that marked her as a seasoned attorney, trusted with higher-level responsibilities and the autonomy to shape her career more directly. It was a recognition of her hard work, a step closer to partnership, but also a reminder of the weighty expectations that came with it.

He waited for her response, but Claire was too in shock to say anything. "Wow, um, I'm not sure what to say, Bob."

This was the last thing she'd expected. The Bates victory was something the firm could leverage to get more business, but she hadn't thought it would result in her promotion. If anything, she was still trying to figure out Bob's involvement in Daniel throwing the trial.

Bob gestured to someone in the hall and a petite middle-aged brunette woman appeared next to him. Claire could tell the woman was a tad shy, but that was normal for people around Bob's big personality.

"This is Sarah. She's going to be your new assistant."

Claire's eyes widened. She merely stared at her mentor for a moment until she remembered herself and walked around her desk. "Nice to meet you, Sarah."

"I'll leave you to it, then," Bob said, turning to leave. But he paused in the doorway, glancing back at Claire with a grin. "Oh, by the way, I volunteered you to be the keynote speaker at the upcoming bar association meeting. It'll be good for you—great recognition for the firm, and it might even help bring in a few clients."

Claire forced a smile, nodding as Bob tapped the doorframe and walked off down the hall. Internally, she groaned. Bar association meetings were dreadfully boring, and pulling together a presentation on top of everything else she had on her plate felt like an insurmountable task. She was already struggling to stay afloat, and now she'd have to find the time to prepare a speech for a room full of lawyers.

She sighed quietly, turning her attention back to Sarah. "Welcome to the firm," Claire said, extending a hand toward Sarah, who still stood at the threshold of her office.

Sarah nodded her head, hesitating briefly before reaching out to shake Claire's hand. Her grip was firm but quick, and she still didn't say anything.

"What was your last name was again?" Claire asked.

"Carver," Sarah said softly.

Claire's thoughts snagged for a moment. Why did that last name sound familiar? She shook her head slightly, deciding she had other things to concentrate on.

"How long have you been a legal assistant?"

"Not long. But I'm excited to learn from you."

"That's great," Claire said, trying to put as much enthusiasm into her voice as she could muster. "I'm pretty easy going. I've never had my own assistant before, but I'm sure we'll get along great."

Sarah nodded. She was about to turn to leave before she hesitated. "Your office smells really nice, by the way."

Claire blinked a bit in surprise. "Thanks."

Sarah wrinkled her nose slightly. "The rest of the office smells like the coffee machine."

Claire chuckled. "Yeah, Bob's pretty fond of the stuff. Keeps it running all day long. I took to putting a little thing of incense in my office to mask the smell. It's Sweet Pea."

Sarah smiled and nodded. "Well, if you need anything from me, please let me know. The firm's got me doing some training on the computer today."

"Great, thanks!" Claire said warmly, then retreated to her desk.

She sat down and pulled the letter out of her bag. Under the fluorescent lights, it didn't seem quite as scary as it had in the darkness of her apartment.

She switched on her computer and pulled up a web browser to find out if any further information had been posted about the new victim. It took her a little over an hour before she finally came across a blurry photo of what was supposedly the letter sent to the victim.

Claire's heart raced as she read over the letter, blowing it up as much as possible to make out any small details. Looking at her own letter, she tried to compare the script. Both were handwritten but the script on Claire's was tidy and concise, whereas the script on the victim's seemed a little messier and rushed.

Claire chewed her thumbnail while she tried to go line by line, comparing the two. The handwriting was different, for sure, but there were other things that were different, too. Her letter had very precise grammar; the victim's did not. Her letter was written with what appeared to be a thin, blue Sharpie; the victim's letter was in some sort of gel pen. At the very least from what she could make out, the ink looked different.

"Did you want anything for lunch?"

Claire jumped at the sound of Sarah's voice. She looked down at the time and realized that she must have been staring at the screen for far too long.

"I'm okay," she said. "I should probably go for a walk or something."

Sarah nodded. "You seemed really engrossed."

Claire nodded and switched off her screen as Sarah walked away. She had to admit that she felt slightly better about the two letters being different. While it wasn't conclusive evidence, it made it possible that her letter really was from an innocent admirer.

Just as she was about to grab her coat and head out to get something to eat, Sarah turned back up.

"There's a large delivery of boxes for you at the front desk," she said. "Do you want me to bring them over?"

Claire furrowed her brow. She wasn't expecting any deliveries.

"No, thanks," she said. "Why don't you go to lunch. I'll see what they are."

Sarah nodded, seemingly relieved that she wouldn't have to delay her lunch plans and hurried out the door.

Claire made her way to reception and looked at the white file boxes on a cart.

"A woman from the law library dropped those off," the receptionist said with a warm smile. "She said she wanted to stay, but she had to run back."

Claire nodded. "Thanks. I'll let her know I got them."

It was nice of Joy to bring back the Bates evidence boxes, not that Claire really wanted to look at them again. Just seeing them made her chest tighten, the memories of late nights, endless coffee, and the overwhelming pressure to dig up the truth rushing back like a wave. Her anxiety prickled at the edges of her thoughts, whispering that she might have missed something, that going back through the evidence might unravel her confidence all over again.

As she wheeled the first one into her office, she grimaced as she looked at it. Then, her stomach sank. The weight of everything this case represented pressed down on her—a mix of dread and determination.

She let her door close behind her and grabbed the letter she had stuffed in her top drawer. Going back over to the box, she rifled through until she found what she was after. She pulled out one of the evidence binders and leafed through it frantically until she found the right page.

There, staring back at her, was a photocopy of one of the original victims' letters. She put her letter next to it. Bile threatened to creep up her throat.

The handwriting matched. The color and marker thickness matched. Even the grammar and length matched.

It all matched.

It was as if the two letters were carbon copies of one another, the only difference being key words used to strike a specific cord. To feel admired.

Maybe the new perpetrator hadn't sent Claire a letter. Maybe Bates had.

chapter
twenty-six

"IF YOU GET any closer to that screen you'll end up inside the computer," Paul Richardson laughed.

Detective Lawson blinked her eyes several times as she tried to adjust her vision to the low lighting of her office. Richardson handed her a cup of coffee and she took it with a "Thanks."

"Any developments?" he asked, sitting down opposite her desk.

She shook her head. "When I became a detective, I didn't really think I'd be spending all of my time scrolling Instagram and Facebook."

"Murders these days."

"It's like the general public gave a key to their lives to every creep out there."

Richardson took a sip of his coffee. "Certainly made the stalkers' jobs easier."

"And ours harder." Lawson groaned and rubbed a hand down her face.

"I'm sure you'll get to the bottom of it," he said. "You always do."

"I hope you're right," Lawson muttered,, her confidence waning.

"You think it could have anything to do with Bates?"

Lawson looked at her supervisor, but his poker face was so practiced. He was the one person she really struggled to read.

"I don't think the timing adds up," she said, narrowing her eyes. "What do you think?"

He shrugged. "It's not my case, so I haven't really thought about it. Just curious to know yours."

"That's bullshit and we both know it," Lawson said. "You always have thoughts on every matter."

"Let's just say I don't envy you right now."

"Is this supposed to be helpful? Because if so, I need to give you some honest feedback about your mentoring sessions."

Richardson chuckled and rose from his seat. "I'll leave you to it."

Lawson sighed as Richardson left, closing the door behind him. The man was too cagey—always offering just enough guidance to point her in the right direction, but never enough to make the path feel clear. It frustrated her no end, but deep down, she knew it was his way of pushing her to grow. He wanted her to solve problems on her own, to develop instincts that couldn't be taught in a meeting or training manual. It was a lesson she appreciated in theory, but in moments like this, she couldn't help but wish for a little more direct advice.

She turned her attention back to the Instagram page of the victim, Ashley Gilford. She'd been a 22-year-old attending college at the University of North Carolina but had returned home for a visit. She had a sizeable following on Instagram, and a larger following on TikTok. With over one million followers, all her posts had tons of comments. Her page was more geared towards men, as indicated by the suggestive poses in her photos, the carefully curated outfits that left little to the imagination, and the captions that flirted with innuendo. Lawson was positive the perp had to have been one of the many men leaving comments on her page, but trying to find the one stalker amidst all of them was proving difficult, if not impossible.

Lawson forced herself to concentrate and scrolled through Ashley's page to get to the beginning, the images of the vibrant young woman staring back at her, blissfully unaware of the fate that awaited her. It left a bitter taste in Lawson's mouth—this strange intimacy with someone who could no longer speak for herself. Each photo felt like a ghost, a reminder of everything Ashley had lost and the life that had been stolen from her.

She scrolled through the posts in chronological order, starting with the oldest first. Photos of her and her friends. A sunset here or there. Then slowly her feed began to transform. Lawson shook her head as the posts became more and more suggestive. More skin, more smirks, and more suggestive content to read in the blurbs.

Lawson paused when she came across Ashley beaming at the camera, surrounded by letters on the bed beneath her. The caption read, "I love getting letters from my admirers! #blessed."

She wrinkled her nose as she thought back to Claire Stevens. She had brushed off Claire's concern over a letter of admiration, perhaps too hastily. If she was being honest, she was somewhat angry over the overturned Bates case and let it cloud her judgment. But now, she wondered if there was more to Claire's letter than just an innocent admirer.

Lawson had told the press that they had possession of everything the perpetrator had sent to the victim, but she wasn't sure that was actually true now.

"Dammit," Lawson muttered under her breath. She should call Claire, tell her the whole truth and let her in, but her pride held her back. Admitting that she hadn't given the letter enough attention would be painful, but if it could help her link things to the new killer, wouldn't that be worth it?

Her hand hovered over the phone receiver, indecision gnawing at her. Lawson let out a frustrated sigh and pulled her hand back. Admitting her oversight would mean acknowledging that she'd let something slip through the cracks—a failure she couldn't stomach, not now. The weight of her reputation, her years of experience, and the respect she'd fought to earn loomed larger in her mind than the need to uncover the truth. Pride and dignity felt like the last shreds of control she had, and in this moment, they mattered more than opening herself up to judgment or vulnerability. As much as she wanted to see Claire's letter again, she wouldn't do it at the expense of her own dignity.

She turned back to Ashley's profile. There had to be something else, some clue hidden among the smiling photos that could lead her to the perpetrator. She clicked through the photos of the letter post, hoping for something that might be useful until one caught her eye. Ashley had taken photos of some of the letters up close. They were mostly out of focus and blurry, but Lawson zoomed in to see what was written.

She shook her head as she tried to scan the words of one. It was an over-the-top, generic message of admiration, the kind you'd expect from some lovesick fan. But something nagged at the back of Lawson's mind.

This whole letter of admiration and Claire's felt a lot like Bates. But the timelines didn't match up. Bates was in prison until the day of the murder. There's no way he could have been stalking someone on social media while under lock and key.

She moved on, searching for more concrete clues in the comment section. As she scrolled, comments started blurring together, forming a sea of compliments, emojis, and cruder content.

Then, one comment caught her eye. "Glad you've been receiving my gifts. Looking forward to seeing you soon." From what Lawson could see, Ashley rarely acknowledged comments on her page, but this one had a little heart with her icon next to it.

"Interesting," Lawson whispered. She clicked on the profile that had left the comment, hoping to find some insight into the person behind the message. The profile username was DarkWanderer87. Lawson's eyes narrowed as she scanned through the profile and photo thumbnails. The content was pretty generic, containing photos of landscapes, city skylines, and the occasional bar scene. Every image seemed disconnected, like scattered pieces of different puzzles.

She was certain the account's owner was male. An older photo taken at a dimly lit bar showed a half-empty glass of whiskey, and just barely visible in the corner of the frame was a man's hand. A tattoo peeked out from the back of his hand, but it was impossible to decipher the design from the angle of the shot.

As she zoomed in on the photo, something else caught her notice. A man in the background, who looked an awful lot like Anthony Bates. She couldn't be sure, because the image was so grainy, but there weren't too many blond men in Savannah who smiled that big.

Her heart skipped a beat when she scrolled back up to click on the most recent photo. It was taken over a week ago from the Blue Sky Preserve, the very place Ashley's body had been discovered.

It could certainly have been a coincidence. A lot of people from the Savannah area made their way out to the trails to get away from the city, but it was the closest lead Lawson had. She grabbed a notepad from the corner of her desk and jotted down the details, underlining the location for later follow-up.

It was entirely possible that Bates had been at that bar at the same time as the account owner by coincidence. It was also one more thing that made her feel like she was onto something.

She went back to DarkWanderer87's main profile to see who they followed. Fourteen people in total, each was a young, attractive woman —just like Ashley Gilford. And Claire Stevens.

She turned in her chair to rifle through a filing cabinet to find a form for filing a subpoena. She slapped it on her desk and fished for a pen in the jar at the corner of her desk to start filling it out. The pen wasn't working right away. She let out a grumble and found a piece of scrap paper to scribble on until the ink decided to flow out and she continued filling the form. She wanted it on a magistrate judge's desk first thing in the morning. It wasn't the easiest to get information from internet service providers, but it wasn't impossible when it came to criminal matters.

As Lawson wrote up the request, her thoughts drifted back to Claire and her letter. She groaned at the thought of calling the woman. In Lawson's eyes, Claire was the reason for all of this. If she had left well enough alone, Bates would still be in prison and there likely wouldn't be anyone trying to emulate him, or worse.

Still, the attorney didn't deserve to get murdered. So, Lawson put her pride aside and decided she'd call Claire in the morning. Now that she at least had a potential lead, she didn't feel quite so bad to ask

Claire about her own letter a bit more. She'd have her come to the station tomorrow.

Maybe by solving this newest murder before things escalated, Lawson could win back some of the public support that Claire had cost her.

chapter
twenty-seven

THE MAGISTRATE JUDGE had issued the warrant first thing the next morning. By early afternoon, Lawson already had the account's owner, Jason Morrison, in custody. The small interrogation room smelled faintly of disinfectant and stale coffee, its bare walls and cold fluorescent lighting giving it a sterile, unwelcoming feel. The metal table between them was scuffed and dented, a testament to countless tense interviews before this one.

The man was in his late thirties and had lived outside of Savannah all his life. So far, he hadn't requested a lawyer, which Lawson was grateful for. She intended to get as much out of him as she could before that changed.

"Is it true your Instagram username is DarkWanderer87?" Lawson asked the suspect, her voice steady, her gaze fixed on him.

He sat with his arms crossed at the table, his posture defensive but his face calm. His long dark hair was pulled back in a ponytail, and the dim lighting cast shadows over his sharp features. A tattoo on the back of his hand—a wolf's paw that made Lawson barely suppress an eyeroll —matched the one in the photo from the account, shoddy angle and all. Morrison remained silent, the faint creak of his chair the only response as he shifted his weight slightly.

"I have a few different accounts on social media," Jason responded.

Lawson pushed a pen and paper over to him. "Can you write them down for me?"

"I guess," he said with a shrug, picking up the pen and writing.

She was surprised at his cooperation, considering he was being questioned regarding the murder of a young woman. Then again, he didn't seem like the smartest member of society.

When he put the pen down, Lawson asked, "Did you know Ashley Gilford? Or is she someone you just followed online?"

"We met once or twice."

"What did you do when you met?"

"Look," Jason said, "I don't know nothing about that girl's murder. I swear it."

"Okay," Lawson replied, shrugging a shoulder. "We're just trying to find out who does. And you knew her. That's why you're here."

"She agreed to meet me when I messaged her," Jason said, eyes not quite meeting Lawson's. "That's all."

Lawson nodded and decided to shift gears. "Do you go to the Blue Sky Preserve often?"

"Sometimes," Jason said, his voice a little more measured now.

"When's the last time that you were there?"

"Couldn't say. A while ago."

"You posted a picture of it online timestamped for last week."

"People post things after they do them."

"So if I asked to see your phone and looked through your photos, the timestamp on the original wouldn't be from last week then?"

Jason didn't answer, instead sinking into his seat. His unease was palpable, but Lawson kept up the pressure.

"You wrote to Ashley and said you were glad she liked your gifts. What else did you buy her?"

"Just things she said she liked."

"How did you know what she liked?"

Jason shifted in his chair. "I may have watched her a bit."

"Online?"

"Yeah... and in other ways." He furrowed his brow. "Look, am I in trouble or something?"

"As I said, we're just here to ask a few questions." Lawson side-stepped his question. She hadn't intended to ask the next so soon, or even at all, but that photo at the bar was gnawing at the back of her mind. "Do you know Anthony Bates?"

Jason seemed to light up at the mention of his name. "I met him once, yeah."

"Can you tell me a little bit about that meeting?"

"It was at a bar. He approached me," Jason said, the blush dusting his cheeks at odds with his rough and tumble exterior. "Everyone wanted to be around him. He had a way of drawing attention."

"I'm sure you heard about his conviction."

"He was acquitted."

"His conviction was overturned due to a technical error."

"I'm just happy he's out."

Lawson furrowed her brow, her thoughts churning. There was something unsettling about this man's obvious infatuation with Bates. It felt too intense, too personal, like an obsession that ran deeper than admiration. She couldn't shake the feeling that there was more to his fixation, something she wasn't seeing yet, and it gnawed at the edges of her mind.

"Did you read about his crimes, Jason?"

Jason just nodded his head slowly in response.

"What did you think about them?"

He shrugged, still not saying anything.

"Were you—" Lawson paused, wondering if she was about to push too hard. She decided any outcome was worth the knowledge. "Inspired by them?"

Jason stared at her, his arms crossed. The silence between them was heavy before he finally replied, "Can't say."

"Did you kill Ashley Gilford, Jason? Did you send her gifts like Anthony sent gifts to his victims?"

"I don't think I want to say anything else," Jason said, but the flicker of fear in his eyes was all she needed.

"That's alright, Jason. Wait here for just a second."

She got up and swiped her card to unlock the door, exiting the interrogation room. Richardson waited for her on the other side.

"Well?" he said.

"You heard it all?" she asked.

He nodded. "That's good enough for me," he said. "Go ahead and cuff him."

Lawson nodded, and a nearby officer entered the room, removing his cuffs as he did so. Lawson caught only a glimpse of Jason and his widening, protesting eyes as she made her way back to her office and sank in her chair. She flipped through the pad of paper and stared at the usernames Jason had written. She would have someone in the department pull information on the accounts first thing tomorrow.

She was more than sure that Jason was the culprit behind Ashley's murder. There was a sense of relief that there wasn't a second Anthony Bates on the loose. She wasn't sure her career, or her psyche for that matter, could take another Bates.

Her phone rang and she picked up. "Detective Lawson."

"There's a Claire Stevens here to see you," the front dispatcher informed her.

Lawson let out a deep breath. She supposed she had to see the woman, considering that she was the one to call her this morning asking her to come to the station with the letter. But now that she already had the perpetrator in custody, she wished she hadn't.

"Be right there."

She tried to put her attitude in check as she walked out to the front. If nothing else, Claire's letter might be used as evidence against Jason at trial, assuming he didn't plead guilty. Lawson was definitely not looking forward to another Bates-type trial and hoped it wouldn't come to that.

Lawson chuckled to herself as she realized that Claire might not be able to represent him, since she had an affinity for representing murderers. If it's true that he sent that letter, or even if it was used as evidence, it would conflict her out.

Lawson reached the front and took a moment to study the attorney before drawing her attention. The woman was far worse for wear since the last time they'd seen one another. If the dark circles under Claire's eyes were any indication, she hadn't been sleeping well, if at all. Her hair was tied back in a messy bun and she wasn't wearing anything that looked like she was coming from or going to an office.

"Claire," Lawson said, finally walking over to her.

Claire's snapped to attention and she stood. "Hello."

"Thanks for coming down to the station." Lawson said, directing her to the conference room they'd used last time.

Claire slipped inside and Lawson closed the door behind them.

"Do you mind if I take a look at the letter?" Lawson asked, holding her hand out as Claire took a seat.

Claire fumbled in her bag a bit before pulling out a folder and handing it to Lawson. Inside was the letter, folded up inside a plain, white envelope. The detective pulled out Jason's list of usernames to cross-reference his script with the letters, but the handwriting was not the same.

Lawson looked up from the papers, setting them down on the table. "Do you have any ideas on who sent it?"

Claire shifted in her seat and tucked a strand of hair behind her ear, her brow furrowing in thought. "At first, I thought maybe it was the new perpetrator. The one who killed that influencer."

It was possible Claire had already done some digging on her own, and Lawson didn't want to risk tipping her hand too soon. She wasn't quite ready to let Claire know she had a potential suspect in custody.

"At first?" Lawson asked.

Claire nodded. "But then I found a picture of a letter the perpetrator supposedly sent to the victim. The handwriting didn't match mine."

Lawson's pulse quickened. How could she have missed something like that?" Can you show me?"

Claire reached into her bag and pulled out her phone, tapping on the screen a few times before handing the device over to Lawson. The picture was grainy, but it was clear that the handwriting was not a match.

"How did you find this?" Lawson asked, taking note of the website on which it was posted.

Claire let out a humorless chuckle. "It took me many hours of anxiously scouring the internet. I don't know for sure that it's real."

Lawson nodded. "We'll look into it and try and get the person who posted in for questioning."

The attorney nodded and stayed silent. Her usual fiery persistence was nowhere to be found today. Lawson waited for Claire to share more, but it was obvious she was going to have to drag information out of the woman.

"Do you have any idea of who this other sender could be?"

Claire shifted in her chair again. In a way, she was exhibiting the same pattern of behavior as a suspect pulled in for questioning, which Lawson thought was odd. The nervous movements, the reluctance to speak openly, the way her responses seemed measured, as if she was weighing every word before speaking—these weren't the actions of someone confidently sharing information. Claire wasn't usually this guarded, and it sent up a red flag. Was she hiding something? Or was she simply unsure of what she knew?

"I do," she said, "but you're not going to like the answer."

Lawson shook her head. "It's okay. At this point, everything is worth exploring."

Claire nodded, letting out a breath, and dug into her bag again. She pulled out another manila folder. She pushed it forward toward Lawson. Lawson tilted her head slightly, eyeing the folder with a mix of curiosity and caution, her fingers brushing over the edge before flipping it open. Opening it up, she recognized it as an evidence file from Bates' case. Inside was a photograph of a letter Bates had sent to one of his victims.

"That letter is almost identical to mine," Claire said.

Lawson blew out a frustrated sigh. "Claire, I thought we addressed this the last time that you were here."

"That was before I compared the letters. You can't deny that they're almost exactly the same."

Lawson stood. "I know I'm the one who asked you down here, Claire, but I really do not have time to entertain this line of thinking. As I said before, the timeline doesn't line up."

"Then why *did* you call me down here?" Claire gave Lawson a look full of derision. "What's the real reason?"

Lawson shook her head. "I'm not sure I follow your question. Obviously, I wanted to look at the letter again."

"Yes," Claire said, folding her arms, "but why?"

Lawson's patience was waning, but she supposed she owed the woman an answer. "Because we've found a suspect in the new case."

Claire scoffed, stood, and grabbed her letter, shoving it back into her bag. "I'm not here to help you on your other investigations, Detective. Especially when you have no intention to help me with mine."

Lawson watched as the attorney stormed out of the room. She sat back down in her seat and blew out a breath. This job was really starting to wear on her.

chapter
twenty-eight

CLAIRE TUGGED at the bangle bracelet against her wrist. Tonight was the welcome home party for Anthony, and she still wasn't sure she wanted to attend. Of course, she really had no choice. Bob would be there, and for Claire to snub the event would almost certainly make waves in the small, tightly knit social circles that dominated Savannah's elite.

Her absence would be noticed, discussed, and spun into whispers that could ripple beyond the party. The media attention surrounding her lately only heightened the stakes. A snub like this could easily catch the attention of a local tabloid, adding another layer of scrutiny to her already tenuous position. In a town like Savannah, appearances mattered just as much as actions, and tonight, showing up wasn't just about Anthony—it was about protecting her own reputation. Her phone buzzed and she fished it out of her far too small purse.

It was Meredith.

Meredith: Hey! Running a few minutes late. My straightening iron crapped out on me last minute 😩

Claire: It's okay, don't stress. There's still plenty of time.

Meredith: Whew, thanks. I'll see you in a few!

Claire: See you soon!

Claire stuffed it back into her bag and smoothed imaginary wrinkles out of her simple black cocktail dress. She had decided on something plain in order to fly under the radar at tonight's party.

She flipped through the television stations and another news report announcing the successful arrest of a suspect in the most recent murder flashed on the screen.

The suspect had been a long-time admirer of Anthony, having met him at a bar a number of years ago. The way the newscaster spoke, it was almost as if they were trying to suggest some form of romantic involvement. Apparently, the suspect had been so enthralled with Anthony that when he'd heard about his release, he thought he would go and murder someone in his signature style as a welcome home gift.

Claire closed her eyes and switched off the television. She knew that watching the news reports likely wasn't good for her already tenuous mental health.

A horn honking outside had her jumping. She looked down from her window to see Meredith waving at her. She waved back, and headed downstairs to the car.

"Hey," she said as she got in and buckled her seatbelt.

"Hey!" Meredith replied, slightly out of breath.

She was wearing a bright red dress to match her red hair, which was pulled back into a tight bun. Claire laughed as she noticed a small twig stuck in the back. She pulled it out and held it up. "Been running a marathon or something?"

Meredith looked at the twig with wide eyes and laughed. She touched the back of her hair and shook her head. "I swear, how in the world did that get back there? I must have brushed a tree branch in my rush to get to the car."

Claire laughed, rolled the window down and tossed the branch out. "Are you really sure you want to go to this? You can still back out."

Meredith brushed Claire's comment aside with a wave of her hand. "Don't be ridiculous. I work in this world. I'm not scared of an ex-convict, and I'm happy to support you. This is as much your party as it is his."

"I'm not sure that makes me feel any better." Claire sighed as they backed out of the parking spot.

"Stop it," Meredith said with a laugh. "Just try and have fun, okay?"

Claire wrinkled her face. "I think I've forgotten the definition of 'fun.'"

"I definitely think that's true. But now is the time to relax a little! You won the case! Honestly, even if the man is a raving lunatic, I doubt he would try and off the attorney that got him released!"

Claire blinked her eyes wide in a mixture of laughter and surprise. "Where do you even come up with these things?"

Meredith shrugged her shoulders. "I dunno. When you work in the industry that I do, if you don't find ways to lighten the mood, it can seriously drag you down."

"Yeah," Claire said. Her fingers fidgeted with the edge of her sleeve as her thoughts shifted. "I just wish I knew who sent me that letter." Claire shook her head. "Lawson called me down to the station yesterday."

Meredith pulled to a stop at a red light. "The detective?"

Claire nodded. "She wanted to take another look at the letter."

"What'd she think?"

Claire sighed. "You know Lawson. She doesn't give anything away. All she did was dismiss my concerns about it being from Anthony. She'd just called me down because she thought that *I* could help *her*."

Meredith rolled her eyes as she stepped on the gas pedal.

"It's like, I'll be sure to let her know if I get murdered."

"Don't worry. I'll let her know, too," Meredith said with a laugh.

Claire shook her head but couldn't stop the smile from creeping onto her lips. The light turned green and Claire turned her gaze to look out the window as they made their way into the upper crust of Savannah real estate.

Meredith pulled the car up to the Bates residence. It was exactly what you'd expect from an old Southern estate. The façade of the mansion exuded Southern charm with its stately columns and a sweeping veranda across the front adorned with ornate wrought-iron railings. The soft glow of gas lanterns illuminated the entrance, casting a warm ambiance that beckoned guests in.

The women exited the car and closed the car doors, one after the other, as the valet approached Meredith for her keys.. Claire looked up at the large mansion and all the guests making their way inside and gulped. She hadn't really prepared herself for this evening. She just hoped to blend into the crowd. She especially hoped that she wouldn't have to interact much with Anthony during the party,

"Ready?" Meredith asked, breaking Claire out of her trance. She nodded, but couldn't bring herself to say, "yes."

Claire stepped through the double doors after Meredith, greeted by a foyer adorned with intricate moldings and a crystal chandelier that cascaded a soft, golden light. The air was permeated with the subtle notes of magnolias. Claire wrinkled her nose at the scent.

Like any good matriarch, Dolores Bates was standing in the foyer, greeting guests as they arrived. She played her part perfectly. Her silver-grey hair was pulled back into a professional updo and she wore a sophisticated forest green wrap dress.

Claire tried to shrink herself, but Dolores' gaze found her before she could disappear. "Claire," the woman said warmly, her hands outstretched as Claire walked inside. "Thank you so much for coming."

Claire did her best to smile. "Thank you for inviting me."

"Don't be silly. None of this would be possible if not for you. You're as much the guest of honor tonight as Anthony."

Claire pressed her lips together and nodded. "This is my friend, Meredith Porter."

Dolores' greeting towards Meredith was a bit more reserved, simply nodding at the woman before returning her attention to Claire. "I hope you both make yourselves comfortable. We're expecting Anthony to arrive soon."

Claire furrowed her brow. "He's not here, yet?"

"You know my Anthony. Always one to make an entrance."

Claire nodded and the two women moved further into the house.

The interior was a seamless blend of old-world elegance and modern comfort. Exquisite chandeliers hanging from high ceilings created an air of grandeur in every room. Rich hardwood floors led the way through lavishly furnished parlors and drawing rooms, where plush velvet sofas and antique furniture hinted at the mansion's storied past.

The women each grabbed a drink from one of the many bars throughout the house before finding a quiet corner.

"Where do you think he is?" Meredith whispered to Claire.

"I don't know," Claire replied, shaking her head. "Don't you think it's a little odd for someone not to be here for their own welcome home party?"

Meredith nodded, but before she had a chance to respond, a voice all but shouted Claire's name. Her cover had already been blown, and she hadn't even been here for ten minutes. So much for the quiet corner.

"Claire Stevens!" Bob's voice boomed above the din of the crowd. Claire cringed, preparing herself for the attention she'd been hoping to avoid. "Woman of the hour!"

"Hi Bob," Claire said in a reserved tone. She toasted her wine glass against his as he held it up.

"Who is your friend here?" he asked.

"Meredith introduced herself and held her hand out, saving Claire the trouble. She was much more outgoing than Claire ever could be.

"Glad to meet you," Bob said. He twisted his lips, his moustache moving from side to side as he clearly grappled with what to say. "It's a great party, don't you ladies think so?"

"Yes," Meredith responded, glancing at Claire. "We were just remarking that the true man of the hour seems to be making a delayed entrance."

Claire gave her friend a "what the heck?" look, but Meredith just gave her a mischievous smile back.

"Yes, yes, I did hear there was a delay," Bob said. "Something about car troubles."

"I'd just heard that he liked to be fashionably late," Meredith said.

Bob seemed a little uncomfortable with the topic, which Claire imagined is exactly what Meredith was after. She was a psychologist after all. Claire supposed that testing people's behaviors was sort of a strong suit for her.

Bob cleared his throat and raised his glass. "I hope you enjoy the party!"

Meredith turned back around to beam a smile at Claire as Bob sauntered off. "I figured you deal with him all day at work. No sense in dealing with him after work, too."

"Thanks," Claire said, feeling a bit relieved.

The two meandered through the party, picking at the trays of hors d'oeuvres. As time waned on and Anthony still hadn't appeared, the tone of the crowd shifted, a discomfort becoming prevalent. More and more people were starting to whisper behind hands. Expressions took on notes of confusion.

The tapping of a fork against a glass drew everyone's attention back to the foyer. Claire and Meredith made their way there to see Dolores standing ramrod straight, looking slightly paler than when they had first walked in.

"Something's wrong," Meredith whispered, nodding to Dolores. Claire had to agree.

When the crowd quieted down, Dolores cleared her throat and put on a forced smile. "I'm sorry to say that we will have to end the party early." Murmurs of disappointment made their way through the crowd, but Dolores put up her hands and people settled back down. "We very much appreciate you coming out to show your support and welcome Anthony back home. The valets are outside and waiting. If anyone feels that they are unsafe to drive, please let one of them know and they will call you a cab. Thank you for coming."

Claire and Meredith shared a confused look as they made their way out to the front of the house with the rest of the crowd. Waiting in line, Claire could see that many people were pulling their phones out and a few were gasping.

"Do you know what's going on?" Claire asked Meredith.

Meredith shook her head. "No. But everyone else seems to."

By the time Claire fished her phone out of her purse, they were next in line for the valet. Meredith turned in her ticket as Claire searched the local news.

And she found it.

Anthony Bates was dead.

chapter
twenty-nine

"IN A SHOCKING TURN OF EVENTS, Anthony Bates, a 42-year-old resident of Savannah, was found dead after a tragic accident on the outskirts of the city." Claire read the report aloud from her phone as Meredith drove back to Claire's apartment.

"According to initial reports from the Savannah Police Department, Bates was driving alone when his vehicle veered off the road, resulting in a fatal crash. The accident occurred on a quiet stretch of highway just outside of Savannah.

"Authorities arrived at the scene promptly after receiving reports from a passerby who discovered the wreckage. Surprisingly, there were no other vehicles involved in the incident, and it appears that Bates' car was the only one affected."

"No other cars?" Meredith repeated, confusion laced in her voice. "How does someone just swerve off the road bad enough to kill them if no one else was involved?"

Claire shook her head. Deer frequented the quieter stretches of road outside of the city, but if a deer had been the culprit, the article would surely have mentioned that. Right?

"The circumstances surrounding the accident have prompted the police to launch a thorough investigation into Bates' death. While no foul play has been officially confirmed, sources close to the investigation reveal that the initial findings have raised suspicions among law enforcement."

"I'd say so," Meredith remarked. "I mean, don't you think it's a little suspicious that the man turns up dead when he's supposed to be at his welcome home party? Plus, he's not exactly the most favorite figure in town right now."

Claire started chewing her fingernails. "You don't think someone was after him because of—well, everything, and that they might come after me next, do you?"

Meredith was quiet for a beat and that was all Claire needed. It was obvious that her friend was trying to save her feelings, but her feelings were already past saving.

"Does the article say anything else?" Meredith asked, pulling into a parking space in front of Claire's apartment.

"Detective e Erin Lawson, leading the investigation, stated, 'At this point, we are treating the case as suspicious. The absence of other vehicles and the apparent swerving off the road have led us to explore all possibilities. We are awaiting the results of a full autopsy to determine the exact cause of Mr. Bates' death.'

"Anthony Bates was a well-known figure in the local community, having just recently been released from prison on a technicality after being convicted of the murder of seven young women. Friends and family are grappling with the sudden loss, and the community is awaiting further updates from the police investigation."

Claire tried to scroll further, but there was nothing else. "That's all it says." She squeezed her eyes shut. "Do you think I should call Lawson?"

"I don't think Lawson is going to help, if your meetings with her are any indication," Meredith replied, her lips twisted in thought. "And, honestly? Something about Lawson feels off to me."

Claire cracked her eyes open to look at her friend. " What do you mean?"

Meredith sighed. "I really shouldn't be saying this since I have absolutely no evidence to back it up. It's just a feeling."

Claire blinked at her friend. "Which is?"

"It just feels like when something goes wrong with Anthony,

Lawson is there. She was there when he got taken to the hospital. The way she questioned him. The way she's been completely dismissing your concerns about your letter. And now, he turns up dead?"

"What are you saying, Meredith?"

"It just feels odd. Like, why dismiss your letter so summarily? How could she know for sure it wasn't him?" Meredith glanced at Claire. "Unless—."

"Unless she knew it was someone else."

"Or at least knew it wasn't Bates."

"You think Lawson is behind the letter?" Claire asked.

It's something she hadn't considered before, but Lawson had the right motive. She was angry over the appeal, that much was evident. She thought Anthony was a danger to society.

Then Claire had a darker thought. "You don't think Lawson is behind his death, do you?"

"I don't know if she'd go that far."

Claire raised her eyebrows. "Yeah, but you wouldn't think she'd interrogate him the way she did, either. People might surprise you."

"I hope I'm wrong. I'm not even sure I believe what I'm saying," Meredith said, trying to laugh it off, but Claire wasn't going to dismiss the thought so easily. Maybe she'd been wrong to go to Lawson with the letter she'd received. Maybe she was playing right into the detective's hands.

"Do you want me to stay with you tonight?"

Claire shook her head. "No, it's okay. You've got work tomorrow and so do I. I'm sure it's fine. It probably was just an accident. The man hasn't driven in some time and he was driving alone on the highway. I'm sure it's just one of those tragedies."

"Okay," Meredith said. "If you're sure."

Claire nodded and climbed from the vehicle, closing the door behind her and waving to Meredith as she pulled out of the parking lot. She sighed and made her way inside, then forced herself to check the mailbox just to put her mind at ease.

She walked up to the little box and inserted the key. Her breath held steady as she looked inside.

It was empty.

Claire let her breath out and closed it with a definitive thud before trudging her way up the stairs. Rather than indulging in her normal nighttime routine of drinking wine, watching TV, and staring at her phone, she decided to triple check that her door was locked, and then crash onto her bed.

THE ALARM SOUNDED FAR TOO EARLY the next morning, its shrill beeping cutting through the quiet stillness of her bedroom. The faint light of dawn seeped through the edges of her curtains, casting soft shadows across the cluttered space. Claire groaned, rolling over in bed and mashing the off button with more force than necessary. She hadn't even changed out of her evening attire, having been far too tired and emotionally drained from the events of the prior day.

As she sat up and rubbed her eyes, she glanced at the half-empty glass of water still sitting on her nightstand, the condensation long gone. She groaned again at the thought of going into the office. The weight of Bates' death hung heavy, and she was sure everyone would be whispering about it. She didn't want to deal with the hushed conversations or the accusatory glances. And then there was Daniel—she hadn't seen him since their last tense conversation, but she knew her luck wouldn't hold out much longer.

Her phone chimed, breaking her train of thought. She reached for it, scrolling through her notifications until the reminder popped up. Lunch with Fiona. She sighed, tossing the phone onto the bed. With Fiona obviously angry with her, she wasn't sure if the lunch was still on, and the thought of another confrontation made her stomach twist. She took a moment to send her sister a text.

Hey. Are we still on for lunch? I'd love to see you.

The last thing Claire wanted was for this case to cause an even bigger rift between her and her family. Things had already been tense since she took the Bates case. Fiona had made it clear from the start that she didn't agree with Claire's decision, and her father's initial carefully worded remarks had been equally frustrating at the time. The unspoken divide had only widened in the weeks that followed, leaving Claire feeling more isolated with every family interaction. She couldn't shake the fear that, if left unchecked, this might become yet another issue her family danced around but never addressed outright.

Fiona's message came back fairly quickly.

Fine. But don't expect me to be all chipper.

Claire couldn't help but smile and shake her head. Her sister always had been a little difficult. Maybe it was something about being a Taurus.

That's fine. Usual place?

Yes.

LUNCH COULDN'T HAVE COME FAST ENOUGH. Not that Claire was particularly looking forward to what was sure to be an awkward hour with her sister, but her job had become increasingly busy. While the majority of Savannah couldn't stand her for getting a now-dead murderer off the hook, the other portion of Savannah was convinced she could get them off the hook for every crime imaginable.

It wasn't the worst problem to have, because being Of Counsel at the firm meant that she would also be responsible for bringing in her own work. But she had never imagined that she would be a criminal defense attorney.

A knock at the door had her looking up. Her new assistant, Sarah, approached, holding a folder. "Is this a bad time?" she asked Claire.

Claire looked at the time. Fifteen more minutes and then she had to leave to meet Fiona.

"I have a few minutes," she replied.

Sarah smiled and walked into her office. She handed her the folder, and Claire noted how much heavier it was than it looked.

"More potential cases," Sarah said. "I worked through them this morning."

"Wow." Claire shook her head and opened the folder. "I haven't even gotten through the first batch you left for me."

"Nice to be popular," Sarah said, although her tone didn't completely match her words.

Claire nodded. "I guess it's just a little unexpected."

"I suppose when you get someone like Bates off the hook for murder, everyone thinks you can do the same for them."

Claire worried her lower lip as she looked at her assistant. "What made you want to work in the legal field, Sarah?"

"My family had a run-in with the legal system a few years ago," she said vaguely, her gaze shifting from side to side. "I guess it inspired me to want to learn it better."

"Makes sense," Claire said before forcing a smile. "Well, thanks. I'll take a look at these."

Sarah left the room, and Claire decided to head to lunch early. Standing up, she stretched her arms over her head, feeling the tension in her shoulders ease slightly. She glanced around the room, scanning for her sneakers. Her eyes landed on them near the corner of her desk, and she took a step toward them, slipping one on and reaching for the other.

As she bent down, the soft click of her office door shutting made her pause. Straightening up, she turned, expecting Sarah or a colleague —but the sight of Daniel standing there made her heart skip a beat. She almost yelped.

He didn't look happy. In fact, he looked downright anxious.

"Daniel?" Claire asked carefully, noting how he stood between her and the door—her only exit. She tried to steady her voice. "What can I do for you?"

Daniel approached her desk, glancing at the door behind him before his eyes locked back on hers. "I told you! I told you this would happen." His voice was hushed, urgent, but carried an edge that put her on high alert.

Claire tried to remain calm, though her heart was pounding in her chest. "Told me what would happen?"

"I told you not to represent him or at least throw the case. And now look. He's dead, and I'm likely to be next. All because of your stupid sense of justice."

Daniel moved closer, rounding her desk. Claire instinctively stepped back, her palms pressing lightly against its edge. The bags under his eyes were a sure sign he wasn't getting enough sleep, and his disheveled appearance only added to the tension crackling in the room.

"Bates' death has so far been ruled a tragic accident—"

"That's what they want you to think!" Daniel interrupted sharply.

"Daniel," Claire said, trying to sound calm as she inched along the wall toward the door. "I think the last few weeks have been really stressful, and maybe you just haven't been getting enough sleep."

"Fuck that!" Daniel all but yelled, making Claire jump. "You're responsible for his death, Claire. You! I told you not to get involved, to let things be. Now you're going to get us all killed."

Claire let him rant, nodding slightly to keep him distracted as she continued to edge closer to the door. Her fingers finally brushed the cool metal handle, and she exhaled silently. Pressing down on it, she sighed with relief as the latch gave way.

"I'm sorry you feel that way, Daniel," she said, leaning against the door as it opened slowly. "Unfortunately, I've got a lunch meeting. Maybe we can talk about this later."

Claire didn't give him a chance to respond before letting herself fall through the door and making her way out of the office and onto the busy public street outside. It was obvious that Daniel didn't want anyone knowing about this, so it was very unlikely that he would cause a scene in public.

Even the humid air of the outdoors felt less oppressive than the conditioned air of the office. Claire all but ran to the restaurant to meet Fiona, still shaken from her encounter with Daniel. How her sister could date someone who was proving to be so unhinged was beyond her.

That confrontation had her back on edge. She hated admitting it, but when Bates death was announced, she'd breathed a sigh of relief. When the letter she'd received exactly matched those he'd sent, she was terrified he might come after her. With his death, that was no longer a possibility. Now, all she had to worry about was the potential of a copy-cat. The thought still left a chill creeping up her spine, but it wasn't the same visceral fear she'd felt when Bates himself was alive. At least now, the immediate threat was gone, replaced by a more distant, but no less troubling, unease.

She never imagined someone could be so desperate to keep Bates imprisoned that they'd go after his defense attorney. If Daniel was telling the truth and someone had threatened him, it wasn't far-fetched to think that same person might resort to murdering Bates once he was released. It even made a twisted kind of sense—they'd remove the problem permanently. And if they were willing to go that far, it wasn't a stretch to think they might also target Bates' defense attorney from the original trial.

Then a thought crossed Claire's mind, stopping her in her tracks. What if the person who sent her the letter was the same one who had killed Bates and threatened Daniel? The connection sent a shiver down her spine, the pieces of the puzzle fitting together in a way she didn't like.

Her thoughts drifted back to her conversation with Meredith. Lawson had all the facts available to her plus the resources to pull it off. Could Lawson have been the one to threaten Daniel? To send Claire her letter? To kill Bates?

She tried to shake the thought out of her mind. There was no evidence that any of these things were connected. And what sort of attorney would she be if she relied on conjecture instead of evidence?

The little coffee shop in Franklin Square came into view. Claire entered quickly and was unable to stop herself from looking behind her to make sure no one had followed her in. She hated how on edge she felt.

Bates is dead and the case is over, she reminded herself as she sat down in one of the red vinyl booths to wait for her sister. "I have no reason to be anxious," she mumbled to herself.

" I don't know if that's exactly true," a voice above her said.

chapter
thirty

CLAIRE BLINKED as she looked up at her sister. "Sorry, what?"

Fiona slid into the booth and raised her hand to flag a waitress over. "I'm saying that I disagree that you have no reason to be anxious."

Claire furrowed her brows as she looked at her sister, her stomach twisting further into knots. "Why do you say that?"

Before Fiona could respond, a bubbly waitress came over to take their order.

"Hey there!" she said. "I'm Melissa! I'll be taking care of you today."

"Great, thanks," Claire muttered.

"Our special for this afternoon is the Ruben served with house made chips or a salad."

"Oh, that sounds good," Fiona said, looking over the menu, temporarily distracted from the conversation she and Claire were about to have.

Claire decided on the same thing she always ordered. "I'll do the Caesar salad."

"I'll do the special," Fiona said, sounding far too chipper for Claire's liking.

"Great! And to drink?"

Claire's patience was wearing thin.

"I'll do an iced tea," Fiona said, smiling wider than Claire had seen in weeks.

Melissa turned to Claire. "And for you?"

"Just water is great, thanks."

After what felt like a century, Melissa finally took their menus, told them she'd be back with their drinks in just a minute, and made her way back to the kitchen.

"Okay, so, what is it you were saying?" Claire asked her sister.

Fiona rolled her eyes. "Nice to see you, too, sis."

Claire did her best to stop the huff that wanted to leave her mouth. She knew her sister far too well. If she pushed, Fiona would clam up and leave without giving her anything.

"You're right," Claire said, forcing herself to play her sister's game. "How have things been for you?"

"Pretty crappy," Fiona said, the chipper façade making a hasty exit.

"Oh, no!" Claire said, trying not to let the words sound too forced. "What's the matter?"

"Daniel and I broke up."

Now that *was* something Claire was interested in, especially given the encounter she'd just had with him. "Why? What happened?"

Fiona made a face. "He just started acting really odd."

"How so?" Claire asked, trying to sound surprised.

"All he could talk about was the stupid case. At the beginning, I got it. He was upset that the family chose you over him for the appeal, considering he was the trial lawyer. But then it started to consume him."

With her exceptional timing, Melissa came by to drop off their drinks. "Now, which one of you had the iced tea?"

Claire tried to hold back a groan.

"Me," Fiona said, raising her hand slightly.

"Right, right." Melissa put the drink down in front of her. "Which means you had the water."

"Yes," Claire said, enthusiasm non-existent. "Thanks."

"Your food will be out in just a minute."

Claire sucked in a deep breath and Fiona gave her a look as Melissa walked away.

"What's eating you?" she asked.

Claire shrugged, trying to act calm, although her stomach was doing flip flops. "Nothing. Just tired."

"Right," Fiona said, narrowing her eyes. "Anyway, like I was saying, at first I understood. But then it was all he could talk about. No offense, the last thing I want to hear my boyfriend talking about is my sister."

Claire chortled into her straw as she tried to suck up some water. "I get that."

"And then when Bates' death was finally announced, things just escalated. He kept going on about someone coming for him just like they did for Bates. Talked about us leaving town even. It was too much. I just don't need that negative energy in my life, so I called it off."

Claire nodded. So Daniel had gone off his rocker. She pushed her water aside. "Makes sense."

True to her word, Melissa came back over with their food promptly, and Claire tried to act a little less exasperated with the waitress this time.

"Can I get you two anything else?" When the sisters shook their heads and muttered "No, thanks," Melissa nodded and left.

"You always order the same thing," Fiona remarked as she dug into her sandwich.

Claire shrugged. "I know, it works."

Both sisters sat in silence as they chewed their first bites. Claire grappled with whether to tell Fiona what had happened on the way here. Part of her wanted to confide in her sister, to explain just how rattled she was by Daniel's confrontation and his spiraling paranoia. But she hesitated. Fiona had already made her disapproval of Claire's choices clear and admitting that things were escalating might only make her sister more critical—or worse, more worried. Did Fiona even need to know? Would it help, or would it just make everything feel heavier?

"I wasn't going to say anything, but I've had a few run-ins with Daniel in the last few weeks. Plus another on my way here."

"What do you mean by 'run-in'?" Fiona asked between bites.

Claire tilted her head this way and that. "When I first took the case, he tried to tell me I should throw it for my own safety." Claire lowered her voice a bit and leaned forward. "Fiona, I think he botched the trial because someone threatened him."

Fiona made a face. "I mean, clearly he thinks someone did."

"Or, maybe he misunderstood?" Claire shrugged. "Purposefully throwing a case is grounds for being disbarred, or worse."

Fiona shook her head. "I don't want to go after him that way."

Claire nodded and leaned back. "No, I wasn't suggesting we should. I just want you to know how serious an offense it is."

"I understand," Fiona said.

"Look, I know our last family dinner didn't go over well," Claire said. "I am sorry if I made you uncomfortable when I took the case. I hope you understand why I felt I had to."

Fiona nodded. "I appreciate that. I get it. You've always had a righteousness stick up your butt."

Claire laughed at that. "Maybe you're right."

"Besides, it doesn't really matter now that Bates is dead." Fiona stopped and cocked her head to the side. "At least we think he is."

Claire's stomach was finally loosening enough to let her eat, but that had it all back in knots. "What do you mean?"

"I was one of the reporters who went out to the scene," Fiona explained. "The car didn't just swerve off the road. It was also on fire... and there wasn't much left of the body."

Claire swallowed hard and set her fork down. "There was enough of the body left to confirm it was him, though, right?"

Fiona shrugged. "Not sure. I haven't checked to see whether an autopsy was ordered or what the results were."

"Wouldn't an autopsy be ordered for something like that automatically?"

Fiona shrugged again as she popped a chip in her mouth and spoke between bites. "I guess? I suppose it depends on how interested the police are. Whether they think it involved foul play or what not." Fiona gave Claire a look. "You're an attorney. Aren't you supposed to know this stuff?"

Claire shook her head. "Before this case, I never really had to deal with the criminal side of things."

"Yeah, but given what happened in high school—"

"Let's not go there, shall we?"

Fiona rolled her eyes. "It's been how long now? And you're still not over it?"

Claire shoved some lettuce in her mouth. "It's not really the sort of thing one just 'gets over.'"

"I guess."

"So what you're telling me," Claire said, trying to turn the conversation back to Bates, "is that the police aren't actually sure that Bates is dead?"

"I mean, they're pretty sure."

Claire closed her eyes and breathed in heavily.

"What's the big deal?" Fiona asked, taking another bite of her sandwich. "It's almost like you really want him dead, which doesn't make sense because you're his defense attorney." She gestured around with her sandwich. "You're the one who got him out in the first place."

Claire worried her lower lip and debated whether to tell her sister about the letter. Before she could even decide, Fiona jumped on the silence.

"There's something you're not telling me," she said, narrowing her eyes. "It's why you got all huffy at dinner on Sunday, too. Like, you're always huffy, but for you this was a cut above."

Claire rolled her eyes. "Gee, thanks."

"Calling it like I see it. Now, spill."

Claire sighed. "I got a letter. A really bizarre and creepy letter from an anonymous admirer regarding the Bates case."

Fiona looked confused. "Okay, but I'm not sure why that's something to fuss over."

"Except for the fact that the first thing Bates used to send to his victims was a letter of admiration and the letter's handwriting and format exactly matched the ones Bates used to send."

"A copycat?" Fiona suggested. "What about the guy who killed that Instagram girl?"

Claire shook her head. "He did send her a letter, but it didn't match."

"Another copycat?"

"God, I hope not." Claire sighed, taking a long drink of water.

"It's certainly possible." Fiona tapped a finger against her lips. "I mean, a lot of victim support groups were really upset with you during the appeal. I imagine they still are."

Claire frowned. "I didn't realize there were whole groups of people."

Fiona nodded. "Yeah. I only know about it because I was writing extensively about the appeal."

Claire grimaced. "Right."

"Speaking of, how's your new assistant working out?"

Claire furrowed her brow. "What do you mean?"

"Sarah Carver?" Fiona asked with a bit of a mischievous smile.

"Fine, I guess? Why?"

"I guess you didn't put two-and-two together then."

"Just spit it out already!" Claire said, starting to lose her patience.

Fiona leaned her head back and sighed. "Her younger sister was Violet Carver."

As soon as Claire heard the name, her stomach dropped. "Sarah was in one of those victim support groups?"

"Uh, yeah," Fiona said. "Still is. And she definitely did not like you at the time."

Claire's heartbeat picked up speed and she put her fork down, knowing she wasn't going to be eating the rest of her salad. "Not sure I'm super comfortable with her working for me in that case."

"I don't blame you," Fiona said, finishing the last bite of her sandwich. "Maybe she's the one who sent you the letter. You know, to freak you out? Make you feel what her sister felt?"

"I think I'd rather it be Bates."

"Well, yeah. Because he's supposedly dead now."

"Right," Claire said with a nod. "Supposedly."

chapter
thirty-one

LAWSON'S SHADOW loomed over the stainless steel autopsy table, her eyes narrowed as she observed the coroner's meticulous movements. The color of the body before them was an unsettling homogeny of charred black, its human features obliterated by the flames that had consumed Bates' car.

She had tried to keep quiet the fact that Bates' car hadn't just swerved off the road but had also been found in a ditch and heavily charred. Unfortunately, a few pesky reporters had made this information public, and the news spread about as fast as an uncontrolled fire through Savannah. Now the conspiracy theories were beginning to surface.

Was Bates really dead? Was he murdered? Was it even him in the car? Brand new Mercedes Benz's weren't particularly prone to spontaneous combustion, so the entire situation was odd.

Damn reporters.

Lawson's gaze never left the corpse. The last thing she needed right now was sensationalism, especially if there was a chance Bates was still out there. His history of manipulation and violence weighed heavily on her mind.

The coroner, Dr. Timothy Martin, was a stout figure with a crown of sandy brown hair slightly disheveled from concentration. He adjusted his glasses and proceeded with an unsettling reverence. His hands, encased in latex gloves, moved deftly with surgical tools, peeling back what remained of the dermal layers to expose the singed musculature underneath. The scent of burnt flesh lingered in the air. This was Lawson's least favorite part of her job.

With each incision, Dr. Martin narrated his findings both to Lawson and the nearby recording device, his voice steady despite the grim tableau. "Epidermis entirely carbonized... underlying muscle tissues contracted and distorted..." He paused, examining a particularly damaged section of ribcage before continuing, "Severe thermal damage to the thoracic cavity."

Lawson watched as he extracted a fragment of bone, placing it delicately into a small evidence bag with tweezers. Dr. Martin worked systematically, documenting the extent of the burns, collecting samples, and measuring the depth of tissue destruction.

"Any luck with the ID?" Lawson asked, her voice betraying a hint of urgency.

"Still working on it," Dr. Martin replied without looking up, his focus unbreakable. "This level of damage...it complicates things."

Lawson nodded, her mind racing with the implications. If they couldn't confirm the identity soon, then she worried about how that might affect the town. Not to mention the police had already indicated it was Bates' body that was found in the wreckage.

Bates' inane killing spree had inspired at least one copycat. If he became some specter for the town, she worried that might exacerbate the problem. The notoriety could embolden others looking to make a name for themselves or justify their own twisted actions.

"Normally we use dental records," the coroner continued, speaking almost to himself.

"And how long will it take to get those?" Lawson asked.

Dr. Martin beckoned Lawson to lean in closer, his gloved hand motioning toward the blackened skull. The overhead light cast an unforgiving glare on what remained of the cadaver's face, or rather where the face should have been.

"Normally, we'd have results in about a week," he said.

Lawson's eyes narrowed, impatience lacing her voice. "Normally?"

"Take a look." Dr. Martin gestured towards the remains of the mouth. Most of the teeth were gone, the jawbone exposed and ashen. Only two molars were present, stubbornly clinging to what was left of the subject's jaw.

"Almost all the teeth are missing," he continued, his fingers hovering just above the molars, careful not to disturb the delicate remnants. "That complicates things."

Lawson's stomach churned at the sight. She turned to the coroner, seeking answers she wasn't sure she wanted to hear. "Cause of death? Can we tell if the fire killed him?"

Dr. Martin's lips twitched into a semblance of a smile, a macabre twist given their surroundings. It made Lawson's skin crawl. She never did understand those who could find a home amongst the dead.

"Still trying to figure that out."

He dug his scalpel into the subject, peeling back the charred remains that once formed a human chest.

"Interesting," the doctor muttered, loud enough for Lawson to hear over the hum of the fluorescent lights. "Take a look at this."

Lawson stepped closer, her gaze following his gloved finger to the cavity that housed the lungs. They were a ghastly pale against the soot-blackened thorax, untouched by the smoke that had engulfed the car.

"Clean," he announced. "Almost pristine internally. No signs of soot or smoke inhalation. If the subject died in a fire, normally we'd see signs of smoke inhalation, which would present as black dust or dirt in the lungs."

Lawson's brow creased in thought. "So, this subject didn't die in the fire?"

Dr. Martin shrugged and gave her a grim smile. "My job is just to report to you what I see, Detective. Your job is to tell me what it all means."

Lawson hated when people played games. "And the teeth?" she asked, her voice betraying her annoyance.

He shook his head, the light catching on his glasses as he peered up at her. "Not much to say about two teeth."

"Could you determine if they were removed pre- or postmortem?"

"Impossible to say." He removed his glasses and cleaned them thoughtfully with a cloth from his coat pocket. "The fire has done its job too well."

Lawson nodded, scribbling furiously in her worn notebook. "Do what you can with those molars. Compare them to prison dental records. Maybe you can get a match on a DNA sample as well."

"Will do, but fair warning, it's a long shot."

Lawson offered a tight-lipped smile. "Long shots are my specialty. I'll speak to Mrs. Bates about releasing Anthony's dental records. Might give us a clearer picture."

"Good luck with that. I'd suspect she won't be so keen to help the police these days, either. From what I've heard, she's not the cooperative type."

"Neither am I."

Her eyes lingered on the body one last moment before she turned to leave, the list of unanswered questions growing longer with each step she took.

The outside air seemed even fresher after breathing in the heavy scent of formaldehyde for the better part of an hour.

Lawson slid behind the wheel of her unmarked sedan, the leather seat cool against her back. She tossed the notebook onto the passenger seat, where it landed with a soft thud, its pages rife with scribbled questions and half-formed theories. Her hands gripped the steering wheel, knuckles pale, as she stared at nothing.

Bates was supposed to be dead. That was the easy conclusion, the one that fit neatly into the puzzle of his high-risk lifestyle.

But nothing about this case was turning out to be easy. The lungs were clean—no soot, no smoke. It painted a picture of a body planted postmortem, or a corpse used as a prop.

Cars didn't just go up in flames and teeth didn't just fall out of someone's mouth.

"Damn it," she muttered to herself, feeling the onset of a tension headache. If Bates was indeed the victim, someone wanted to delay identification. But for what?

The detective turned the key in the ignition, and the engine hummed to life. It was clear this wasn't just some random accident. Someone had gone to great lengths to make sure the truth was as scorched and buried as the teeth in that charred skull.

The question now was whether Anthony Bates was truly the man in the ashes—or if someone was playing them all for fools.

chapter
thirty-two

CLAIRE AND FIONA gave each other an awkward hug before parting at the end of their lunch. If nothing else, Claire was happy to at least start the mending process with Fiona. With Daniel out of the picture, she supposed that might be a little bit easier.

Claire decided the office was the last place she wanted to return to today. Hearing that Sarah was a sister of one of Bates' victims had her on edge in a way she hadn't anticipated.

Claire was aware of victim support groups, but she wasn't aware these groups were strongly against her. She had assumed they were neutral, focused on healing and advocacy for victims, not rallying against the legal process. Learning that her name had become a target for their ire was unsettling, a blow she hadn't seen coming. And that wasn't even the *most* disturbing thing she'd learned from Fiona at lunch.

Assuming that her sister was actually telling her the truth and not just trying to freak her out as some sort of prank, then Bates may very well be alive. Or he may have been murdered. Either scenario made the hair on Claire's neck stand up straight. If someone was after Bates, then she could easily be their next target. And if Bates was alive, then she could definitely be *his* next target.

"I seriously need some coffee," Claire said to herself.

She slipped into a café down the street, a short walk from the restaurant, and walked up to the counter to order. The shop was small, but it was a local favorite. A hodgepodge of art from local artists was hung on the exposed brick wall. The owners of the shop clearly had a thing for giraffes because anywhere you looked, you could find the spotted mammal.

A small group of teenagers huddled together in a corner, mostly staring at their phones. A few of them looked up at Claire as she walked in, but Claire tried not to pay attention to them.

"What can I get for you?" the woman at the counter asked Claire.

"Just a latte is great, thanks."

"Any flavors?"

Claire shook her head.

"Name?"

"Claire," and the woman wrote her name in big letters on the cup.

As she waited for her drink, the four teenagers continued to look at their phones and then look at her. Finally, she couldn't take it anymore. She walked over to them, and they all looked up at her, but none of them said anything.

"Is there something I can help you with?" Claire asked.

A girl with short red hair and freckles was the first to respond. "You're Claire Stevens, aren't you? That defense attorney?"

Claire frowned. "Who's asking."

One of the girl's friends reached over and gave her a slight shove on the shoulder. "Miranda, that's totally her. Look." She pushed her phone towards her friend.

The girl, apparently named Miranda, took the phone, looked at the screen, and then at Claire. She stifled a giggle behind her hand, but not very well. "That's pretty unfortunate."

Claire crossed her arms over her chest and was about to ask for the phone when her order was called.

"Latte for Claire."

The teenagers almost burst out laughing as Claire pressed her lips together and walked over to the counter to get her drink. By the time she made her way back to where they were, they had all hurried out of the cafe.

Claire sat down heavily in one of the abandoned seats and pulled out her phone. She grimaced but forced herself to Google her name. It didn't take her long to figure out what the teenagers were laughing about.

At the top of the search results was an article that read, "Legal Eagle or Arson Avenger?"

The article was written in a tabloid-like style and posted on a website known for its sensational—and often untrue—stories. Still, as Claire began to read, the whole thing made her blood boil.

In a shocking twist hotter than a Hollywood scandal, legal maestro Claire Stevens, celebrated for dodging the judicial bullet for her client Anthony Bates, may now be dancing with the devil herself. Allegations are blazing like the fire that consumed her former client, accusing the sassy defender of playing pyromaniac puppet master in the tragic car fire that torched Bates.

Burning questions linger as Stevens now faces her own trial by fire. Did she use her legal prowess to ignite a fiery revenge plot? Sources say Stevens might have cooked up more than just legal briefs as her defense strategy.

As the courtroom drama unfolds, tongues are wagging faster than a Taylor Swift breakup song, and speculation is spreading like wildfire. Is Claire Stevens the legal phoenix rising from the ashes, or did she set the whole damn thing ablaze? Buckle up folks, because this legal saga is heating up faster than a Kardashian Instagram feud! #LawAndOrder-InFlames

Claire blinked at the screen several times before tears welled in her eyes. Her heartbeat raced as she tried to make sense of what she'd just read. The city wasn't the fondest of her after she got Bates acquitted, but this was just a whole new level of uncalled for vitriol.

She wiped the tears from her eyes and stood, keeping her head down and heading for the door. Her phone began to vibrate in her hand. Of all people in the world to call her now, it was Detective

Lawson. She stopped just outside the door, a little apprehensive to even answer.

Naturally, curiosity got the better of her. "This is Claire."

"Claire, it's Detective Lawson."

"How can I help you?" Claire asked, stepping to the side to allow patrons to enter the shop.

"I need you to come by the station."

Claire's stomach dropped. "Detective, you have to know I didn't have anything to do with the fire. That piece is just trying to get the community worked up against me."

"Calm down," Lawson said dismissively. "There's no evidence to suggest you were involved. I couldn't even get a warrant issued for your arrest if I wanted to and you should know that."

Claire breathed out a sigh of relief. Of all people to take her side, the last person she expected was Lawson. "Thanks."

"But I do want to talk to you about Bates. I heard you went to see him before his release. I'm hoping something he said might help piece together what happened to him, but I'd rather do it off the record."

"I can be there in about thirty minutes."

"See you then," Lawson said curtly before breaking the connection.

The police station was a bit of a walk, so Claire opted to get her car from the apartment and drive to the station. On the walk to her apartment, her mind had plenty of time to wander. Should she really be trusting Lawson? What if all of this was just a ploy by the detective to set Claire up to take the fall for Bates' murder—a murder that Lawson herself perpetrated?

After all, Lawson had already obscured the truth about Anthony's car crash during the press conference. She could be calling Claire to the station to feed her information, only to turn on her later. Was Lawson trying to manipulate her? Was she setting her up to look complicit, or was this all part of some larger agenda Claire couldn't yet see?

The closer Claire got to her apartment, the more her mind spun out of control with worry over Lawson's motives. Could she really trust a detective who seemed to appear at every critical moment but offered few real answers? Was Lawson genuinely trying to solve the case, or was she protecting someone—or something—bigger than either of them?

As she drove to the station, she reminded herself that she just needed to stay vigilant. The chances that Lawson was behind the threats to Daniel, Bates' disappearance, and Claire's letter were thin, but they existed. Her gut told her Lawson wasn't innocent in all of this, even if her exact role remained unclear.

After arriving, Claire waited in the lobby of the police station, working on biting one particularly stubborn nail. Her visits to Lawson were becoming her least favorite hobby of late, given that she was never quite certain how they would turn out. The detective's attitude seemed a little volatile, especially when it came to Claire. Unless, of course, she needed something from Claire. Then, she was marginally tolerable.

"Ms. Stevens." Claire heard the detective call her name from just past the front desk. She stood and met Lawson half-way, the two of them shaking hands awkwardly. "Thanks for coming."

"Sure," replied Claire, uncertainty coating her words. She started to walk toward the familiar conference room, but Lawson stopped her.

"Actually," the detective said, pausing before they reached the doorway, "I'd like to take a little field trip."

Claire furrowed her brows. "To?"

"The morgue."

Claire blinked a few times before she finally registered what Lawson said. "The morgue?"

Lawson nodded her head. "Yes."

"Why?"

"We can talk on the way. I'll drive." Lawson gestured for Claire to follow her further into the station. "I'm parked in the back."

Claire hesitated before finally following the detective. She reminded herself that she was a lawyer, after all. If Lawson was trying to pull something to get Claire to incriminate herself, Claire was mostly confident she'd be able to spot it.

Lawson led her down a long, sterile hallway with white vinyl flooring before they finally exited through an unmarked steel door. She pressed the button on the key fob and an older, blue Crown Victoria nearby unlocked. Claire looked at the car with a bit of a frown.

"Were you expecting something different?" Lawson asked her as they climbed inside.

As Claire buckled her seatbelt, she looked around the interior. The only real thing that made it seem like a police car was the laptop mounted to the center console and the extra radio wires trailing here and there.

Claire shrugged. "Not sure I really expected anything. Just happy you asked me to sit in the front of the car, and not the back."

Lawson chuckled. "There's still time."

chapter
thirty-three

THE STERILE SMELL of the morgue burned the back of Claire's nose as she stared down at the charred remains on the cold metal table.

"What am I supposed to be looking at?" she asked Lawson, her voice barely a whisper.

The blackened, twisted figure barely resembled anything human. Its limbs were contorted in unnatural angles, the flesh charred and falling away from the bone. The face, or what was left of it, seemed to have an eerie grin frozen in place.

Before Lawson could answer, the coroner walked in clad in a white lab coat and a friendly smile. Off-putting, given the circumstances.

"Hello," he said, extending his hand for Claire to shake. "I'm Dr. Timothy Martin. You're looking at the human remains of a middle-aged man who was severely engulfed in flames."

Lawson looked a tad bit annoyed, but she thanked the coroner anyway. "Dr. Martin, could you give Claire and me a few moments alone?"

"Actually, it's against protocol to leave anyone else alone with the subject," Dr. Martin said, hesitating. "We need to reduce any chance of tampering with evidence."

"Trust me, doctor, I have no intention of tampering with evidence for my own investigation." Lawson sighed, her tone firm yet reassuring.

Claire resisted the urge to make a face. In her estimation, Lawson had the sort of ethical compass that could *exactly* lead to tampering with evidence. Claire also didn't like the idea of being alone in the room with the detective and, presumably, a murder victim. Claire imagined a scenario where her DNA was found on the body and what that could lead to.

"I don't see any harm in the doctor staying," Claire replied.

Lawson gave Claire an exasperated look. "The doctor is very busy," Lawson said in a terse tone. "We don't want to take up too much of his time."

"I may work mostly with dead people, but I can still read a room." The doctor stepped out, leaving the two women alone with the grisly sight.

Claire's mind raced as she tried to make sense of the situation. Her stomach churned as she tried to piece together what this could mean for the case, for Bates, and for herself. The overwhelming weight of not knowing pressed down on her, leaving her desperate for clarity in the midst of chaos. She looked between the charred remains and Lawson, her eyes pleading for some sort of explanation.

"Do you recognize this body?" Lawson asked.

Claire looked between the body and the detective, trying to keep her voice from wavering. "Is this a trick question?"

"No, it's not," Lawson said firmly. "This was the body found at the scene of Bates' car accident."

"You mean, this is Bates?"

Lawson shrugged. "I've spent a considerable amount of time with these remains. I'm sure it's him, but technically speaking, we haven't confirmed it yet."

"How is that even possible?" Claire asked, incredulous.

"Someone went to great efforts to obscure the identity of the body." Lawson pointed to the skull, where only two teeth remained. "For example, someone pulled out the rest of the teeth. Dr. Martin also mentioned the flames were much hotter than they should have been, completely charring the body. It suggests interference. So on the off chance we get matching dental records based on two teeth, and with no fingerprints to speak of, we can't confirm for sure whether Bates is dead, despite what the media is saying."

Claire's stomach dropped as she processed Lawson's words. The thought of Bates still being alive sent shivers down her spine. "Do you mean Bates could still be alive?"

Lawson's expression was unreadable, but she responded, "No."

"You're just saying that, though. You just said you don't have evidence."

Lawson looked a tad exasperated. "I know this is your first foray in criminal law, but I've been doing this for quite some time. I don't need a pathologist to confirm that this is Bates."

Claire shook her head, unable to accept Lawson's response. "But there's no way to really know for sure. Isn't that why you called me here?"

"Not exactly," Lawson said. "You were one of the last people to see him and speak with him at length during the appeal. I thought maybe you might be able to recall something he said that might help guide us in the right direction."

"What do you mean by that?'" Claire asked.

Lawson stared at the body for some time. "Like I said, someone interfered. Given Bates' record, it's highly unlikely that this was some sort of suicide. Even less likely when you factor in the teeth situation." Lawson shook her head. "Someone wanted this man dead. He was murdered. I'm sure of it."

Claire closed her eyes, trying to block out the horrific image before her as she recalled her encounter with Bates before the appeal. His chilling smile, the intensity in his eyes, and the unsettling feeling he left her with all came flooding back. She tried to remember if he'd said anything helpful, but she was drawing a blank.

She opened her eyes and forced herself to look at the charred remains, feeling the bile rise in her throat once more. "Nothing comes to mind. But when I return home, I'll look through my notes from the interview."

What Claire didn't say was that even if she were to remember anything useful, she wouldn't have told it to Lawson without thinking it over first. She really didn't trust the detective. Lawson bringing her here to look at the remains by themselves only made her even more wary.

Lawson's gaze never left the remains. "Thank you, Claire."

As they exited the morgue, the cold air outside was a relief compared to the atmosphere inside the sterile room. Claire shivered and wrapped her arms around herself, trying to steady her nerves.

"Do you have any leads at all?" she asked Lawson, seeking to distract herself from the dark thoughts swirling in her mind.

Lawson didn't look at Claire, her brow furrowed in concentration. "No."

"God," Claire muttered. "I know you're convinced that Bates is dead, and that that's him in there, but I don't know if I am. And I hate the idea that he might still be alive."

Lawson gave her a quizzical look. "I'm sorry Claire, but did you just infer that you'd prefer Bates to be dead?"

Claire's breath hitched as she realized what that sounded like. She put her hands up in front of her. "No, it's not that. The uncertainty must be so difficult for his family to go through." Claire felt a flicker of guilt as she used the family's struggles to mask her own conflicted feelings. She didn't want to admit, even to herself, that a part of her had felt relief when she first heard about Bates' death. Admitting it to Lawson—someone she already suspected of ulterior motives—was out of the question.

Lawson studied Claire, as if considering her words and weighing their implications. The scrutiny sent a chill down Claire's spine, and she felt the urge to distance herself from the detective. She already thought Lawson might want to set her up. She really didn't need to give her any ammunition to do so.

"Erin, I really need to get back home," she said, her voice cracking slightly. "There's a lot I need to do."

"Of course." Lawson's gaze still lingered on Claire just a moment longer before they both climbed into the car and drove back to the station in silence.

CLAIRE'S HAND trembled as she unlocked the door to her apartment, each click of the tumbler echoing her mounting anxiety. The weight of what she had learned from Lawson pressed on her chest, making it difficult to breathe. Her heart raced as she considered the possibility that Bates could still be alive. When Fiona mentioned it in the cafe, it didn't seem like an actual possibility. Now seeing what Lawson claimed was Bates, the reality of the situation was sinking in.

Was he staging his own death to resume his gruesome killing spree?

She made her way over to the corner of her kitchen where she'd stashed anything Bates-related, but not before grabbing a glass of water to down one of the pills Meredith had given her. She figured if there was ever a time to take anxiety pills, it was after seeing the charred remains of your former client and potential stalker. She'd been given a prescription for them after leaving New York, and she had to admit they did help a bit. She wondered how frantic she would feel without them.

She looked down at the white cardboard in the corner of the kitchen. She really did not want to reopen this file box, but she also didn't want to delay. If she did have something that could help Lawson, she wanted to hand it over and fast.

She rummaged through the clutter until she found the notebook from the day she'd interviewed Bates. She began to flip through the pages. Her mind raced back to the interview, the memory chilling. She shivered involuntarily as she recalled Bates' unsettling comments–how she reminded him of his mother, the way he'd noted the scent of her perfume. It made her skin crawl, and she wished more than anything that she'd never taken on the case when Dolores first approached her.

"Why didn't I say no?" she asked herself.

Claire's heart pounded in her chest, the silence of the apartment amplifying her unease. Her fingers trembled as she flipped through the pages of the notebook, desperate for answers. Then, a knock at the door caused her to jump.

"Who could that be?" she whispered to herself, closing the notebook and standing slowly up. As she approached the door, her mind raced with possibilities. Was it Lawson? A neighbor?

Peering through the peephole, she saw no one. Hesitant, she cracked open the door, scanning the hallway for any sign of movement. Still nothing. She was about to close the door when her eyes caught sight of a small, unmarked box on the floor.

"Maybe it's just a package," she told herself, trying to quell her anxiety. But she couldn't shake the overwhelming sense of dread. Against her better judgment, she picked up the box and took it inside, placing it on the kitchen counter.

"Okay, Claire... just open it." She took a deep breath, her hands shaking as she slowly lifted the lid. Horror took over. The second gift, customary to the murders was something personal to the victim.

Inside, nestled among crumpled pink tissue paper, was a bottle of her favorite perfume: Sweet Pea.

chapter
thirty-four

LAWSON SHOVED her key into the lock, turning hard until the thing finally gave way with a click. She pressed her shoulder into the door to give it an extra nudge. The damn thing always stuck to the swollen doorframe. She'd told the landlord about it countless times but had long-since given up on expecting him to fix it.

Her apartment greeted her with a blend of stale air and a mustiness permanently etched into the walls. It'd been so long since she'd spent more than just a few hours here to catch some sleep.

Flicking on the light, she took in the living room that doubled as a dining area, both spaces sharing the same look of neglect. The sofa, an outdated plaid she'd found at a thrift store, looked even older than she remembered.

A glance toward the kitchen revealed a counter full of empty beer bottles, a testament to how her sobriety had all but disappeared. She'd fought a difficult battle to get sober the first time. She wasn't sure that she was up to the task again.

"Home sweet home," she muttered under her breath. She stepped inside and slumped her shoes off, letting her bag drop to the floor.

The place really didn't feel much like home anymore. Not that any place did. If anything, she felt more comfortable at the precinct, with its constant hum of activity, ringing phones, and the aroma of burnt coffee and copier toner. Even when she was alone in her office, there were always people around. Here, the four walls seemed to shrink in on her the longer she was alone.

Lawson made her way to the fridge and pulled it open. She blinked against the harsh light as she looked inside. A couple cans of beer huddled next to a Chinese takeout box that she knew better than to open. Aside from that, emptiness.

She sighed and snagged a can of beer. Her fingers traced the label as she settled onto the sofa, a plume of dust rising against her weight. As she cracked open the can, she felt the guilt well up inside of her.

"Damn job," she whispered, tipping the can to her lips. With every gulp, the guilt gnawed more and more at her, but she couldn't stop herself from drinking the cursed liquid. She preferred the guilt over the relentless pressure from her badge.

The sun was setting outside, casting eerie shadows on the walls, as she got up to get her second can. Sitting back down in the same spot, she let her mind drift to Bates. The whole situation was grating on her.

The entire appeal and the way it had been handled had been a giant slap in the face to her credibility. As far as Lawson was concerned, the only reason she was even speaking to Claire Stevens was because the woman might be able to help her solve this new mystery surrounding the cursed man.

The woman's entire appeal hinged on Bates' unlawful confession. Sure, Claire had couched it in terms of an error of the trial court to admit it into evidence. But at the end of the day, the real error, so she'd argued, had been the way Lawson extracted Bates' confession.

Lawson crumpled the empty beer can in her fist and stopped herself from throwing it against the wall. The only saving grace to all of this was that Claire didn't come out so clean from the appeal, either. The media had its fun poking at Lawson for the few days after the appeal. But all of that stopped when Lawson had managed to apprehend the Bates copycat relatively quickly.

Of course, the real issue confronting Lawson now was Bates' killer. So many people had wanted him dead. Lawson chuckled to herself. Even perfect-miss-Claire admitted she'd rather him be six feet under.

As if on cue, Lawson's phone buzzed. She fished it from where it had fallen out of her pocket in between the sofa cushions. She squinted at the caller-ID: Claire Stevens. Lawson very nearly didn't pick up, but then she remembered Claire promised to look through her notes from her last encounter with Bates. It's possible that what she was calling with would be useful.

"Hello?" Lawson answered.

"Something's happened," Claire said, her words tumbling over each other, rushed and frantic. "I came home to it, the bottle, the box."

"Slow down," Lawson interrupted. "What's going on?"

"Right after I got home, there was a knock at my door.....it's a bottle of perfume. Just sitting there, in an unmarked box, no one around."

Lawson could hear Claire's labored breathing through the phone.

"Perfume?" she repeated, her confusion genuine. "I'm sorry, Claire, but you lost me."

"An unmarked package, delivered right to my door. No one there when I opened it. Just the box. You remember, don't you? What Bates would do?"

"Claire, I..."

"The second gift. It was always something personal to his victim. It's Bates, Lawson. It has to be."

"Anthony Bates is dead," Lawson said flatly.

"You don't know that!" Claire almost yelled through the phone. "That body lying in the morgue could be anyone!"

Lawson shook her head, unable to contain her annoyance. "Anyone could have sent it, Claire. You're not exactly the most popular right now. Maybe it was even just a friend who forgot to leave a note."

"No friends," Claire said. "Who would know that's my favorite perfume?"

Lawson rolled her eyes. "I don't know, people who are around you? Maybe you mentioned it to someone?"

"Bates. He commented on it in the interview."

"What?" Lawson asked.

" He commented on my perfume."

Lawson rubbed at her temple, feeling the onset of a headache. "Like I said, maybe a friend."

"My friends don't send me gifts like this," Claire insisted, the fear and anger evident in her voice. "You can't tell me you're one hundred percent sure that Bates is dead."

Lawson nearly growled in frustration. "I don't need a signed confession from the Grim Reaper himself to know a corpse when I see one."

"Then explain the perfume!"

"Listen, Claire," Lawson said, her tone flat. "I can't chase shadows with you tonight. I just don't have the energy for it. I get that you're probably a little shaken up from seeing the body, but a bottle of perfume doesn't mean anything. If you have actual information you think might help with the Bates homicide, call me tomorrow at the office."

"If I'm still alive by tomorrow," Claire said, her jaw clearly clenched on the other end.

"Drop it, Claire," Lawson said. "Bates isn't coming for you because Anthony Bates is dead. End of story."

Lawson ended the call before Claire could respond and switched the phone on airplane mode. She could do without any more calls for the evening. With a sigh, she dragged herself up off the couch to grab a third beer from the fridge.

Falling back into the couch, she clicked the top off the beer and started the bad habit of hers. Opening the photo app, she started scrolling through her photo reel, reliving memories that should be as dead as Bates.

"Here's to you," she muttered as an image of her old partner lit up the screen. She tipped the can in a silent toast before taking a long, deep gulp that did nothing to relieve the ache in her chest.

Her eyes remained on the image. The beer grew warmer in her hand as time seemed to stand still. Lawson found herself sinking deeper and deeper into the sofa, the darkness of sleep mixing with the alcohol just enough to bend reality and crack open the floodgates of her memory.

"Oh, God, no!" she had screamed upon hearing the gunshot.

It was dark, but the flood light illuminated directly behind the perpetrator. It made it impossible to get a good visual. But what she could see clearly was her partner's body drop to the floor.

Lawson had run over to her, her hands trying to apply pressure to a wound that seemed to gush crimson the harder she pressed.

"I've got a 10-999," she cried frantically into her radio. "Officer down. Send help immediately."

The dispatch's response didn't even register. All that mattered to her was the woman bleeding out in front of her. She was more than a colleague, and more than a partner. No one else in the unit knew the two were something more to one another. No one else needed to know.

Lawson blinked, trying to dispel the tears that had welled in her eyes. The apartment was dark now, the sun having set as she stumbled down memory lane. She took another swig of beer, hoping the liquid would stop the memories that were consuming her, but it only seemed to make it worse.

She remembered the days after the incident. How her badge felt heavier each day. No one could give her any information as to who was responsible for her partner's death. So Lawson had taken it upon herself to find out, growing frustrated when the leads led nowhere.

That frustration led her moral compass to spin wildly. She started crossing lines no officer should. Drinking more to try and forget. Each day she fell further and further from her oath, yet no closer to finding out her partner's killer.

She crushed the empty beer can in her hand, feeling that familiar surge of rage as she recalled when she'd received notice of her suspension. Richardson had told her she was lucky to only receive a suspension.

"Use the time to get sober," he had said to her. "Your badge will be waiting for you when you get back."

Lawson scoffed. Maybe she should have just walked away from all of it right then and there. Gotten a job at Starbucks or something that didn't cause her to spiral daily. She tossed the can onto the carpet, too tired to put it in the trash.

Her fingers fumbled with the power button on her phone as she kicked her feet up onto the sofa. The screen glowed and then went black, and she threw it onto the coffee table.

With a weary sigh, she closed her eyes and let the darkness wrap around her. Maybe in her dreams she could chase down the ghosts that haunted her waking hours.

Her breaths grew shallow and her consciousness slipped. Images of her old partner blurred with the charred remains of Anthony Bates on a metal table. And then, finally, she drifted off to sleep, her body succumbing to exhaustion.

chapter
thirty-five

THE PHONE CLICKED dead in her hand, and Claire's grip tightened until her knuckles whitened. She tossed the device onto the desk with a clatter. Lawson, with her damned practicality and infuriating calm, had once again ignored Claire's instincts.

"Unbelievable," she muttered to herself, pacing the length of her living room. The detective might as well have patted her on the head and told her to run along and play while the grown-ups handled the real detective work. The nerve! Anthony Bates was still out there. Claire was certain of it. And here she was, feeling like the only one seeing through the fog.

She stopped short, considering her next move. Her sister was a journalist with a nose for scandal and a penchant for stirring the pot. Claire was sure that if she let it slip to Fiona that Bates' body hadn't been clearly identified, it would be all over the front page of tomorrow's news.

Her fingers hovered above her phone, an itch in her brain compelling her to call her sister. But her brain had her resisting. Once that bell was rung, there was no un-ringing it. If she needed Lawson down the line, that would be one hell of a bridge torched and left smoldering in her wake.

She exhaled slowly, dropping her hand and raking it through her hair in frustration. Maybe Lawson was right. Maybe it wasn't Bates who'd sent her the gift. But, if not him, then who?

Claire was far too spun up to even think about sleep. What she needed to think about was who else might have sent her the bottle. Who knew her well enough...?

Her mind began to rifle through the Rolodex of faces—friends, colleagues, fleeting acquaintances. But none of it seemed quite right. Her favorite perfume was highly personal. Whoever sent it had to know her in an intimate capacity.

Her sister would know the fragrance, of course. They shared everything growing up—clothes, makeup, secrets. But would Fiona really pull a prank like this on her sister? Claire knew their relationship had soured, but she felt good about today's lunch. For her sister to try and mess with her mental health in such a drastic way would be low, even at their worst moments.

Could it be Lawson? Claire had already suspected her of threatening Daniel and maybe of even sending her the letter. She shook her head. How would Lawson know her favorite perfume? The woman didn't strike her as someone who frequented Bath and Body Works regularly.

She brushed Erin Lawson aside as Jamie's image crept into her thoughts unbidden. Claire was still a bit bitter over the breakup. They hadn't spoken since things had ended.

Jamie certainly would have known Claire's favorite perfume if he'd paid attention. He'd been to her apartment a few times. Stayed over once or twice. She kept the bottle right on the bathroom counter, beside the sink. It was hard to miss, if you were looking for it.

But why send a bottle of perfume if they were over? Was this some warped attempt at an olive branch? Or was he trying to prove a point that Claire had made a mistake in taking the case?

The idea sent a shiver down her spine. Jamie was many things—stubborn, passionate, even reckless—but to frighten her? That was new territory. An attempt at a makeup gone awry didn't quite fit either. They were beyond the point of salvaging anything.

With a heavy sigh, she sank into her sofa and massaged her temples, her mind spinning with the scent of the mystery perfume still lingering in the air. The Jamie theory was a stretch. She needed something concrete, someone closer to her everyday life.

She played back her recent interactions and that's when it hit her. Her new assistant, Sarah. Her comment about how lovely her office smelled, compared to the rest of the place. Claire had shared the name of the fragrance without a second thought.

Sarah, who belonged to the victims' support group with a bone to pick with Claire's courtroom victory.

The room spun a little as anxiety nibbled away at Claire's composure. " Sarah had access to Claire's personal information through the firm's computer system. She also would have known about the sorts of gifts Bates sent to his victims, given that her sister was one of them.

It wouldn't be hard for her to send an unmarked gift to Claire's doorstep if she were properly motivated. It was a bit brazen, but entirely within the realm of possibility for someone with an axe to grind.

The more Claire thought about it, the more she was convinced that Sarah could be the culprit. It made no sense for a woman like that to want to work for the very attorney who'd successfully appealed her sister's killer.

Claire was entirely too ramped up to sleep. She rummaged through her purse until her fingers closed around an oblong pill case. It had been some time since she'd needed to take an Ambien. In fact, her original prescription had been given to her during her senior year of high school.

"Sweet dreams or no dreams," she quipped to the silence of her apartment before swallowing the small white tablet.

THE SUN HAD BARELY BEGUN to rise when Claire walked through the doors of office. The clock on the wall ticked with an unrelenting rhythm as she planted herself firmly by Sarah's desk, her eyes narrowing as she awaited the inevitable confrontation.

Her sleep had been dreamless last night, but she had still awoken early and anxious. As she got ready for the day, she had decided the best course of action was to confront Sarah first thing in the morning. There was no way she would be able to work around the woman until she got some answers.

Besides, this gave her the perfect opportunity to do it in a public space. The secretaries' desks were mostly clumped together in the main area, so Claire resolved to have the conversation out in the open, where everyone could hear.

As Claire waited, a few of the other employees began to filter through the doors. Janet gave Claire a bit of a confused look.

"Good morning," she said, stopping in front of Claire.

"Hi," Claire responded, not really wanting to engage in any back and forth.

"I don't think Sarah's here yet," Janet commented, clearly confused by Claire's presence.

"I see that."

" I can let her know you're looking for her. I'm sure you're quite busy. No need for you to just wait around."

Claire gave Janet a forced smile. "I'm good here, thanks."

Janet sighed and walked away, muttering something about "stubborn attorneys," as she made her way to the coffee machine.

"Hello Janet," Claire heard Sarah say a little way down the hall.

Claire's heartrate picked up upon hearing the woman approach. Even though Claire was an attorney, she actually hated this sort of confrontation.

"Good luck," was Janet's greeting to the girl.

Sarah approached her desk with a confused look on her face. Upon seeing Claire, she startled a little but recovered quickly.

"Good morning, Claire. Is there something I can do for you?"

Her voice was sugary sweet and the more Claire watched her unpack her belongings, the more she was convinced that Sarah was hiding her true intentions behind a fake exterior.

"Actually, yes," Claire said, deciding not to exchange pleasantries. "About the perfume bottle."

"Perfume?" Sarah's brow furrowed as she switched on her computer and took a seat. "I have no idea what you're talking about, Claire."

"Cut the crap, Sarah," Claire shot back. Sarah froze and Claire could hear a few gasps from further back in the office, but she didn't care. "I'm really not interested in hearing your lies."

"Really, I don't—"

Claire leaned forward over Sarah's desk. "You're a member of that victims' support group, aren't you? The one that's been after my hide since the Bates appeal?"

Sarah shifted in her seat, discomfort etching lines into her face, tears welling in her eyes. " I am."

"Then why on earth would you want to work for me?" Claire's question hung heavily between them. "I'm the woman who helped acquit the man accused of killing your sister."

Sarah's hands clenched into fists in her lap, her confused and sad look starting to lift as she finally understood what was happening.

"This isn't appropriate, Claire," she murmured, looking down at her hands. Her voice was a whisper, but still carried a hint of indignation.

"What's not appropriate is you trying to scare me by sending me an unmarked personal gift. Did the group put you up to this? Did they think it would be funny to make me feel the same terror as your sister?"

"I don't feel comfortable discussing this here," Sarah responded, still not looking up.

"Comfortable? I could honestly care less about your comfort level right now."

Sarah stood and for the first time looked Claire straight in the eyes. "I'm sorry, but I'm not going to sit here and take this from you."

As Claire held the woman's gaze for a moment, her confidence that Sarah was actually the one responsible for the unmarked package began to waver.

Sarah brushed past her, leaving Claire sitting there. The office was deadly quiet as Claire looked around the room. Everyone was staring at her in disbelief.

Her frustration boiling over, she put her head down and tried to make her way back to her office.

"Claire," came Bob's booming voice over the quiet just as Claire was going to close herself in. "A word."

chapter
thirty-six

CLAIRE STARTLED as Bob barged into her office, his usual jovial demeanor replaced with a stern glare. "Sit down."

Claire lowered herself into the chair opposite her desk, pulse racing. Bob's friendly smile was nowhere to be seen today. He had apparently even abandoned his cup of coffee for this conversation.

He slammed the door behind him. "What the hell was that out there?"

Claire swallowed, her mouth dry. More than anything she wanted to tell Bob everything she had been experiencing since Bates' acquittal, but she knew that would be foolish. From the outside looking in, people didn't seem to understand.

Before Claire could respond, Bob continued. "Because it looked an awful lot like you just harassed one of my employees. You better have a damn good explanation, or I can't guarantee your job is safe, Claire."

"I just found out Sarah's sister was one of Bates' victims," Claire said. "It...it made me uncomfortable."

Bob's eyes narrowed. "So you thought that gave you the right to attack her? And publicly? Why not have a conversation with her in your office? Would you like me to have this conversation with you out in the open?"

"No, of course not," Claire replied, shaking her head. "It's just...Sarah is part of this victim's rights group that's been very vocal against me. I guess I got paranoid she was targeting me."

Claire bit her lip. She couldn't tell Bob about the letter, the gift. He'd think she was crazy.

"I received a strange package," she said instead. "I thought maybe Sarah sent it to rattle me. That maybe the group had put her up to it." Even as Claire said the words, she wasn't sure she believed them anymore.

Claire held her breath, searching Bob's face. The last thing she wanted was trouble with her job. If anything, her job was the only thing that helped to occupy her time and keep her mind off her personal life.

Bob sighed, running a hand through his salt and pepper hair. "Look, I knew about Sarah's history when I hired her. But that doesn't disqualify someone from a job."

Claire's eyes widened in surprise. "Why would you hire her then? As *my* assistant?"

"Because she had a damn good reason for wanting to work here," Bob said pointedly. "She wants to help other victims like her sister and make sure they get justice. I can respect that motivation."

"I really think this should have been disclosed to me ahead of time."

"I presumed you would do your own investigation when she was assigned to you. And that if there were any issues, you would come to me like a professional and voice them. I certainly didn't expect this sort of behavior from you."

Claire looked down at her lap, chastened. She should have known Bob would see the good in hiring Sarah. He was just like that. In a way, maybe that's the only reason she had gotten a job here, as well.

"I still don't see the logic in her working for me, specifically."

"She wasn't the one who asked to work for you. I assigned her to you, and she didn't object. I thought it would be good for the both of you. She could learn that there's more to a defense lawyer than the cases they work on, and you could benefit from humanizing your work."

Claire didn't say anything. She wasn't sure how to respond. Bob was far too idealistic for her liking and she still felt it should have been disclosed to her ahead of time. But he was never going to agree with her on that point, so it made no sense to argue with him.

"I doubt Sarah is the type to send threats or play games," Bob continued. "If you're really being harassed, you need to go to the police. Not take it out on your coworkers."

Claire shifted in her seat. "I did notify the police. But they're not doing much about it."

Bob shook his head. "Then you need to be patient and let them handle it. I know Bates' death has you on edge. But lashing out at his victims' families won't help."

Bob's demeanor softened and he put a hand on Claire's shoulder. "Why don't you take some time off? This case was hard on you. Get some rest."

Claire opened her mouth to argue but Bob cut her off.

"It's not up for discussion. I don't want to see you back here for two weeks. Daniel can handle your cases while you're gone."

Claire slumped back, defeated. Two weeks away from the only thing that kept her mind occupied and her body out of the apartment. She felt much safer in public, surrounded by people. In her mind, having a predictable routine made her less of a target, as it created the sense that others were always aware of her whereabouts.

It seemed unbearable. But one look at Bob's stoic face told her arguing was futile.

She had no choice but to accept his mandated time off. Even if it killed her.

CLAIRE PUSHED through the heavy glass doors of the office building, the bright midday sun momentarily blinding her. She blinked against the glare, adjusting the heavy bag of files slung over her shoulder. A hollow pang in her stomach reminded her she hadn't eaten since the bagel she'd scarfed down as she rushed out of her apartment, intent on beating everyone to the office.

She wondered if her job would still be there in two weeks when she was scheduled to return. Lawyers pulled that crap all the time—suspending someone under murky circumstances and then silently removing their position while they were gone. Sneaky and underhanded, but that was the legal world for you.

Claire pulled out her phone, shielding the screen from the sun with her hand. An earlier text from Meredith was waiting for her.

Haven't heard from you in a bit. Free for lunch?

Claire tapped out a quick reply.

I know it's short notice, but if you're still free I could meet up.

Meredith's response was instant.

Just finishing up a case then I'm free. Anywhere downtown work for you?

They settled on a hole-in-the-wall deli neither of them had tried before. The heavy bag of files dug into her shoulder on the way over, and she briefly considered stopping back home to drop them off. When her stomach rumbled again, she decided to make her way straight to the deli.

A few blocks' walk and Claire pushed open the door of the deli, a bell jingling overhead. The place was narrow, with a long counter running along the left and a few small tables crammed together on the right. The scent of roasted meat and fresh bread had her mouth watering. Her stomach rumbled loudly.

She chose a table in the back corner and slid into the chair, setting her overstuffed bag on the floor with a thump. While she waited for Meredith, she scrolled through her phone. An unanswered text from her dad glowed on the screen.

Hey kiddo, how are you holding up?

Claire hesitated. Bob would call her dad—if he hadn't already—to tattle about her "episode." But she couldn't bring herself to tell her father she'd been suspended. She ignored the text for now. She didn't have the mental energy to figure out how to respond.

"Claire!"

Meredith breezed through the entrance, red hair swirling around her shoulders and the sunlight behind the door illuminating her like a halo. Meredith slid into the chair opposite her with an easy grin.

"Hey you," Claire said, trying and failing to match her enthusiasm.

Meredith's forehead creased. "You okay? You look wiped."

Claire sighed, rubbing her temples. "I had a shit morning at work. Ended up getting suspended for two weeks."

"What? Even after you won them the appeal? Ungrateful bastards." She shook her head. "What happened?"

Claire gave a weak smile at Meredith's attempt to cheer her up. "I found out my assistant, Sarah, is part of some victims' support group. Pretty sure it was them that sent me the perfume bottle."

Meredith's eyebrows shot up. "Perfume bottle? What are you talking about?"

"I guess I forgot to tell you about that." She leaned forward, lowering her voice. "Yesterday Detective Lawson asked me to identify a burnt body they think is Bates. But I'm not convinced it's actually him."

"Why not?" Meredith asked, intrigued.

"The body was too damaged to ID. But here's the extra weird part - someone removed all the teeth. And the pathologist said that the temperature of the fire indicated it wasn't just a standard car fire."

"Holy shit. You really think it's not him?"

Claire shook her head firmly. "Lawson says she's sure it's him, but I'm not. And then, when I got back to my apartment last night, I got an unmarked package delivered to my door. Inside was a bottle of my favorite perfume."

Meredith shook her head, her expression confused. "I don't understand."

"Bates sent his victims gifts," Claire explained, sitting back. "The second gift was always something personal to the victim."

Meredith looked a little worried. "Didn't you say the first gift was a letter of admiration?"

Claire nodded. "Yeah. So, either Bates is still alive and he sent me that bottle, or the group put Sarah up to it. She would have my address. It makes sense."

"Well, she *and* Lawson have your address," Meredith pointed out.

Claire grimaced. She hadn't considered whether the detective could be behind the second gift. It wouldn't have been hard for Lawson to get

Claire's address and plant the bottle at her door. But why would Lawson do something like that?

"I don't blame you for asking Sarah about it," Meredith continued. "I'd be pretty shaken up, too."

Claire shoved the concern about Lawson aside. "Maybe I could have gone about it in a better way, but I still think I was right to confront her. And so Bob suspended me."

Meredith reached over and squeezed her hand. "You've had a lot to deal with—seeing that body, all the questions surrounding it, and everything else this case has thrown at you. It's no wonder you're shaken." She gave Claire a small, reassuring smile. "This whole thing stinks worse than Bob's coffee breath."

Despite everything, Claire chuckled.

"I tried to explain it to him," Claire continued. "I mean I left out the part about the letter, but I told him I thought the group put Sarah up to it to rattle me."

"What'd he say to that?"

"He told me to go to the police." Claire scoffed. "Which I've done. I told Lawson about the perfume bottle, but she brushed me off. Said I was being paranoid, and that Bates is dead."

Meredith clicked her tongue in disapproval. "That's ridiculous. There's clearly something strange going on here."

"But what can I do? The cops have already made up their minds."

Meredith thought for a moment, her forehead creased in concentration. "Maybe you could go to someone above Lawson? Or try talking to another detective?"

Claire shook her head. "They'll just refer me back to her. Once cops decide you're a nutjob, there's no changing their minds."

Meredith chuckled lightly. "Yeah, you're probably right." She absently ran her finger along the edge of the menu. "What are you going to do with your time off then?"

"No idea." Claire hunched over the table. "Normally work consumes my life, so I'm not sure what to do with myself."

Meredith's eyes lit up with an idea. "This could be good for you,

Claire! A chance to do something fun, something you've always wanted to try but never had time for."

Claire just stared at her friend with a blank expression.

"Oh come on. Isn't there anything you've been wanting to do outside of work? Take up a new hobby? A trip somewhere exotic? Maybe getting out of town would be good for you!"

Claire wracked her brain but came up empty. "I really have no clue. My career has been my sole focus since law school."

Meredith patted her hand. "That's okay. Just take some time and think about it. Come up with at least one fun thing to do, okay? You deserve it."

"Alright, alright," Claire conceded with a small smile. "I'll try to come up with something."

"Good." Meredith flagged down a waiter. "Now let's order some food. I'm starving."

chapter
thirty-seven

AS CLAIRE SAID her goodbyes to Meredith and started her walk back to her apartment, she realized that maybe Meredith was right. Claire really hadn't taken much time to relax after the appeal. Maybe a good getaway was what she needed to help put all of this behind her.

She slowed as she passed the law library. She hadn't seen Joy since the appeal and she felt a bit bad about that, especially since the woman had even trudged all her files back over to the firm. Given that she was currently in an unemployed state with nowhere to really go, she decided to stop in and pay her friend a visit.

Claire pushed open the heavy oak doors of the library, the familiar scent of old books washing over her. She spotted Joy behind the receptionist counter, her bright blonde hair brushing her shoulders as she sorted through a stack of papers.

"Hey stranger," Claire said, walking up to the counter. "Long time no see."

Joy's head snapped up, her eyes lighting up behind her dark-rimmed glasses. "Claire!" Her smile was genuine, and she rushed around the desk for a hug.

As the two embraced, Claire realized the feeling that someone was actually happy to see her felt odd these days. It was a nice reprieve from everything else going on in her life.

L.T. Ryan & Laura Chase

"How have you been?" Joy asked, pulling away and searching Claire's face. "How have you been holding up?"

Claire figured Joy meant, "how are you holding up after finding out the man you just got acquitted is dead?"

"Oh, you know." She shrugged, suddenly interested in a chipped edge on the counter. "Taking it one day at a time."

In some ways, Claire didn't have the heart to tell Joy just how messed up everything had been since the appeal. On the other hand, Claire very much wanted to divulge everything to a woman she considered one of her few friends.

"I'm sure everything has been so overwhelming for you," Joy said. She leaned in and whispered, "especially regarding the news about Bates."

Claire debated telling Joy about the unidentified body that may or may not belong to Bates. She knew Lawson wanted to keep this under wraps right now, but she wasn't particularly fond of the detective of late. Besides, Joy was a trustworthy friend. Maybe she could provide some insight.

Claire motioned for Joy to follow her into the study room they had used to work on the case. The irony of the location wasn't lost on Claire.

"The cops found a body in Bates' car," she told her friend. "But they haven't been able to make a positive identification yet."

Joy's mouth fell open. " What happened?"

Claire briefly looked out the glass window of the study room to make sure they were truly alone before continuing in a hushed tone. She told Joy about the car fire, the charred body, and his missing teeth. That there was no real way to know if this dead man was actually Anthony Bates.

"If it's not Bates," Joy said, "then who is it?"

Claire shrugged.

Joy put a finger on her chin. "Someone else must be involved."

"That was my instinct too." A knot formed in Claire's stomach as she said the words. Her mind drifted back to the letter and the bottle of perfume sitting on her counter at home, triggering a spiral of anxiety that she couldn't stop. An involuntary shiver ran down her spine.

"Are you okay?" Joy asked.

Claire pulled out one of the chairs and dropped down in it. "Yes?" she said, then shook her head slightly. "No."

She found herself wanting to open up to Joy about the gifts, even though she wasn't sure she should. But of all people, Joy knew about the Bates case in an intimate way. Maybe the woman could offer some guidance.

Claire looked up at her friend. "You know when we were going through the pre-sentence report, how it talked about Bates' method for stalking his victims?"

"Yes," Joy said slowly, taking a seat across from Claire.

"You remember how it described him sending first a letter, then a gift?"

"Yes. If I remember correctly, it was five things in total, the last being a bouquet of flowers the victim was always found with."

Claire swallowed hard and nodded. "Yeah, that's right. Well, I've gotten a letter and a gift."

Joy's eyes widened. "Have you gone to the police? Told them what happened? Do you have any idea who it might be?"

"Yes, yes, and not really," Claire replied. "I've told Detective Lawson, but she seems unconcerned. I told her I thought it was Bates, but she is convinced that the body they found in the car is him."

"But she can't know that for sure!"

Claire nodded. "I know. But the detective seems unwilling to help me."

"Who else could it be, then?" Joy pondered. "Someone who has to know you really well."

"I thought it might be my assistant."

"Your assistant?"

"I just found out her sister was one of Bates' victims. Plus she's in that victim's rights group that isn't particularly fond of me."

Joy nodded and pushed her glasses up the bridge of her nose. "She would have the right motivation. But do you really think she's capable of doing something like that?"

"Maybe? It's hard to tell. Bates never seemed like the type of person to go around murdering people."

"Yeah, that is true," Joy said, almost as if to herself. "I'll be honest with you; the whole case still bothers me from time to time for exactly that reason. I could never put my finger on it, but there were just things that didn't line up, and things that never got explained. Like the two different psychological reports. How we were never able to track down the second doctor."

Claire nodded, feeling even more anxious about the whole situation. "I know what you mean."

Joy jumped up from her chair and walked over to a little desk at the side of the room. She grabbed a pen and a piece of paper and jotted something down, then turned back to Claire. "That's my cell phone. If you're ever feeling unsafe or if you just need someone to talk to who doesn't think you're crazy, just call me, okay?"

Claire took the little sheet of paper and tucked it in her bag. "Thank you, Joy. That is very kind of you."

The two women stood and embraced once more before walking out of the study room.

"I'll be at the Bar Association meeting on Friday," Joy said as she made her way around the front desk. "You're presenting, right?"

Claire's stomach dropped. She'd completely forgotten and hadn't done a thing to prepare.

"Yeah," she said, shaking her head. "Thank God you reminded me."

Joy waved a hand. "You'll do great. You always do."

Claire forced a smile. "Thanks."

"Take care, and let's make sure we get together soon."

"I'd like that," Claire said before the two women said their goodbyes.

Claire kept her head down as she walked out of the library and back to her apartment building. The sun was starting to set, as it did so early in the winter months.

As she approached the front entrance, she pushed the door open and surveyed her surroundings. She almost wished there was something out of the ordinary. At least then she could come up with a better explanation for the perfume bottle, but her street was quiet, with just a few people milling about in the distance.

She took a deep breath before heading up the stairs and unlocking her door and closing it behind her. She leaned against it for a moment, eyes closed. The stillness of the apartment pressed down on her, offering no answers, only amplifying her unease. She felt the tension in her shoulders refuse to ease, her mind still replaying the unanswered questions from earlier. When she opened them, her eyes drifted to Bates' case file, which was strewn across her kitchen table.

Was it really Bates behind her letter and gift? Or perhaps another copycat?

A car horn blared on the street below, jolting Claire from her thoughts. She took a shaky breath, trying to collect herself. She peeled herself from the door and made her way over to the kitchen and flipped a switch, flooding the room with light. She gathered all of Bates' files and tossed them back into the box and instead set her heavy bag of files down on the kitchen table.

She began pulling the disorganized files from her bag. Sorting through things always made her feel a bit better, and she needed to prepare for her presentation on Friday. As she worked, her thoughts drifted back to her conversation with Joy. She felt a pang of guilt for involving her friend in this mess.

For a moment, she wondered if Joy could have been behind the letter and perfume bottle. Joy knew Bates' history. Maybe the woman was a secret supporter of the victims, like Sarah. Claire chuckled to herself. Maybe Lawson was right, and she really was losing it.

As she opened one of her folders, a FedEx envelope was wedged inside. That was weird. She didn't recall putting it into her bag, but to be fair, the stack of papers she needed to sort was substantial. It's possible she missed it.

Tearing it open, she initially thought it was empty, the lightness of the envelope adding to her confusion. Her pulse quickened as she reached inside, her fingers brushing against something thin and smooth—a piece of paper.

She pulled it out, her breath catching as she unfolded it and saw that it was a receipt. The crinkling of the paper seemed deafening in the silence of the room, and she scanned it with widening eyes. It was from the deli where she had lunch with Meredith earlier that day.

Her stomach twisted as her gaze traveled to the top of the receipt. The date and time-stamp were for today, matching almost perfectly with the time she and Meredith had been sitting at the table. Paid for in cash.

This wasn't her receipt. She hadn't paid in cash, and she'd discarded her copy at the deli. A chill ran down her spine as she realized what it meant. Someone else had been there, close enough to observe them, close enough to know exactly when and where they had lunch.

Her fingers trembled as she held the receipt, her eyes darting toward the locked door as if expecting someone to burst through it at any moment. She could almost feel the weight of unseen eyes, watching her even now, as the realization sank in—whoever had sent this wasn't just sending a message. They were following her.

The room suddenly felt stifling, the air thick as her breaths grew shallow. She gripped the edge of the counter to steady herself, her heart hammering in her chest. The receipt felt heavier in her hand than it should, as if it carried the weight of a thousand unanswered questions. Who had been there? Why had they followed her? And what did they want?

Claire's pulse roared in her ears. This couldn't be a coincidence. She flipped the envelope over to find a tracking number. Rushing to her computer, she typed it in.

"No record of this tracking number can be found at this time, please check the number and try again later. For further assistance, please contact Customer Service."

She stared back at the words before refreshing the page and trying again.

"No record of this tracking number can be found at this time, please check the number and try again later. For further assistance, please contact Customer Service."

No matter how many times she tried the number, she got the same message. She dialed the number for FedEx customer service. Maybe because the envelope had only been shipped today it wasn't in the system.

"Thank you for calling FedEx, how can I help you?" the agent said on the other side of the line as soon as Claire made it through the automated menus.

"Yes, hi. I'm trying to find information on an envelope I received."

"Go ahead with the tracking number," the agent replied, clearly not picking up on Claire's frantic energy.

Claire read out the number. There was a pause, and then the agent came back on the line. "I'm sorry," the woman said, "but I have no information on this label. I see it in the system as being generated, but it looks like it was purchased from a store in Savannah, Georgia. That's all I can find out about it."

"Was it shipped?" Claire asked.

"No. Just a label that was purchased."

"Can you tell me which store it was purchased from?" It was at least something to go on.

"5 West Broughton Street."

Claire wrote down the address and thanked the agent before hanging up the phone.

Panic clawed at her chest as she all but ran over to where she'd thrown Bates' files. She rifled through until she found his pre-sentence report. There—the third item he sent his victims was proof he was watching them.

Claire's hands shook so badly, she could barely hold onto the report. Someone was sending her a message. Bates? The victims' group? Lawson?

Someone was watching her, and she had never felt more terrified or alone.

chapter
thirty-eight

THE SMELL of toner and fresh reams of paper permeated the air of the FedEx store as Claire shoved open the door at 9 a.m. She took long steps to the counter and slapped the envelope down, startling the agent in front of her.

The man behind the counter eyed Claire warily. "Can I help you?"

"Someone bought this label from this store yesterday," she said, urgency wrought within her voice. "I need to know who."

The agent furrowed his brows and started typing away on his keyboard. "Usually we aren't able to give away too much information about a sender, but I'll see what I can do for you."

Claire tapped her fingers against the counter, her eyes never leaving the man. If she looked away, he'd surely move on from her request..

"Sorry ma'am," he said, turning his gaze to Claire. "It was paid for in cash."

Her jaw tightened. Of course it was. "Can you at least pinpoint when it was paid for?"

A few more keystrokes, the noise grating against Claire's ears.

"Looks like it was at 11:14 a.m."

"I want to see your security footage from yesterday at that time," Claire demanded.

The agent's eyes widened slightly. "I'm sorry, but I'm going to have to refer you to my manager for that."

Claire gave him an exasperated look. "Well then," she said, shooing him away from the counter. "Go fetch your manager."

The agent walked away from Claire and into the back of the store. She could hear him speaking to someone in a hushed tone. This was going to be a problem when it really shouldn't be. People were beyond irritating to her of late.

The manager, a forgettable woman in her mid-forties approached Claire with a forced smile and a voice sweeter than sugar. "How can I help you today?"

Claire rolled her eyes, frustrated that she was being forced to repeat herself.

"I want the security footage from yesterday morning. I'm an attorney and I need to take a look at the film to see if I can identify who purchased this label." Claire smashed her finger into the envelope on the counter, as if that would help everyone see it better.

The manager's smile stayed plastered on her face. "I'm afraid we can't release footage without proper authorization. Do you have a subpoena?"

Clare clenched her fists, her nails digging into her palms. "No, but I'd be happy to get one. I thought we could just save ourselves the trouble."

"It's no trouble. Unfortunately, it's our policy. Those sorts of things have to be reviewed by our legal department." The manager's eyes twinkled and Claire could swear her mouth quirked up in a smirk. "As an attorney, I'm sure you can understand."

"Unbelievable," Claire muttered under her breath.

She spun on her heel and marched out of the store, the glass door slamming shut behind her. Fine. She'd go to the cops again, even though she knew they'd be useless.

If it weren't for the fact that she was on atrocious terms with the city's prosecutor, she would have gone straight to him. If things escalated and Lawson continued to stonewall her, she might still try.

"Oof!" A man grunted as he collided into Claire.

"Watch it!" she said, before she looked up to see who it was. She blinked a few times. "Jamie?"

Jamie gave her a small, awkward smile. "Hey Claire."

Claire just stared at him, not returning the greeting. The more she looked at the man, the more a creeping suspicion began to form in her mind. Maybe she'd been right to suspect Jamie originally. He knew where she lived, and her favorite perfume. Perhaps he'd followed her into the deli yesterday without her noticing.

He'd always been against her taking the appeal in the first place. Maybe he was bitter that she hadn't listened to him and was trying to prove a point.

"What are you doing here?" she demanded sharply, folding her arms.

Jamie blinked, clearly taken aback by her tone. "I was just about to mail something for work. But that's not really any of your business."

Claire stepped closer to him, her voice rising with accusation. "Did you send me that perfume bottle, Jamie? Did you follow me into the deli yesterday?"

Jamie held up both hands. "Claire, I honestly don't know what you're talking about. I think you need help. You're really not acting like yourself."

He tried to step around her, but she moved to block him.

"Don't lie to me! Just admit what you're doing! Trying to teach me a lesson or something!"

"I have no idea what's going on with you, but I can't deal with this right now." He deftly side-stepped her, gave her a wide berth, and hurried away without looking back.

Claire stood frozen in place outside of the FedEx store. Jamie's abrupt departure left Claire reeling on the sidewalk. Passersby gave her odd looks as she stood there unblinking, breathing heavily.

She couldn't believe Jamie would just walk away like that. She shook her head. That settled it for her, he must be hiding something. Why else would he run off so quickly?

Her hands curled into fists as anger bubbled inside of her. How dare he act like she was the crazy one when he was doing all of this to her?

Claire stomped down the street and headed straight for the police station. She didn't care if Lawson brushed her off again. She would demand the security footage from the FedEx store and prove Jamie had been there yesterday morning.

When she arrived at the station, Claire burst through the front doors and made a beeline for Lawson's office. Another officer stopped her.

"Ma'am," he said, "I need you to calm down."

Claire turned to look at him. "I need to speak with Lawson. It's urgent."

A look of recognition flickered on the officer's face. "Just wait right here," he said, leaving Claire to pace back and forth in the lobby.

Her chest heaved as she walked back and forth across the dirty tile floor. Just as she was about to try and go back to Lawson's office, the doors opened and out came Lawson.

"Claire," Lawson greeted, that ever-present annoyance on her features. "What's going on?"

"I need a warrant for the FedEx security tapes from yesterday morning," Claire said, stepping a little too close to the detective. "Jamie was there and I need to prove it!"

Lawson guided her firmly into the conference room, her grip steady and unyielding. The echo of their footsteps on the tiled floor filled the hallway, amplifying the tension in the air. The heavy door creaked slightly as Lawson pushed it open. The fluorescent lights buzzed softly overhead, casting a harsh glow on the polished table and the chairs arranged neatly around it. Claire hesitated for a moment before stepping inside, the weight of the detective's presence urging her forward.

"Okay, just take a breath," Lawson said, her tone softening. "What's going on?"

""I got another gift!" Claire reached into her bag and slammed the FedEx envelope on the table. "I'm being stalked, Erin. Whether you want to admit it or not."

Lawson picked up the envelope carefully and looked inside. She pulled out the receipt. "Anita's Deli?"

"I met a friend for lunch there yesterday, then found that in my bag when I got home. And no, it's not mine or my friend's." Claire tapped her foot against the floor, her eyebrows lifted into her forehead. "The third gift was always proof that he was watching."

"I'm sure this is just a mistake." Lawson closed her eyes and shook her head. "Claire, have you considered talking to someone? You seem very stressed."

"You think I'm crazy too!" Claire cried. "I'm not making this up! I need those tapes. It was either Jamie, or Sarah, or Bates!"

"Bates is dead," Lawson said firmly.

"Fine, then it's Sarah, or Jamie, or I don't know, maybe even Joy. I don't know who it is but if I could just get those tapes, I could figure it out!"

Lawson shook her head. "I'm sorry, Claire. But a receipt from a deli doesn't rise to the level of probable cause. I can't ask for a subpoena on this and you know it."

"Why?" Claire narrowed her eyes and moved in closer to the woman. "Is that because if those tapes were pulled, they'd show you walking into that FedEx store? What are you trying to hide, Erin? You've been dismissive of this from the beginning. Is that because you're trying to set me up for something?"

Lawson smirked at her. She walked over to the phone and picked up the receiver. "I need someone to show Ms. Stevens out."

"You can't do this!" Claire shouted to Lawson as the door to the conference room swung open and the officer from earlier strode in. He grabbed Claire firmly by the elbow and began to lead her toward the door.

"Get some sleep," Lawson said. "Talk to someone."

"I'm not crazy!" Claire said, as she was all but thrown out of the station.

The officer left her on the curb and walked back into the precinct, looking back over his shoulder at the *not* crazy woman wearing an incredulous expression. He shook his head as he continued inside.

———

CLAIRE PACED BACK and forth on the sidewalk outside the police station, fuming over Lawson's dismissal of her concerns. What she had seen and experienced over the past few days was real, not some paranoid delusion brought on by stress. But she didn't know who was targeting her, or why. The only reason she could think of was because they were angry over Bates' release and the part she played in it.

Glancing up at the station windows, she considered barging back inside and refusing to leave without a warrant for the tapes. But she knew that would only land her in more trouble, and possibly lead to her arrest.

Maybe that's what Lawson wanted. Maybe Lawson was pulling the strings on all of this just so Claire would unravel enough so Lawson could reel her in. Pin her with something to ruin her reputation and restore her own.

As Claire made the walk back to her apartment, she tried to decide her next move. FedEx wouldn't release tapes to her, but maybe the deli would. She could try and see if they had footage of who entered the restaurant while she and Meredith were having lunch. Maybe the staff had seen something or maybe if she was lucky, she'd be able to see who slipped the envelope into her bag.

It was a long shot, but she had to follow every lead. She changed course to head to the deli. Getting those tapes was her first priority, and Claire always got what she wanted.

chapter
thirty-nine

CLAIRE SAT at her kitchen table, staring in frustration at the three items in front of her—the letter, the perfume bottle, and the deli receipt. She had gone back to the deli, hoping for security footage, but they claimed not to have any cameras.

Who the hell didn't have security cameras these days? Since that option had been removed, she'd all but interrogated the wait staff, but no one could remember a specific person or what they'd ordered. Claire had even pulled out the receipt, but with the constant stream of customers moving through the deli, none of the staff had any time to look at it.

Claire was simply helpless now, fixating on pieces of a puzzle no one else thought existed.

She should be preparing for her speech at the bar association dinner tonight, but her obsession remained over the three items in front of her. The irony was that her speech was on properly documenting criminal cases to preserve appeal rights. Yet, here she was, living a case study in what not to do.

Claire shoved the letter, bottle, and receipt aside, forcing herself to stare at the empty table and clear her mind. Glancing at the clock, she realized time was running short if she hoped to get ready and arrive on time.

She spent the next hour hastily pulling together her presentation notes, her desk cluttered with legal pads, sticky notes, and half-empty coffee cups. Every time she thought she had her points organized, she'd remember a key fact or argument she hadn't included, sending her back to shuffle through the pile of papers again.

Midway through, her laptop froze, the spinning wheel of doom mocking her as she tapped the keys in frustration. "Of course," she muttered under her breath, reaching for her phone to jot down her ideas before she forgot them. When the laptop finally rebooted, she stared at the screen with a sigh.

"Well, it is what it is," she muttered, resigning herself to the time crunch as she quickly typed out her final points. Her presentation might not be perfect, but at least it would be finished.

Once she had it ready to go, she rushed to the bathroom, quickly showering and brushing out her sopping wet hair, running a towel over it out of hope it would air dry in the next hour.

Out of habit, she reached for the perfume bottle on her bathroom vanity, but just as her fingers brushed the glass, she recoiled as if it'd burned her. She shook her head and decided to go without perfume for the evening.

She jogged to her closet and grabbed the first dress she spotted. The skinny black fabric had her shimmying inside and fighting with the zipper on the back. Was it tighter than when she'd last worn it? She wasn't even sure when she'd last worn it. Her hands were behind her, one crossed around the bottom of her back and working the zipper, the other around her neck to pinch the fabric together and will the zipper into place. After what felt like an eternity, the metal gave way.

She attempted to tame her hair one last time before she surveyed herself in the mirror, turning to each side to make sure the dress was in place and her hair wasn't too wild. But no matter what angle she looked at herself, she was as tired and frazzled on the outside as she felt inside. And she was sure people would be able to see right through any attempt to hide it.

Claire checked the clock again and burst out of the room. She had half an hour. She threw on a pair of heels, grabbed her keys and purse, and hurried out the door. Her car sat waiting in its usual spot, and she climbed in, tossing her purse onto the passenger seat. Turning the key, the engine roared to life as she backed out of the driveway.

The city blurred by as she navigated the streets, her grip tightening on the steering wheel each time she caught a red light. She tried to control her thoughts, taking deep breaths in between muttered rehearsals of her key points. The rhythmic sound of the tires against the asphalt should have been calming, but it only seemed to amplify her nerves.

As she pulled into the hotel parking lot, Claire glanced at the clock on her dashboard. She had just enough time, but the knot in her stomach wasn't loosening. She turned off the engine and sat for a moment, gathering herself before stepping out.

Her heels clicked against the pavement as she made her way toward the entrance. Smoothing down her dress with one hand and clutching her purse with the other, she took a deep breath before stepping into the lobby, her pulse quickening as she prepared for the evening ahead. The glass double doors gave way to a sea of lawyers congregated in the lobby, most wearing black suits, and most of them with drinks in their hands. Claire had only inched her way inside before a few acquaintances made their way over to her. With each handshake and hollow smile, her anxiety grew. Everywhere she turned, she wondered if she had overlooked something, if each person she spoke to had been responsible for the items sitting on her kitchen table.

Finally, one of the hosts gathered the crowd's attention and encouraged them to enter the ballroom. Claire made her way inside, electing to stay to the back of the hoard of lawyers, and sat down at one of the tables in the back. A few people she didn't recognize ended up sitting with her and she greeted them with a forced smile and a nod.

As dinner was being served, the bar association president stood and tapped the microphone, his voice cutting through the low hum of conversation. "Good evening, everyone," he began, flashing a practiced smile. "Before we conclude tonight's meal, I'd like to go over our agenda. We'll start with a brief discussion of this year's initiatives, followed by a special recognition ceremony for our distinguished members. And then, the highlight of the evening—our keynote address."

Claire barely registered the rest of his words as her stomach twisted. She'd gone over her speech a dozen times, yet the thought of standing in front of the packed room made her heart pound.

Finally, the president introduced her. "It's my pleasure to introduce our keynote speaker for this evening. A brilliant legal mind and compassionate advocate, Ms. Claire Stevens fought tirelessly for the rights of the accused. She is an insightful and accomplished attorney, someone we are all fortunate to have speak with us this evening."

Polite applause echoed through the banquet hall, a steady rhythm that felt both distant and overwhelming. Claire rose from her seat, her legs feeling heavier with each step toward the podium. Her chest tightened, and her palms were damp as she clutched her notes.

She couldn't help but think about how much she would have preferred to be anywhere else. She wished Bob hadn't volunteered her for this. She didn't need another spotlight moment—not tonight, not with everything else going on.

The weight of hundreds of judging stares settled on her shoulders as she stepped behind the podium, her fingers gripping the edges for balance. She forced herself to smile, but inside, all she could think about was getting through the next twenty minutes without falling apart.

As the applause died down, she shuffled her notes with trembling hands. She looked back up, out at the sea of expectant faces. Her anxiety spiked. She recognized a few—Bob, Daniel, Joy.

Bob sat near the front, arms crossed and a confident smile on his face. He nodded approvingly as if silently reminding her this was her chance to shine for the firm. He looked comfortable, completely at ease.

Daniel, a few rows back, leaned forward slightly in his chair. His expression was harder to read—an odd mix of curiosity and unease. His eyes darted between Claire and his program, as though he couldn't decide whether to focus on her or the printed schedule in front of him.

Joy sat farther to the side, scribbling something on her notepad.

Even in this formal setting, she couldn't sit still, her pen tapping rhythmically on the edge of her chair as she alternated between jotting notes and glancing up at Claire.

With every set of eyes that looked at her, Claire wondered whether they were responsible for her torment. The paranoia nipped at the edges of her confidence, making her question every gesture, every expression, every whispered word she saw in the crowd.

She cleared her throat and forced herself to begin her presentation. "The right to a fair trial is the cornerstone of our judicial system."

Her voice wavered as she continued her speech. She made the mistake of glancing up from her notes, making eye contact with Bob. Her mind won out as it raced with paranoid thoughts. She went silent for a moment, and then continued despite her mind being somewhere else completely.

"This principle ensures that every defendant, regardless of the accusations against them, has the opportunity to present their case without prejudice. But what happens when that principle is compromised? When the scales of justice are tipped before a trial even begins? It is our duty as attorneys to fight against those injustices, even when the odds feel insurmountable."

Perhaps Bob was the culprit. Perhaps secretly he was angry over the way she had accepted the appeal without his permission. Maybe he thought it put the firm in a precarious position within Savannah society. He could have written the letter to look like it was Bates. He might have recognized the brand of perfume she wore to the office and left it at her door.

Maybe the promotion was all a hoax. A way to cover up his true motives. Then on top of that, he allowed her to be piled up with work after the appeal, knowing she would be sleep deprived and stressed.

"Appellate work is a critical part of this process. It is where we can challenge errors made in the courtroom, where we can demand accountability and fairness. It's not just about the individual case—it's about protecting the integrity of our system as a whole."

He knew her. He had access to her information.

Claire's mouth went dry as the notes in front of her started to blur.

She lost her place, stumbling over a sentence about the appellate process. A few confused murmurs rose from the crowd. Her fellow lawyers began to share glances and whisper to one another behind their hands. Claire gripped the edges of the podium, her knuckles turning white. She tried to will herself to stay in control. The room seemed to grow warmer, the air heavier, as if every eye in the audience were a spotlight fixed on her.

Not here. Not now. Not in front of all these people.

But there was no helping it. She stammered into the microphone. "I...I'm sorry, I just... Excuse me."

Before she knew what she was doing, Claire found herself rushing from the stage. She had to get out of here now. She couldn't take everyone's stares.

Gasps of surprise followed her as she flew down the aisle and out the lobby doors. The cool night air hit her clammy skin as she gulped it down, heaving heavy breaths.

But she couldn't stop there. Someone could be watching. She had to keep moving. Her heels clicked against the pavement as she hurried toward the parking lot, fumbling with her keys as she reached her car. She yanked the door open and slid into the driver's seat, her hands gripping the wheel tightly as she tried to steady her breathing.

Claire managed to pull out of the lot and onto the street, her mind racing as fast as her heartbeat. She kept it together, mostly, focusing on the road ahead, but her grip on the wheel was too tight, and her thoughts too erratic. Her chest heaved as she felt the weight of what had happened pressing down on her.

As the tension built, her car began to swerve slightly, the tires brushing the edge of the lane. A horn blared behind her, snapping her back into focus for a moment. She tightened her grip, blinking back tears as she forced herself to stay in control just long enough to make it home.

When she finally pulled into her parking space, her hands trembled so violently she could barely turn off the engine. She sat there for a moment, the silence in the car deafening, before forcing herself to grab her bag and head toward her apartment.

Her keys jingled loudly as she fumbled to unlock the door, her hands shaking uncontrollably. When the lock finally gave way, she burst inside, slamming the door shut behind her. Leaning back against the closed door, her chest heaved as she tried to catch her breath.

The panic hit her like a freight train, and she slid down the door, her knees giving out beneath her. Tears streamed down her face as the emotions she'd held back during the drive crashed over her all at once. She tried to breathe, but it was like there was suddenly not enough air in the room. Her hands pressed down into the cool floor, but the world was shaking beneath her. Her heart pounded, threatening to beat out of her chest. She closed her eyes as the room began to spin.

Finally, she drew her knees to her chest and began to rock back and forth, sobbing into her skirt. The tears stained it but she kept her eyes closed, trying to slow her breathing. The episode took its time, but it finally passed. She blinked her eyes open and tears spilled from them, and the room was finally still again.

Claire wished the paranoia would have subsided with the attack, but it was still at an all-time high. Fear clouded her mind.

"It could be anyone," she said to herself, running through the list of those closest to her. "Bates, Daniel, Joy, hell even Meredith."

It hurt her to suspect her friends. People like Joy and Meredith who had done nothing but support her through difficult times, yet here she was, borderline accusing them of murdering Anthony and plotting to kill her.

That thought seemed to ground her. Perhaps it couldn't be everybody. It was still just one person, she said to herself, and that helped to loosen the grip the anxiety had on her heart.

She forced herself to stand as her heartbeat slowed and the tears stopped flowing. Her feet were unsteady beneath her and she used the wall for support. She wiped at the tears streaking her face and took a few deep breaths.

And that's when she noticed it.

Straight ahead, a picture she didn't recognize hung on the wall. Her steps were measured as she approached it cautiously, heart sinking into her stomach.

She reached out with a shaky hand to touch it, half-convinced it was just some hallucination. But the glass was real and cool beneath her fingertips. She stepped back to read the lettering.

It wasn't a picture, but a copy of her high school diploma.

Someone had been here.

In her home.

Left this calling card as proof.

chapter
forty

LAWSON PULLED APART the chopsticks to dig into a takeout container of Chinese food. The smell of sesame chicken filled her apartment and her stomach rumbled in response.

Just as she was about to take the first bite, her phone vibrated. She tried ignoring it, letting it ring once, twice. When it rang for the third time, she couldn't ignore it anymore. She sighed and fished the phone out of her back pocket.

Claire Stevens' name lit up the screen. Lawson scoffed and rejected the call. The last thing she needed was to deal with another of Claire's wild outbursts.

She took her first bite and then the phone lit up again.

"Claire Stevens," the screen said, as if she didn't know who was calling her a second time.

"For the love of Christ," Lawson said, this time letting the call go unanswered.

She shoved a chopstick full of noodles into her mouth, savoring every full bite of flavor, closing her eyes to enjoy the moment of peace.

Then, the damn thing rang a third time. Lawson let out an audible groan as she put her dinner down. As much as she wanted to ignore Claire, there was the slim possibility that the woman had something to help her with the Bates case.

"This better be important," Lawson said as she held the phone to her ear.

"There's been a break-in," Claire said, her voice shaking and breathing labored. "In my apartment."

Lawson wasn't sure whether to believe the woman. She'd claimed so many outlandish things since the appeal. "A break in? Did you call 911?"

"No! I called you!" Claire bit back.

"You need to call for a dispatch. Are you safe?"

"They're not here anymore," Claire said. "I need you to come over and see what they left. It has to do with Bates."

Lawson gritted her teeth. Claire had claimed this a number of times, and it had always been a bust. But she couldn't deny that it got her attention.

"If you're safe, then I can stop by in the morning," Lawson said, picking her takeout container back up.

"No," was Claire's terse response. "I need you to come now. And if you don't come now, I'm just going to tell the dispatch when I report the break-in that it has to do with the Bates matter, and then they'll send you here anyway. At least this way you can look at things yourself first without other officers hanging around."

Lawson almost growled in frustration. It was obvious Claire knew how to work the system. "I'll be there in 15 minutes."

The call ended and Lawson got off her couch and put her dinner into the refrigerator. She sighed and looked at the other container that had long since spoiled.

For once, she'd been looking forward to a quiet night at home, feet up, bad reality TV, and a cold beer. But of course, Little Miss Defense Attorney had to interrupt her evening. And probably all for nothing.

AS SHE STARTED her car and made her way toward Claire's apartment, she tried to think through the different "gifts" Claire had received. While they undeniably aligned with the profile of a Bates case, that alone wasn't enough to prove Claire was being stalked by Bates or even a copycat.

Lawson had been in the force long enough to know that sometimes people wanted something to fit a case so much that they willed it to be that way. Claire's letter was likely nothing more than an actual letter of admiration from a Bates supporter who was too embarrassed to use their real name.

And the perfume bottle? That could have been anything. Heck, it could have been a delivery man getting the address wrong. It's not like Claire's "preferred scent" was some difficult-to-find perfume. It was sold everywhere. She'd seen it on display shelves herself, even in the kind of stores she barely paid attention to perfumes in—department stores, grocery chains, even airport duty-free shops. It wasn't exactly the sort of thing that required insider knowledge to track down.

Lawson parked in front of the apartment building and took a deep sigh before getting out of the car. As she climbed the stairs up to Claire's apartment, she mentally prepared for this confrontation to test her patience.

She raised her hand to knock on the door, but Claire opened it before she even had a chance for her knuckles to make contact. The woman backed up into her unit, chewing her thumbnail into oblivion. "Alright, what's so important that it couldn't wait until morning?" Lawson asked, irritation creeping into her voice.

She stepped inside and frowned. The place looked like a bomb had gone off. There were papers strewn everywhere. It was not what Lawson expected of the—until recently—put-together defense attorney.

Claire's usual polished appearance had degraded as well. Her makeup was smudged, her eyeliner slightly smeared beneath her eyes, and her hair, which was typically neat, was pulled back into a messy ponytail with loose strands framing her face. The cardigan over her dress was buttoned wrong, making the fabric sit awkwardly on one side. She looked like someone running on fumes, every bit as disheveled as the chaos around her.

She grabbed Lawson's arm with a shaking hand and led her toward the wall in her living room. They stopped in front of a giant frame with cursive writing. Claire looked at it like there was a monster hiding behind it.

Lawson raised an eyebrow. "What am I supposed to be looking at?"

Claire pointed straight ahead.

"This is what couldn't wait?" Lawson asked. "A diploma?"

Claire's eyes were wide, darting around the room. "Don't you get it? The fourth gift was always about the past. Something the victim wanted to cover up."

Lawson considered the diploma and Claire's words. "And what is it you want to cover up about high school, Claire?"

Claire was quiet, her eyes searching Lawson's features. She was visibly shaking. It was obvious that something was getting to her. Whether it was a stalker was the real question.

"It doesn't matter," she said finally. "What matters is that this was a message."

Lawson pinched the bridge of her nose. "Is it possible that you just forgot that you hung this here?" she asked. "Or a family member did it for you?"

"No," Claire said, shaking her head wildly. "No one's been here. Bates put it here while I was at the bar association dinner. That's the only explanation. Of everyone I thought might be doing this to me, he's the only one that makes sense."

Lawson's frustration boiled over again at the mention of Bates. Claire's lack of sleep was clearly impacting her mood and her mental well-being. Before Lawson decided to act on this information and make herself look like a fool to the rest of the precinct, she wanted to rule out any other possibilities. She hated to say it, but she was still more than skeptical that Claire was really being stalked. "Claire, you need to get a grip," she scolded. "This isn't some crime novel. Bates is dead. No one is breaking into your apartment to leave some cryptic message about your past."

Claire's face flushed. "You think I'm making this up? I come home and find this here, and you accuse me of what, framing myself?"

"All I'm saying is that we need solid evidence before jumping to wild conclusions."

"Evidence? You want evidence?" Claire marched over to the kitchen table and began rifling through a stack of papers. She pulled out a stapled document and shoved it back at Lawson. "Right there. The fourth gift is about the past."

Lawson skimmed the page. It was Bates' psychological report. This section discussed the order of gifts for each victim. She looked back at Claire skeptically. "So, you think that Bates is alive and he's chosen you, his defense attorney who got him acquitted for his crimes, to stalk and murder?"

Claire crossed her arms defensively. "I don't know who else would do this. It had to be him."

"Or you hung it up yourself and forgot."

Claire's eyes flashed in anger. "I did not hang this here! I'm telling you that someone is after me!"

Lawson shook her head. "I think you need to speak to someone, get help dealing with this irrational fear." She held up a hand to stop Claire's impending outburst. "But right now, I'm going home. You have no evidence a crime occurred here tonight."

She turned and made her way to the door, but Claire followed her, grabbing her arm just as she reached for the handle.

"You can't just leave!" Claire cried, her fingers digging into Lawson's jacket sleeve. "I'm telling you that my life is in danger here!"

Lawson gently removed Claire's hand. "And I'm telling you nothing has happened that warrants police involvement. No sign of a break-in, no threats made, nothing stolen or damaged. Just a diploma hung on a wall."

"None of Bates' victims experienced those things, either! It's all right here," she said, grabbing the psychological report. "The next gift is going to be a bouquet of peonies and you're going to find me dead!"

Lawson held Claire's desperate gaze. "Lock your doors and windows if it makes you feel better. But don't go looking for trouble where there is none."

Claire's eyes filled with angry tears. "So what, you're just going to

abandon me? You're not even going to file a report? Some detective you are."

Lawson softened slightly. "I know you're scared. But I can't indulge this...episode. For your own good, let it go. Get some rest tonight."

She pulled the door open and slipped out before Claire could respond. Claire's quiet sobbing echoed down the silent hallway.

As much as Lawson felt a pang of guilt for leaving the woman in such a state, there wasn't anything she could do. She couldn't help someone fight their own demons. Claire would have to do it herself. Lawson knew that all too well.

chapter
forty-one

The music was blasting, the drinks were flowing, and Claire was drowning in it all. She scanned the crowded room, trying to find Matty out of habit among the sea of bodies, but he was nowhere in sight. She took another sip of her beer and scanned the scene in front of her. Who needed Matty when she had all this?

That's when Kendra stumbled over. She was draped over some tall guy, one Claire recognized as being on the football team. Another of his teammates followed behind them. Claire was pretty proud of the fact that a couple of football players had decided to come. Football players at Country Day were basically their own level of royalty.

"Hey, Claire!" Kendra slurred. "You gotta meet Evan here," she gestured to the guy behind her. "He's a catch." She winked at Claire and made a beeline for the nearest shot glass. The guy she was with followed her, leaving Claire alone with Evan.

Claire surveyed the big guy. He looked like he belonged on a field rather than at a party, with his broad shoulders and chiseled jawline. Claire recognized him. His family was old money and now operated one of the more successful wealth management firms in the city.

Evan wasn't just a pretty face, though. Claire had heard that he'd gotten a full scholarship to the University of Georgia to play football. He wasn't her usual type, but she couldn't deny an attraction to him.

Her irritating inner conscience told her—in Matty's voice, of course —that maybe it was because his family was loaded and connected. She shook her head. It was probably just the alcohol doing the talking.

"Hey there," he said, leaning against the wall next to her. "I'm Evan."

"Claire."

"Kendra tells me your dad's a lawyer."

"Yep," Claire replied, taking another swig of her drink. Even though she understood it, she never quite liked the fact that kids in this crowd seemed to care more about what your parents did than who you were.

"Sounds exciting," Evan said, his eyes lingering on her for a moment too long. "It's a great party."

"Thanks," Claire said, feeling a bit awkward around the guy. She decided a bit more alcohol might help her feel more at ease. She looked over at Kendra to see her taking shots. "Wanna join?"

He shrugged. "Why not?"

The two made their way over and Claire nudged Kendra. "Hey, pour me one, too!"

"That's the spirit!" Kendra said, pouring clear liquid into the shot glass, spilling it all down the sides, and handing it back to Claire. The two toasted two more times, taking three shots in all. The room started to spin around Claire..

She tried to walk away from the table where they were all sitting, but she was unsteady on her feet. Evan stood to catch her. "Hey, you alright?"

She smiled up at him. "Yeah," she said, before leaning in to try and kiss him. Maybe Matty wouldn't kiss her, but who needed him anyway?

"Whoa," Evan said, pulling away from her just the same. Even in her inebriated state, Claire wanted to scream.

"What's the issue?" Claire huffed through slurred words.

"Aren't you dating that Matty kid?" Evan asked.

Claire rolled her eyes. "No, we're just friends."

Evan kept her at bay with his strong grasp. "The entire school thinks you two are dating. You hang out constantly."

Claire shook her head but regretted it. The room started spinning even faster. "We couldn't be dating even if we wanted to."

Evan furrowed his brow. "What do you mean by that?"

"Matty's gay."

Evan's eyes widened at the news. Claire instantly regretted letting it slip and clapped a hand over her mouth.

"Are you serious?" Evan asked.

"Please don't tell anyone," she said, her tone taking on a panicked desperation. "No one is supposed to know."

"Okay," Evan said. "I won't."

Claire smiled and tried to move back in. Evan leaned in to kiss her but the moment their lips touched, Claire felt totally sick to her stomach. This time she pushed away from Evan and ran to the nearest bathroom.

"CLAIRE, CLAIRE!" a voice crashed into her sleeping mind. "You need to wake up!"

Someone was shaking her roughly. She blinked her eyes several times, trying to clear the haze the alcohol had left in her system.

As the world started to make sense around her, she realized that she was passed out in the downstairs bathroom. But where there was once lively music of a roaring party outside the room, there was now an eerie silence over the whole place.

She looked up to realize that it was Kendra shaking her awake.

Claire sat up slowly and Kendra helped her to her feet, leading her out of the bathroom. No one was in the house anymore. There was no more party. Blue and red lights were flashing from somewhere outside.

"What's going on?" she asked, her head pounding.

"The police are here," Kendra said, her tone serious. "They want to talk to you."

Claire's stomach dropped. "Do you think I'll get arrested for throwing the party?"

Kendra frowned before realizing why Claire was asking that question. "No, Claire. Something's happened."

"What?" Claire asked again.

"Something about your dad's shed," Kendra said. "Some of the football players found guns or something. Someone got shot."

Claire's heart started beating out of her chest. She already knew the answer but had to ask anyway. "Who?"

Kendra sniffled and looked away. "Matty."

chapter
forty-two

CLAIRE CLUTCHED the blanket tightly around her as she sat on the front porch to her house. Blue and red lights lit up the pitch-black night. She couldn't take her eyes off the scene unfolding around her, straight out of a horror movie. Medics wheeled a gurney with a black body bag on top into the ambulance. She knew who was in that bag and wanted to throw up all over again.

"I can't believe this is happening," she began to say to herself over and over as she rocked back and forth.

An officer approached her as the doors to the ambulance were being shut. "Claire Stevens?"

"Yes," she said, but didn't look up at him.

"I need to ask you some questions."

Claire stayed quiet.

"Can you tell me what happened at the party?"

Still, Claire didn't answer.

"Whose guns were in the shed?" the officer asked. "Did you know anyone was planning on shooting them?"

Claire's mind was blank. The shock of the night numbed her thoughts. The officer was talking to her, but nothing was registering.

"I need my dad," she said to him.

"You can talk to your dad later," the officer replied. "Right now, we need some information from you."

"No," she replied. "I need my dad here. Can I just call him?"

"Later," the officer said, his tone growing firmer.

"He's a lawyer," Claire said, looking down at her feet. "He can help."

The officer shook his head and walked away for a minute. Then he walked back over to Claire, his tone gentler. "We think it'd be best if you come down to the station so we can get some things sorted."

Claire didn't respond again. Instead, she allowed the officer to lift her by her elbow and guide her into the back of the squad car. The ride to the station was a blur as the city's night lights flashed around her, all jumbled together with the static from the police radio.

When she got to the station, the florescent overhead lights almost blinded her and she tried to blink her vision clear. She clung to the blanket around her like a lifeline as she was led down a long hallway and into a small room. The walls were made of white cinder blocks and enclosed a small table and two chairs pressed up against one side.

Her hands shook as she was directed to take a seat. The officer who had tried to talk to her at the house directed her. "Wait here and someone will be in to help you."

Claire didn't know how much time had passed before the door finally opened and a middle-aged man with graying hair and a large moustache walked in.

"Claire Stevens," he said. "I'm Detective Rodgers. I'd like to ask you some questions."

"I want my dad."

"I understand that. But in the meantime, maybe you can help me piece together what happened this evening. Tell me about the party you threw last night."

Claire just wanted this to stop. Maybe if she answered some of his questions, he would leave her alone and let her call her dad.

"It was just a small get-together with some friends," she replied, trying to keep her voice steady.

"Didn't seem like a small get together," the detective said. Claire just shrugged and he frowned. "Did you know that there were guns in the shed?"

Claire hesitated for a moment before answering. "I knew they were there, but I didn't think anyone would use them."

"Did you lock the shed?"

"No," Claire admitted, feeling a wave of guilt wash over her. "I didn't."

"Seems like a pretty big oversight for someone who's supposed to be top of her class. How old are you now, Claire? Eighteen?"

Claire nodded her head.

"Tell me about your relationship with the victim."

Tears started to well in Claire's eyes as she thought about Matty. Matty, the victim. She shook her head, unable to answer.

Rogers leaned forward. "I heard the two of you got into a fight just before the party started."

"Look, I don't know what happened," Claire said, her voice wavering.

"Don't lie, Claire," he said sternly. "If you don't start cooperating with us and answering some questions, you're going to be in a world of trouble." He flipped pages over in his notepad. "You know you can be charged as an adult now, right? An involuntary manslaughter charge would be a piece of cake to bring against you. But, if you cooperate, maybe I can convince the prosecutor to cut you a deal."

"I want my dad," Claire repeated through gritted teeth. " He's a lawyer. He can answer your questions. Why can't I call him?"

Just as she said those words, her father burst into the interrogation room like a raging bull. His features were contorted with anger. "Get the hell out of here," he growled at the detective. "She's my client and I won't let you interrogate her without me present."

Claire got up and ran to her father, collapsing into his arms and sobbing uncontrollably. "I'm sorry, Dad," she choked between sobs. "This is all my fault."

Roy held her tight, but didn't take his eyes off Detective Rogers. "You better have a damn good explanation for why you denied someone a phone call and interrogated them when they were clearly asking for their attorney to be present."

"She wasn't asking for her attorney," Rogers said defensively. "She was asking for her father."

"That's not what I was told," Roy spat back. "And I'm sure body camera footage of the officers will prove me right."

Rogers paled a bit.

"I suggest you leave and let me speak to my client before I decide to file a suit against you for violating her constitutional rights."

Rogers all but ran out of the room. The moment the door slammed shut behind him, Roy's demeanor softened as he leaned down to hug his daughter.

Claire sobbed into his embrace. "What's going to happen to me?"

"Nothing, Claire Bear."

"That's not what the detective said. He said they want to charge me with involuntary manslaughter."

Roy scoffed. "Let them try. They violated your rights by questioning you without an attorney present and they know it. I'll talk to the prosecutor. The case will never move forward."

"But Matty..." Claire trailed off, unable to finish the thought.

Roy held her tight. "It's not your fault, honey," he said soothingly. "You made a mistake by throwing that party, but what those boys did is not your responsibility. They were old enough to know better. They made a choice to use those guns, and they're going to be the ones to live with the consequences."

"No, Dad, you don't understand." Claire shook her head, wiping her running nose against the blanket. "Matty told me he was gay just before the party started. I was mad at him for keeping it a secret. I was drunk. I let it slip." She looked down and choked on another sob. "That's why they killed him."

"Claire, look at me." He pulled away from her briefly so that she was forced to make eye contact with him. "This is very important."

Claire nodded her head.

"I don't want you telling anyone else what you just told me, okay?"

"Why?" Claire asked, but Roy just shook his head.

"Can you do that for me, Claire Bear? If anyone ever asks you, those boys went after Matty on their own, okay? You never told them anything about him."

Claire nodded slowly, her mind racing with guilt and fear. She took a deep breath, trying to calm herself down. Her father was one of the best attorneys in the city. He would save her from this.

But the guilt would haunt her for the rest of her life.

chapter
forty-three

Claire watched through her window as Lawson's taillights disappeared into the night. A chill ran through her as she hurried to the front door and locked it, then moved methodically from window to window, checking each lock. All secure. Yet someone had still managed to break in without leaving a trace. She understood Lawson's skepticism. There were no signs of forced entry.

But the perpetrator always slipped up somewhere.

She moved back to the living room, eyes landing on the diploma hanging perfectly straight on the wall. Her hands trembled as she reached for it. She hesitated just before her fingertips could touch it, withdrawing them slightly.

Should she leave it? Fingerprints could still be lifted if Lawson changed her mind. But the detective's trust in Claire had clearly eroded —if it had ever existed in the first place. She wasn't coming back. And besides, whoever staged this break-in didn't strike her as someone careless enough to leave prints behind.

Claire lifted the frame off its hook and carried it to the kitchen table. She turned it over, scrutinizing the back for any sign of tampering. Nothing. A standard frame from any craft store.

With a deep breath, Claire carefully moved each tab one by one until she was able to pop open the back of the frame. Her eyes widened. On the reverse side of the diploma, a message had been typed.

YOU KILLED MATTY.

Claire recoiled from the table, bile rising in her throat. Long suppressed memories flooded her mind. Matty's smile, their fight, watching the medic wheel his lifeless form in a body bag. She collapsed to the floor in sobs, the diploma fluttering to the floor beside her.

Claire didn't know how long she stayed curled up on the floor, rocking back and forth as the traumatic memories overwhelmed her. Flashing lights, loud music, sirens permeated her mind and she couldn't make them stop. Gun shots, screams, people fleeing from the house. All of this had been tucked safely away in the deep recesses of her mind, even though she hadn't been conscious for any of it. She had been passed out in the bathroom during all of it.

She never should have thrown that party in the first place.

Her father's embrace was the last memory to surface. His protection over her. The way he'd saved her life.

Eventually, the sobs subsided. She sat up slowly, wiping her eyes. The diploma still lay next to her, message side up.

YOU KILLED MATTY.

She picked it up with a shaky hand. Even if Claire had wanted to share this new piece of evidence with Lawson, she wouldn't risk it. She couldn't bear yet another dismissal from the exasperated detective. She'd carried this secret with her for over a decade and she wouldn't let it out now.

Claire was on her own. She had to figure out who was behind this attack on her psyche, or they would continue tormenting her until she ended up in the body bag.

The only person she could trust with something like this was her father. He was the only one who knew the whole truth. But she couldn't risk him becoming a target, not if she was really in danger.

She rose to her feet, her knees wobbling and threatening to give out, and returned to the kitchen table. After clearing it off, she found a blank sheet of paper and began compiling a list of potential suspects. She would start with the obvious and work her way to the improbable.

One by one, she would analyze their means and motive until only the guilty party remained.

For the first time, she felt confident that she could figure this out. No one was supposed to know about her connection to Matty's death. This message was a dead giveaway.

Claire clicked her pen and wrote the first name: Bates.

She stared it and tapped the pen against her chin. For the first time, she considered the possibility of whether it could be Bates. He couldn't possibly know about Matty.

Bates had no connections in law enforcement. As far as Claire knew, his family wasn't connected to Matty's in any way other than just being a part of the same social circles.

No, the more Claire thought about it, the less sense Bates made as a suspect. Whether he was alive or dead, it seemed Lawson had been right to dismiss him as the culprit.

With a sigh, Claire moved down to the next name on her list: Sarah.

Now there was someone with a clear motive. Sure, she acted really dodgy about the perfume, but Sarah had no way of knowing about Matty, either.

That eliminated her from suspicion. Claire looked at the next name on the list. Could it have been Daniel?

A knock on her door had her nearly jumping out of her skin. Claire tensed, her heart pounding. She froze, listening intently for any sound outside the door. As quietly as she could, she got up and grabbed the largest knife from the kitchen and positioned herself beside the front door. She waited, barely breathing, before another knock made her jump.

"Claire!" came Meredith's muffled voice from the other side of the door. "It's Meredith! I tried calling. Open up!"

Claire lowered the knife and opened the door. "What are you doing here?"

Meredith looked at her with wide eyes. "Why are you holding a knife?"

Claire looked down at it sheepishly, but didn't loosen her grip. "Um, it's been a long night."

"I heard you ran out of the bar event mid-speech," Meredith said stepping into the apartment. She handed Claire a bouquet of flowers. "They were going to give you these at the end."

"Thanks." She tossed them onto her kitchen counter along with the knife.

Meredith looked at the mess in Claire's apartment and gave her friend a worried look. "Are you sure you're okay?"

"Yes. And no." She was about to hand Meredith the copy of her diploma, but realizing what was on the back of it, she brushed it under her list of suspects. "I've just been trying to work out who could be behind these gifts."

"Did you get another one?" Meredith asked, eyes wide.

"Sort of," Claire replied. "More of a message."

"Can I help?"

Claire handed her the list of names. Meredith scanned the list. "Wow, you really went all out here. Even Bob and Daniel?"

Claire sighed. " I'm grasping at straws. But I just want to make sure I'm not overlooking something." Claire shook her head. "I just feel so lost. My life feels like it's unraveling and I have no idea who I can trust."

Meredith reached over and wrapped an arm around Claire's shoulder. "You can trust me. We'll figure this out. Do you want to walk me through your thought process on your list of suspects?"

Claire looked at the clock on her stove. It was nearing ten o'clock. She already felt bad that Meredith was worried enough to make the drive over to her apartment.

"No, it's okay. I probably should just get some sleep," she said, knowing that sleep was the last thing she was going to do when Meredith left.

"Okay," Meredith said, heading to the door. "But if you need me for anything, I want you to call me, okay? I don't care what time it is."

Claire nodded. "Thank you."

Meredith slipped out the door and Claire made her way back to the kitchen table and took a deep breath.

"Okay, so Sarah," she mumbled to herself. "I thought maybe because her sister was one of Bates' victims, she'd want revenge. But there's no way she could have found out about Matty. So, it can't be her." Claire crossed the woman's name off her list.

"And for the same reason, Jamie shouldn't know anything about my past with Matty, either. So, he's out too." Another line drawn on the paper.

Claire hesitated a moment as she looked at Bob's name. Her father and Bob had been working together at the time the incident happened. Was it possible that Roy let it slip to Bob?

Claire looked down the list at Daniel's name. Was it possible that Bob eventually let it slip to Daniel? Until Claire had won the appeal, Daniel had been the favored associate at the firm.

She considered the chain possibility a bit more and then shook her head. Her father was far too principled to gossip about something like that. Besides, he'd made it very clear to Claire that *no one* was ever to know. Roy wouldn't have gone behind her back that way.

Claire crossed both Bob and Daniel's names off the list. She slumped in her seat and looked at the remaining names on the list.

Joy, Fiona, and Kendra.

Claire crossed out Joy and Fiona's names. There was no sense in even lingering on how ridiculous it would be if they were the culprits. She paused on Kendra for a moment, tapping her pen against the paper.

Kendra knew about Matty, but she didn't live close anymore and she'd known about Matty for a long time. Why would she start things now? And in Bates' footsteps?

Plus, Kendra didn't know about Claire and Matty's fight, unless Matty had told her, but that would have been unlikely. He hadn't wanted anyone to know he was gay, and Kendra had been known for being a bit of a gossip.

Besides, Kendra had been hanging out that evening with the football players who ultimately were responsible for Matty's death. Why would she think Claire was responsible for it?

Unless, Evan had told Kendra what Claire had told him.

Claire paused for a moment as she thought about the boys responsible for Matty's murder. A true tragedy, yet no one had ever been charged. There'd been too much finger pointing and their families had too much influence. The prosecutor had basically brushed the entire thing under the rug, claiming it'd been a horrible accident.

She ran through the names she remembered off the top of her head. Evan Cooper, Michael Thompson, and Christopher Carver. Claire made her way to the living room and fished out her high school yearbook. She opened it to the page of the football team and ran through the rest of the names and faces. Alex Parker may have been there, and maybe Ben Johnson.

Claire went back to the kitchen table and pulled out the list of Bates' victims. Her eyes rapidly scanned the names and the connections dawned on her.

Olivia Parker, Emma Johnson, Mia Martinez, Violet Carver, Ava Cooper, Isabella Thompson, and Charlotte Davis.

Several of the victims' last names matched the names of the football players.

Claire's eyes landed on Violet Carver before her eyes swiped over to her yearbook and the name Christopher Carver. Was Christopher her assistant's older brother?

But why would Bates go after the siblings of the boys who killed Matty? There had to be something in Bates' file that connected this all together. Something Claire had overlooked when she first began this case.

Claire all but ran back over to the box of files on the floor and fished out the original psychological report, the report that said Bates was a fully functioning adult with no mental illness. She thought back to her phone call with Dr. Fields.

As far as I understood it, the prosecutor requested a second evaluation of the defendant following a recommendation from another psychologist. It wasn't my place to question why.

Claire's head shot up and her breath caught. Matty had a sister. A sister who, according to him, was studying psychology.

Claire stood and walked over to the bouquet she'd tossed on the kitchen counter. She didn't have to look at them to know. They were a bouquet of peonies.

chapter
forty-four

PAST

Claire's hands trembled as she opened the letter, the crisp white paper feeling suddenly heavy in her grasp. She read the words on the page before they started to blur together from the tears that were leaking down her cheeks.

She reached for her phone to call her father.

"Dad?" she said as he picked up the phone.

"What is it, Claire Bear? What's wrong?"

Claire swallowed hard, willing her voice not to crack. "They denied my admission to the New York bar. They said there's an issue with the background check."

"What?" Roy sounded incredulous. "Can you read it to me?"

Claire took a deep breath and began to read the letter in a flat monotone. "We regret to inform you that we are unable to admit you to the state bar due to a failed background check. It has come to our attention that on Sunday, June 4, 2017, at 2:53 a.m. you were arrested. Although this arrest record has been expunged, pursuant to the General Instructions of the Application for Admission to Practice as an Attorney and Counselor-at-Law in the State of New York, this arrest should have been disclosed. As a result, your character and fitness has been called into question and we cannot admit you to the New York State Bar Association."

"Bastards," Roy muttered.

Hot tears spilled down Claire's face. "Dad, what am I going to do? I'll lose my job when they find out I wasn't admitted. And they'll want to know why. I can't tell them about...that."

Roy sighed. "I know it's not what you want to hear, but you'll have to leave your job in New York. Resign tomorrow. Don't give them a chance to find out about this on their own. We need to control the narrative."

Claire winced. She had worked so hard to get where she was. The thought of throwing it all away made her stomach churn.

"I can get you set up to take the bar exam here in Georgia," Roy continued. "You'll have to study and retake it, but once you pass, I'll get you a job with my old partner, Bob Greene. You remember Bob, right?"

Claire sniffled. "Yes. But I don't want to just pick up and move back home. There are just...too many bad memories."

"I know," Roy said gently. "But if you want to practice law, there are really not many other options. I have friends at the Georgia State Bar. I'll make sure that the expunged record doesn't cause you any problem. Let me handle the logistics. You just focus on getting yourself back down here as soon as possible."

Claire stared out the window of her New York apartment, watching the city buzz below as she held the phone to her ear.

"I know this is difficult," her father said. "But try to look at the bright side. This could be a fresh start for you. A chance to move on from the past."

"I thought New York was going to be my fresh start," Claire replied.

"Sometimes things don't work out the way we want them to."

Claire was silent. Her mind churned with a dozen conflicting thoughts, none of them clear enough to voice. Was this really a fresh start, or just another chance to fail? Did she even want a clean slate, or was she too tangled up in the past to let it go? She chewed on her fingernail absentmindedly, her gaze fixed on a spot on the floor as if it held some kind of answer. In the end, she said nothing, letting the silence hang between them.

"Your mother will be thrilled to have you back, too," he said, but Claire knew that was a lie. "And we finally moved into that house in the North End like she always wanted. It'll be nice for you to come visit."

Claire clenched her jaw. The only reason her parents had sold the home in Ardsley Park was because of what happened at her party. Her father had confessed to Claire some time ago that Gretchen had complained about not being able to sleep, knowing that someone had been shot on the property.

"Can't wait, Dad." She tried to sound enthusiastic, though it came out flat and hollow. No matter what promises her father made, going back home felt like anything but a step forward.

"Hey, just think—soon you'll be back down South enjoying some real sweet tea and barbecue. Not that Yankee stuff they try and pass off up there."

Claire huffed a small laugh. Her dad always knew how to make her smile. Maybe he was right. Maybe this could be a second chance, an opportunity to mend fences and heal old wounds.

Still, the thought of returning home stirred up memories better left buried. The house, the party, that night...

Claire shuddered, a chill running through her. Some ghosts refused to be exorcised.

chapter
forty-five

It was a moonless night, and it didn't take much effort to hide herself in plain sight. She watched from the safety of her car as Detective Lawson pulled up to Claire's apartment, squad lights blazing. She'd been here since before Claire had run into her apartment frantically, coming home from her botched speech at the Bar Association dinner.

The whole thing made her chuckle.

Lawson was clearly agitated. She had to give Claire credit, though. Most people would have given up begging Lawson for help by now. But Claire kept dialing. If Lawson was a more careful and observant detective, maybe she would have figured it out by now. But she was a screw-up. She'd screwed up the Bates case and she was screwing up his murder case, and that made her all the happier.

Not even a full fifteen minutes had passed before Lawson was coming back out the front door of the apartment complex, letting it slam behind her. It was obvious that she was irritated—the woman was always irritated—and she was letting the world know it. She watched as the detective yanked open the door of her squad car and threw herself inside, peeling out onto the street.

Lawson had always been hotheaded. Made it so much easier to stay two steps ahead.

Up in the apartment, Claire's silhouette appeared in the window. She watched Claire's head swivel, tracking Lawson's departure. Then one by one, Claire went to each window, checking to ensure they were all locked.

Everything was finally falling into place now. Fifteen years of waiting, fifteen years of planning, and she was finally down to the last name on her list. Claire Stevens. Claire, who had no clue she'd been living on borrowed time all these years.

After tonight, it would all be over, and Claire Stevens would be dead.

chapter
forty-six

CLAIRE BLINKED at the peonies sitting on her kitchen counter. How had she not seen it? The flowers, the letter, the perfume, the diploma. It all traced back to one person. One person who had been right under her nose this whole time.

Claire grabbed her keys off the counter, hands shaking. She had to get out of here. Now. Staying in her apartment made her an easy target. Once outside among people, she would be safe. Or, safer.

Taking the stairs two at a time, Claire burst out of her building into the cool midnight air. The world around her was shrouded in darkness. Claire's eyes darted around the parked cars as she rushed to hers. It was hard to see anything, but she could feel eyes on her. It was probably just that paranoia that seemed to stick with her.

Fumbling with the lock, Claire finally managed to wrench open the door and slide inside. She quickly locked the doors and jammed the keys into the ignition. The engine sputtered to life as Claire's breathing grew rapid and shallow. She gripped the steering wheel tightly and threw the car into reverse, then peeled out of the parking spot. She narrowly missed sideswiping the adjacent vehicles in her haste to escape.

Once on the main road, Claire tried to focus on getting somewhere well-lit and crowded. She decided to drive to the station. At this point she didn't care if Lawson tried to arrest her. She'd at least be safe from her stalker there. At least for a time.

Claire's eyes kept flicking up to the rearview mirror as she drove. Was that a car behind her? It was hard to tell in the darkness, but she could've sworn she saw a shadowy vehicle keeping pace with her own.

Her heart pounding, Claire took a right turn down a side street, hoping to lose her pursuer. But as she checked the mirror again, the car was still there. Claire took another sharp turn, tires screeching as she whipped the wheel around. Still, the car followed stealthily behind.

She strained to make out any details of the vehicle tailing her, but just as she tried, the driver turned on their headlights, blinding her in the process.

She blinked to try and clear her vision, but it was no use. Worse than that, she was lost now, the streets unfamiliar as she tried in vain to find her way back to a main road. But with each turn, her stalker mimicked her moves, the car behind followed, getting closer and closer.

Claire's breath came in ragged gasps as she tried to keep her cool. It was useless, though. Claire's mind raced as she stepped on the accelerator. If she couldn't make it to the station or at least somewhere public, her life was forfeit, just as all the other victims' had been.

Just as she was about to take another random turn, the car behind her accelerated, ramming hard into her rear bumper. Claire's head lurched forward and then hit the headrest. Her tires spun out, the car sliding into a roadside ditch and coming to a halt. A sickening crunch of metal filled the silence.

Dazed, Claire lifted her head from the deflated airbag. The front of her car was crumpled inward, trapping her legs. Warm blood trickled down her forehead.

Claire prepared herself for the worst. Despite her previous panic, a sense of calm overtook her as she realized that there was no getting out of this situation. If anything, she just hoped her death would put an end to this whole mess. Maybe this was her final penance for everything that had happened with Matty.

Fighting the spinning in her head, Claire fumbled for her phone.

She briefly considered calling 911 but ruled it out. The dispatch wouldn't know the history and her stalker wasn't going to keep her here at the scene long. Her only hope was to call Lawson. The detective likely wouldn't even pick up, but Claire had to try. She had to give the woman some clue before it was too late.

With trembling fingers, Claire dialed and waited as it rang. Just then, her window was shattered. Claire dropped the phone as she came face to face with her attacker. Claire struggled weakly as a cloth came down over her mouth. Her world went black.

chapter
forty-seven

THE FLUORESCENT LIGHTS of the office buzzed overhead as Lawson stared at the clock. It was nearly 11 p.m. She rolled her eyes and cursed under her breath. Claire had gotten her so riled up that she'd made her way back to the precinct out of habit rather than back home. Now she was past going to bed.

Besides, Lawson couldn't deny that there was something strange in the way Claire had tensed up at the vision of her high school diploma. A deep shame had flashed across her face before she recomposed herself. What was she hiding?

Curiosity gnawed at the detective as she logged into the system. She started with Claire's background around her high school years. A quick search told her Claire had attended the ritzy Country Day School. Of course she had. Little Miss Privilege.

She scanned the system, filtering by time frame and location. At first, the list of crimes seemed innocuous enough. Petty vandalism— kids breaking windows or spray-painting graffiti on the school gym. She skimmed past a minor drug bust that listed a few students caught with marijuana at a party. It was the kind of thing that got cleaned up quietly with the right lawyers and a few well-placed donations. Typical stuff for teenagers with too much money and too little supervision.

But then—a homicide.

Lawson's brows knitted together as the word leapt off the screen. Her stomach tightened as she clicked on the file. The unresolved case of Matthew Brown. A senior at Claire's elite prep school, dead under suspicious circumstances just months before graduation.

The further she read, the more unsettling it became. It wasn't just the death itself—it was the other cases on the list leading up to it. A series of escalating incidents painted a troubling picture.

One report detailed a string of harassing anonymous notes discovered in students' lockers. Some were scrawled with slurs, others with veiled threats. One note in particular stood out: "WATCH YOUR BACK." The victim, Matthew Brown, was among those who had reported receiving one of these notes.

Another incident described a violent altercation during a football game. Matthew had been shoved into the bleachers by a fellow teammate during halftime. The scuffle was chalked up to "boys being boys," but witnesses described the confrontation as far more intense, with shouts of, "You'll regret it!"

As Lawson clicked through the reports, her unease deepened. Weeks before Matthew's death, police had responded to a 911 call about a trespassing incident at his home. The details were vague, with no suspect ever identified, but Matthew had told responding officers he'd heard someone outside his window late at night.

And then, the homicide itself.

The official report described a chaotic house party—too much alcohol, dozens of teenagers, and no adults. Matthew had been found outside, shot once in the chest. Witnesses claimed it was an accident, the result of reckless handling of a family heirloom firearm. But the details didn't add up.

The gun had supposedly been locked in a shed, yet it had somehow ended up on display during the party. There were conflicting statements about who had touched it and when. Some witnesses said Matthew was holding the gun moments before the shot was fired. Others swore they saw someone else, though no one could agree on who or even where this incident occurred on the property.

Her brow furrowed as she read through the reports. Something didn't sit right. The lead detective had recommended closing the matter with several loose ends. He hadn't done half the investigative work that this sort of case would warrant.

Lawson pulled up the arrest records of the case to see if there had been any suspects at all. She blinked in surprise as the name stared back at her. Claire Stevens.

It had been expunged, but Claire had been arrested in connection with the shooting. Perhaps that explained why Claire always seemed jumpy every time she came to the station. It wasn't abnormal for high school students to get arrested for attending parties. It was just a little out of character for perfect Miss Stevens.

The shooting took place at a residence in Ardsley Park. She copied and pasted the address into the city's land records. The home had been purchased about three years before the shooting by the Stevens family. Claire's family.

The house had been listed for sale less than a year after the shooting, but it had taken a few years to eventually sell, and at a significant loss for the family. They'd even taken the listing off and reposted later on. Even then, it had taken months for anyone to bite.

Lawson leaned back in her chair, mind racing. This wasn't just Claire attending some high school party and getting trashed. This had been her house. She'd obviously thrown the party, the shooting happened, and then she'd been arrested in connection with his death.

Lawson started looking into the victim, pulling up every record and file she could find on the system. Matthew Brown came from a wealthy family himself. His father, George Brown, had been a successful financial advisor in Savannah. Following Matthew's death, he'd decided to shutter the business and retire. Records indicated that the family home in the North End had been sold. The family moved to a different state. Lawson wondered if the pain of losing a child had been too much for him to stay. Sometimes that kind of loss could make your entire family feel like a crime scene.

According to records, George Brown had another biological child by a different woman, an elder daughter named Elizabeth.

Elizabeth Brown. The name was so familiar. She searched for it, not expecting to find many hits. Both first and last names were common, but she was surprised when it generated a hit in the police's system.

Elizabeth Brown was a registered psychologist, most recently working at Augusta Medical Facility. Lawson pulled up the list of criminal cases she had been assigned to. She blinked her eyes rapidly, trying to comprehend what she was seeing. The woman had only ever been assigned to one case. And it was Anthony Bates'.

A deeper look into the file revealed a private memo between the prosecutor and the judge. The prosecutor had requested a second opinion on Bates' mental state. The psychologist they consulted had previously worked with Bates in the private sector. Bates had a long history of being committed, something his family had worked hard to keep hidden.

The judge had granted the motion, and Dr. Elizabeth Brown constructed a new psychological report, discarding the first one.

Lawson paused for a minute as she tried to piece together the information. Matty Brown had been a classmate of Claire's in high school. Claire had thrown a party where some drunk teenagers had found guns and shot Matty. Matty's sister, Elizabeth, had been Anthony Bates' psychologist.

And now Claire was being stalked in the same fashion that Bates stalked his own victims.

That's when Lawson froze, her breath catching in her throat. The pieces snapped into place, and she realized with chilling certainty—she had been wrong. Claire wasn't imagining things. She was being targeted.

But not by Bates. It couldn't be him.

The revelation all but knocked the wind out of Lawson. Bates had been a victim himself, dragged into a deadly game he hadn't even seen coming. Someone else had been pulling the strings all along, and now they had their sights set on Claire.

Panic surged through her as she grabbed her keys off the desk, her mind racing. Claire had been right to fear for her life, and Lawson had wasted precious time dismissing her concerns. She practically bolted out of the station, her shoes slamming against the linoleum floor, her heart pounding louder with each step.

Sliding into her squad car, she fumbled with the ignition before finally getting it started. The engine roared to life, and she floored it out of the lot, tires squealing against the pavement. The streetlights blurred past as she sped through the city, gripping the wheel so tightly her knuckles turned white.

She pressed harder on the gas. She had to get to Claire before she turned up dead.

chapter
forty-eight

CLAIRE BLINKED her eyes open slowly. She tried to move but her limbs were weighed down, sunken into the earth and numb. Her vision attempted to adjust to the dim light. After a time, she could make out wooden walls and shelves. The musky scent of damp early morning filled her nostrils. This was a cellar of some sort, possibly a shed.

Turning her head, she spotted a small, blurred light in the corner. Beside it was the silhouette of a familiar woman, her red hair tucked tight into a bun.

"Awake at last, Claire?" The woman turned and flashed Claire a wicked grin. "You're probably wondering where you are, how you got here, yes?"

She sauntered closer and leaned in, as if whispering a secret. "I pulled you from the crash and brought you here to this lovely shed. Do you recognize it?" She waited for Claire's answer, but Claire stayed quiet. "It's your old family home. In Ardsley Park, remember?"

Claire's heart hammered in her chest. Her eyes darted around the shed, searching for anything that might help to free her. But the dim light and her blurred vision revealed little besides dusty shelves and cobwebbed corners.

"You really should relax, dear. You certainly did make things easier for me by taking those antidepressants I gave you." The woman moved to Claire's side and adjusted something. Claire tracked her movements and noticed an IV bag with clear liquid flowing through the tube jabbed inside of her arm.

"Just a little fentanyl for you," she said sweetly. "Mixed with those happy pills you've been taking, it'll cause you something called serotonin toxicity. But it won't kill you right away. I want you to suffer, Claire. To know your end is coming and be able to do nothing about it."

The woman leaned down, breath hot against Claire's ear. "I could end this fast, but that'd be too kind. Your agony will be exquisite, lasting hours or maybe even days. However long it takes." She straightened. "A quick death is too good for you, Claire Stevens. I want you to really feel what it's like. To suffer like I've suffered."

Claire fought against the pull of the drugs, struggling to focus her fuzzy mind. She had to stay awake. She put all her effort into trying to focus on the person in front of her. Her vision responded, clearing enough so that she could see. She studied the woman's face. Those green eyes were now cold and filled with hate. And that voice, usually so warm and reassuring, now chilling and sinister.

With great effort, Claire forced out a single cracked word. "Meredith?"

"Very good, Claire!" Meredith leaned down and patted Claire's cheek. "I'm impressed you figured it out, even doped up as you are. Took you long enough though. Sometimes book smarts aren't everything, huh?"

Meredith laughed, the sound grating against Claire's ears. "I left so many clues. But you were too self-absorbed to notice anything amiss with your dear old friend."

Claire shook her head weakly. She hadn't wanted to believe that it was Meredith. Even when she'd figured it out earlier that evening, there was still a part of her that hoped she was wrong.

"Why?" Claire rasped.

Meredith's eyes hardened. "Why do you think? You're the last loose end, Claire. The final name to cross off my list." Meredith laughed. "You really shouldn't have gotten Bates acquitted. Shouldn't have kept digging. I was never going to kill him, but now you'll join him in the grave."

Claire squeezed her eyes shut against a wave of nausea and dread. Bates had been innocent? And now he was dead because of her?

Meredith let out an exaggerated sigh. "I suppose you still don't understand. I guess I'll have to explain it to you."

She walked over to the IV bag and adjusted something as she began to speak. "My real name isn't Meredith Porter. It's Elizabeth Brown. You know, Dr. Elizabeth Brown from Anthony's psychological report. And Matty Hodges was my half-brother."

Claire's eyes widened. Despite the drugs invading her system faster now, Claire couldn't stop the sob that lingered in her chest. She tried hard to move her body again, but her limbs just wouldn't cooperate.

"Matty was the sweetest soul," Meredith continued, her voice taking on a wistful quality. "He had so many dreams. But because of you, he ended up dead at eighteen."

Claire flinched, unsure if her eyes were spilling tears or if the drugs were making them feel fuzzy .

"It took me some time to piece it all together. I knew Matty was shot at your party, but I thought it was just a freak accident, just like everyone said it was. But something didn't sit right about that with me." Meredith put a finger on her chin, the image of her oscillating between clear and blurry. "Matty wasn't the type of boy to play with guns. He also wasn't the type of boy to hang out at parties with football players. So, I started digging.

"As expected, it wasn't hard to find out that Matty hadn't died from some accident. He'd been shot on purpose. The autopsy records showed that without too much effort, but a few well-placed inquiries of people at the party who saw the incident confirmed my suspicion.

"At first, I just went after the football players. I wanted them to feel the same loss I did. I wanted to take a younger sibling away from them. Someone they loved dearly. But I needed someone to take the fall. And then I found Bates."

She smirked. "Poor, stupid Anthony. So desperate to be liked. I met him when I was in my residency at Augusta. His parents were constantly admitting him because of his outbursts. What they didn't want to admit was that he was mentally fine. They were the ones who'd made him unstable by not accepting the fact that he was gay."

"But as bad as I felt for him, he was just who I needed." She paused and sighed. "Well, I didn't feel too bad for him. He was part of high society. The same society that ostracized me for the mistakes of my father. The same society that killed Matty." Meredith chortled.

"Bates was easy to manipulate. He became unstable because no one accepted him for who he was. But that worked to my benefit. I gave him all the details of the victims. His memory was very suggestive. By the time our therapy was finished, he was convinced that he was the one to carry out the murders.

"He wasn't, of course. I would never have left that up to him. What's the saying, if you want something done right, you have to do it yourself?" Meredith laughed. "I gave him the psilocybin and dropped him off on the street that day. Called in the anonymous tip to the police, because they were so desperate for any lead. Worked like a charm and they picked him up just like I knew they would.

"You were right and wrong to suspect Lawson. She bends the rules to suit her needs. But she wouldn't be bothered to stalk you just because she was angry over the appeal," Meredith laughed. " I did love letting you run away with that possibility."

Claire's heart hammered against her ribs. She thought of all the misery Meredith had caused in Matty's name. All the innocent lives destroyed. And Claire had unknowingly played right into her hands.

Meredith looked at Claire, brushing the hair sticking to her sweaty forehead back with her hand in a way that was far too gentle given the current situation. "I thought I would be satisfied to just take out the ones who killed Matty. But you see, when I got to one of the football players, a boy named Evan, he was wracked with guilt. I barely had to drug him to get him talking. He was happy to tell me that it was you who told him that Matty was gay. That they had targeted him because of it." Meredith's features hardened. "Matty had never told anyone but me. But apparently he trusted you enough to share his ultimate secret.

And how did you repay his trust? By blabbing it to the first boy that gave you any attention."

Meredith shook her head in disgust. "When I learned you had everything to do with Matty's death, I decided I couldn't let you live, Claire. Evan may have pulled the trigger, but you were the one who killed Matty. And Bates for that matter. He wouldn't have had to die. That fool Daniel was scared off from trying too hard on his original case by a few anonymous phone calls. But you, you had to stick your nose in. Get him acquitted. Force me to improvise. You should have let sleeping dogs lie."

"Who's Meredith?" Claire managed to rasp.

"You know how easy it is to steal an identity these days? Well, it is if you know the right people, which I do." Meredith smirked. "Dr. Meredith Porter really does exist. She graduated from Augusta, just like me, practiced psychology for a time before she burned out of the field. Her credentials were easy enough to snag without anyone paying too close attention. Even her." Meredith spoke the words as if she were proud of them.

Her eyes bore into Claire's. "And in case things are too hazy for you to piece it together, yes. It was Bates' body in that car. He was placed there ahead of time. And I did remove most of his teeth to slow the police down in their identification. Plus, it had the added benefit of making you seem even crazier when you kept going around convinced that Bates was alive."

Claire opened her mouth to speak, but no words came out. Just a thin trail of blood from the corner of her lips. The taste of metal lingered in her mouth.

Meredith smiled softly. "There now. It will all be over soon. You can finally atone for what you did."

Claire tried to summon anger, outrage, anything to fight the encroaching darkness. But she was so tired. And maybe this was justice, in a way. Punishment for her sins.

"He loved you, you know," Meredith said softly. "Matty thought you hung the moon. That's why he told you his secret."

A tear slid down Claire's cheek as she remembered Matty. Sweet, kind Matty who'd only ever wanted to do good in the world and be Claire's best friend. She wished she could take it all back. Undo the damage she'd caused. But it was too late.

"You were always so selfish," Meredith said. "Only cared about your career, your ambitions. Never about the people you stepped on along the way." She stroked Claire's hair, almost lovingly. " I hope all your success was worth it. Because now you have nothing. And soon, you'll be nothing."

Claire tried to cling to consciousness, but it slipped through her fingers like sand. The edges of her vision faded inward, and the last thing she saw was Meredith's cold, triumphant smile.

chapter
forty-nine

MEREDITH WATCHED as Claire's eyes drifted shut, her breathing slowing. Soon, those pesky vital signs would stop altogether, and Meredith would finally have her vengeance.

She thought back to when she'd first met Anthony, so desperate for connection that he'd latched onto anyone who showed him kindness. She'd played the part of the caring confidante, listening to him pour his heart out about his troubled relationship with his mother and his struggle to hide his sexuality.

It had been Meredith who picked him up at the prison on the day of his release. She couldn't risk him being out and getting actual help. It would have come out quickly that he wasn't the one to commit the murders. It would only have been a matter of time for people to figure out that Elizabeth Brown was Meredith Porter.

Poor, pathetic Anthony. He'd gone to his death still believing she cared for him. If only he knew he was just a means to an end, a tool she'd used and discarded. But he hadn't been the first. Anyone that got in her way would meet the same fate.

His mother had been easy to manipulate as well. An anonymous letter delivered to her doorstep pointing out the flaws in Daniel's legal work during Anthony's case had led her down the path of hiring Claire. Meredith had wanted Claire involved with Anthony's case so she could torment her along the way. She just hadn't anticipated that Claire was competent enough to actually get Anthony released.

But it all worked out in the end. Bates was dead and Claire would be too. And the detective—Meredith chuckled—the detective had once again let it all slip through her fingers, unable to do her job to even the smallest degree.

For now, Meredith just had to wait. Another twenty minutes and it would finally be over. And then, she could give Matty the peace he deserved.

chapter
fifty

LAWSON'S FEET pounded up the stairs, taking them two at a time. She reached Claire's apartment door and pounded her fist against it. "Claire!" She shouted, banging again. Silence.

Lawson cursed under her breath. She never should have left Claire alone. Now who knew where she could be?

She tried to remember everything she just learned. If she was right about who was stalking Claire, then there were only a few places they could be. She wracked her brain trying to figure out which was more likely, but a buzzing from her pocket distracted her.

She grabbed it, heart leaping when she saw the name. She swiped to answer. "Claire? Where are you?"

Muffled sounds came through the speaker. Lawson pressed the phone harder to her ear, straining to make out the words. A voice in the background, too distorted to identify.

"Shit." She sprinted for the stairwell, keeping the call connected.

She jumped into her squad car, adrenaline surging through her veins as she fumbled to flip on the GPS tracker. Her hands trembled slightly, and she cursed under her breath, willing the device to respond faster. The screen flickered, the loading icon spinning agonizingly slowly as it worked to triangulate the call's location.

"Come on, come on," Lawson muttered, her fingers tapping impatiently on the steering wheel.

After what felt like an eternity, the device beeped, and a location finally blinked onto the screen. She leaned in, squinting at the map as a small red beacon appeared, pulsating softly against the gridlines. Her heart sank.

Claire's location didn't make sense. It almost looked like she had been heading toward the station before suddenly veering off course. The detour was abrupt, the path erratic, zigzagging through side streets and cutting away from the main roads.

Lawson hit the gas, tires squealing as she tore onto the street.

A few miles up the road and a few minutes of driving through twisted backroads brought Lawson to the location blinking on her GPS tracker. Her squad car skidded to a stop on the gravel shoulder. Up ahead, a car lay crumpled in the ditch, its front end still steaming and taillights blinking.

Lawson leaped out of the squad car, careful to keep her balance on the uneven ground.

"Claire?" she called out, but she was met with silence. She trotted over to the car. Glass crunched under her boots with each measured step that she took. The driver side door was slightly ajar and the glass had been busted through, shattered all over the interior. The driver's seatbelt had been cut too. Sunken airbags rested on the driver's seat.

Lawson reached inside, spotting Claire's cell phone sitting on the passenger seat. The phone was unlocked as the call was still active. Ending the call, she quickly swiped through the phone to find any messages or numbers dialed that could help piece this together.

It was obvious that Claire had dialed Lawson's number around the time of the crash. Had she done it to try and let Lawson know her last location? Had she known someone was after her when she made the call? Or had she been distracted? None of that could explain why Lawson was staring at an empty car. That muffled voice must have been the perpetrator, here at the scene. Snatching Claire from the wreckage before she could arrive.

Jaw clenched, Lawson ran back to her squad car. She had a good idea who was behind this, and a hunch as to where they might be.

She grabbed the radio. "Detective Lawson requesting immediate backup and an ambulance to 516 East 44th Street, Ardsley Park. I have reason to believe a kidnapping has occurred, and there's also been a car crash. I need medical assistance on standby. Please expedite."

Tires spinning, Lawson sped away from the crash site. She raced down the dark country road, her headlights cutting through the night. It was only a couple minutes' drive but it felt like an eternity getting out to the Stevens' old residence.

When she finally pulled up to it, she was met with an intricate wrought iron gate. It was locked and for a moment she thought she may have made a mistake. She shook her head, pushed off her doubt, and stepped on the gas, ramming the gate open with the grill of her car.

The metal gave way with a squeal of protest and her tires tore through the damp night grass as she circled the car to the back of the property. A small shed came into view. She breathed a sigh of relief as she saw a glimpse of light creeping through the panels of the shed.

Opening her door, she exited her car quietly and drew her weapon. She approached the door of the shed cautiously. Her heart pounded as she put her ear against it, listening to see if she could hear anything inside.

Nothing.

She reached for the door and tried the handle.

Locked.

She pounded her fist against it. "Police! Open up!"

More silence. She pounded again, harder. "Police! Open up!"

The shed was either vacant, or the occupants weren't going to open the door. She took a step back and braced herself before delivering a powerful kick with her boot. The door burst open, the wood splintering as her foot went clean through the door.

She held her breath and stepped to the side, gun outstretched and ready, but no one attempted to shoot at her. She reached her hand to the inside of the door through the hole she had just made and unlocked it. The door swung open.

Weapon raised, she swept inside. At first, the shed appeared empty. Then her gaze fell upon a dark shape crumpled in the corner.

Lawson hurried over and knelt down to find Claire, unconscious, an IV line taped to the crook of her elbow. Lawson quickly removed it and checked for a pulse. It was there, but dangerously faint. Claire's skin had a deathly pallor.

She looked at the IV bag. It was unmarked, clear liquid. There was no way that Lawson could know just what had been given to Claire based on that alone. She turned her over gently and tried to get a response, but Claire was more than unresponsive. Lawson carefully lifted the woman's eyelids to check her pupils. Heavily dilated. There was a bit of vomit on the floor where she'd been curled up.

Jaw set, Lawson sprinted back to her squad car. She threw the trunk door open, the sound of the latch clanging echoing in her ears as she grabbed the medical kit. Heart pounding, she raced back inside, dropping to her knees beside Claire.

She ripped the bag open, the contents spilling out in her haste. Her fingers fumbled as she grabbed a vial of naloxone, her breath coming in short, panicked bursts. "Focus," she muttered to herself, forcing her hands to steady enough to prepare the syringe.

She stuck the first injection into Claire's upper arm, the needle piercing the skin with practiced precision. "Come on, Claire," she whispered, her voice strained as she checked her watch, counting down the seconds.

Claire didn't move.

Lawson clenched her jaw, her pulse roaring in her ears. "Damn it," she hissed under her breath, glancing down at Claire's pale face. Her chest wasn't rising. No breath, no movement.

She grabbed another dose, her hands shaking again as she loaded the syringe. "Stay with me, Stevens," she muttered through gritted teeth, injecting the second dose and leaning back, staring at Claire as if sheer willpower could force her to wake up.

The seconds stretched into what felt like hours. Lawson leaned closer, her hand hovering just over Claire's chest feeling for movement. Nothing.

She glanced at her watch again. Thirty seconds. Forty. A minute. Still nothing.

The room felt suffocatingly silent except for Lawson's ragged breaths. Her mind raced, a dozen worst-case scenarios flashing before her eyes. Had she been too late? Had the dose been enough?

Finally, after what felt like an eternity, Claire's eyelids fluttered. A shallow gasp escaped her lips, and her chest heaved weakly.

Lawson let out a ragged breath of relief, her knees buckling beneath her as she crouched lower beside Claire. "Claire? Can you hear me?"

Claire's squinted gaze found Lawson's, glazed with confusion.

"Help is coming. Just try to stay still," Lawson said. She doubted Claire understood anything.

True to form, Claire struggled to rise. Lawson pressed her back down firmly.

"Not this time. You need to rest."

Claire's eyes blazed, but she relented. She tried to speak, but all that came out were faint whispers and coughs full of dry blood.

Finally, her lips formed a name. "Meredith."

chapter
fifty-one

MEREDITH PEERED THROUGH THE TREES, her heart pounding. She watched as Detective Lawson's car made deep tire marks in the soft mud as she made her way to the shed. She'd heard a loud bang minutes earlier, which prompted her to abandon the shed and hide. Claire was still alive, but she'd turned the IV drip to full, hoping that it'd be enough to end her quickly. It was only a matter of time before the drugs overwhelmed her system.

Meredith watched as Lawson approached the shed cautiously. She had to stifle a laugh as the detective tried to announce her presence. No one would be answering, especially not Claire. She watched Lawson kick in the door and a few minutes later, run back out to her squad car. No doubt she'd found Claire unconscious inside.

Sirens wailed in the distance as Lawson sprinted back inside the shed, a medical kit under her arm. Meredith shook her head and tried to tell herself there was no way Claire could still be alive in there. That Lawson was wasting her time.

The next few minutes passed like hours as Meredith waited to see what would happen. An ambulance and five cop cars raced onto the property, lights rotating furiously and sirens wailing. Paramedics entered the area under the strobe lights and hurried into the shed.

Meredith risked being caught if she stayed much longer. The police would start combing the area soon.

But she had to see Claire wheeled out of that shed in a body bag, otherwise she'd never feel at peace. Several minutes stretched on until finally, the shed door opened back up and the first sign of paramedics emerged.

Except, Claire wasn't in a body bag. She was alive, with an oxygen mask over her face. Meredith nearly screamed in frustration as she watched them load her into the ambulance.

Police and their K9s exited their vehicles, the dogs already with their heads low to the ground, taking every command of their handler. This was Meredith's cue to leave the area and quickly. She ran the short distance to her car and prayed that firing up the engine wouldn't alert the entire police force of her location. Pulling out onto the back road, her hands shook as she tried to grip the steering wheel.

She tried to keep her breathing and driving steady. She'd failed and Claire was still alive. What would she do now? The police would be hunting her relentlessly if they figured out it was her. Even if she managed to escape tonight, Claire would certainly tell them when she awoke.

She needed somewhere to lay low and think about her next move. Meredith drove aimlessly for a while, her mind racing.

She berated herself for deciding to go after Claire. She should have targeted Fiona like she had intended when all of this started. But with Claire coming back to the city, and ultimately responsible for Matty's death, she couldn't help herself.

After about twenty minutes, she was on the outskirts of the city, pulling up to a graveyard that had mostly been forgotten.

In the early hours of the morning, there was no one around, not even on the nearby roads. She was safe enough here for now. Meredith pulled up to the front gate and stepped out into the damp morning air. She clicked on a small flashlight and wove her way through the tombstones, walking a path she had memorized.

Matty's grave was under a large oak tree, tucked away in a far corner of the plot. Meredith sighed and sank down onto the damp grass in front of his tombstone, letting the flashlight fall onto the earth. It illuminated the reflective, shining gray stone and she could make out his birth date and the words, "Matthew 'Matty' Hodges. Beloved son, brother, and friend."

"Hey, Matty," she whispered, pulling her knees to her chest. "I'm so sorry. I tried, I really did. But that damn Claire just won't die."

She chuckled ruefully and the wind whistled through the bare branches above, as if in response. Meredith sighed.

She reached out and traced the letters of his name carved into the cold granite. "Don't worry. I'll make this right. I'll finish what I started. Then you can finally rest in peace."

Meredith wasn't sure how much time passed as she sat there, the chill seeping into her bones. But she was calmer now. She lost track of time as the sun made its appearance, warming her slightly. She closed her eyes, heavy with fatigue and leaned against the trunk of the tree. She just needed a few minutes to rest after fifteen years of unrest.

"Why'd you do it?"

The voice cut through the early morning haze, making Meredith jump. She pushed against the tree, trying to stand, but exhaustion had finally overtaken her. She stumbled back against the oak, gripping the bark for support.

Detective Lawson approached her, her hands in her pockets and her expression neutral, curious even. She waited for an answer but Meredith was still too stunned at her failure to speak.

"Why'd you kill them, Meredith?" Lawson asked again, her tone stern but not unkind. "Or, should I say, Elizabeth?"

How did Lawson find her? She'd checked to make sure she wasn't followed the entire ride out to the cemetery. Claire shouldn't have been conscious enough to even speak.

Was it possible that Lawson really figured it out on her own?

"I...I don't know what you're talking about."

Lawson stepped closer. "I think you do. I found Claire in the shed overdosed on fentanyl. Found another vial of the stuff in your car parked out front. It's over."

Meredith's shoulders slumped in defeat. No point in pretending anymore.

"I did it for him," she said softly, gesturing at Matty's grave with her chin. "His death destroyed me. I wanted them to feel that same pain. Not just Claire, but all of them."

Lawson nodded slowly. "So you targeted their loved ones for revenge?"

"Yes," Meredith replied. "They deserved it after what they did to Matty."

"Why not just kill the ones who killed Matty, then?"

"Because a quick death is too generous. There's so much more suffering that can be had through life," she explained, unsure the detective would understand. "For years, I lived with the pain of losing a younger sibling. The guilt in knowing that maybe I could have saved him if I'd been more present. I wanted them to know that pain. Live with it all their lives."

"Maybe so," Lawson said, her hands still in her pockets. "But killing innocents, destroying more families? Do you really think Matty would've wanted that?"

Meredith shrugged her shoulders. "Matty's not here. That's the whole point." After a long pause, she asked, "Is Claire dead?"

Lawson hesitated before answering. "No, she'll recover."

Meredith closed her eyes. At least she had gotten close. Caused Claire some of the stress and anxiety that she'd felt over the last decade and a half.

Lawson stepped forward and put a hand on her arm. "Come on, let's go."

Meredith didn't resist as Lawson led her away from Matty's grave. She placed Meredith in the squad car and started up the engine, driving away from Matty's resting place. Meredith stared out the window as the sun came up, the skyline of Savannah coming into view, its church spires and historic rooftops silhouetted against the soft pink and orange hues of dawn.

She knew it might be the very last time that she was able to visit

Matty's grave for a very long time, and she wanted to savor the way the morning looked.

She looked up and caught Lawson's gaze in the rearview mirror. The detective was watching her.

Lawson broke the uncomfortable silence as she shifted her eyes between the mirror and the road. "I have to ask...the gifts you left at each scene. What was the meaning behind them?"

Meredith took a shaky breath before responding.

"They were inspired by a gift Matty had put together for Claire before he died. It was supposed to be her graduation present. I found it in his room—a letter telling her how much he valued their friendship, a bottle of her favorite perfume, a friendship bracelet she'd given him when she'd first gotten to the school. And the police report said he brought her flowers the night of the party."

Meredith's voice broke with a sob. "It was one of the last things he did. So I decided to do the same for the victims, in that order—the letter, the personal item, the memento, and then the flowers."

"You understand how insane this sounds, right? That poor boy is gone, and killing others won't bring him back." Lawson shook her head, her expression not unkind. "It's not what he would have wanted. I think you know that, too."

Meredith's eyes flashed with anger. "You don't get it. I did what I had to do. What they deserved."

"And I'm doing what I have to do," Lawson said firmly. "I'm bringing you in because I believe in justice, not vengeance. One of us is doing right by Matty's memory. The other is soiling it."

Meredith shook her head. She didn't need to argue with the detective. She'd done the right thing. She was just sad that she hadn't been able to see it all the way through. Fiona. Claire. They should have been her last victims. Instead, they would live their lives and never think about Matty, or the pain Meredith would have to live with for the rest of her life.

chapter
fifty-two

THE CEMETERY WAS BATHED in a dreary grey light, matching the somber mood of the mourners gathered around the casket. Claire scanned the crowd, taking in the blank faces and bowed heads. She noted Dolores Bates' stony expression, not a crack in her stoic facade as she stared straight ahead. Daniel stood solemnly beside Fiona, gently squeezing her hand in support. Claire's parents were composed, her mother attempting to act distraught by clutching a crumpled tissue. Even the city prosecutor had shown up, leaving Claire to wonder whether such an appearance was appropriate.

The casket was made from a gleaming, polished wood. She thought of the charred remains inside, the secrets and trauma that had shaped Anthony's twisted life. Sure, she had been successful in overturning his conviction, but guilt still gnawed at her for her suspicions of him afterward.

When she'd finally gotten home from the hospital, she'd revisited her notes one last time from their interview. Now, after knowing he had never been the culprit, and hadn't even been a murderer, the words he'd spoken now carried a very different meaning. His comments about his mother, his remarks about her perfume, his playful attitude. He was simply a man suffering under the weight of his family's expectations. That was all.

The pastor began speaking, his words hollow in her ears. Her thoughts turned to Meredith. It was weird to think about her sitting in a prison cell. So much had happened while Claire recovered from her forced overdose in the hospital.

Following Meredith's arrest, the judge had denied her bond, as she was a clear flight risk. Claire would need to testify against her former friend, if she could even be called that. While she wasn't looking forward to reliving the nightmare she'd just been through, she would do what needed to be done.

She wasn't sure how to process her false friendship. Looking back, the woman had been truly helpful and supportive at times. Had everything just been an act? Claire shook her head, trying to shake loose the thoughts that were swirling around inside. It didn't help to dwell on these things.

She'd also realized she had a stronger support system than she'd thought. Fiona and her mother had come to visit several times, and her father had been there almost every day. Even the detective had made an appearance at her bedside.

Claire had admitted her guilt to Lawson for ever suspecting Anthony. Had she just looked beyond the picture the city had painted of him, maybe she wouldn't have been so blind to the true culprit right under her nose.

"We're both guilty of that," Lawson had sighed. "And at the end of the day, you were the only one who agreed to take his appeal and fight for him. Be grateful you're on that side of the equation, unlike me who will go down in history as being on the other side."

Claire had felt a pang of sympathy for the detective. She still didn't like the woman, but perhaps this experience had led her to better understand her.

Claire's attention drifted back to the pastor's droning voice.

"Though Anthony struggled with inner demons," the pastor intoned, "he was a child of God, worthy of compassion and empathy."

Claire scanned the crowd, taking in the stony faces of Savannah high society. Their carefully curated appearances couldn't hide the judgment in their eyes. She doubted many of them had compassion for Anthony Bates. Most had likely come to the service out of obligation or morbid curiosity rather than genuine grief.

The pastor continued. "We must not judge those who walk a different path, for we all carry secret burdens..."

Claire noticed heads turning and whispers being exchanged. Word of Anthony's sexuality had spread through the grapevine. Claire turned to look at Dolores sitting rigidly, humiliation clearly washing over her as her son's "shameful secret" was hinted at.

Claire felt a swell of pity for Anthony, imagining the torment he must have endured, unable to be his true self. He was a broken man who had strayed down a dark path, only to be betrayed and murdered by someone he trusted. She may not have been able to save him, but she could still honor his memory by ensuring his killer was brought to justice.

The pastor concluded the eulogy with a passage from Corinthians. "Would anyone like to say a few words?" he asked the crowd.

Despite the large number of people in attendance, no one came forward to speak on the man's behalf. Not even his own mother.

Awkward silence ensued. The pastor was about to give the signal to lower the casket, when Claire stood and walked forward. She wasn't sure what she was going to say, but the man deserved more than a silent send-off.

As she stood beside the casket, Claire's eyes swept across the faces in the crowd. For much of the service, those faces had been downcast, eyes fixed on the ground or their hands, their expressions unreadable. Now, they were turned upward, watching her with expectant and hungry gazes. The air was heavy with curiosity and judgment, a force that pressed against her chest as she stood there. She felt the weight of their stares, their need for her words to fill the uncomfortable silence that had hung over the service.

"I'd only met Anthony once," Claire began, her voice trembling slightly. She paused, clearing her throat and gathering her composure. "But even in that short time span, I allowed our city's perceptions of him to cloud my own." Her words hung in the air, and she could almost feel the tension ripple through the crowd. "Anthony was a man who needed acceptance, not judgment. His tragic life story has taught me to look deeper, with more empathy, and to promise myself to do better. I hope all of you will do the same."

Her voice cracked slightly on the last sentence, and she took a deep breath to steady herself. Blinking back tears, Claire stepped away from the front and returned to her seat. The pastor caught her eye, offering a slight smile and an approving nod.

After a final prayer, the attendees began to filter away. Quiet murmurs rippled through the crowd, heels clicking against the stone paths as they departed.

Claire remained seated, her hands folded tightly in her lap. Her gaze lingered on the casket. His life had been a storm of struggle and pain—crushed by expectations, tarnished by betrayal, and weighed down by secrets that no one could fully understand. It wasn't just Anthony's death that haunted her; it was the reminder of how easily people could be dismissed, reduced to nothing more than whispers and rumors in a town like Savannah.

Claire waited a few more minutes, saying a silent goodbye, before she finally took a deep breath of the cool air and started making her way to the car.

Fiona came up next to her and grabbed her hand. "What you said was nice."

"Thanks," Claire said with a small smile.

She was glad that she and her sister had reconnected, despite everything. She was especially glad that Meredith hadn't decided to go after Fiona.

What Meredith hadn't understood was the depth of Claire's pain. Losing Matty had been a blow that shattered her, leaving cracks in places that had never quite healed. It wasn't just grief—it was guilt, anger, and a profound sense of helplessness that had consumed her for years. While Meredith had every right to feel betrayed and to seek justice, she hadn't seen how close Claire had come to breaking under the weight of it all.

"You did right by him today," a voice said, stirring Claire from her reverie. She turned to see Detective Lawson, her expression unusually kind.

"I'll meet you at the car," Fiona said and headed toward the parking lot.

Lawson placed a hand on Claire's shoulder. "Don't beat yourself up over the past. Just keep seeking the truth."

Claire nodded. It was a good way to put it.

"I think I've been looking for a purpose," Claire found herself admitting. "A reason to wake up and go to the office each morning. Maybe that's what this whole experience was for me." She shook her head. "Learn from my mistakes. Use them to become a better advocate for the vulnerable among us."

Lawson nodded. "I hope it works out for you, Claire. And I hope that moving forward, we're on the same side of the equation."

"Me too." Claire smiled at the detective's words of reassurance before turning to search the dispersing crowd for her sister who was waiting by the car.

Claire made her way through the headstones, the crunch of gravel under her heels punctuating the heavy silence. She caught snippets of hushed conversations as she passed mourners, their voices tinged with both relief and regret now that the truth about Anthony had come to light.

She was nearly to the parking lot when a voice called out behind her. "Claire!"

Claire paused and turned to see Dolores Bates walking towards her. Anthony's mother looked weary, her usual composure somewhat fractured.

"I just wanted to thank you for speaking on Anthony's behalf," Dolores said once she caught up. "It meant the world to me."

Claire gave her a sad smile. "Of course. I'm so sorry for your loss."

Dolores waved a hand. "It's quite alright, dear. At least now people know he was truly innocent. As I'm sure you're aware, many didn't believe he should have been released. Our family name would have carried that stigma around for many years to come had you not successfully removed it." Dolores looked pensive for a minute. "I do think the gossip surrounding his... preferences is something that we can manage and will eventually fade from public eye. We have you to thank for all of it."

Claire tensed, suppressing a flare of annoyance. Even in mourning, Dolores seemed preoccupied with status and reputation, rather than the loss of her son. As if her son's life was meaningless apart from how it affected people's perception of her family name.

"I'm sorry his life was so lonely," Claire said bluntly. "If only you had accepted him as he was, perhaps he wouldn't have had to suffer in both life and death, and I wouldn't have had to be involved at all. There's more to the world than status and money, Dolores."

Claire turned on her heel, leaving a stunned Dolores Bates behind without another word. She strode towards the parking lot, irritation still simmering in her chest. She understood grief could make people act strangely, but Dolores' preoccupation with status was nothing new.

She didn't notice her father until he fell into step beside her.

"That was quite a conversation back there," Roy said. "I'm proud of you for speaking your mind."

Claire huffed a humorless laugh. "Well, we can kiss goodbye any more dinner party invitations from the Bates family."

"Good riddance. Those affairs are dead boring anyway." He chuckled and nudged her with his elbow. "You still coming for dinner at our house tomorrow? Your mom's making pot roast." He paused. "Well, your mom's making someone else make pot roast."

Claire smiled slightly, remembering Meredith's advice to take time for herself. The woman may have been unhinged, but she made some good points.

"I was actually thinking of heading to the beach," Claire said. "Clear my head a bit."

Roy nodded. "A fine idea. The ocean air will do you good."

They reached the parking lot. With a final squeeze of her shoulder, Roy headed for his car and turned to look at Fiona. "Riding with me or your sister?"

Fiona looked at Claire. "Did you want some alone time?"

Claire nodded. "Actually, if you don't mind, I have somewhere I want to go quickly."

"Catch up for lunch next week?" Fiona asked.

"Of course," Claire said as she gave her sister a hug.

Claire took one last look at the cemetery before getting into her car and started the engine. Her next visit was long overdue.

chapter
fifty-three

CLAIRE PULLED her car off the main road and onto a narrow dirt path leading up a grassy hill. She had driven far outside the city limits, past the subdivisions and shopping centers, until the urban sprawl gave way to stretches of open farmland. This was the first time she had come out here. She had always wanted to, but until today, she could never bring herself to visit.

Claire shifted the car into park and stared out at the rows of weathered tombstones dotting the hillside. Her hands gripped the steering wheel tightly even after she shut off the ignition.

With a deep breath, Claire let go of the wheel and stepped out of the car. The wind whipped strands of hair across her face as she made her way up the hill, each step heavier than the last. Her sneakers sunk into the soft earth as she wove between the graves. She knew which one was his before she even saw the engraving.

Claire stopped before the simple tombstone. Matty's name was carved across its face in sharp letters. She stood there in silence, the lonely hillside cemetery stretching out around her. After all this time, she was finally here.

Claire knelt in front of the grave, not caring that the damp ground was soaking through her stockings. She reached out and traced her fingers over the letters of his name.

"Hey Matty," she said softly. "I'm sorry it took me so long to visit."

Claire's voice caught in her throat. She blinked back tears, taking a moment to gather her swirling emotions.

"I'm so sorry about everything. I never should have told Evan what you confessed to me. I was young and stupid."

Claire paused, picturing Matty's face the last time she saw him alive.

"I'm going to have to live with that regret for the rest of my life. And live with the guilt of all that came after. I know none of it would have happened if I had just been a good friend and kept your secret."

Claire laid her hand on top of the cool, solid gravestone.

"I promise I'm going to try to make things right, Matty. I'm going to honor you and I hope...I hope somehow you can forgive me."

Claire's voice broke off into a sob. She stayed there kneeling in the dirt before his grave, grieving for the friend she had lost so many years ago. She placed her hands on the sides of his tombstone and bowed her head. The tears fell from her eyes and mingled with the damp soil beneath her.

Her tears slowed as she traced her fingers over the engraved letters of Matty's name. A soft breeze rustled through the cemetery, drying the wet tracks down her cheeks.

She heard a scuff of shoes on the gravel path behind her and turned to see Detective Lawson approaching. Claire stood quickly, swiping at her eyes.

"I followed you out here. Don't worry. I'm not stalking you," she said, clearly trying to lighten the mood.

Claire glared at the detective.

Lawson took the hint and sobered immediately. "This is actually where I arrested Elizabeth for her crimes."

Claire's brows rose in surprise. "I didn't realize that."

Lawson nodded, her eyes flickering to Matty's gravestone. "I wanted to apologize for not taking you more seriously through this whole ordeal. I should have trusted your instincts."

"I'm sorry too," Claire replied. "I didn't make it easy for you."

Lawson sighed, stepping closer. "I know now...about what happened back in high school. With Matty and Evan."

Claire's shoulders slumped. "Yeah, I guess I can't run from it anymore."

"There's no running from these things, Claire." Lawson looked far off for a moment and then sat down next to her. "I lost my partner a while back. I carried that guilt for a long time. Led me to do things I shouldn't have. But I learned it's better to try and make a positive change in their honor, instead of wallowing in the guilt."

Claire nodded slowly, considering her words. The breeze gusted stronger and she shivered against the chill. They sat in silence for a moment, gazing at the tombstone in front of them.

"I should get going," Claire said finally.

"I have a proposition for you," Lawson said. "Come work with us. Put your skills to use taking down criminals instead of protecting them."

Claire stared at her in surprise. "Anthony wasn't a criminal."

"No, he wasn't," Lawson said. "But maybe if you had been on the other side with me, you would have helped me see what I couldn't."

Claire was silent as she mulled over the detective's words. The idea was absurd on the surface—switching sides, stepping away from the career she'd worked so hard to build. But was it? Part of her wondered if Lawson was right. Would being on the other side offer her the chance to seek truth and justice more directly?

"What do you say?" Lawson prodded. "Will you join me in fighting for the victims?"

Slowly, Claire felt a smile spread across her face. She knew then what her answer would be. What it had to be.

"Yes," she said firmly. "I think Matty would be proud of that."

Lawson grinned and extended her hand. As Claire shook it, she felt lighter than she had in years. She was ready for this change. Ready to make Matty proud.

Lawson touched her shoulder gently. "Take care of yourself, Claire. My office will be in touch."

Claire offered a small, grateful smile. Then she turned and walked away.

Ready for another gripping thriller set in Savannah? Click below to get your copy of *The Silence Before*, or continue to the next page for a sample.
https://www.amazon.com/gp/product/B0DWZ8TTS5

Join the LT Ryan reader family & receive a free copy of the Alex Hayes story, *Trial by Fire*. Click the link below to get started:
https://ltryan.com/alex-hayes-newsletter-signup-1

the silence before: chapter 1

The Pitch

By mid-March, Savannah was already shedding the cool embrace of winter, trading it for a tentative warmth that hinted at the sultry days ahead. The breeze carried the faint perfume of early-blooming jasmine, mingling with the earthy scent of brick-lined streets still damp from last night's rain. Fiona Stevens stepped into the newsroom of *The Savannah Chronicle*, her heels clicking on the scuffed linoleum, her mind racing faster than her heart.

The *Chronicle* was a relic of Savannah's past, much like the city itself—a newspaper steeped in the charm and scandal of its genteel society. Its glossy front page often featured vibrant photographs of garden parties, debutante balls, and ribbon cuttings, with headlines hinting at social intrigue just scandalous enough to sell papers but polite enough not to offend its upper-crust readership.

Fiona had long ago grown weary of covering stories about who wore what to the annual Azalea Gala or whose feud had spilled over during a garden club luncheon. She craved meatier stories, the kind that unearthed secrets and peeled back the layers of Savannah's polished veneer. But here at the *Chronicle*, the priority was keeping readers entertained with gossip, fluff pieces, and just enough exclusivity to stay relevant. It paid the bills, she reminded herself, even if it didn't always nourish her ambitions.

She glanced at the clock: 9:15 a.m. Just enough time to grab coffee before her meeting with Jacobs.

"Stevens, on a mission, I see," Denise quipped from her cubicle, her head popping up like a meerkat's. The features writer held a mug with a faded *I'd Rather Be at Tybee* slogan and a pen tucked behind one ear.

"Mission's an understatement," Fiona replied, tugging at her blazer to smooth out the wrinkles from her walk. "Jacobs is going to need convincing, and I'm ready to do it."

"Ah, the famous Jacobs gauntlet. What's the pitch this time?" Denise leaned forward conspiratorially, her curiosity almost palpable.

Fiona hesitated. Sharing her idea now felt like bad luck, as if giving it away too soon would jinx her chances. "You'll hear soon enough," she said with a grin. "Assuming I survive."

Denise laughed, leaning back in her chair as Fiona continued her trek to the break room. The coffee pot, predictably empty, sat abandoned on the counter. She sighed, abandoning the idea of caffeine and instead bracing herself for what she hoped would be a productive morning. As much as she loved the rush of pitching a story, the stakes felt higher today. This wasn't just another society profile or a feature on Savannah's latest garden craze; this was her chance to elevate her work beyond the *Chronicle*'s usual fare.

Jacobs' office was a relic of an era where smoking indoors was the norm, even if no one dared to light up anymore. The air still held a faint scent of tobacco and leather, mixing with the sharper notes of the man himself—a combination of aftershave and cheap cologne. Fiona knocked twice on the half-open door and waited.

"Come in, Stevens," Jacobs barked without looking up from his desk. His reading glasses perched precariously on his nose, and a stack of proofs sat to one side, forgotten.

She stepped in, clutching her leather-bound notebook. "Good morning, Jacobs."

"Depends on what you've got for me," he said, finally looking up. His weathered face betrayed years of deadlines and red pens. "What's this earth-shattering idea you're so eager about?"

Fiona crossed the room and set her notebook on his desk, flipping it open to the notes she'd spent hours refining. "The Savannah Tour of Homes and Gardens," she began, watching his expression carefully. "It's coming up next month, and Dolores Bates is participating. I want to do a feature on her estate."

Jacobs raised an eyebrow, the skepticism already apparent. "The Bates family? The same Bateses whose serial killer son was murdered last year? That Bates family?"

"He was framed for those crimes," Fiona corrected him, "But yes, that's the one," Fiona said, holding her ground. "But that's exactly why this could work. The estate has a fascinating history—centuries of intrigue, old Savannah money, and connections to the Wesley fortune. Plus, it'll draw attention to the Tour itself, which hasn't had great press in recent years."

Jacobs leaned back in his chair, rubbing his chin. "Dolores isn't exactly known for her charm. How are you planning to convince her to talk? Or are you hoping for one of those 'exclusive exposés' everyone's obsessed with?"

Fiona allowed herself a small smile. "Neither. I plan to pitch it as a profile. A feature piece showcasing her home and her involvement in the Tour. It's not about prying into her personal life—at least not at first. The goal is to let her control the narrative, focus on the grandeur of the house. Once she's comfortable, we might dig a little deeper."

Jacobs snorted. "You're not just dealing with a guarded socialite. Mrs. Bates has a reputation for being outright hostile. You think she'll let you into her house, much less her past?"

"She might," Fiona countered. "If I position this as an opportunity to highlight the history of her estate, to frame her as a cornerstone of Savannah's elite... I think she'll bite."

Jacobs tapped his pen on the desk, his gaze fixed on her. "This is risky. If she shuts you out, it's dead in the water."

"If it works, though, it'll sell papers. People love a peek behind the curtain of Savannah's high society. And if I can frame Mrs. Bates as more than just the tragic widow or the woman whose family legacy has been tainted... it could be a game-changer."

Jacobs tapped his pen against the desk, his eyes narrowing as he considered her pitch. "This still feels like a long shot."

"Let me sweeten the deal," Fiona said quickly. "My sister is on a first name basis with Dolores."

Jacobs narrowed his eyes. "Oh, that's right. The sister that defended her serial killer son."

Fiona deadpanned. "For an editor at a news agency, you sure don't pay attention to the news. I told you, he was falsely accused."

Jacobs waved a hand, dismissing the information. "So, what? You think your sister is going to be able to secure this story for you?"

Fiona hesitated. "I wouldn't go that far. But worst case, if Dolores shuts me out, Claire might be able to pull a few strings to help me at least get in the door."

Jacobs let out a sharp laugh. "Ah, nepotism. Journalism's old reliable."

"It's not nepotism if it gets the story," Fiona shot back with a faint grin.

Jacobs let out a long breath, nodding slowly. "Fine. Go for it. But don't waste too much time on this if she's not willing to play ball. The second she shuts you down, move on to something else."

Fiona's shoulders eased as the tension left her body. "Thank you. I won't let you down."

"Make sure you don't," Jacobs said, already returning to the stack of proofs on his desk. "And Stevens? Make sure you get a fresh angle. Don't recycle last year's fluff about the Tour."

Back at her desk, Fiona felt the first pangs of nerves creep in. The Savannah Tour of Homes and Gardens was a staple of springtime in the city, drawing locals and tourists alike to the grand antebellum houses that lined the historic district. The Bates estate, a sprawling mansion with its pristine white columns and lush gardens, was the crown jewel of this year's lineup.

It was also a place steeped in shadows—rumors of affairs, a mysterious death, and the tangled legacy of family fortune. Fiona had no doubt Mrs. Bates would be a challenge, but the thought of peeling back the layers of that woman's carefully curated facade made her pulse quicken.

"Did Jacobs sign off?" Denise appeared at the edge of her cubicle, holding a bag of bagels. "You look like you just scaled Everest."

"He did," Fiona said with a smile. "Now the real work begins."

"Well, enjoy your climb. Want a bagel?"

Fiona laughed, reaching for one. "Thanks. I'll need all the carbs I can get for this one."

As Denise wandered back to her desk, Fiona opened her laptop and began drafting her email to Mrs. Bates. Her fingers hovered over the keys for a moment before she began to type:

Dear Mrs. Bates,

My name is Fiona Stevens, and I'm a journalist with the Savannah Chronicle.

She paused, her mind drifting to the stories she'd already heard whispered over coffee and cocktails—about the missing woman, the almost-divorce, the whispers that Mrs. Bates' temper concealed more than just her disdain for the press. Fiona shook her head, refocusing on the task at hand. First, she had to get Mrs. Bates to agree. Then, she'd see where the story led.

As the hum of the newsroom faded into the background, Fiona felt a flicker of excitement. If this story turned out the way she imagined, it would be the kind of piece that defined careers.

the silence before: chapter 2

Lunch with Claire

The café on Forsyth Park was already filling with its usual midday crowd when Fiona arrived. She spotted Claire sitting at a small table near the window, her hair swept back into a practical ponytail, a steaming cup of tea cradled in her hands.

Fiona slid into the chair across from her sister, placing her bag on the floor. "Thanks for meeting me. I figured I'd need backup."

Claire smirked, her eyes glinting with amusement. "Backup for lunch? Or for whatever you've gotten yourself into now?"

"Both," Fiona admitted with a grin. She flagged down a server and ordered an iced coffee and a chicken wrap before turning her attention back to Claire. "I pitched a new article to Jacobs today."

Claire arched an eyebrow. "Let me guess. It's not another piece about Savannah's most eligible bachelors or the latest rooftop bar trend?"

"Not even close." Fiona leaned forward, excitement sparking in her voice. "It's a feature on Dolores Bates and her estate, tied to the Savannah Tour of Homes and Gardens."

Claire's reaction was immediate—a sharp intake of breath followed by a wary shake of her head. "Dolores Bates? Are you serious, Fiona?"

"Completely serious. Her estate is a centerpiece of the Tour this year. It's the perfect opportunity to delve into the history of the house and—maybe—her family. I think she might actually agree to it."

"Agree to what? Being interrogated by you in print?" Claire's tone was skeptical, but there was an undercurrent of concern. "You realize she's notoriously private, right? And after everything she's been through." Her voice trailed off.

"Okay, fine. Maybe it's a bit of a long shot," Fiona said quickly, pulling her laptop out of her bag. "But I already drafted an email to her. I figured it was worth a try."

Claire stared at her sister, incredulous. "An email? Fiona, how did you even get an email address for Dolores Bates?"

"It's listed on the website for the Tour tickets," Fiona said, opening the laptop and spinning it around to face Claire. "Look, it's straightforward and professional. No pressure. Just an invitation to tell her story on her terms."

Claire squinted at the screen, reading aloud in a deadpan voice. "'Dear Mrs. Bates... highlight your estate... celebrate your contributions...' Fiona, this is fine—if she actually uses email. Which she doesn't."

Fiona frowned. "How can you know that?"

"I only worked with her during the entire time I put together Anthony's appeal. And, because she's Dolores Bates," Claire said, as if that explained everything. "Even if she did use email, do you really think she's the one monitoring a random address tied to a public website? It's probably being managed by some assistant—or worse, it's just sitting in an inbox no one checks."

Fiona deflated slightly, sitting back in her chair. "Well, it's better than nothing."

Claire sighed, softening. "I'll make a call on your behalf. It's been a little while since we spoke, but maybe she'll still pick up the phone for me. It's at least worth a try."

Fiona's eyes lit up with gratitude. "You'd do that for me?"

"Of course." Claire's expression softened further. "You're my sister. And if you're determined to take on Dolores Bates, you're going to need all the help you can get."

"So," Fiona said, leaning on her elbows. "What have you been up to since the Bates case? Still taking time to figure things out?"

Claire hesitated, her tea poised midway to her lips. "I guess you could say that. I've been," she paused, "selective about the cases I take. It's not like before, where I'd just take anything that came my way."

"That makes sense. After what happened with Anthony, I wouldn't blame you for being cautious." Fiona's tone was gentle, but she watched her sister closely, curious if Claire would open up.

Claire set her cup down, her fingers tracing the rim absently. "It's not just caution. It's—" She paused again, searching for the right words. "It's wanting to make sure I'm doing something meaningful. Something I can actually handle. I don't want to dive into something overwhelming and end up back where I was."

Fiona nodded, understanding. The weight of Anthony Bates' case had left its mark on her sister, both professionally and personally. His death after his release from prison, the truth about the real culprit of the crimes he was accused of, it was enough to haunt anyone.

"Detective Lawson keeps asking me to come work with her," Claire added, breaking Fiona's train of thought.

Fiona's eyebrows shot up. "Really? That's big, Claire. Are you considering it?"

"Not really," Claire admitted, though there was a flicker of uncertainty in her voice. "She means well, but working with her would mean diving headfirst into the kind of cases I'm trying to avoid. She keeps saying I'd bring something new to the team, but I don't know if I'm ready for that."

"You'd be great at it," Fiona said earnestly, smiling as the waitress sent her lunch in front of her. "But if it's not what you want, don't let anyone pressure you."

Claire offered a small smile as Fiona took a bite of her wrap. "Thanks. For now, I'm happy taking things one step at a time. The world of high-stakes legal drama can survive without me for a while."

Fiona chuckled, but her mind was already spinning with the possibilities. If Claire still had connections to Detective Lawson, that might come in handy down the line—especially if Dolores Bates turned out to be as difficult as everyone seemed to think.

"Aren't you going to order something?" she asked.

Claire shook her head. "I'm good with the tea for now, thanks."

Fiona shrugged. "Suit yourself. So," she said, spearing the last piece of chicken from her wrap, "any big plans this weekend? Or are you still pretending to be a hermit?"

Claire smirked, setting her tea cup down with a delicate clink. "I'm not pretending anything. But I was thinking about heading out to Tybee for the weekend. Maybe rent a kayak, read a book by the water. You know, just decompress."

"Sounds idyllic," Fiona said wistfully. "Meanwhile, I'll probably be chained to my laptop trying to figure out how to charm Savannah's resident fortress."

"Probably," Fiona replied, her tone half-joking. She tilted her head. "Speaking of vacations, have you thought any more about that road trip we talked about? The one to Shenandoah?"

Claire smirked, pushing her empty tea cup aside. "I thought you were joking about that."

"I wasn't joking! A cabin in the mountains, some hiking, maybe a wine tour—doesn't that sound perfect?" Fiona leaned forward, a playful glint in her eyes. "You could use the break, and I could use a partner who won't judge me for trying to mix work and relaxation."

Claire raised an eyebrow. "Work? On a vacation?"

"I mean, the Shenandoah's got a history. There's bound to be a story hiding in one of those old estates or tucked into a quirky art gallery," Fiona said with a grin.

"Of course you'd find a way to turn a vacation into research," Claire said, laughing. "But honestly, I haven't ruled it out. After Anthony's case and everything that came with it, I've been trying to keep things... simple. Staying in Savannah makes that easier."

Fiona's smile softened. "That's fair. You've been through a lot. But don't stay stuck. You deserve to get out there—just maybe not straight into another high-stakes situation."

Claire nodded, her expression contemplative. "I know. One day at a time, right? But I'll admit, the idea of a quiet cabin in the mountains sounds tempting."

"I'll take that as a maybe," Fiona said with mock solemnity, raising her hands in surrender. "Whenever you're ready, let me know. In the meantime, if you hear anything from your network, especially about Dolores, let me know. I feel like this is my big chance to prove myself. To break out of the *Chronicle's* fluff mold, you know?"

Claire tilted her head, studying her sister. "I get it. Just don't forget —Dolores Bates isn't just some society matriarch. There are people who've gone out of their way to keep her skeletons buried. You might be walking into something bigger than you realize."

"Bigger stories sell papers," Fiona said, her grin sharp. "But I'll be careful, I promise."

Claire sighed, but there was a trace of affection in her exasperation. "You better be. And don't overthink the email thing. I'll make the call, and we'll see where it goes. Just... be ready for the possibility that she might slam the door in your face."

"Or throw me out on the lawn," Fiona added with a dramatic flair. "Still, thanks for the help. I owe you one."

"You owe me about ten," Claire replied with a smirk. "But let's start with this. I'll call tonight and see what I can do."

As they gathered their things and headed out, the conversation settled into comfortable silence, but Fiona's mind was already racing ahead, spinning with possibilities. Dolores Bates might be a fortress, but Fiona had always been good at finding cracks in the walls.

the silence before: chapter 3

The Meeting

The ringtone jarred Fiona awake from the half-daze she'd been in, her coffee cooling untouched on her desk. She grabbed her phone, her heart leaping when she saw Claire's name.

"Hey," Fiona said, tucking the phone between her ear and shoulder. "What's up?"

"You're going to want to drop whatever you're doing," Claire said without preamble. "I just got off the phone with Dolores Bates. She agreed to meet with you—but she wants to do it now. This woman waits for no one, Fiona."

"Now?" Fiona bolted upright, her pulse quickening. "Like, right now?"

"Yes. Her exact words were, 'If this woman wants to waste my time, she'd better be punctual.' So, yes, now. You're welcome, by the way."

"Claire, I could kiss you," Fiona said, grabbing her bag and keys in one motion. "Thank you."

"Save it. Just don't blow this," Claire warned. "And Fiona? Be prepared. Dolores isn't exactly warm and fuzzy."

Fiona hung up, her mind racing as she scrambled to grab her bag. She was halfway to the door when Denise appeared, a mug of coffee in hand and curiosity etched on her face.

"Where's the fire?" Denise asked, leaning casually against the edge of a nearby desk.

"I'm meeting Dolores Bates," Fiona said, trying to keep the tremor out of her voice as she checked her phone for directions. "Claire just called—she got me a last-minute meeting, and apparently, Mrs. Bates waits for no one."

Denise's eyebrows shot up, her interest piqued. "The Dolores Bates? The one who practically owns half of Savannah? You're kidding."

"Wish I was," Fiona muttered, slinging her laptop bag over her shoulder. "I don't even have time to prep. I just have to show up and hope I don't blow it."

"Good luck with that. She's infamous for being... let's say, difficult." Denise sipped her coffee, her tone more amused than concerned. "What's the angle, anyway? Please tell me it's something juicier than flower arrangements and antique armoires."

Fiona paused, glancing over her shoulder. "It's a feature on her estate for the Tour of Homes and Gardens, but if I can get her to open up, it might be more. Her story, her family... There's a lot under the surface, and I want to dig into it."

Denise gave her a sly grin. "You and your 'under the surface' missions. Just don't come back in pieces. I've heard stories about her temper."

"Noted," Fiona said, her nerves tightening. "If I'm not back by tomorrow, send someone to check for claw marks."

Denise laughed, waving her off. "Go get your scoop, Stevens. And hey—if she does throw a vase at you, take notes. That's the kind of gossip our readers love."

"Thanks for the vote of confidence," Fiona shot back, but she couldn't help smiling as she hurried out the door.

The drive to Dolores Bates' estate was a blur, her thoughts bouncing between potential talking points and worst-case scenarios. By the time she pulled up to the sprawling mansion, her nerves were taut as piano strings.

Dolores Bates' house loomed ahead, its white columns and manicured gardens an ostentatious display of old Savannah wealth. As

Fiona stepped out of her car, she adjusted her bag over her shoulder and glanced toward the grand entrance. The house was just as impressive as she'd imagined, with its stately columns and meticulously trimmed hedges. But as she approached the door, small details caught her eye—the paint on the doorframe looked uneven in spots, and the brick pathway had a few cracks she hadn't expected. Nothing major, but in a city like Savannah, where appearances meant everything, it felt slightly... off. Fiona tucked the thought away as the door opened.

The heavy door opened before Fiona could knock. Dolores Bates stood in the doorway, her presence as commanding as the house itself. She was tall and angular, with silver hair swept into a chignon and piercing blue eyes that pinned Fiona in place.

"You're late," Dolores said, though Fiona knew she was at least five minutes early.

"Thank you for seeing me on such short notice, Mrs. Bates," Fiona said, stepping forward with a polite smile. "I appreciate the opportunity."

Dolores waved her inside without a word, turning sharply on her heel. Fiona followed, her eyes darting around as they walked through the grand foyer.

The house was as grand as she'd imagined, with its gleaming hardwood floors and antique furnishings. But there were oddities, too—scratches on the baseboards, a faint crack in one of the windowpanes. And then there were the personal touches: a framed photo of a younger Dolores at the helm of a sailboat, her face alight with determination, and another of a boy with sandy hair, his grin wide and carefree. Anthony, Fiona guessed, her chest tightening at the thought.

Dolores moved with brisk precision, leading Fiona toward a sitting room. But before they could settle, the sound of a vacuum hummed to life somewhere down the hall.

"Karen!" Dolores snapped, her voice sharp enough to make Fiona flinch. A moment later, a woman in a crisp cleaning uniform appeared, looking sheepish.

"I'm sorry, ma'am," Karen murmured, clutching the vacuum.

"Not now," Dolores said with a dismissive wave. "We'll finish later."

Karen disappeared down the hall, and Dolores turned back to Fiona, her expression unreadable. "Where were we?"

"You were about to sit," Fiona offered lightly, hoping to ease the tension. Dolores didn't smile, but she did take a seat on the edge of an armchair, her back ramrod straight.

Fiona sat across from her, pulling her notebook out. "Thank you again for agreeing to meet with me. I wanted to discuss a potential feature for the *Savannah Chronicle* ahead of the Tour of Homes and Gardens. Your estate is such a centerpiece of the event, and I think our readers would love to know more about its history—and about you."

Dolores tilted her head, her eyes narrowing. "Why me? There are plenty of other homes on the Tour. Why single me out?" She brushed imaginary dust off her skirt before folding her hands, clasping them tightly.

Fiona hesitated, choosing her words carefully. "Your home is one of the most iconic in Savannah. It's a reflection of the city's history, its elegance, and its resilience. And, honestly, people are curious about you—about the woman behind the estate. This is a chance to share your story, on your terms."

Dolores' lips pressed into a thin line. "I've seen what curiosity does. It turns into speculation, gossip."

"That's not my goal," Fiona said quickly. "This isn't about prying into your personal life. It's about celebrating your contributions to Savannah's history and culture. The Tour is a perfect opportunity to showcase that."

Dolores was silent for a long moment, her gaze flicking to the window. Outside, the garden staff moved about, pruning hedges and tending to flower beds with mechanical precision. Finally, she turned back to Fiona.

"And what happens when people ask questions about... other events?" Dolores' voice was low, almost a whisper, but her meaning was clear.

Fiona swallowed, careful not to meet her gaze too directly. "This piece isn't about that. But I do think this could help refocus the narrative. It's a chance to remind people who you are beyond recent events."

Dolores leaned back slightly, her posture stiff. "And you think writing about my home is going to do that?"

"I think your home is a starting point," Fiona said. "It's a way to tell a story that's about legacy and resilience, not tragedy. And I think people want to see that side of you."

Another interruption cut through the air as Karen reappeared with a dust cloth, hesitating at the doorway. Dolores waved her off again, irritation flickering across her face.

"Forgive the disruption," Dolores said, though Fiona wasn't sure the words were meant as an apology. "It seems the entire household is in a state of disarray today."

"It's fine," Fiona said, though she couldn't help but notice the nervous energy radiating from Dolores. As they moved to the next room, ostensibly to discuss scheduling, Dolores began plucking at small imperfections—a vase slightly out of place, a corner of a rug that had folded under.

Fiona followed her, taking mental notes as they walked. More photos lined the walls of the next hallway—Dolores at various sailing competitions, a framed newspaper clipping about her late husband's business ventures, and, tucked almost out of sight, a small painting of Anthony as a child. There was warmth in the images, but it was distant, like a memory held at arm's length.

They stopped in a study that smelled faintly of lemon polish. "We can schedule a formal interview next week," Dolores said brusquely. "But I'll need to review your questions beforehand. My lawyer will be in touch with whatever documents you need to sign and you can provide a list to him then."

"Of course," Fiona said, jotting it down. "And, what's his name?"

"Henry Caldwell."

"Got it. Thank you again, Mrs. Bates. I really think this will be a great opportunity," Fiona said, writing down the name and clicking her pen off.

Dolores gave a curt nod, her gaze drifting to the doorway. "We'll see."

As Karen passed by with a mop in hand, Fiona caught the way

Dolores' hands twitched, her fingers gripping the back of a chair as if anchoring herself. It struck Fiona that the house, with all its grandeur and imperfections, mirrored its owner—meticulously maintained on the surface, but with cracks hidden just beneath.

Fiona offered one last smile as she stepped toward the front door. "I'll look forward to next week, then."

Dolores didn't respond, simply closing the door behind her with a decisive click.

Get your copy of *The Silence Before* now:
https://www.amazon.com/gp/product/B0DWZ8TTS5

also by l.t. ryan

Find All of L.T. Ryan's Books on Amazon Today!

The Jack Noble Series

The Recruit (free)

The First Deception (Prequel 1)

Noble Beginnings

A Deadly Distance

Ripple Effect (Bear Logan)

Thin Line

Noble Intentions

When Dead in Greece

Noble Retribution

Noble Betrayal

Never Go Home

Beyond Betrayal (Clarissa Abbot)

Noble Judgment

Never Cry Mercy

Deadline

End Game

Noble Ultimatum

Noble Legend

Noble Revenge

Never Look Back (Coming Soon)

Bear Logan Series

Ripple Effect

Blowback

Take Down

Deep State

Bear & Mandy Logan Series

Close to Home

Under the Surface

The Last Stop

Over the Edge

Between the Lies

Caught in the Web (Coming Soon)

Rachel Hatch Series

Drift

Downburst

Fever Burn

Smoke Signal

Firewalk

Whitewater

Aftershock

Whirlwind

Tsunami

Fastrope

Sidewinder

Mitch Tanner Series

The Depth of Darkness

Into The Darkness

Deliver Us From Darkness

Cassie Quinn Series

Path of Bones

Whisper of Bones

Symphony of Bones

Etched in Shadow

Concealed in Shadow

Betrayed in Shadow

Born from Ashes

Return to Ashes (Coming Soon)

Blake Brier Series

Unmasked

Unleashed

Uncharted

Drawpoint

Contrail

Detachment

Clear

Quarry (Coming Soon)

Dalton Savage Series

Savage Grounds

Scorched Earth

Cold Sky

The Frost Killer

Crimson Moon (Coming Soon)

Maddie Castle Series

The Handler

Tracking Justice

Hunting Grounds

Vanished Trails

Smoldering Lies (Coming Soon)

Affliction Z Series

Affliction Z: Patient Zero

Affliction Z: Abandoned Hope

Affliction Z: Descended in Blood

Affliction Z : Fractured Part 1

Affliction Z: Fractured Part 2 (Fall 2021)

about the authors

L.T. RYAN is a *Wall Street Journal* and *USA Today* bestselling author, renowned for crafting pulse-pounding thrillers that keep readers on the edge of their seats. Known for creating gripping, character-driven stories, Ryan is the author of the *Jack Noble* series, the *Rachel Hatch* series, and more. With a knack for blending action, intrigue, and emotional depth, Ryan's books have captivated millions of fans worldwide.

Whether it's the shadowy world of covert operatives or the relentless pursuit of justice, Ryan's stories feature unforgettable characters and high-stakes plots that resonate with fans of Lee Child, Robert Ludlum, and Michael Connelly.

When not writing, Ryan enjoys crafting new ideas with coauthors, running a thriving publishing company, and connecting with readers. Discover the next story that will keep you turning pages late into the night.

Connect with L.T. Ryan
Sign up for his newsletter to hear the latest goings on and receive some free content
➜ https://ltryan.com/jack-noble-newsletter-signup-1

Join the private readers' group
➜ https://www.facebook.com/groups/1727449564174357

Instagram ➜ @ltryanauthor
Visit the website ➜ https://ltryan.com
Send an email ➜ contact@ltryan.com

LAURA CHASE is a corporate attorney-turned-author who brings her courtroom experience to the page in her gripping legal and psychological thrillers. Chase draws on her real-life experience to draw readers into the high-stakes world of courtroom drama and moral ambiguity.

After earning her JD, Chase clerked for a federal judge and thereafter transitioned to big law, where she honed her skills in high-pressure legal environments. Her passion for exploring the darker side of human nature and the gray areas of justice fuels her writing.

Chase lives with her husband, their two sons, a dog and a cat in Northern Florida. When she's not writing or working, she enjoys spending time with her family, traveling, and bingeing true crime shows.

Connect with Laura:

Sign up for her newsletter: www.laurachaseauthor.com/

Follow her on tiktok: @lawyerlaura

Send an email: info@laurachase.com

Made in the USA
Monee, IL
05 March 2025

54f6d9bd-f1b7-4a0b-b5b1-fd9896c9bb9eR01